Also available from Delores Fossen and HQN

Lone Star Ridge

Tangled Up in Texas

Coldwater Texas

Lone Star Christmas
Lone Star Midnight (ebook novella)
Hot Texas Sunrise
Texas at Dusk (ebook novella)
Sweet Summer Sunset
A Coldwater Christmas

Wrangler's Creek

Lone Star Cowboy (ebook novella)
Those Texas Nights
One Good Cowboy (ebook novella)
No Getting Over a Cowboy
Just Like a Cowboy (ebook novella)
Branded as Trouble
Cowboy Dreaming (ebook novella)
Texas-Sized Trouble
Cowboy Heartbreaker (ebook novella)
Lone Star Blues
Cowboy Blues (ebook novella)
The Last Rodeo

The McCord Brothers

What Happens on the Ranch (ebook novella)
Texas on My Mind
Cowboy Trouble (ebook novella)
Lone Star Nights
Cowboy Underneath It All (ebook novella)
Blame It on the Cowboy

To see the complete list of titles available from Delores Fossen, please visit www.deloresfossen.com.

DELORES FOSSEN

TANGLED UP
IN
Texas

HQN

HQN

PLEASE RECYCLE

THIS PRODUCT IS RECYCLABLE

ISBN-13: 978-1-335-01408-5

Recycling programs
for this product may
not exist in your area.

Tangled Up in Texas

HQN
22 Adelaide St. West, 40th Floor
Toronto, Ontario M5H 4E3, Canada
www.Harlequin.com

Printed in U.S.A.

To Luke and Ruth.
Thank you for bringing so much light to my life.

TANGLED UP
IN
Texas

CHAPTER ONE

Sʜᴀᴡ Jᴀᴍᴇsᴏɴ sʟᴀᴍᴍᴇᴅ on his brakes when he spotted what appeared to be a red bra in the middle of the road.

This wasn't an ordinary bra, either. This one had cantaloupe-sized cups, was made of shiny leather and had three-inch gold lightning bolt spikes on the nipples. The spikes arrowed up to the sky and looked lethal enough to have taken out a tire or two had he run over it. Good thing he'd seen it in time to stop.

Of course, it would have been darn hard to miss.

He pulled his truck onto the shoulder, putting on the emergency flashers in case another vehicle came around the deep curve in the road. He didn't want anyone ramming into him even though there wasn't likely to be much traffic at this time of the morning. Heck, at any time for that matter.

The narrow two-lane road led from his hometown of Lone Star Ridge to his family's ranch, which he could see from across the pasture. This was hardly the beaten path, but obviously that odd bra was proof that someone had *beaten* it.

He got out and walked to the garment for a closer look. Yep, it was a bra all right, and a few feet away was a matching pair of thong panties, complete with more spikes that were on the sides of the slick red leather. If these were someone's actual garments, then the wearer obviously had a more adventurous spirit than most people. As a general rule, he didn't wear anything that could maim him or others.

There was a huge cardboard box not far from the underwear. It was on its side, crushed and gaping open. Other items of underwear were spilling out from it. He saw more spiked bras, a thong made of what appeared to be a Hefty trash bag and a bustier with rhinestones and feathers. No spikes on that one but rather bright yellow duckbills in the nipple regions.

Yeah, definitely someone who was more adventurous. And possibly bat-shit crazy.

Shaw looked up when he heard the sound of an approaching vehicle. Not coming from behind but rather ahead—from the direction of the ranch. It was a dark blue SUV barreling toward him, and it screeched to a stop on the other side of the intimate apparel.

Because of the angle of the morning sunlight and the SUV's tinted windshield, Shaw couldn't see the driver, but he sure as heck saw the woman who stepped from the passenger's side.

Talk about a gut punch of surprise. The biggest surprise of the morning, and that was saying something considering the weird underwear on the road.

Sunny Dalton.

She was a blast from the past, a kick to the balls and a tangle of memories, all rolled into one. And here she was walking toward him like a siren in her snug jeans and loose gray shirt.

And here he was on the verge of drooling.

Shaw did something about that and made sure he closed his mouth, but he knew it wouldn't stay that way. Even though Sunny and he were no longer teenagers and didn't exactly have a good history in the sex department, his body steamed up whenever he saw her.

Sunny smiled at him. However, he didn't think it was so much from steam as a sense of polite frustration.

"Shaw," she said on a rise of breath.

Her voice was smooth and silky. Maybe a little tired, too. Even if Shaw hadn't seen her in a couple of years, he was pretty sure that was fatigue in her steel-blue eyes.

She'd changed her hair. It was still a dark chocolate brown, but it no longer hung well past her shoulders. It was shorter in an unfussy sort of way that would have maybe looked plain on most women. On Sunny, it framed that amazing face.

"Sunny," Shaw greeted back. "Is that your stuff?" he asked, tipping his head to the bra.

She gave a quick laugh, not exactly from humor, followed by a somewhat weary head shake. "Not mine. I was bringing it to my grandmother's house for Hadley. She shipped me a bunch of stuff to bring to Em's, but the box fell off the top of the SUV. We had to find a place to turn around before we could come back for it."

Well, since her sister, Hadley, was a costume designer, that explained some things. Not why Hadley would have made such garments in the first place, though.

And especially not why Sunny was here.

Sunny and her sisters hadn't lived in Lone Star Ridge in years. Why the heck would she be bringing weird underwear out to her grandmother's? Better yet, why had she taken it first to his ranch, because that's obviously the direction she'd been heading?

Before Shaw could ask her those puzzling questions, the driver's side and back doors opened, and a young man got out from behind the steering wheel. He didn't say anything to Shaw. Just as Sunny was doing, he began picking up the stuff.

The other person who stepped out, however, didn't do any underwear gathering. It was a teenage girl, and with her gaze zooming in on Shaw, she started toward him.

Shaw took one look at her and cursed under his breath. She had trouble written all over her, and while she wasn't exactly a bouncing baby girl, he was almost positive that she was here to tell him something.

And the something was that she was his half sister.

A half sister he hadn't known squat about.

Shaw figured that most grown men didn't encounter news like this in their entire lifetimes, but the possibility of it stood a much higher occurrence if your dad happened to be a washed-up country music star named Marty Jameson.

He wasn't a good judge of age, but Shaw figured the girl was about sixteen or so. Her hair was a swirl of radioactive green and fluorescent orange, a mix that looked as if a tropical bird had squatted on her head. It spiked out in some places, was slicked down in others, and it matched the backpack she had slung over one arm.

Unlike Sunny's unfussy hairdo, the girl's was probably a fashion statement. Ditto for the red crop top and the short skirt that was the color of the meds you took when you had a really bad stomach flu.

Shaw didn't help the girl close the distance between them. He stayed put and let her clomp her way to him in pink-tasseled cowboy boots. Yeah, pink. If she'd been older, he might have thought the spiky, duckbilled underwear belonged to her since it would mesh with her over-the-top clothes.

Along with the tassels flinging and flying on her boots, the girl clanged and jangled as she walked. The noise was because of the various chains hanging from or studded on various parts of her rail-thin body. A chunky silver dragon necklace, along with the multiple piercings in both ears, her nose and her eyebrows.

"Are you Shaw Jameson?" she snapped. Her tone leaned toward angry with a touch of badass.

Shaw badassed her right back. "Are you here for an autograph?"

Sweet baby Moses in a basket, let her be a fan wanting his dad's autograph. That was darn sure better than the alternative, but Shaw couldn't hold out even a glimmer of hope.

The girl huffed, rolled her blue-mascara-laden eyes and propped her hands on her hips. Shaw saw it then. The tat scrolled on the top of her right wrist. A single word.

Trouble.

Hell, he hated being right about predicting this sort of thing. Hated the gut punch he got, too, when he combed his gaze over her face and spotted the familiar features. Those stone-gray eyes. The shape of her chin, complete with a dimple. It was a face that Shaw knew all too well.

His father's face.

Shaw didn't know why seeing those features on offspring still managed to throw him off-kilter, not when there'd been so many occasions for those offspring to pop up. But even with the sheer number of kids, he had a hard time wrapping his mind around the fact that his father, Marty, was an idiot when it came to birth control.

Along with Shaw, there was his brother, Austin, his sister, Cait, and their adopted brother, Leyton—who was also Marty's biological son. But there were others, no doubts about that. Shaw figured even Marty didn't know the actual count, but Shaw knew of six more. Miss Pink Boots would make seven.

Well, maybe she would.

He got another gut punch when he looked over at Sunny, who was putting the underwear in the SUV.

Oh, shit.

Shaw remembered hearing that condoms failed something like 15 percent of the time. He hoped that's what hadn't happened—he quickly did the math—fifteen years ago, the one and only time he'd had sex with Sunny.

Hell, had he pulled a Marty Jameson and also been an idiot when it came to birth control?

"Yeah, she's from that stupid show about triplets

that used to be on TV," the teenager griped, glancing over her shoulder at Sunny. "The reruns are still on."

Shaw hadn't needed Pink Boots to fill him in on that. He was well aware that Sunny and her sisters had been the stars of the reality show *Little Cowgirls*, which had been filmed right here at her grandmother's ranch in Lone Star Ridge. He was well aware, too, of the reruns. And, like her sisters, Sunny had moved away the day after they'd graduated from high school.

That had been just a month or so after she and Shaw had had sex.

They'd lusted after each other for a couple of years before that, but since Shaw was two years older than Sunny and hadn't wanted to spend time in prison, they'd waited until she'd turned eighteen and was no longer jailbait. Playing it safe.

Well, maybe *safe* had come back to bite him in the butt.

"Her name's Sunshine or something like that," the girl provided. "I remember that from the show."

"Sunny," Shaw and Sunny corrected together.

Their responses were as rote as swatting at a buzzing fly, and something that Sunny had no doubt had to do many times in her life. Sunshine was her mother's name. Yeah, Sunshine, which he supposed was a hippie–flower child acknowledgment from Sunshine's mom, Em, who had once been a hippie–flower child. And unless there'd been some big changes, Sunny would want to minimize the connections between her and the woman who'd given birth to her as well as being her costar on the show.

Not trusting his voice, Shaw volleyed glances between the girl and her, looking for any hints of Sunny's DNA in the mix. Sunny followed his gaze, gave him a ghost of a smile and went closer to him.

"Rest assured, Shaw, you didn't knock me up when I was a teenager," Sunny whispered in his ear. "She's not ours."

The relief felt like an ice water monsoon and he made a sound of relief that disgusted him. He had a reputation of being a hard-nosed boss. A real cowboy. And it was best not to let anyone know that he'd just had one big-assed scare that'd vised an internal organ or two.

"But you can probably guess that she's Marty's," Sunny added, still whispering.

"Yeah," Shaw admitted.

The relief suddenly took a turn with the realization that while the teenager wasn't his kid, she did share his gene pool. He was betting the girl hadn't come here to celebrate that particular fact, either.

"Who is she?" he asked Sunny.

"I'm Kinsley Rubio," the girl spit out before Sunny could answer. "Where's the bio-dad, sperm donor, country music singer butt hole who planted me in my mom? Is he in there?" She pointed to the sprawling two-story white house that loomed on the hill above the pasture.

Shaw decided to overlook the mild profanity and the shitty attitude. He'd gotten similar reactions from some of Marty's other kids, and he preferred those to the demands for the gobs of money that two of the offspring had made.

Marty had money, maybe even gobs of it if he

hadn't blown it, and Shaw wasn't hurting in that department. In fact, Shaw owned the majority share of the ranch. No thanks to Marty but rather Marty's father, Sam, who'd divvied up the place in his will to Shaw and his then-known siblings. Sam hadn't had a lot of faith in his only child—had basically thought Marty was a screwup and not deserving of the ranch that'd been in the Jameson family for six generations.

"The bio-dad doesn't live there," Shaw explained to the girl. "He and my mom got a divorce when I was a kid, and she lives there. And no, I don't know where he is, but I can call him and let him know you're here."

Or better yet, leave a message to let Marty know that Kinsley Rubio existed. Informing his dad of that, however, wouldn't guarantee Marty would answer the call or do anything more than tell Shaw to handle it. Marty wasn't exactly a coldhearted bastard, but he often believed that a check for a couple of thousand dollars and some "let's keep in touch" consolations would be enough to soothe ruffled feathers and fulfill his parental obligations.

"Then call him and tell him to get out here," Kinsley demanded. "I want him to look in my face and explain why he never told me he was my father."

"And why didn't your mother tell you?" Shaw asked. Not that he was giving Marty a pass on this, but he wanted to know what he was dealing with.

Kinsley huffed as if that was the most unreasonable question in the history of unreasonableness. "Call him now," she repeated, and with what he had to admit was impressive speed and some surprising athletic ability, the girl jumped the ditch, climbed over the fence and started toward the house.

The very house where his mother lived.

Now it was Shaw's turn to huff, and he knew he'd have to go after her. His mother was home, and while she'd want to know this was happening—again— Shaw didn't want her to have to deal with all this surliness alone.

"I was in town about to go into Fred's Grocery and get some things for my grandmother," Sunny explained, following Shaw to his truck. "I heard Kinsley asking how to get out here to the ranch. Apparently, she'd hitchhiked from San Antonio to Lone Star Ridge."

Great. So not just angry but also stupid if she'd done something that risky.

"I noticed the family resemblance so I offered to bring her here," Sunny went on. "I think she's broke. I know she's angry." She paused, checked her watch. "And I'm sorry to dump all of this on you, but I have to go. I still need to get those groceries, and Granny Em's expecting me. I don't want her to worry."

No, she wouldn't want to do that. Her grandmother was in her late seventies, and while Em wasn't feeble, the woman would indeed worry if Sunny was late. Especially since Sunny and her siblings didn't visit that often. However, Em did keep the town informed about her girls. Sunny lived in Houston and was an illustrator for a graphic novel series that apparently had quite a following.

According to the latest intel Shaw had heard from Em, Sunny was also going through a breakup. Not her first, either. Over the years Em had mentioned two breakups, and once Shaw had seen a tabloid headline labeling Sunny as the Runaway Fiancée. He wasn't sure how many times she'd been engaged or did any running away, but it was possible this last one had hit her hard. So maybe not tired but depressed.

"Bye, Shaw," Sunny muttered.

Then she did something that surprised him. She gave his arm a gentle squeeze. It was the kind of absentminded gesture from a woman to a friend who'd never French-kissed her or attempted to give her an orgasm.

It was the gesture of someone who felt sorry for him.

That seemed only reasonable because at the moment Shaw was feeling a little sorry for himself. He was, well, lower than a gopher hole about once again having to clean up after his father. Still, the friendly arm squeeze from Sunny got his attention and bothered him. At the feel of her hand on him, he got a jolt of the attraction that had caused them to be more than friends in the first place.

The attraction might be older than dirt, but it still nudged the wrong part of him. The part right behind the zipper of his jeans.

Sunny's gaze practically collided with his, and either she'd developed ESP or else some wrong parts of her had gotten a sizzler of a nudge, too, because she seemed to know exactly what had gone through his mind. She sighed, shook her head.

"Two words that you should remember," she whispered. "Sore nuts."

Yeah, those were good words to remember all right. And it should have cooled him right down, considering that's exactly what he'd gotten—not once, but twice—when he'd been with Sunny. A man's dick just didn't seem to think straight, though, when nudges and heat got involved. Still, Sunny was hands-off.

At least she was until he'd dealt with the more immediate problem in the pink boots.

Shaw pushed his pity party and groin-tightening aside, started his truck and headed for his house. However, that didn't stop him from glancing at the man who'd strapped what was left of the box back on top of the SUV and then had gotten behind the wheel. The guy was young, very young, but maybe this was the new man in Sunny's life. After all, Sunny wouldn't want to stay in her own personal gopher hole any longer than necessary.

Dragging in a long breath that he was certain he'd need, Shaw turned his attention away from his old flame and drove home. The moment he was there, he went straight into the house. He immediately spotted his mother, Lenore, standing in front of the open door of the fridge.

"Pineapple tuna casserole or tofu hot dog fondue?" she asked. "Which do you think Kinsley would like?"

Neither was the correct answer. He loved his mother, but Lenore was the worst cook in the tristate area, and that's why the fridge was always filled with leftovers. There were a dozen choices in there that no sane person would eat.

"Hold off on the food," Shaw advised her. "Where is she?"

Lenore tipped her head to the adjacent dining room, the motion causing her long gray hair to swing like a curtain. She and Kinsley had a little in common in that his mother clanged some, too. Lenore always wore an assortment of bangles and beads.

"Did she happen to mention who her mother is?" Shaw pressed.

Lenore shook her head. "All she told me was her name, and then she insisted I call Marty."

That was the same demand the girl had made to him. "I'll take care of it," Shaw assured her. "Just wait here."

"But Kinsley looks hungry," Lenore protested.

"I'll make sure she gets fed when I take her back home." Wherever home was.

Shaw took off his cowboy hat, hung it on the peg by the door and went into the dining room. Kinsley was seated at the huge table, her arms folded over her chest and that temper still flaring in her eyes.

"Well, did you call the A-hole sperm donor?" she snarled.

"Not yet. But even when I do call him, it could be days before he comes." Shaw was being optimistic. It could be years.

Or never.

Marty still did singing gigs and occasionally even went on tour, and it was often hard to track him down, especially if he didn't want to be tracked down.

"I'll talk to him or his manager," Shaw said, "and then take you home—"

"No." Kinsley jumped to her feet as if the chair had

just scalded her butt. "I'm not going back there. My mother lied to me. All this time, she lied."

Oh, crap. Her voice cracked on that last word, and Shaw could practically feel himself getting reeled in on a wave of emotion. And really bad pissed-off anger. Why couldn't Marty just keep his jeans zipped? Or do something to cut down his sperm count?

The man needed to be neutered.

"Who's your mom?" Shaw asked. When Kinsley only glared at him, he added, "I might know her."

That wasn't a stab in the dark. After all, Kinsley had asked him if he was Shaw, so her mom had maybe told her about Marty's son.

"You don't know her. I don't know her, not really, since she spent my entire life lying to me," Kinsley proclaimed with a heavy dose of teenage angst.

"Do you want some sunshine surprise salad?" Lenore called out to them from the kitchen.

"Say no," Shaw advised the girl.

"I'd love some," Kinsley answered loud enough for his mom to hear. She gave Shaw the metaphorical finger with her defiant glare.

Her defiance was going to cost her. Maybe with mere indigestion. Perhaps with the food so god-awful that it would cause her taste buds to self-destruct. But hey, that was her problem for agreeing to be served any food with the word "surprise" in it.

"So," Shaw said to move this conversation along, "you recently found out we have the same father."

"Sperm donor," she corrected. "And my mom didn't bother to tell me. She let me believe my ex-stepdad was my father. She was like a groupie or something when the bio-dad knocked her up."

Shaw figured there'd been one hell of a blowup to go along with her mom revealing that information. "And your mother's name?" he pressed.

The girl went through with some sneering and scowling before she said, "Aurora Elmore Rubio. We're from San Antonio."

Shaw mentally tested out the name, but it didn't ring any bells. "How old are you?"

More sneering and scowling. "Fifteen."

It was the second time in the past ten minutes or so that he'd had to do some math. He was thirty-five, but when he was a teenager, Marty had taken him to meet some of his "women." Because Marty was at the height of his music career then, there'd been a long string of them. However, by the time Marty had met Kinsley's mom, Shaw had long given up on wanting to spend time with his dad.

"Fifteen," Shaw repeated. "And you what...ran away from home and hitchhiked your way here?" He didn't wait for her to confirm that. "Does your mom know where you are?"

"No, and I don't want her to know. I never want to see her again."

"Yet you want to see Marty, the A-hole sperm donor who hasn't bothered to get in touch with you at any point in your life?"

Shaw let that hang in the air as Lenore came in with the...whatever the hell it was. It looked like crushed Cheetos on top of cloudy lemon Jell-O.

"Here you go, sweetheart," Lenore said, setting

the dish in front of Kinsley. "It's a recipe I got off the computer, but I had to make some substitutions."

Kinsley definitely lost some of that surliness when she poked at the food and it jiggled, sending the Cheetos crumbs spilling off the top.

"So, have you worked out everything with Kinsley?" his mother asked him.

"Pretty much." That wasn't anywhere close to the truth, but Shaw had decided to try to finish this fast so that it would indeed be *worked out*. "Kinsley will tell me her address, and I'll take her home so her mother, she and I can talk about all of this."

Of course, talking wasn't going to help, not with the anger coming off Kinsley in hot greasy waves. Using quick jabs, she was taking out some of the anger on the salad surprise.

"I told you I'm not going back to my mom's," Kinsley insisted. Her eyes shifted to Lenore. "You can understand that, right? I mean, she lied to me, never had any intentions of telling me. I wouldn't have ever known that Marty Jameson was my sperm donor if I hadn't found some old letters in her dresser drawer. They were like some stupid kind of fan mail."

"Oh, dear." Lenore reached over and patted her hand. "What a terrible way to find out."

"Yeah, it was. Then, she gave me this bull crap story about not knowing how to get in touch with Marty after they broke up. Well, all it took was a little poking around on the net. I tried to call his manager, but I couldn't find the number. Then, I read about Marty Jameson being raised on this ranch way back when, that it'd been in his family for a long time. The stories said his son, Shaw, was running the place now. So, I left and came here."

Lenore muttered, "Oh, dear." She added, "But I'm sure your mom's worried about you."

"She's not worried," Kinsley argued. "She's just pissed because I found out she's a big fat liar."

"Your mother's probably already reported you missing, and she'll figure out that you've made your way to the ranch," Shaw supplied. "The cops will come here looking for you. They'll force you to go back home."

That finally seemed to sink in, and Shaw had another *oh, crap* moment when Kinsley started blinking back tears.

"Going home's not a bad thing," Shaw continued. "You don't have to forgive your mom, not right off anyway, but you can wait there until Marty comes to see you."

That sure didn't help with Kinsley's tears, and one spilled down her cheek, cutting its way through the layers of makeup.

"Oh, sweetheart," Lenore said, getting up to go around the table to Kinsley.

Shaw was always amazed that his mother could feel no resentment for her ex-husband's love children who kept showing up. Lenore would have had the girl in her arms if Kinsley had also stood, but she backed away from his mother.

"I need to go to the bathroom," Kinsley blurted out. She did a fast swipe with the back of her hand to remove that tear.

"I'll show you where it is," Lenore volunteered,

and she led the girl out of the dining room and toward the hall powder room.

Sighing, Shaw took out his phone to call his brother Leyton. This was one of those times when it was good to have the town sheriff in the family. It was also good when Leyton answered right away.

"Another of Marty's kids showed up," Leyton said before Shaw could speak. "I just heard she was at Fred's asking for directions to the ranch."

"Yeah. Her name's Kinsley Rubio, and it's possible she's been reported as a runaway."

"I'll check."

Lenore came back into the dining room, and her right eyebrow was already arched in a questioning expression. Shaw just shook his head, hoping he'd have answers for her soon.

"Her mother, Aurora Elmore Rubio, reported her missing about four hours ago," Leyton verified several moments later. Shaw heard his brother sigh, too. "Is she looking for money or just for Marty?"

"So far only Marty. You've got her mom's address in San Antonio?"

"I do." He rattled it off to Shaw. "You want to drive her home, or do you need me to do it?" Leyton asked.

Shaw thought of all the work he had on his plate today. A meeting with a cattle broker and tax paperwork, and he wanted to spot-check some fence repairs that were being done by a new ranch hand. All of those things were important but were outweighed by the single tear on Kinsley's cheek. The girl was hurting, and he needed to step in and clear up yet one more of his father's messes.

"I'll take her," Shaw answered. "But you call Marty. If he doesn't answer, call his friends and his manager until you track him down. Then tell him to get his ass out to Kinsley's house and fix this."

Leyton grumbled some profanity, followed by a sound of agreement. Shaw figured it would take his brother much longer to locate Marty than it would for him to drive the girl home. One hour to get to San Antonio. Another couple of hours to try to smooth things over as best he could. Another hour to get back.

"I'll get my purse from the living room so I can go with you to take her home," Lenore volunteered after Shaw had ended the call.

He didn't nix that even though he doubted it would help with the smoothing. Still, if Kinsley started crying again, it might be a good thing to have his mom there with them.

Shaw put his phone back in his pocket and waited for Kinsley. And waited. When too much time had passed, he went to the bathroom and knocked on the door. It swung open.

No Kinsley inside.

He was about to call out for her when he heard his mother's hurried footsteps coming from the living room.

"My purse is gone," Lenore blurted out. Her eyes widened when she looked into the empty bathroom. "You don't think that sweet girl stole it, do you?"

Well, shit on a stick. This smoothing over had just gotten a lot more complicated.

CHAPTER TWO

Sunny hated to state the obvious, but having surgery hurt. So did the ill-advised Brazilian she'd let her former almost-stepdaughter talk her into getting the day before she'd gone under the knife. Now she was hurting in two places.

Two intimate, personal places.

She pushed the red leather bra to the side in the back of the SUV so she could make room for the groceries. But Sunny kept her attention on the garment for several moments. Considering it. Considering her sister, too. She'd often been puzzled over Hadley's costume designs, but she wondered in this case if she could modify the bra to suit her own needs.

Specifically, as a way to cut down on potential boob pain.

If she sanded down the sharp spikes, the cups wouldn't rip her clothes or impale anyone who happened to hug her. And the remaining metal padding could act like a shield over her incision. Still, that was probably the extreme way to go. An easier solution would be to just avoid hugs. And accidental contact. And moving or excessive breathing.

She tried not to wince when she opened the back of her SUV. She failed and not only winced but wasn't able to bite off the throaty grunt of pain that escaped. A grunt that immediately got her traveling companion's attention.

"Are you all right?" Ryan asked, hurrying to take the bags from her. His forehead bunched up when her gaze drifted down to her left breast.

Boob pain wasn't a comfortable subject for a sixteen-year-old boy. Especially when the pain was connected to the boob of his stepmother.

Well, his almost-stepmother anyway.

Sunny hadn't actually married Ryan's father, Hugh Dunbar, but she'd been with him for two years before breaking off the engagement. Ending the relationship had only added more fodder to her runaway fiancée reputation, but a little gossip was a small price to pay for not making the mistake of going through with the marriage. And Sunny was positive it would have been a mistake.

Ryan, however, definitely wasn't a mistake.

He was a good kid. The best part of the deal when it came to Hugh.

"I'm okay," she assured him, and that was true—if she discounted the pain. Which she would do since she didn't want Ryan to worry about her. The stitches had come out that morning. According to her doctor, her recovery was fine and dandy, and she would soon be right as rain.

Sunny had decided that if she needed a surgeon again, she'd look for one who didn't speak in overly cheerful clichés.

At least Dr. Sanchez was correct about her physical recovery. Her body would get to the *dandy* stage soon enough. Perhaps even the *fine* stage. However, as far as the mental stuff, it was going to take her a while to get over the scare of coming face-to-face with the possibility that a part of her body could have killed her.

Death by left breast.

It hadn't been a joking matter, of course, but joking about it even to herself helped stave off the darkness. *Sometimes.* Maybe being back here in Lone Star Ridge would help, too. After all, Granny Em had a knack for chasing away the bad stuff.

"Sunny Dalton?" a man shouted from across the street. "Or is it McCall? Definitely not Hadley."

Even after all these years, fifteen of them to be exact, she had no trouble recognizing that voice. It belonged to none other than Carter Bodell. This time the sound she made was a groan of a different sort. Not from boob pain. But more of a reaction to someone who was a pain in the rear.

"Sunny? McCall?" Carter continued to yell out as if she might not have seen him. Or as if she might bolt. Which she considered doing. She was tired, hurting and just wanted to get to Em's so she could take some meds.

"A friend of yours?" Ryan asked as he put the last of the grocery bags in the back of the SUV.

"A friend in only a generic sense. I went to school with him from kindergarten all the way to high school. Whatever you do, don't shake his hand."

That got Ryan's attention, and she would explain later that unless Carter had, well, actually grown up, he was still a prankster. An annoying one who had crossed too many lines too many times. Ironic, since he was also a mortician. A mortician who, according to Em, had a bumper sticker on his truck proudly announcing that My Other Car Is a Hearse."

Wearing a T-shirt that boasted My Clients Give Me the Cold Shoulder and jeans with a rodeo buckle the size of a 1960s Buick hubcap, Carter darted across Main Street. That didn't take much effort, considering it was just two lanes and there was little traffic.

"Sunny? McCall?" Carter repeated, trotting to her.

"Sunny," she confirmed.

"Funny Sunny." He grinned, exposing overly bright teeth. The man had obviously gone through a vat of whitening strips, and the enamel looked radioactive. "Tell me a joke," he added with a wink.

Those were four words she'd come to hate. Four words she'd probably heard more often than Carter purchased whitening strips. Most people might not be able to pinpoint the exact moment such a comment had become an annoyance, but Sunny could. It'd been the catchphrase on *Little Cowgirls*, started when she'd been five years old and had fancied herself a stand-up comic.

Things had gone downhill after that.

She'd stood up. She'd performed a five-year-old's version of comedy, and the producers had loved it so much, they'd built it into the show.

"I'm sort of joked out at the moment," she muttered.

That refusal and what had to be a sour expression on her face didn't deter him. Still grinning, Carter stuck out his hand for her to shake, and she caught a glimpse of the little metal device on his palm that would no doubt shock her or make farting noises if she touched it.

Sunny just shook her head and sighed. "Sorry, but I don't have time to visit. Or to be pranked. Granny Em's waiting for me."

Carter nodded and stuck out his hand to Ryan. "Carter Bodell," he greeted. "And you are?"

"Ryan Dunbar."

He didn't shake Carter's hand. Didn't explain either that he was her almost-stepson. Of course, if Ryan had mentioned that little detail, there'd be questions about why he was with Sunny and not his father. Why he was an *almost* and not an actual stepson. Those questions would come soon enough anyway, but she hoped to delay them until she'd at least had a nap or two.

"I guess you know all about your mom once being a big star around here," Carter commented. "*Little Cowgirls* was the number one reality show back in the day."

Obviously, he'd assumed that Ryan was her son, and Sunny didn't correct him. In fact, she got in the SUV and motioned for Ryan to do the same. Carter didn't pick up on the not-so-subtle signs—her repeated sighs, disinterested expression and under-the-breath mutterings—that he should say his goodbyes and let them get on with their day.

"Your mom was always the funny one of the *Little Cowgirls*," Carter went on. "Funny Sunny, that's what folks called her. McCall was the prissy pants good girl, and Hadley... Well, she was *bad*." He added a laugh and a wink to that.

There it was in a nutshell. The labels the producers had put on the Dalton triplets. Labels that had become self-fulfilling prophesies in a ball-and-chain, live-up-to-the-hype sort of way.

Sunny figured she'd gotten the so-so deal out of those labels. Funny Sunny was much better than Prissy Pants, especially after it'd become a childhood taunt of "pissy pants" for McCall, who'd lagged behind in toilet training. And Funny Sunny was better than Badly Hadley, as well. That had always sounded like a grammatically challenged outlaw name to Sunny, which would have been okay until the teenage years when it'd taken on a smutty tone.

One that Hadley had reveled in.

"Of course, these days I hear you're called Runny Sunny," Carter said, winking at her.

As if she might not have caught the dig that had been in the tabloids, Carter looked at her bare ring finger. The one that would have had a wedding ring if she hadn't run. Sunny wished she had wizard powers to make Carter, stupid labels and the tabloids vaporize.

"Did you see the episode where your mom said she wanted to grow a weenie like her brother?" Carter hooted with laughter. Apparently, so had many viewers. Since that'd happened when she was three, Sunny had had three decades of folks reminding her of that particular toddler pipe dream.

Ryan didn't respond, and neither did Sunny, but that didn't stop Carter from keeping it up.

"And how about the episode where she wore her mother's lace panties on her head and announced that she was now a redhead?" Carter did more hooting.

Sunny gave him as polite a smile as she could manage. But she needed no such reminders that camera crews had followed her and her family and captured every embarrassing moment there was to capture.

Including *the kiss*.

The one that'd given Shaw sore nuts. Judging from Shaw's reaction, she could surmise that sore nuts was even worse than boob pain. Possibly worse than a first-time Brazilian.

"Let's go, please," she told Ryan the moment he'd started the engine.

"Say, don't you want to visit a while longer so we can catch up?" Carter said.

Since she was the funny one, Sunny wasn't rude, though she wanted to be, and she merely said, "Some other time."

"But I wanted to ask you out," Carter went on. "How about dinner tonight?"

Sunny shook her head. "I can't—"

"Tomorrow night then. Or anytime this week." Carter wasn't actually begging, but it was close.

Sunny didn't think she was a great beauty, but her "fame" seemed to prompt men to hit on her. Sometimes she hit back. But she wouldn't be hitting back in Carter's case. Not in anyone else's for that matter. Two broken engagements was enough. A sort of reverse charm. She obviously sucked at relationships and needed to put a stop to any future suckage.

After Sunny muttered a goodbye to Carter, Ryan

drove off, lurching the SUV only a little when he put his foot on the accelerator. A huge improvement since his starts and stops were usually a lot shakier. Still, he was a good driver, especially considering he'd only had his license for four months.

"Carter's a real charmer," Ryan remarked. "I'm betting it's been a while since someone's fallen for the hand buzzer?"

"Not since ninth grade. I think Carter has a hope-springs-eternal mind-set that we'll all develop severe memory loss so he can play his tired pranks on us." Sunny motioned to the stop sign just ahead. "Take a left there," she instructed, since Ryan didn't know the way to Em's.

The speed limit was twenty-five miles per hour, which meant that even the short distance gave Sunny a chance to take a look at the shops and businesses that lined Main Street.

There were no chain stores here. They were all mom-and-pop businesses and services that covered the basics for a small town. Fred's Grocer, a small hospital, the Lickety Split Ice Cream Parlor, the police station and Breakfast at Tiffany's, a diner that also served as a bakery and coffee shop.

The owner wasn't a Tiffany but rather Hildie Stoddermeyer, who was obsessed with the author Truman Capote. Not only had Hildie painted the diner the signature Tiffany color of robin's-egg blue, but she had items on the menu like Holly Golightly pancakes, Moon River gravy fries and even Capote cranberry compote.

The diner itself was filled with movie posters,

quotes and Capote's other books, which Hildie also adored. While the woman took things to extremes, Sunny figured that most people were just happy that Hildie hadn't insisted the diner be called by the title of one of his other famous books, *In Cold Blood*.

"Who was the cowboy back on the road earlier?" Ryan asked after he took the turn off Main Street. "The one whose arm you touched?"

Oh, so he'd caught that. "Sorry I didn't introduce you. That was Shaw Jameson."

Ryan didn't exactly get an aha expression, but it was close. "The guy you kissed on *Little Cowgirls* when you were a teenager?"

Yep, the very one, and the hidden cameraman had managed to capture that embarrassing and painful moment when her braces had cut Shaw's mouth so deep that he'd gushed blood. Then trying to help, she'd smacked him on the nose with her elbow hard enough that he'd cursed a string of cuss stew that had to be bleeped out of the footage.

For the finale of the attempted kiss, Shaw had staggered into her, causing her to lose her balance, and during her fall, she'd kicked him in the groin with her seriously pointy-toed cowboy boots that the producers had insisted she wear.

That's when Sunny had burst into tears.

The tears had gotten a whole lot worse when the cameraman had stepped out from the shadows, announcing that he'd "caught it all." All her crying and begging had nearly caused him to delete it, but then her mother had gotten involved. Sunshine had insisted that it be aired, just as Sunshine had done with other moments that Sunny and her siblings had begged and cried not to be used.

Later, Sunny had let people believe that the scene had been scripted, as so many of them were, but that one had been the real deal. As spontaneous as spontaneity could be. And Shaw had gotten the sore nuts to prove it.

"Shaw and I go way back," Sunny added.

Unlike Carter Bodell, Shaw wasn't a friend in the generic sense. He'd been the source of many teenage fantasies. Not just hers, either. If tall, dark and hot were what you went for, then Shaw was the right guy for every one of those, and a couple of decades hadn't changed that. If anything, he was taller, darker and even hotter.

She frowned.

Thinking like that wouldn't stop future relationship calamities. Besides, she liked Shaw and didn't want him caught up in her emotional baggage that was now the size of a cargo ship.

Sunny motioned for Ryan to turn into the driveway. And there it was. Granny Em's house.

Home.

Sunny supposed that most adults had mixed feelings when making a long overdue visit like this. So many memories, both good and bad. Em thankfully fell on the good side when it came to the images and memories that started to do a slippery slide through Sunny's head. So did her siblings. Mostly anyway. But there were clearer images, those preserved in reruns that she'd never quite come to terms with.

Now, on top of all of that, she needed to try to help

Ryan work through his issues with his dad. Oh, and heal both mentally and physically from a health scare that had shaken her all the way to the marrow. And try to get her own life back on track.

All of that might be more than too much for her Funny Sunny personality self to come back from.

Ryan pulled to a stop in front of the two-story yellow Victorian where nothing had changed for as long as Sunny could remember. There was something comforting about that. If a house could weather stuff, then maybe she stood a chance, too. Of course, she couldn't be fixed with a fresh coat of paint and occasional new roof.

"Remember not to mention anything about my surgery," Sunny reminded Ryan. "I don't want Em to worry."

He nodded and didn't say anything about her already having warned him multiple times. "I'll bring in the suitcases and then come back for the groceries," Ryan offered.

She thanked him, gave his arm a gentle squeeze and went up the steps. Before she even made it to the door, it opened.

"You're here," the woman in the doorway announced. It wasn't a happy announcement, either. It sounded more like a scolding, one doused with enough dread to erase any ray of sunshine.

The woman was Bernice Biggs, her grandmother's part-time housekeeper and someone else who hadn't changed. In fact, Bernice had the same iron-gray hair styled in the same tight bun as it had been when Sunny was a kid. It had always reminded Sunny of a lump of jagged ice, which was also a fitting description for the woman.

At least Sunny wouldn't have to deal with a painful hug from Bernice. The housekeeper wasn't the sort to dole out any affection.

"Tell me a joke," Bernice grumbled.

The woman knew that the request felt like the equivalent of a poke to sore ribs, but two could play this irritating game. Sunny picked through the repertoire of lame jokes that were branded in her memory and came up with a bad one.

"What do you call an apple that falls on your head?" Sunny asked, and didn't pause before she gave her the answer. "A fruit punch."

Yeah, it was lame enough to make Bernice probably wish that she hadn't gone for rib poking. The joke hadn't been worth the energy that Bernice had to expend for an eye roll.

"Bernice, this is Ryan," Sunny said. She kept her Funny Sunny tone and expression to bug Bernice even more. Sunny also secretly hoped that some of that sunniness would rub off on the woman. A thin temporary veneer of fake pleasantness would do.

"Your boyfriend's son," Bernice muttered. That sounded like another scolding. "Your boyfriend who didn't come with you."

Bernice no doubt knew about the breakup, knew that Hugh Dunbar and Sunny hadn't parted on friendly terms after she'd ended their engagement one week before the wedding.

"Hugh's traveling around the country on buying trips and meeting with investors for some new stores,"

Sunny settled for saying, and that was possibly the truth.

Possibly.

Hugh often traveled looking for rare and antique books for his small chain of bookstores, One More Chapter, that were scattered throughout the major cities in Texas. However, he hadn't seen fit to fill in either Ryan or Sunny on his plans.

Sunny got why Hugh wouldn't have cc'd his ex-fiancée his travel itinerary. He was pissed off at her. Likely hated her guts. But, unfortunately, Hugh had let his broken heart and sour feelings spill onto his son.

Hugh had just assumed that Ryan would stay with her as he normally did when his dad was traveling. And Ryan and Sunny had indeed wanted that particular arrangement to continue. But this time Hugh hadn't bothered to clear it with either of them. In Sunny's opinion, that made Hugh a giant, smelly turd who should be subjected to a Brazilian.

On a huff and as if it were a great chore, Bernice stepped back to let Ryan bring in the bags. "Any reason this boy isn't in school?" Bernice asked. "It's April. Kids should be in school this time of year."

"I graduated from high school early." Ryan set the suitcases on the floor. "I'm taking some online college classes, but I'll be moving to the campus dorm in the fall to start a premed degree."

"You're staying until the fall?" Bernice asked, her mouth tightening more than some prunes past their expiration date.

"To be determined," Sunny supplied as Ryan went back to the SUV for the groceries.

When Sunny had spoken to Em, she'd been vague about how long she'd be staying, and she hadn't offered any explanation about Ryan other than he would be coming with her to the ranch, too. Of course, Em hadn't wanted explanations or the length of the stay and had instead said they were "welcome there forever."

"What about work?" Bernice asked. "Or did you ditch the job when you ditched your fiancé?"

"No job ditching," Sunny assured her. "I can work from here."

It wouldn't be hard to do since she normally did her illustrations from home anyway. And, thankfully, she was so far ahead that she could determine her own workload for a few months, which was a good thing considering her low energy level.

"Still working on those comic books then," Bernice commented.

"Graphic novels," Sunny corrected. "Yes, I still work on them."

Well, she did the illustrations for one anyway. One very odd graphic novel series that had taken on a life of its own. *Slackers Quackers*, a lazy duck who woke up every morning in a new time and place.

Sort of like Doctor Who with feathers.

J.B. Whitman, the reclusive author, had originally written the stories for kids, but many adults—especially college students—had decided *Slackers Quackers* could be enjoyed on many levels. Levels that likely included huge amounts of tequila and other party enhancers.

After ten years or so, *Slackers Quackers* now had a huge cult following, which in turn gave Sunny a paycheck. But it was more than that. So much more. Most people wouldn't understand that the often silly drawings were on a different level for her, too.

"You can put those in there," Bernice said, tipping her head toward the kitchen when Ryan returned with the bags. "Though if Sunny did the shopping, I'm betting there's not much in there that the rest of us will eat."

Since Sunny's mouth was starting to hurt from all the fake smiling and teeth gritting, she went in search of Em. She threaded her way through the place. No modern open floor plan in this house. The rooms tumbled into each other with no rhyme or reason to the design. The living room fed into a guest bedroom, then into the dining room, then into a library/study.

And that's where she spotted Em.

Her grandmother was at the window, earbud headphones in place, which meant she was listening to music. Not songs from her generation as many would expect. No, Em preferred rap, specifically Lil Jon's "Get Low." Sunny chose to believe that Em didn't understand the curse words and sexual references in the song but merely liked the beat.

She had binoculars pressed to her eyes, and her attention nailed to whatever she was watching. Probably some insect, bird or other critter. Em had a butterfly garden, birdbaths, squirrel feeders and even an area planted to draw bees and ladybugs. There was a lettuce patch planted just for rabbits, too.

If it flew, fluttered, flounced or looked like something that belonged in a hobbit village, Em liked to encourage it to drop in for a visit. The only insects she hated were mosquitos, and she'd invested plenty of money in the metal traps to catch them and keep them away from her and the other animals.

Em was wearing her usual cowboy boots and jeans, these with puckered-up rhinestone-red lips on the back pockets that likely hadn't been targeted to the over-seventy shopper. She turned at the sound of Sunny's footsteps and smiled. Not an ordinary smile, either. Em wasn't capable of ordinary. The woman could make things feel like, well, like a magical hobbit village.

"Come over here," Em said. She pulled out her earbuds and motioned for Sunny to come to the window.

She did, brushing a kiss on Em's cheek before her grandmother handed her the binoculars. "Have a look at that hiney."

Although she was a little confused, Sunny obliged. And her tongue nearly landed on her kneecaps when, amid the gardens, lawn gnomes and gazing balls, she spotted the half-naked man on a ladder by the barn. Definitely no flying, fluttering or flouncing. And he darn sure wasn't a hobbit. The guy was shirtless, his jeans way low on his hips, and he didn't appear to be wearing any underwear. Sunny could see the top of the crack of his butt.

"Josiah Cowan," Em provided, taking back the binoculars for another look. "You remember him from high school?"

Sunny nodded. He'd played football. Sunny was reasonably sure she'd never seen this much of him.

"He does some handyman work for me," Em explained. "But he's doodling around with some boards that in no way need such doodling or fixing. You can bet your Sunday britches he's here to see you. He'll want to ask you out now that you're free and single."

Sunny's stomach dropped a little. She didn't want to be asked out. She didn't want men to think of her as free or single.

"And Josiah's not the only one," Em went on. "In the past thirty minutes, I've gotten three calls and two texts from men who want to know if I need something fixed or if they could run errands for me. One of them was Elmer Goggins, who's sixty if he's a day. He wants to take you on a picnic."

Em's phone rang, and she frowned when she looked at the screen. "Bennie Harper. He's a volunteer fireman," she explained, hitting the decline-call button. "He'd better not start another fire in the birdbath just so he can get your attention."

Since Sunny suspected Bennie had done that their junior year of high school, she hoped he wouldn't try the ploy again. Or any ploy, for that matter.

"Now, now," Em said, giving Sunny's hand a squeeze. "Don't get that look on your face. The look that says you're thinking about turning tail and running. Once menfolk understand you're still getting over your ex, they'll leave you be."

Maybe. But Sunny was indeed thinking of run-

ning. Briefly thinking it anyway. Then she remembered all the reasons she'd come here in the first place.
She needed to be home. She needed to heal. What she
didn't need was a cowboy with a great hiney, a picnic
or a man loony enough to start a fire for her.

"Are you really still getting over your ex?" Em
came out and asked.

Even though she was wallowing somewhat in her
own pity party, Sunny had no trouble hearing the
concern in her grandmother's voice. Em was worried about her, and causing worry was not one of the
reasons Sunny had come back.

"I'm fine," Sunny assured her. But because Em
had an especially good BS meter and was picking up
on something, Sunny added, "I'm just having some
trouble dealing with the way Hugh's ignoring his son.
I don't want Ryan to be punished because I called off
the wedding. I want Ryan and his dad to be close, the
way it should be between father and son."

Em nodded and paused as if giving that some
thought. "You're right. But if the boy's as bright as
you say, then he already knows his dad's all hat and
no cattle."

So true. Well, it was true if all hat and no cattle
was a put-down for someone who was a lousy father.
And that was one of the reasons Ryan needed some
TLC. It was a tough time in a kid's life when they
figured out they had a butt hole for a parent. Sunny
knew that firsthand because both of her parents fell
into that category.

It was something Shaw knew, as well, when it
came to his own father, and she thought about what

he might be going through right now with another of Marty's kids.

"Don't know why you got engaged to Hugh in the first place," Em muttered.

Sunny was having trouble figuring that out, too, and she thought she finally had a handle on it. "I'd see him in one of his bookstores, and I think I got my feelings for him mixed up with all those cool books. Plus, he's moody and mysterious like Heathcliff and Mr. Darcy."

Of course, that was being generous. With his handsome, distinguished face, Hugh had indeed looked like those fictional characters. But moody and mysterious were just other ways of saying *grouchy* and *secretive*. At first she had blamed that on him being a widower. But in hindsight, Sunny could see that Hugh's greatest asset, the thing that had drawn him to her, was Ryan. Her engagement to Hugh might have been a bust, but Ryan was a prize that she hadn't had to give up.

What she had had to give up was the dream of having a baby with Hugh.

Of course, she hadn't specifically wanted *his* but *a* baby, and that was part of the problem.

Sunny had wanted a child for as long as she could remember, and she'd thought that since Hugh was already a father, he would want other children. With her. That'd been the same faulty logic she'd applied to her first engagement, too. It turned out that getting involved with a single father didn't necessarily lead to more fatherhood.

Or motherhood.

"Let me look at you," Em said, taking her hands and giving Sunny the once-over. Her smile dimmed. "Other than calling off your latest wedding, is there something else I should know about?"

"I'm fine," Sunny assured her with the best lie she could manage. "Just a little tired."

Em continued to stare at her as if she might press to get at the truth, but she finally nodded. Then she gave Sunny the hug that she'd been dreading. Plenty of boob pain came with it, but Sunny held her ground. Held her breath, too, until Em finally put an end to the torture.

"Okay," Em concluded, her eyes pinned to Sunny. "Go on up to your room and take a nap. I want you all rested up for lunch so we can have a good sit-down and gab. I want to gab some with Ryan, too. Go on," she insisted.

Sunny did, noticing that Em went back to watching the handyman. The one who would no doubt soon ask her out. She wouldn't be able to say no fast enough. Even if she hadn't been recovering, he'd be hands-off. Besides, if she wanted a rebound guy and was in any shape to have one, she'd look in Shaw's direction.

Especially since he'd already looked in hers.

She hadn't missed the glimmer of heat in his eyes or the old attraction that snapped at them like a rubber band. A little painful but definitely an attention getter.

When Sunny made it back to the foyer, she saw Ryan heading up the stairs with their suitcases. "This is the last of our things," he said. "I left your sister's stuff in the SUV because I wasn't sure where to put it."

Neither was Sunny. The weird underwear and several other boxes had arrived in a huge shipping crate along with instructions: "Store this at Em's the next time you're there. Had."

Apparently, her sister had been in such a hurry that she hadn't bothered to use her whole name, and Hadley definitely hadn't mentioned why she'd needed such things stored. Sunny didn't want to speculate about that why, either, because with Hadley it could be anything.

"Miss Bernice told me which room was yours, and the one I'd be using, so I'll put my stuff in there," Ryan added.

Sunny hoped the woman hadn't doused the info with a coating of more gloom, but she knew Bernice had when Ryan added, "Look, if it's a problem with me being here, I can find someplace else to stay."

She wanted to throttle Bernice for putting that idea in Ryan's head. Especially since there was no *someplace else* for him. His mother had died eight years ago, and while his paternal grandparents were still living, Ryan had never even met them because they were estranged from his dad.

And as for staying with his dad, well, Hugh had nixed that, saying that he'd needed some "me time" to get over Sunny crushing his heart into a million pieces. Yes, he'd used those exact words. He'd added that Ryan was plenty old enough to be on his own. While Ryan was more mature than most sixteen-year-old boys, she'd seen the worry all over him when he'd thought he was going to have to fend for himself for God knew how long.

Me time could go on for a while.

"You're staying here," Sunny assured the boy. "Just ignore Bernice like everyone else does. The producers wanted a crotchety housekeeper to contrast with Granny Em's cheer and sass so they talked Em into hiring her. Bernice has stayed in character for three decades."

Well, either that or the woman had been going through menopause and PMS, simultaneously, for just as long.

"And besides," Sunny went on, "Bernice is normally only here a couple of hours each day, so you won't have to put up with her too much."

Pushing thoughts of Bernice aside, Sunny stepped in the doorway of her childhood bedroom and did something she always did when she came back for a visit. She froze, then muttered, "Sheez, Louise." Somehow, she always seemed to forget that the room was like a time capsule.

Or maybe the scene of a crime.

Obviously, Em hadn't done an ounce of redecorating here. Neither had Sunny on the many visits she'd made back. Simply put, she hadn't stayed long enough to get rid of the things that now brought back too many memories.

The large loft-style room was divided into three distinct areas, like a rectangular pie cut into a triangle, with beds, chest of drawers and tables forming each section. Her section was in the right corner, where it'd been for as long as Sunny could remember. According to Em, it'd been where their mother had put them shortly after she'd brought them home from the hospital.

Ryan didn't remark on the teenage girl decor. Perhaps because he didn't even recognize the posters tacked onto the walls of the respective areas. Sunny's had the boy bands. NSYNC, Backstreet Boys and 98 Degrees. But there were also ones of the stand-up comics of the day, Robin Williams and Jerry Seinfeld.

Even though Sunny had come back to the ranch many times over the past fifteen years, something just now occurred to her. The things she had on display were like those labels the producers had given her and her sisters.

Maybe her brush with possible death had given her some kind of insight. Or maybe her mopey attitude was causing her to peer through non-rose-colored glasses. Either way, her triangle screamed Funny Sunny, so much so that it made her want to toss it all into the trash. Made her want a fresh do-over. Of course, some would say that's exactly what she'd attempted when she'd become a runaway fiancée.

Not once but twice.

She was guessing when it happened twice, it was no longer a do-over but a sign that she should stay celibate and become a youngish crazy cat lady.

Sighing over the possibility, Sunny shifted her attention to McCall's area. Hers screamed prissy pants/good girl, what with her pink lace comforter. Princess Diana and Jane Austen posters were on her walls—all precisely framed, of course—and her trophies and awards were for all the good service and the civic-minded stuff she favored. *Still favored*, Sunny mentally amended. After all, McCall had become a relationship counselor. A very successful one.

And then there was Hadley's triangle.

Living up to the hype, Badly Hadley had painted her walls glossy black. Not especially well, either, since the long-dried paint was glopped in places, making it look as if it were oozing down like an oil spill. The posters were of *Thelma and Louise* and heavy metal bands, including one band member gripping his own crotch with an Edward Scissorhands-type glove. Sunny wouldn't have been surprised if it had deballed the guy.

There were no trophies or awards in Hadley's space since there hadn't been any. No framed high school graduation diploma, either, because she'd flunked out and gone the GED route. The only sign of things to come for Hadley was a stack of dark superhero graphic novels that the producers had given her as props and the basket of fabric on the floor next to her bed. The scraps were black, too, with some grays and bloodreds tossed in, but maybe whatever Hadley had been sewing before she turned eighteen had led her to become a costume designer.

Pulling herself out of the decor memory lane, Sunny turned to Ryan, who was taking in the space as if it were a museum, art gallery or—yes—a crime scene.

"You didn't take any of this stuff with you when you left?" he asked before she could say anything.

"Not really."

Basically, she'd packed some of her clothes and hightailed it to college. Anything in the dresser drawers, she'd boxed up and put in the attic. Including the diaries. Yes, she'd been one of those girls who'd written daily, complete with titles, dates and even a memento or two that she'd taped onto some of the pages.

Daily whinings, laments and angsts punctuated by lustful fantasies about Shaw.

It was depressing to think that if she continued writing in diaries, there'd be too many similarities between now and then. As far as she was concerned, they could stay boxed up. She'd gone into too many details, bared too much of her soul. Written way more than she should have.

Including the one and only time she'd had sex with Shaw.

That one she'd titled "Hot Dreamy Shaw," and she'd taped one of his chest hairs to the page.

Sunny cleared her throat and her mind of the images that came. Shaw had indeed been hot and dreamy. "I just wanted a fresh start," she added.

Which she hadn't gotten, of course. Not when her college classmates had discovered her "celebrity" status. It hadn't been fandom like a real actor or rock star would have gotten, either. Because that's when Sunny had realized that she, her life and her childhood had been one big joke.

"What was it like?" Ryan's voice pierced through the silence and her thoughts. "Having a camera follow you around all the time?"

"It sucked," she answered readily. "Most of the time," Sunny amended. "It made me feel special because it wasn't the norm. And it made me feel like a freak because it wasn't the norm."

Ryan made a sound to indicate he got that. And he

likely did. Boy geniuses probably didn't always fit in with the rest of the kids.

"It wasn't like what you saw on TV," Sunny added a moment later. "Things that happened were often edited, and we were prompted…pushed."

Yeah, that was the right word. And her mother had usually been the pusher. Sunshine had been driven by the need for high ratings, and she'd learned darn fast that the way to do that was for her little cowgirls to do something funny. Sunshine hadn't cared a rat's butt if it was also embarrassing.

Unless it was her, of course.

Sunshine had added many conditions to her contract as to how she'd be filmed. One of them was that no footage of her would be used when she was without her Spanx and makeup.

Ryan went to the side of her bed and bent down to pick up something from the floor. It was a necklace containing her name etched in silver. Since Sunny was certain she'd packed that away, it meant Em had likely taken it out. Why, Sunny didn't know. She didn't particularly need a reminder of who she was.

On the other hand, maybe that was exactly what she needed.

"The necklace was something I had to wear nearly every episode," she explained to Ryan. "Just as Hadley and McCall had worn theirs. It was so the viewers could tell us apart. Hadley used to turn hers backward so that it spelled Yeldah. She told people she'd been possessed by a Ukrainian peasant."

Ryan smiled, then got quiet for a moment. "How'd

you feel having a face that's exactly like two other people?"

She'd gotten a lot of variations on that question over her thirty-plus years, and she'd never had an easy answer. "It made me feel both special and like a freak," she said, paraphrasing her earlier response. "It was nice though to be able to see how new makeup, a hairstyle or new clothes would look on me without ever having to try it out."

For instance, she knew without a doubt that she hadn't wanted any of Hadley's black Goth lipstick and the safety pin piercings on her eyebrow.

Ryan took another glance at the diverse corners of the room. "Did you ever like swap places or things like that?"

"A couple of times," she admitted. "McCall and I swapped anyway. She sucked at math so I took some of the tests for her." Sunny winced. Cheating in school probably wasn't something she should confess to a kid. "And a couple of times Hadley tried to pretend she was either McCall or me so she could leave the house after being grounded. It didn't work."

Which was another reason not to get a pierced eyebrow. Those holes showed even without the safety pin.

"Sorry," Ryan muttered. "You probably just want to go to bed, and here I am peppering you with questions."

"It's okay. I don't mind *your* questions." But she did motion for him to follow her. "You'll be staying in my brother's old room."

It was at the other end of the hall with her parents' bedroom and Em's in between. Hayes had wanted to be as far away from his triplet sisters as the Victorian floor plan allowed. Even that hadn't been far enough though because Hayes had also created his own getaway in the attic, which had easy access for him since the attic stairs were in his closet.

There were no posters on Hayes's wall. Nor any of his personal things lying around. He'd cleared that out long ago when he'd left town, left the ranch, left his sisters. And he'd never come back after going to Hollywood to be an actor. Still, Sunny thought she should give Ryan a warning.

"It's possible you'll find some old *Playboy* magazines stashed in here," she said. That got his attention. Of course, it did. Ryan was sixteen after all. "The most likely place is the bathroom." She tipped her head toward the en suite. "If you find any, hide them again. Bernice will have a hissy fit if she sees them."

Ryan made a sound of agreement and looked around the room before his gaze came back to her. "You want me to get you a glass of water so you can take your pain meds?"

She smiled, feeling the warmth of his concern brush away some of the mopey cobwebs. "No, thanks. But I'm going to grab a nap before lunch. You'll be okay on your own?"

He returned the smile. "I can unpack, search for porn. That's plenty to keep me busy."

That humor was why she loved him. Why she wanted to make sure Hugh's "me time" didn't screw him up six ways to Sunday.

Drawing in a long breath, Sunny made her way back down the hall toward her room. She had one thing on her mind. Well, two actually. Meds and sleep. Since she'd need that water for the meds, she stopped by the hall bathroom to get a glass. She opened the door.

And froze.

Because the room wasn't empty.

There on the floor, the girl sat, wedged between the bathtub and the toilet. It would have been hard to recognize that tear-streaked face, but Sunny had no trouble recalling the cowboy boots.

The pink-tasseled ones.

"Please don't tell anyone I'm here," the girl blurted out in a whisper. And with that, Kinsley burst into more tears.

CHAPTER THREE

SHAW DROVE HIS truck at a snail's pace. And looked. He kept his eyes peeled to the sides of the road, the woods, pastures—heck, even the ditches. There was no sign of Kinsley.

Just how far could a purse-stealing teenager get in less than two hours?

Apparently pretty far, since Shaw hadn't seen hide nor hair of her.

And he'd looked hard, too. First in the barns and the immediate area of the ranch house. When he hadn't spotted her, he'd called in a few hands to help with the search. There were no missing horses, no missing vehicles, either, so that meant Kinsley had walked out on her own booted feet or else she was hiding somewhere.

When Shaw didn't spot her on the road, he continued to drive into town. If Kinsley had made it this far, then it meant she had even more places to hide, in the shops and alleys. Of course, no local was just going to ignore a girl who looked like Kinsley. Nope. Once folks eyed her outfit, they would notice that she had Marty's looks and would call Shaw or his siblings.

So far though, there'd been no such calls.

There wasn't a bus or taxi service in Lone Star

Ridge so leaving by those methods was out, but the
girl could try hitchhiking again. Shaw didn't like the
idea of her doing that, though maybe it meant she
was heading home. In case that's what she'd done,
he tried calling her mother again, using the number
that Leyton had given him. The call went straight to
voice mail, just as his three other calls had.

As the ones to Marty had, too.

Of course, Shaw hadn't expected anything else
from his quick-zippered dad, but since Kinsley's mom
had filed a missing person's report, he'd figured she
would have her phone right next to her, waiting to
hear news about her daughter.

Shaw slowed to a stop when he saw Leyton on the
sidewalk outside the police department. His brother
was pacing while he talked on the phone. Maybe he
had some good news. But when Shaw lowered the
window on the passenger's side, Leyton just shook
his head.

"No one knows where she is," Leyton relayed.
"But there have been a couple of sightings. From
what I can piece together, she walked through town
and was heading west."

Well, at least they had something. Not much of
something because "west" covered a lot of territory,
but it meant Kinsley wasn't hiding out at the ranch.
Of course, if she had been doing that, at least she
was safe.

Shaw cursed the concern he felt, but there was no
way to avoid it. It didn't matter that Kinsley had stolen from his mom and was almost certainly a general

pain in the ass. She was still a kid. One who needed to be home with her mother in San Antonio.

"Let me know if you hear anything," Shaw told his brother. "I'll keep looking for her."

Shaw got a jolt of hope the moment he pulled away from the curb because his phone rang. The hope faded and his curiosity ballooned when he saw what was on the screen.

Unknown caller.

He took the call using hands free, and Sunny's voice poured through his truck. "Shaw," she said, not so silky and smooth this time. "Kinsley's here at Em's. She's stuck between the tub and toilet, but other than that, she's okay."

Of all the things Shaw had anticipated Sunny might say, that hadn't been one of them. Not just the part about Kinsley's being stuck, either, but the entire explanation.

"How the hell did she get there?" he asked, already doing a U-turn to head that way.

"I think she walked. I just found her in the upstairs bathroom. Heaven knows how she got past Bernice."

Yeah, that was a good question that Shaw had an answer for. Obviously, Kinsley was sneaky, because she'd managed to lift Lenore's purse and leave the ranch without anyone there laying eyes on her. And it wasn't as if Kinsley blended in with the surroundings.

"Oh, good," Sunny said a moment later. "Ryan managed to get her unwedged. Her backpack was caught on something."

Shaw ignored that and went with his next question. "Did she say why she went to Em's?"

"Not really, but I gather she asked somebody in town where I'd gone, and she got directions. At least I think that's what she said. It's been hard for her to talk what with her crying so hard."

Great. Tears. Whenever possible, Shaw liked to avoid those and the emotions that went along with them.

"I'll be there in a few," Shaw told her, and he hung up so he could call Leyton. "She's at Em's," he said the moment his brother answered. "Try to get in touch with her mother to let her know."

Shaw figured he'd have his hands full with Kinsley. No need to add a distraught mother to his to-do list.

When Shaw pulled up in front of Em's house, he got confirmation of his "hands full" prediction. Bernice was waiting on the porch, and he didn't think it was his imagination that the woman was scowling even more than usual.

"Your sister's upstairs." Bernice said *sister* as if it was an unidentified fungus. "Any idea when your father's going to stop procreating?"

"That's a question for the ages." As long as Marty was drawing breath, he could and likely would reproduce.

Bernice didn't invite him in, though Em certainly did when Shaw stepped into the foyer. The woman hugged him, poking him with the binoculars she was holding. "Good. Glad you're here. You can fix things."

The woman had a gallon of faith in him when Shaw didn't have an ounce of such confidence in himself. He wasn't reasonably sure he could fix anything, but at least the girl had been located and wasn't in a vehicle with a serial killer.

"Maybe you can fix things with Sunny, too," Em continued, following him up the stairs. "You don't happen to know what's wrong with her, do you?"

That stopped Shaw in midstep. "Something's wrong with Sunny?"

Without hesitation, Em nodded. "Something more than the breakup with that slicker-than-a-slop-jar ex-fiancé of hers. Sorry," she quickly added. "I shouldn't bad-mouth that pile of malarkey in case his boy hears."

Em whispered that last part, or rather her version of a whisper, which meant folks in Oklahoma could have still heard it. "His boy?" Though Shaw didn't like adding another question to this conversation when what he really wanted was to get back to the part about Sunny and something being wrong.

"Ryan," Em supplied. "He's sixteen and the ex's son, but the ex doesn't want to spend time with his own boy 'cause he's boo-hooing over his broken heart too much to remember he's got a kid who needs him." She shook her head, obviously in disgust. "Sunny brought Ryan here with her…to work out whatever was troubling her."

So, the guy he'd seen with Sunny earlier was her ex-boyfriend's kid. For reasons Shaw didn't want to explore right now, that made him feel marginally better. Then more than marginally worse. A bad breakup and a teenager could definitely be the reasons for feeling troubled. Plus, there was another possibility.

"You think Sunshine's giving Sunny some problems?" Shaw asked.

Em huffed, and her mouth tightened. "Maybe. My daughter has a knack for trying to bleed as much money from her kids as possible. That makes her even worse than her worthless malarkey of an ex-husband."

Shaw couldn't argue that. Willard had walked out on the family after *Little Cowgirls* had been canceled and the big bucks had stopped flowing in. Sunshine, on the other hand, had exploited their triplets, trying to earn as much money off them as possible. Still, that was the norm and not something that would give Sunny any concern out of the ordinary.

If you'd spent your entire life around a particularly sucky leech, then it wasn't much of an uproar when the leech surfaced again.

"Sunshine came to see me about a month ago," Em went on.

That got his attention because it was a rare thing for Sunshine to come to town without word spreading. "How much money did she want?" He didn't bother speculating about any other possibility for a visit.

"Plenty more than I was willing to give her. She whined and cried when I said I'd only pony up a thousand and that she had to consider it a loan. She finally agreed and took it. Then, she spent the night, probably figuring she'd convince me to give her more, but I didn't cave."

Good, but it would have been better if Em had flat out refused to give her a dime. From what Em had said over the years, Sunny and her sisters had cut their mother off; obviously Em hadn't done that. Sunshine might not have gotten the bucks that she wanted on this latest visit, but the dribble of cash from Em would bring Sunshine back for more.

Em gave him a motherly pat on the back. "Do some poking and figure out what's eating away at Sunny. Oh, and do the same for the girl, too, of course. Bernice got a look at her and said she was one of Marty's."

"Yep," he verified, which made Kinsley one of his, too. His problem anyway. One that he hoped he could fix by driving her home to her mother.

Shaw started up the stairs again. Em didn't follow, proving that she was indeed a wise woman not to involve herself in this any more than she already was. Besides, Em clearly had her own worries what with Sunny.

Since Shaw had been in Em's house too many times to count, he knew his way to the bathroom. He immediately spotted Ryan sitting on the floor outside the door.

"They're in there," the boy volunteered. "Crying."

Judging by the way the kid's forehead bunched up, he felt the same about a weeping female as Shaw did. "Sunny, too?"

The boy nodded but offered no further explanation.

"You're Ryan?" Shaw asked, and when he got another nod, he added, "I'm Shaw Jameson."

"Yeah. The bloody kisser," Ryan muttered.

Well, that was better than how most folks described it. Usually there was a "sore nuts" remark. Before Shaw knocked on the bathroom door, he took a moment to try to clear up something.

"Is anything wrong with Sunny?" Shaw asked. "Em seems to think there might be."

Deer in the headlights. That was the look on the boy's face, and he swallowed hard. "Sunny's okay," he said without a whole lot of conviction.

Well, hell. Something was wrong, and he might or might not have to do something about it. First things first, though. He needed to deal with his crying half sister.

Shaw rapped on the bathroom door and listened. No audible sobs, thank goodness, but he knew from his experience with a kid sister that sometimes silent tears were worse. Several moments later, Sunny opened the door, and he saw that Ryan had been right. Her face was splotchy, her eyes red, and she swiped a fresh tear off her cheek.

"What the heck did Kinsley say or do to make you cry?" Shaw whispered.

Sunny shook her head, still wiping her eyes and waving off the question at the same time. "Nothing really. I just got weepy when she did. I'm a little overly emotional, I guess."

Well, along with Ryan's weak "Sunny's okay," that was a big-assed red flag, proving that Em had been right to voice concern. Sunny wasn't the overly emotional sort. Or at least she hadn't been before this latest breakup.

Sunny stepped back, fully opening the door so he could see Kinsley. The girl was sitting on the floor, and there were wads of what were no doubt tear-dampened toilet paper dropped around her like a weird mushroom garden.

Shaw received a jolt of fear when she lifted her face because at first he thought she'd been bruised. Then he realized they were not bruises but streaks of mascara. Clearly the girl hadn't gone for the waterproof variety.

"I don't want to talk to you," Kinsley said immediately.

There wasn't nearly as much snarl in her voice as there had been at the ranch, and some of the defiant body language was gone, too. Of course, it was hard to look badass while practically cowering on the floor and with a face that looked like a revival of the rock band Kiss.

Shaw took cautious steps closer, the way he would approach a spooked calf. He knew what to murmur in a hushed voice to a calf. *You're all right, girl...boy... or it for undetermined sex.* He tried that with Kinsley, making certain he inserted "girl," and he got a dagger-sharp glare from her.

"I'm not all right," she insisted, which brought on some fresh tears. "My whole life has been a lie, and I'm not the person I thought I was."

"Sometimes, that's better than being the person you actually are," Shaw said, thinking of his father. But, judging from the way Sunny's head whipped up and her gaze met his, that wasn't the way to go here. "Probably not in your case," he amended.

Shaw sat down on the edge of the tub, wishing that Sunny would give him some guidance. Considering she had two sisters, she could likely soothe better than a cowboy who tried to avoid shit like this. As if reading his mind, Sunny shrugged. Then, she winced.

Yeah, winced.

He was certain he hadn't mistaken that, and it was the kind of wince a person made from pain.

Hell.

That nearly got Shaw focusing on her, but there was no way he could ignore Kinsley's sobs. "I know things look pretty bad right now," he told the girl. "But I'm sure we can work this out."

"How?" Kinsley challenged. "By making my bio-dad want me enough to call me or come and see me?"

"Marty doesn't call or come to see me, either," Shaw pointed out, and at least that didn't earn him another whipped-up-head look from Sunny. "This probably isn't what you're going to want to hear, but no one is ever going to accuse Marty of being father of the year. Well, not unless that's judged by the sheer number of offspring," he added under his breath.

"Shaw's right," Sunny piped in. "Marty's not worth crying over. You said you had a stepfather—"

"He left," Kinsley interrupted, snapping out the words. "He left my mom and left me, too. I wondered why he didn't bother trying to see me and now I know. I'm not his. I'm nobody's unless you count a bio-dad butt hole singer with too many kids."

"You have your mom," Shaw reminded her.

That was a reminder for himself, too, and he took out his phone again to call Aurora Rubio. Still no answer. The moment he'd finished leaving another voice mail, Leyton called.

"I'll step out in the hall to take this," Shaw said, doing just that. Ryan wasn't there, but the boy was peering out of the room that used to belong to Sunny's brother, Hayes.

"Please tell me Aurora Rubio's on the way here," Shaw said to Leyton.

"Sorry. I haven't been able to reach her, but someone finally answered Marty's phone. Not Marty," Leyton added quickly. "The woman introduced herself to me as his girlfriend. Her name is Carmen Sibley, and she said Marty and she had been together a whole two weeks."

For Marty, that could be considered a long-term relationship. "Why didn't Marty answer his own phone?" Shaw asked.

"Because Carmen said Marty left it behind when he went out to jam with friends. *Yesterday*," Leyton emphasized. "Carmen didn't know where he was, but she was sure he'd be back."

Shaw wouldn't lay odds on that, and judging from Leyton's huff, neither would he.

"Carmen lives in Tulsa," Leyton went on. "So, at least we have a recent last location for Marty. I've reached out to his manager and asked him to check and see if there's any sign of him. Maybe something will turn up." He paused a moment. "How's the girl?"

"Crying," Shaw provided, and he felt the brotherly comradery with Leyton's groan.

"You want me to send in Cait?" Leyton asked.

Shaw debated that for a moment. Their sister, Cait, was a deputy who worked for Leyton along with doing more than her share to run the ranch. She was good at training horses and dealing with the often stupid crimes that happened in a small town, but Shaw thought his sister was already tapped out when it came to dealing with situations like Kinsley's. Still, he'd hold Cait in reserve.

Ditto for holding his other brother in reserve, too, though Austin was a widower with kids of his own. Two little girls. And, unlike Marty, Austin was actually a good dad who wanted to spend time with his kids. However, Austin was also grieving and might not ever get over losing his wife. As Austin had put it—you don't get lucky finding your soul mate twice.

What a mess, Shaw thought as he ended the call with Leyton. And Marty being Marty just kept on piling on the reasons why Shaw had never felt the need to expand his own personal gene pool. Nope. There was enough Jameson DNA out there already.

Shaw was about to go back in the bathroom to start round two when his phone rang. He nearly sagged with relief when he realized it was Aurora. Finally! Kinsley's mom definitely wouldn't be reserve reinforcements. She was the front-runner for solving this situation.

"Mr. Jameson?" the woman greeted.

"Shaw," he offered. "You're Aurora Rubio?"

"I am. I gather from your voice mails that Kinsley went to your ranch, and then she left and ran away again."

"Yes, but we found her. She's pissed off and upset, but she's safe."

Judging from what Shaw heard, the woman uttered a sound of agreement. A rather mild one, considering what was going on.

"Kinsley's mad at me for not telling her about

Marty," Aurora admitted. "But with Kinsley, there's always something to be mad at."

"Well, she's fifteen." Shaw tried to sound sympathetic. Best not to piss off the mom with some offhanded remark about Kinsley having a right to be angry. "I've got a younger sister so I know it comes with the territory."

"I'm betting your sister was never as bad as Kinsley." This time it sounded as if she huffed. "Look, I reported her missing when she stormed out of the house last night and took off running."

The girl had been gone since then? Well, crap. "Where'd she spend the night?" Shaw asked.

"To heck if I know. My neighbor's a cop, and when Kinsley wasn't back by morning, he insisted I report her missing so I did. But you should know that Kinsley's run off before."

Shaw wanted to continue to dole out some sympathy, but he was getting a bad feeling here. This felt like…trouble.

A moment later, that trouble was confirmed.

"I'm fed up," Aurora said. "I've had enough. You find Marty and give Kinsley to him." And with that order, the woman hung up.

CHAPTER FOUR

Sunny had no trouble hearing Shaw curse outside the bathroom door. She didn't know who he'd been talking to, but obviously the conversation wasn't going well. Neither was what was happening in the bathroom.

Kinsley had stopped crying, which some would have considered a good thing, but she didn't like the dark resignation in the girl's eyes. Sunny didn't have a clue about her past or her home life, but she was betting that Kinsley had experienced enough frustration and disappointment to make her believe that only frustration and disappointment would continue.

"I don't know how much you know about the TV show, but this was one of the few rooms where the cameraman wasn't allowed," Sunny said while she glanced around at the dated mint-green tiles. "It became my sanctuary of sorts. Well, for the fifteen-minute blocks that I was allowed to hole myself up in here."

Kinsley looked at her and frowned. "You were only allowed fifteen minutes?"

"Yep. I shared this with my sisters, and there were enough arguments that it forced my grandmother to come up with a schedule. Em tried to include my brother's bathroom in the rotation so we'd get more time, but holing up near a boy's toilet didn't have a sanctuary feel. When I'd get desperate, I'd use Em's bath in her room downstairs."

It had smelled like lavender and lemons. Unlike her brother's, which had reeked of eau de gym socks and pee.

"I'm not going to feel sorry for you," Kinsley declared. "You grew up rich."

"No, I didn't." But Sunny knew most people believed that.

There'd been some money, but it hadn't lasted. And that was the reason Sunny still had some student loan debt from graduating with her art degree. Also the reason she'd come back here after ending her engagement.

After the surgery.

She'd moved out of the house she'd shared with Hugh, a sweet Colonial in an upscale Houston neighborhood, and into a small condo in a not-so-upscale area. Sunny had had the money to buy a bigger place, but it would have been a stretch of her budget. Especially if she ended up helping Ryan with his own college expenses, which she would do if Hugh didn't step up to the plate. Hugh had plenty of money, but if he was still in me-time mode in the fall, he might not be man enough to realize his son would need to eat and sleep under a roof.

"Well, you grew up with people who loved you and didn't lie to you," Kinsley grumbled.

"Not exactly," Sunny grumbled back. There'd been lies. But some love, too—from Em. Thank God for Em or they would have all turned out as messed up as many other child actors had.

Out in the hall, Sunny heard Shaw do more cursing and make another call. This time she heard him say Leyton's name.

Sunny would have tried to hear what bits and pieces of the conversation she could manage to if her own phone hadn't jingled with a call. She checked the screen and immediately hit the decline button when she saw it was from a reporter who'd been bugging Sunny for info on an article she wanted to write about the grown-up *Little Cowgirls*. Something she always did when it came to reporters. The request for articles had dwindled over the years, but she still got at least one a month.

It was a blessing that few people in town had her phone number. Em and Shaw, that was it. And Shaw had only gotten it today when she'd called him to let him know that Kinsley was there. That meant Josiah and the other men Em had mentioned wouldn't be able to contact her directly. However, that didn't mean they wouldn't just show up. Or set a fire to get her attention.

"You knew my dad?" Kinsley asked after Sunny had put her phone back in her jeans pocket.

Sunny nodded and left it at that. Since she'd been born and raised here in Lone Star Ridge, she knew pretty much everybody, and most folks were decent enough. Marty, however, didn't fall into the decent category, and that's why Sunny hoped the girl wouldn't want to know anything else about the irresponsible man who'd fathered her. She didn't feel right bad-mouthing Marty, even if he deserved it. Besides, that sort of thing should come from Shaw.

"What's my dad like?" Kinsley pressed.

Sunny sighed. So much for hoping Kinsley wouldn't ask her for more details. "He can be charming," she said, after pausing long enough to give her time to decide how to answer. "And he's talented. He used to make up songs for me and my sisters when we were little, but then he hit it big and left town."

"What else was he like?" Kinsley said when Sunny didn't elaborate.

Again Sunny had to think about it. "Well, he's good-looking or at least he was last time I saw him. It's been a while." She added one of Em's favorite sayings. "Marty likes to try out lots of churns for his dasher."

"Huh?" Kinsley said.

Obviously, the girl wasn't schooled in Texas-speak. "It's an ice-cream maker reference." A sexual one that she shouldn't have brought up. Em's sayings were always G-rated but often with R-rated subtext. "Marty sleeps around," she clarified.

Kinsley made a sound of frustrated agreement, and Sunny could see more questions brewing in her eyes. Questions that the girl thankfully didn't get a chance to ask because Kinsley's phone rang. Kinsley fished it from her pocket and groaned. Because Sunny was so close, she had no trouble seeing "Mom" pop up on the screen.

"She's probably worried about you," Sunny pointed out when Kinsley just stared at it.

This time Kinsley made a sound of frustrated disagreement, and she hit the answer button. "You don't have to go," the girl told Sunny when she got up to leave, and she started the conversation before Sunny could even move. "I don't want to hear anything you've got to say," she said to her mother.

"Well, you're going to hear it anyway," the woman snapped. Along with being plenty loud enough for Sunny to hear in the small room, there was no maternal warmth and fuzziness in the woman's tone, but then Kinsley's mom was probably stressed-out.

Or not.

Sunny got confirmation that this was about more than just stress when Aurora continued.

"I've already told your *brother* this, but you should hear it, too. I'm fed up, Kinsley, and you should stay there with your dad's family. That's the best thing all the way around. If they need me to sign papers or something, I will, but I don't want you coming back here."

Maybe Kinsley was too dumbfounded to respond. Sunny certainly was. But Kinsley regained her ability to speak much sooner than Sunny could.

"You lied to me," Kinsley said to her mother.

"So?" Aurora tossed back. "If you hadn't been snooping in my things, *my personal things*," the woman emphasized, "then you wouldn't have found out the cold hard truth about your so-called father. The man walked out on me. He didn't want me, and he sure as hell didn't want you."

Good grief. Aurora's parenting style seemed very similar to Sunny's own folks. Kinsley didn't start crying again, but Sunny could practically feel the anger expanding inside the girl like a steam cloud about to explode.

"My father knew you were pregnant with me?" Kinsley snapped.

"Yes, he knew. Or at least he knew that was a possibility," Aurora amended. "He left anyway. Left me to deal with you. Well, I'm tired of dealing with you, Kinsley. You can spread your sunshine and sparkling personality there with your dad and his family."

Even after Aurora ended the call, Kinsley just sat there and continued to stare at her phone.

"I'm sorry," Sunny muttered because she had no idea what to say.

She wanted to add that maybe Aurora would call back and apologize once the fit of temper had run its course, but that might not be true. The woman could have meant every single word she said.

Including the part about dumping Kinsley on Shaw and his family.

Sunny was betting that Shaw wouldn't put up with that. For years when they were growing up, she'd listened to Shaw vent about never wanting kids. That had plenty to do with Marty and his penchant for procreating. It also had something to do with the fact that getting Austin and Cait through the teenage years had fallen mostly to him. Lenore was a sweetheart, but she was, well, a ditz. Cait had once told Sunny that she'd survived on bananas, Ding Dongs and the triweekly pizza deliveries that Shaw had set up.

"I'll talk to Shaw," Sunny said, getting to her feet. She'd tell him about Aurora's call and let him vent before he chatted with Kinsley. That might not be a fast or easy process.

"No," Kinsley snapped. She got to her feet, too, and she did it a lot faster than Sunny. On a repeated and very mean sounding *no*, Kinsley threw open the door, banging it against the wall and the edge of the tub. The girl stormed out, nearly knocking Shaw over in the process.

Shaw groaned out more of that same profanity she'd heard from him earlier. "Did her mother call her, too?" he asked.

Sunny nodded, and while Shaw would want to compare the conversations Kinsley and he had had with the woman, this wasn't the time. "Kinsley will probably try to run away again."

"I'll go after her," Ryan said, coming out of his room. Obviously, he'd been listening, and judging from the quick glance at her chest, he didn't want her having to chase down a teenager.

Ryan barreled down the stairs, taking the steps two at a time as Kinsley had done. Sunny and Shaw followed but at a slower pace. And with a lot of heavy sighs.

"Any sense that Aurora will change her mind and come and get Kinsley?" Sunny asked.

"None," Shaw answered readily. "But I have to believe she will. The woman's raised her for fifteen years. Hard to think she could wash her hands of her now." He froze, his forehead bunching up. "Sorry."

The apology was because Sunny's father had done exactly that. Hand washing, walking out, vamoosing.

The timing for her dad's departure had been particularly bad, too, because it'd happened mere hours after they'd lost the *Little Cowgirls* show and therefore their income. It hadn't helped either that her father had drained as many of the bank accounts as possible. It especially hadn't helped that those accounts had been in his name and there hadn't been any way to recoup the funds he stole.

There was some new money coming in from the reruns, and Sunny had made sure her father's name wasn't anywhere on that account. Nor had she or her sisters touched it. In a rare show of agreement, they'd decided to keep it tucked away in case Em needed long-term care or a nursing home.

"No worries," Sunny said. "We both got screwed over in the daddy department."

At least Marty hadn't stolen from his family, but then again her own father didn't continue to slam the family with indiscretions from his past.

Once they'd made it downstairs, Sunny didn't see any signs of Kinsley. She went to the front door when she noticed it was wide open, and from there it didn't take long for her to hear Kinsley.

"No, I don't want to see your bunny garden," Kinsley snarled.

Obviously, the offer for that particular viewing experience had come from Em, who was in the front yard. So were Bernice and Ryan, though Bernice seemed more to be viewing the scene like a train wreck than someone willing to step in and try to help. The housekeeper was holding the red spiked bra.

"This was on the ground," Bernice told her. "You should have left your sex stuff in Houston."

Sunny snatched the bra from her and didn't bother to explain what she couldn't explain. Just saying it was Hadley's wouldn't have clarified the reason the garment had been made in the first place. As for why it was on the ground, it'd likely fallen out when Ryan had been getting the grocery bags.

Em moved closer to Kinsley and gave the girl a once-over as if sussing out something. Then the woman leaned in, whispering at a volume that in no way qualified as a whisper. "There's a hot cowboy back there by the barn who's nice to look at. We could ogle him while you watch the hummingbirds. He came here to ask out Sunny, but I don't think she's feeling up to hot cowboys."

As offers went, it was a bad one what with Kinsley only being fifteen. Also, what with her ready to blow a fuse. Or cry. Or run.

"We can talk if you want," Ryan said to Kinsley in that quiet voice of his. "It might help."

Kinsley's huff and eye roll let him know she didn't believe that for a second. Still, she didn't run, cry or do any fuse blowing. The girl just stood there, eyeing them as if they were all participants in the hurtful crap her mother had just doled out.

It was a contrast seeing the teens there, facing each other as if in an angst-ridden standoff. There was angst on Kinley's part anyway. Ryan had been brushed off by his dad, too, and he wasn't acting out like this.

Then again, being brushed off was Ryan's norm.

Maybe it was for Kinsley, too, but this time the girl had gotten it with an extra topping of having the rug pulled from beneath her feet. Kinsley was hurting, and whether she wanted to or not, she should talk with someone. Then they could figure out what to do.

Sunny suspected they'd need to involve Leyton so he could try to convince Aurora to take her daughter back. Maybe Leyton could even work in the suggestion of counseling.

"Nothing can help," Kinsley finally declared, just as Sunny stepped closer to the girl.

And just as Kinsley moved forward. Maybe to step around Sunny, but that wasn't what happened. With what felt like the move of a seasoned linebacker, Kinsley plowed into her, knocking the tit spikes right into Sunny's chest.

The pain sent Sunny to her knees. She could have sworn she saw entire constellations, but the pain was too much for mere stars. The sound that left her mouth was a garbled gasp.

"Help her," Ryan begged to no one in particular. He ran over and held on to her. Shaw did the same thing on her other side. "Help her," Ryan repeated, sounding frantic.

"What's wrong with her?" Em asked, hurrying in front of Sunny and stooping down.

"She had surgery," Ryan blurted out, his wide,

frightened eyes nailed to hers. "Surgery because the doctors thought she had cancer. We need to get her to the hospital. Now."

CHAPTER FIVE

SHAW PACED THE ER waiting room, the plastic Fred's Grocery shopping bag he carried occasionally bopping against his leg. Normally, that wouldn't have been a particularly risky thing, but the bag held the spiked bra.

He hadn't been the one to think of bringing the blasted garment. That'd been Em's doing. While they'd been getting Sunny into her SUV to drive her to the hospital, Em had said she thought that maybe the doctor would want to see it. Sort of like some weird weapon preserved from a crime scene. Em had thought the doctor might want to examine it so he could better treat Sunny's injury.

It hadn't seemed right to make the teenagers haul around what might have been designed for S and M or some other sexual shenanigans. Ditto for giving that "burden" to Em because it could throw her off balance and send her into the ER, as well. Since Bernice hadn't made a move to come with them, and Shaw hadn't wanted to just leave the bra lying around, he'd done the honors.

Definitely not a scenario he'd imagined first thing that morning.

Of course, he hadn't thought he'd be in a hospital

waiting room, either. Or that he'd be worried about Sunny. Or that he'd have another half sister sobbing in one of the chairs. This was a day for the unexpected, all right.

Thankfully, Em was tending to the girl by patting her hand and giving her assurances that all would be well. Of course, Em wasn't keeping it simple, and she was using a lot of phrases that he doubted Kinsley understood. Things like, "This will turn out to be as big of a deal as a popcorn fart, you'll see."

That had only caused Kinsley to sob louder.

Shaw wasn't sure if Kinsley was crying because she was feeling guilty about hurting Sunny or because of what her mother had told her. He'd probably find out soon enough; for now he wanted to focus on Sunny. Well, that's what he'd do once he saw her and made sure she was truly all right. He was afraid it would be much bigger than farting popcorn.

Cancer.

Hell.

And now it was cancer with an injury. Shaw had had no trouble seeing that on her shirt after the bra spike had nailed her. There'd been some blood. Maybe it was from the surgery incision, but it was just as likely that Hadley's lethal lingerie had caused serious damage.

Ryan was pacing right along with him, and he gave occasional glances at the closed door of the exam room where the nurse had taken Sunny. What the boy hadn't done was spill anything else after dropping his bombshell.

Surgery because the doctors thought she had cancer.

Shaw had asked Ryan for more, of course. So had Em. Heck, even Kinsley had. Ryan had insisted he'd already said too much and that anything else would have to come from Sunny herself.

Of course, when Shaw finally managed to ask her about it, Sunny might just tell him to mind his own business, and, like Kinsley, he was feeling guilty, too. If he'd handled the situation better with Kinsley, then she wouldn't have run off to Em's, and she wouldn't have been anywhere near Sunny or that damn bra.

As he paced, Shaw glanced around again, and he was certain that word had already spread that there'd been some kind of trouble at the Dalton place. Either that or there'd been an epidemic of some sort because in the half hour they'd been there in the tiny ER, Shaw had seen no less than thirty people come in and out. All reasonably healthy-looking people whose only ailment was nosiness.

Or in search of a date.

Yeah, there'd been those all right. The single guys. The divorced ones. The ones who'd likely be willing to get a divorce if Sunny gave them a come-on look. Which there was no way she'd do to a married man. Still, they came, all leaving their numbers with Em when they learned they wouldn't be seeing Sunny anytime soon. Em shoved the scribbled-down numbers in her purse.

Shaw didn't know if Em would actually give the numbers to Sunny. She probably would. And even if the woman didn't, that didn't mean the horde of suitors wouldn't just go to Em's and try to see Sunny there. Shaw could definitely see why the men would persist. He wasn't blind and knew that Sunny was beautiful. Always had been, still was. But it was a lousy time to try to start up a romance.

He glanced behind him when the ER door opened again, and after the stream of guys who'd come in, Shaw wasn't particularly surprised to see yet one more. Carter Bodell, the town's mortician. Since Carter was smiling, it didn't appear he was going to feign an illness.

"Good to see you," Carter greeted, extending his buzzer-rigged hand for him to shake.

Shaw gave him a look that could have frozen the entire city of El Paso in July. The look wasn't just for that stupid buzzer, either. It was because Carter was no doubt here to try to scout out a date with Sunny.

Carter went to Ryan next. Greeted him. Extended his hand. The boy shook his head and paced in another direction.

That sent Carter to Em.

"My legs don't work as good as they used to," Em told Carter, getting to her feet. She, too, ignored the offered handshake. "When I get startled or surprised, my right leg jerks and kicks about yea high." She leveled her weathered hand with Carter's crotch. "Best not to do anything to startle me."

Carter lowered his hand, and while his smile dimmed some, he didn't look completely put off by the not-so-veiled threat of a kick to the balls. "I was hoping to see Sunny," he said. "I wanted to see if she'd like to go to the Lickety Split with me."

The look Em gave him wouldn't have chilled El Paso, but the woman managed to question Carter's

IQ with the simple lift of her eyebrow. "Sunny's here in the ER. I'm thinking ice cream will have to wait."

Carter bobbed his head. "I didn't figure she'd want to go right now but maybe in an hour or two. Say, what's wrong with her anyway? No one seems to know for sure."

That set Kinsley to crying again.

Frowning, Em took his hand carefully, as if she might give it a grandmotherly squeeze, and then without warning, she smashed Carter's palm against his own arm. Along with the farting noise the buzzer made, it caused Carter to jolt as if he'd been electrocuted.

"I'll tell Sunny you dropped by," Em said as if nothing had happened.

Carter opened his mouth, but it took him a few seconds to recover. When he had, he stripped off the buzzer, flicked a button on it and jammed it into his pocket. He didn't come out with an empty hand, though. He came out with a business card that he gave to Em.

"My number," Carter said, still sounding a little shaky. "Please tell Sunny to call me."

Em shoved the card in her purse with the other numbers and muttered all the right things that a polite lady would say. *Good of you to drop by. Thanks for coming.* With the underlying message of *Don't let the door hit you in the ass on the way out.* Carter left, taking his annoying self and buzzer with him. The man had certainly chosen the right profession since there was no way he could bother the dead.

Carter had been gone only a few minutes when

the exterior door opened again, and Shaw automatically turned in that direction. He'd thought maybe it was another guy out for a date or that he would see Leyton. He had hoped it'd be his brother, since Shaw had given him the task of trying to talk Aurora into coming here and picking up her daughter.

But it wasn't Leyton or his sister, Cait. It was a tall woman with ginger hair. Wearing jeans that were ripped and torn in all the fashionable places and a rhinestone tee, she looked like a been-there, done-that rock star. She had a huge leather bag hooked over her shoulder and what appeared to be a red spiked thong dangling from her fingers. Either that, or she liked really big and unusual rings. She glanced around the room, spotted Shaw and walked straight toward him.

After the day he'd had, he immediately looked for any signs of Marty's features. None, thank God. He'd had all the DNA surprises he could handle for one day.

"This was on the ground outside the SUV that you used to drive Sunny Dalton here to the hospital," she said, extending the red leather spiked thong for him to take. "It must have fallen out."

Shaw hesitated, but on a huff, he snatched it from her and crammed it into the Fred's bag. "Thanks," he mumbled in a dismissive sort of way.

The woman didn't budge. "I'm Tonya Pryor." She extended her hand again, this time for him to shake. He didn't. Because he recognized that name.

"You're the reporter looking to do a story on *Little Cowgirls*," he grumbled. It wasn't a question, and it wasn't friendly. The woman had called him just a few days earlier. "This isn't a good time."

"I gathered as much." Tonya gave him a thin smile. "I can wait."

Shaw supposed that was her way of saying she wasn't giving up. Well, neither was he. "You're wasting your time."

"It's my time to waste," she countered, giving him what he was pretty sure was a variation of the stink-eye.

He would have given it right back to her if the door to the examining room hadn't finally opened, with Dr. Mendoza emerging. That sent Ryan practically running toward the man.

"How is she?" Ryan asked, taking the question out of Shaw's mouth. Obviously, out of Em's as well because she muttered a variation of that.

The doctor was about to answer, but then he looked over Shaw's shoulder at Tonya. "A friend of Sunny's?"

"No," Shaw quickly assured him. "A reporter who has no business being here."

The doctor's eyes narrowed. "Then, skedaddle," he warned the woman.

Huffing, the woman did move but not very far. She went about ten yards away and leaned against the wall. Shaw ignored her and turned back to Dr. Mendoza.

"Is Sunny okay?" Shaw asked just as Ryan repeated, "How is she?" and just as Kinsley asked, "Did I stab her with that stupid bra?" and just as Em asked, "You didn't ask her to tell you a joke, did you? Because Sunny doesn't really care much for that."

Shaw seriously doubted that Em was so unruffled by all of this that a possible joke request would be at the top of her concerns. But maybe it was easier for Em to think about that than what Sunny might be going through in the examining room.

"Sunny's going to be okay," Dr. Mendoza answered without addressing the joke comment. "But she didn't want me to give you any details. While she's waiting on a scrip for her meds, she wants to tell you those details herself. You first," he said, looking at Ryan. "Then you," he added to Shaw. "Then you," he said to Em. "Sunny wants to see you, too." The last request was aimed at Kinsley.

"She wants to kill me because I stabbed her with that bra," Kinsley concluded. That brought on more tears, and the girl went back to the waiting area where she dropped down into one of the chairs.

"This girl stabbed Sunny Dalton with a bra?" Tonya questioned from behind them, causing Shaw to groan. He didn't want to know how the reporter could work something like that into a story.

Ryan took off to the examining room, leaving the rest of them standing there. Well, not the doctor. He didn't offer any more info, but it did give Shaw some thoughts about the designated order of the visits. And he decided he needed to address that designation when Em looked even more troubled than she had minutes earlier.

"Sunny likely just wants to make sure the boy's not feeling too bad about what he blurted out," Shaw told her, keeping his voice low since Tonya was nearby and obviously had ears like a bat.

Em nodded and sighed. "I'm betting Ryan wished he'd had a zipper on his mouth right after he said it." She looked up at Shaw. "We'll need to do some soothing over there. Soothing over with her, too," Em added, tipping her head to Kinsley. "Maybe Lenore can cook her up something special?"

That wouldn't fix squat, but for whatever reason Em had never been put off by his mom's cooking the way everyone else had.

"And I can maybe take Kinsley to the ladybug garden," Em went on, her weary eyes fixed on the examining room where Ryan had disappeared. "That's a surefire way to cheer her up."

Nope, it wasn't. It was going to take a lot more than beetles with a cute name to get the girl out of this crying jag. Shaw was hoping that whatever Sunny had to tell her would help because he was tapped out here. If Leyton didn't come through with Aurora, well, Shaw might take that trip to the ladybug garden just to see if he'd been wrong about it helping.

It seemed to take an eternity, but Shaw figured it was only a couple of minutes before Ryan came out. The boy looked a little shell-shocked and still worried, but didn't seem to be reeling from regret.

"She wants to see you now," Ryan told him.

Shaw didn't exactly run as Ryan had done, but he didn't dawdle, either, steeling himself for whatever he might see in the room. Blood, an IV maybe. Maybe a pasty-pale Sunny in a great deal of pain. But none of that was going on. Wearing a bloodless green scrub top, she was sitting on the examining room table, her legs dangling over the side, and she was dragging a mascara wand over the lashes of her right eye while she peered into a palm-sized mirror.

"I don't want to look washed-out," she said, not looking at him as she finished with the black goo. She'd obviously already applied some lipstick because her mouth was cherry red. "It'll worry Em."

"That ship's already sailed." Shaw went closer and dropped the bra bag in the chair beside the examining table. "She's worried. We all are. You okay?" he added when she didn't say anything.

She muttered a curse when she poked herself with the mascara, then blinked hard. That put some spidery black marks below her eye that she tried to smear away with her pinkie. *Smear* being the operative word because it turned the spider marks to more of a wave.

"I have four stitches just below my armpit, but the doctor numbed it so I'm not hurting," she explained, capping the mascara and dropping it into her purse— yet something else that Em had thought to bring to the hospital.

"Stitches," he repeated, silently cursing the damn bra. "And the surgery for cancer?"

She made an *oh, that* kind of dismissal, but there was nothing dismissive about the look she gave him when she finally lifted her head and met his gaze. He supposed she was giving him a very serious expression, which was somewhat diminished by the makeup. She'd only put the mascara on one eye, and that cherry-red color only covered half of her bottom lip.

"Do you owe me any favors?" Sunny asked.

Shaw had to admit he hadn't expected her to ask

that, and it certainly didn't address his question about surgery and cancer. Still, he'd see where it went. It wasn't going to lead anywhere if she thought it would get her out of giving him some answers. Or at least giving Em some anyway.

"I was thinking *you* might owe me a favor or two. Sore nuts," he added as a reminder.

Sunny huffed. "That was an accident, and it traumatized me. So, I'm going to count that as you owing me a favor."

"Okay." He could see it from her angle though he wouldn't mention that he'd taken years of ribbing over being nut-kicked and blooded-up by a girl. "Spill it. What favor do you want from me?"

The corner of her mouth lifted a little, only emphasizing the badly applied lip stuff. For just a moment there was a naughty glint, but he thought maybe that was more of a reflex than actual lust. Hard to be lustful with armpit stitches and possible cancer while sitting in an ER. Still, the glint stayed.

"Can you look at me as if you want to gobble me up?" Sunny asked.

Shaw opened his mouth to answer and realized he didn't have a clue how to respond to that. "Why?" he settled for saying.

"Because if we have the hots for each other, then it'll help Em focus on something else. Something other than her worry. It'll stop some of the gossip about my health issues. And best of all, it'll stop guys from trying to hit on me."

He had to give that some thought. "It might help with those things. *Might*," he qualified. "But what else it'll do is start a whole bunch of gossip about us hooking up again." He groaned. "This is your solution to deal with Em? Because I think a better fix would be for you to tell us what's wrong and how we can help you."

She looked him straight in the eyes. "You can't help with that."

Oh, hell. Shaw felt as if an entire team of pissed-off mules had kicked him. "You have cancer?"

"No." She glanced away, shook her head and clamped her teeth over her lip for a moment. "But I thought I did." Sunny motioned toward her breasts. "I had a lump removed, and for a while I thought it was cancer."

Shaw released the breath he'd been holding, and he expelled enough air to cause strands of her hair to flutter. "So, you're okay? Well, as okay as you can be with stitches?"

"As okay as I can be," she verified.

Still, he didn't see any verification in her eyes or expression. "Are you worried a lump could come back?" Because something sure as hell was eating away at her.

She stayed quiet a snail-crawling moment. "I'm afraid I won't get past the fear of the fear. If you know what I mean."

Shaw thought he did. The health scare had shaken her. "How long ago did you have the surgery?"

"Last week." She made a circling motion with her finger to her left breast. "The stitches came out this morning."

"Shit," he grumbled. Well, that explained the wince

he'd seen her make. That wasn't nearly long enough for her to have recovered either mentally or physically. "And now you have new stiches."

"I can deal with that. There are plenty of Funny Sunny jokes I can come up with to stop any real concern folks might have. That won't work with Em," she added. "But giving her something else to think about will. That's where the favor comes in. If she believes I came here to rekindle things with you, it'll give her something else to focus on."

Shaw wasn't so sure of that. "It could also give her something else to worry about. Em might see straight through something like this and then worry about why you're trying so hard give her the kid-glove treatment."

"She won't see through it because the heat is there between us." She frowned when he groaned, shook his head and gave him narrowed eyes. "Deny it, Shaw Jameson, and I'll French-kiss you to prove it."

Shaw stopped and considered. And he hated that he considered pushing to get that tongue kiss from Sunny. Of course, that only confirmed she was right about the heat.

"This won't cost you much time or energy," she went on.

"No, but it might cause me a hard-on or two," he grumbled, causing her to smile. And that smile caused his own mouth to move in the direction of what could be interpreted as a cocky grin.

"We'll try to keep the hard-ons to a minimum," Sunny assured him. "We can stick with kisses, touches, some long, lingering looks."

All of which could lead to hard-ons. He knew it. Sunny knew it. Heck, his dick especially knew it.

"You'll do it?" she asked.

Shaw did the whole mental argument with himself. Then he did what he'd known he would do from the moment she'd asked for this favor. He nodded and heard himself say, "I'll do it. We'll keep it low-key. Just enough to satisfy Em."

That didn't earn him the tongue kiss he was starting to fantasize about, but Sunny did rub his arm, as she'd done when they were on the road. Chaste and friend-like. Not the gesture of a woman who'd just gotten him to agree to what would no doubt be a string of cold showers in his immediate future. Even if a faked romance could lead to actual sex, Sunny wasn't in any shape for that.

In fact, it might be a really long time before she was ready.

"Is your recent breakup playing into this?" he asked.

"Possibly. Probably," she amended. "I don't want anyone feeling sorry for me about that, either. Or trying to get me into therapy because I've ended two engagements or have that stupid label of Runaway Fiancée. It's too much attention, and I've had enough of that to last me a couple of lifetimes. Okay?"

Shaw had to give her a nod for that, too. He wasn't big at being on the receiving end of sympathy, but thankfully he didn't have to deal with it very often.

Not Sunny, though.

She'd practically been born into the spotlight and had had to deal with way too many people knowing

way too much about her. Shaw had gotten a taste of
that when they'd been a couple, and it hadn't been a
good thing. He doubted it would be this time, either,
but the show would be all for Em and no one else.

Speaking of Em, he turned to leave so the woman
could come in, but Sunny caught onto his hand.
"What will you do about Kinsley?" she asked.

Well, he certainly couldn't give her anything positive when it came to this. "Don't have a clue. Got
any advice?"

Her forehead bunched up. "Don't pee outside in
a windstorm." Sunny smiled and gave his hand a
squeeze. "Sorry, but that's about as good as you're
going to get from me right now."

Her voice cracked. The smile vanished, and Shaw
saw something he didn't want to see. Sunny's eyes
suddenly had a shimmer in them. Tears. She was
blinking back tears.

Hell.

"Pain?" he asked.

She shook her head and squeezed her eyes shut.
"Just more of those emotions that I know you don't
want to deal with."

Maybe that was it, but Shaw wouldn't rule it out.
Another thing he couldn't rule out was that he was a
sucker for those tears, which was why he reached out
and gently eased Sunny into his arms. He brushed a
kiss on the top of her head just as the sob broke from
her mouth.

And just as Shaw heard Kinsley.

"I knew it," the girl said. Shaw looked up and saw
her standing in the doorway. "She's crying because

I hurt her. Sunny was just trying to help, and I hurt her."

"Oh, dear," Em muttered. She was also there, standing right next to Kinsley.

"I'm fine," Sunny insisted, and Shaw had to hand it to her—she did a fast job in the tear-drying-up department. She wiped them from her cheeks, did some more heavy blinking and faced Em and Kinsley with a plastered-on smile.

Sheez, it was a bad one. As fake as some of the scenes she'd played in *Little Cowgirls*. Obviously, all those scenes hadn't helped with her acting abilities because Shaw could tell that Kinsley and especially Em weren't buying it.

"My poor girl," Em said. She went closer, but she didn't reach for Sunny. It was as if the woman was afraid Sunny would break if she touched her.

"Good grief," Sunny whispered, the words hitting against his neck. She didn't have to come out and say it, but this was what she was trying to avoid.

And Shaw had a fix for it.

He hadn't intended for Kinsley to be in on this charade, but that was okay since the girl likely wouldn't be around Lone Star Ridge for much longer. That's why Shaw leaned back enough to locate Sunny's mouth, and he kissed her. No peck of friendly reassurance. Nothing that smacked of fakery. Nope. He went full in, tongue and everything.

Shaw instantly got a nice buzz. The kind that alerted his body to start getting ready for a whole lot more. He reined in the *more* when he sensed some movement in the doorway. Sunny must have, too, because at the same moment and with her still in his arms, they looked in that direction.

"I hope you didn't get a bloody mouth this time," Em murmured. "And Sunny, you make sure you don't kick him in the privates again."

Good advice. But Em wasn't the only one witnessing this. Dr. Mendoza was behind Em and Kinsley. And Ryan.

And Tonya, the reporter.

Who clicked their picture.

Apparently, this "all for show for Em" had just gone up some Texas-sized notches.

CHAPTER SIX

SHAW RARELY HAD the urge to throttle a person, but he had that urge now. Damn Tonya. And damn how she would almost certainly try to use Sunny and her pain and misery to get a story.

Since he wasn't sure he could hold on to his temper, Shaw went back into the waiting room and well, waited. There wasn't enough distance, though, between him and the examining room, because he heard plenty of the conversation now that the door was wide open.

Dr. Mendoza handed Sunny a piece of paper. "The scrip for your meds," he said, and he immediately took out his phone. Without sparing the reporter a glance, he called the police station and requested an officer come ASAP to escort Tonya out of the building. "I'll be filing charges against her for violation of patient's privacy and applying for a restraining order."

Tonya might have been a pesky jerk, but apparently she wasn't a complete idiot. She turned and left, likely deciding that a run-in with a small-town police force wasn't a good idea. Whether she would stay gone was anyone's guess. For that matter it was also a guess if Mendoza could get that restraining order.

All of that was food for thought, but Shaw had his own food and thoughts to worry about.

News of the kiss would get out, no doubt about that. This was a small town and Tonya could possibly still be in the waiting room, probably hanging on every word she could make out. As soon as she thought she had all she could get, she'd start the gossip. Gossip that Sunny hadn't especially wanted, but the kiss might do its job and distract Em.

It seemed to have distracted Ryan, too, because he had a puzzled look on his face when he left the examining room and walked toward Shaw.

"Don't hurt her," Ryan warned him, and suddenly he didn't sound so much like a teenager. "Sunny's been hurt enough already."

Agreed, and he nearly blurted out that there'd be no hurting, not in the romantic sense, because Sunny didn't have those kind of feelings for him. However, if he said that, he'd have to explain the favor he was doing for Sunny.

Okay, the lie.

If the truth got around, he'd be reneging on the favor he'd agreed to do. So, Shaw figured on this particular subject, silence coupled with an agreeing nod were the best responses here.

"She wants a baby, you know?" Ryan threw out there.

"Still?" Shaw wished he'd kept his silence on that, too. Yes, he'd known since they were teenagers that Sunny wanted a baby, but he didn't see how that applied here. "Did Sunny have a miscarriage or something?"

"No. She never got that close to having one with my dad." Ryan paused. "But I think that's why she got involved with him. She thought he'd give her a baby." He opened his mouth to say more and then waved it off. "She wouldn't want me to talk to you about this."

Again they were in agreement, because Sunny knew that fatherhood wasn't in the cards for him, either. In all those long chats they'd had as teenagers, they'd only disagreed on two things. Kids and Garth Brooks. Sunny had been a fan of both and Shaw wasn't.

"You'll make sure that Sunny and Em get back to the house?" Shaw asked the boy.

Apparently, silence and a nod were Ryan's preferred responses, as well, and several moments later when Sunny, Em and Kinsley came out, Ryan went to Sunny to take hold of her arm.

"We'll talk soon," Sunny told Shaw, hesitating as if she didn't know what to say or do. There was a lot of that going around today.

Shaw and Kinsley walked out behind Ryan, Sunny and Em, and they watched as Ryan helped Sunny and Em into the SUV. The boy then took the bra bag from Em and tossed it in the back. Maybe someone would bury the darn thing so it couldn't do any more damage.

What now? Shaw asked himself as Ryan drove away. He and Kinsley couldn't just stand there, and since he still hadn't heard from Leyton, that left Shaw with limited options as to what to do about Kinsley.

Shaw turned to the girl. "Should I drive you to your mom's and see if we can—"

"No, she doesn't want me," Kinsley snapped. "I can't go back there." She took his mother's purse from the backpack and thrust it into his hand. "I'll be fine on my own." And with that completely untrue, BS last sentence, she started walking away from him.

Shaw sighed, something he figured he'd be doing a lot until this situation was resolved. There'd likely be plenty of groaning, too. Still, he couldn't just let her hitchhike to God knew where.

"You're coming back to the ranch with me," he said, and Shaw made sure it didn't sound optional. Then, he added some sweetener to the sting of his order by tacking on, "If Marty comes to Lone Star Ridge, that's where he'll go."

As he'd figured it would, that stopped her in her tracks. She turned, and he saw something that made him want to curse. Way too much hope on her face. "You think he'll come?"

Rather than out-and-out lie with a yes or bash her hopeful expression with a no, Shaw shrugged. "Leyton, my brother...*our* brother," he amended, "is the sheriff, and he's trying to get in touch with him. If anyone can find Marty, it's Leyton."

That last part was the truth, but it was because at this exact moment, Leyton was the only person who was pressing to contact Marty. Shaw would get in on that and make some calls, too, but first he had to get Kinsley back to the ranch, where she'd be safe. For the rest of the afternoon anyway. Maybe that would give Aurora time to cool off and remember that Kinsley was her responsibility.

"Come on," Shaw said, heading toward his truck.

He didn't exactly hold his breath, but it was somewhat of a relief when he heard her clomping boots follow him. There'd be no breaths of relief for him though until he had the girl back safely where she belonged. Then, maybe he'd make a voodoo doll of his father and use some very large pins to jab Marty in the dick.

Before he started the engine, Shaw fired off a text to his mother to let her know he'd be coming back with Kinsley. He added another text to Leyton to press him for an update on Marty or Aurora.

"You're not going to yell at me for hurting Sunny?" Kinsley asked when she climbed in the truck's passenger seat.

"No, it was an accident. A stupid one but still an accident." He paused, then drove toward home. "Did Sunny yell at you?" But he already knew she hadn't. If so, Shaw would have heard it. Plus, he'd never known Sunny to be a big yeller.

"She said she didn't blame me, that it wasn't my fault." She glanced over at him. "Was that kiss for real, or do you feel sorry for her or something?"

"For real." And he wondered how many more lies he would have to tell to keep up with this favor. Of course, it wasn't a total lie since there'd been some real honest-to-goodness heat behind the kiss.

Heat that bothered him.

He wasn't sure how much pain Sunny was in. Probably a lot. He also didn't know how fast she'd recover. Or if she would. Really, the only thing he knew right now was that she'd had surgery and that it hadn't been cancer. Good news, but it could have a big-assed asterisk next to it if this had shaken Sunny to the core. And it appeared to have done just that.

"I've never had more than a bad cold," Shaw grumbled, not aware he was going to say that aloud until it came out of his mouth.

Kinsley gave him a funny look but didn't press him on it. Which he was thankful for. He definitely didn't want to talk to the girl about the woman who'd rung his sexual bell for two decades.

When Shaw pulled into the driveway of the ranch, he saw exactly what he expected—his mother standing outside waiting for them. So was his head ranch hand, Rowley Blake. That was a reminder to Shaw that he'd let some work slide to deal with Kinsley and Sunny.

"Give my mom back her purse and apologize to her for taking it," Shaw said, thrusting it at Kinsley as she'd done to him in the parking lot. "And you sure as hell better not steal another thing."

Shaw couldn't add "or else" to that because he couldn't think of a punishment or consequences he could actually enforce. That was even more reason he shouldn't be handling stuff like this, because he obviously sucked at it.

Maybe out of habit or to try to save face, Kinsley huffed, got out and went to his mother. Shaw couldn't hear what Kinsley mumbled, but it caused Lenore to smile and slide her arm around the girl.

"Come in," Lenore insisted. "I've made you a special sandwich."

As Lenore started leading her into the house, Kinsley glanced back at Shaw, and he shook his head, hoping the girl would pick up on the concept that "special" and "mystery" were alert words for something she definitely wouldn't want to eat. Thankfully, there was fruit and milk in the fridge so Kinsley wouldn't go hungry before Shaw could get her out of there.

"A problem?" Shaw asked as Rowley made his way to him.

"Some," the hand verified. "That guy we hired last isn't working out and needs to be let go. He's just plain lazy. There was also a problem with the pickup of those Angus. Problem with the feed order, too." Rowley paused. "But it looks as if you've got your own worries," he said, eyeing Kinsley as Lenore and the girl went inside. "She's Marty's?"

Shaw nodded, and he heard Rowley blow out what appeared to be a breath of relief.

"I won the bet then," Rowley went on. "About half the hands thought she was yours and Sunny's, but I figured on Marty."

So, that's the direction the gossip was going. Shaw nearly told Rowley to set the record straight with those who believed he'd been the one to screw up and get a woman pregnant, but it wouldn't do any good. Sometimes, protesting too much just made folks dig in their heels.

Shaw's phone dinged with a text, and when he saw Em's name on the screen, he wanted to read the message right away. It could be an update about Sunny. But it wasn't.

Come over tomorrow night around six. I'll fix Sunny and you a nice romantic dinner. She could use some cheering up.

Shaw frowned, especially at the last sentence. He seriously doubted he could help much in the cheering-up department, but it'd give him a chance to talk to Sunny, to see how she was really doing. At least that's what Shaw told himself when he answered with, Thanks. I'll be there.

As soon as Shaw hit Send, his phone rang. Not Em this time but rather Leyton, thank God.

"Deal with whatever problems you can fix," Shaw told Rowley as he stepped away. "I'll be in my office soon to handle the rest."

"Well?" Shaw said, the moment he answered the call. "Where are you and what have you found out?"

"I'm in San Antonio. And it's not good." Leyton added after a pause, "Aurora's gone."

"Gone?" Shaw repeated.

"Yeah. A neighbor, the cop who pressured her into reporting Kinsley missing, told me that he saw Aurora putting some suitcases in her car about an hour ago. When the neighbor asked if she was going somewhere, Aurora said she was. She wouldn't tell him where she was going or when she'd be back."

"Hell," Shaw managed to say.

"Yeah… Hell," Leyton repeated. "I'm heading over to talk to SAPD right now, but it looks as if Kinsley's going to be staying with you for a while."

SITTING CROSS-LEGGED ON her bed and with her back against the headboard, Sunny swished the point of the graphite pencil over the sketch pad, trying to get the right angle of Slackers's prominent tail feather.

The very one that had become a phallic symbol to drunks and pervs.

Yes, it was sort of erect and pointed, just as any tail feather should be, but in hindsight, Sunny could see how some—i.e., drunks and pervs—could believe it was a woody. A tiny fat one that looked non-woodyish when Slackers was standing or walking, but since he was a lazy duck, that meant plenty of sitting with the tail feather poking out between his spindly web-footed legs.

Eight years ago, she'd tried to correct the woody misassumption by changing the design and minimizing the tail feather to a mere nub, but the author and publisher had gotten gobs of hate mail. Some death threats, too. And in the end the powers that be had insisted Sunny go back to the original design.

Even though Slackers was her meal ticket, Sunny had to shake her head and occasionally let out a snort of laughter at how seriously some people took a fictional waterfowl with few redeeming qualities.

From the corner of her eye, Sunny saw the screen of her silenced phone flash with another text message. As she'd done with the other two dozen or so messages and calls over the past five days since the now infamous bra-stabbing incident, she only glanced at the sender.

Bennie Harper, the arsonist fireman.

Sunny didn't actually have Bennie's name in her phone address book, but Em had helped her ID it when he'd first called the day before. Ditto for helping her ID the jokester mortician, the hiney-exposing cowboy and the other assortment of men who'd tried to get in touch with her. Sunny had hit the decline button on all of the calls, ignored the texts and had turned off the ringer on her phone.

Avoiding date requests and the men who were trying to make them had also meant her not answering the door because some of them hadn't taken their unanswered calls and texts as brush-offs. That was where Bernice came in handy. The woman didn't relish visitors or door openings, which came through loud and clear when she greeted the men and then sent them on their way.

It wouldn't last, of course. Sunny knew that eventually she'd have to venture out if for no other reason than to get this latest round of stitches removed. Maybe by then she'd be on a better mental footing and could dissuade the date askers without sounding like Bernice or, better yet, Hadley.

Badly Hadley would have had some stinging comebacks strong enough to cause balls to shrivel. Sunny didn't aspire to be her sister, but she figured sometimes a ball-shriveling skill set could come in handy.

Especially when dealing with Tonya, the reporter.

Tonya had called Sunny, too, after wheedling her phone number from one of Sunny's friends. The reporter had probably called Shaw, as well. What Tonya hadn't done was print the picture she'd taken or a word about what was going on with Sunny's return to the scene of her childhood. Maybe Tonya had lost interest in doing an article. Or maybe she wasn't going to print anything until she had more of a story. If so, that'd be an easy fix because Sunny had no intention of giving the reporter more.

There was only a handful of people who Sunny wanted to hear from. Ryan, Em and Shaw. The first two hadn't been an issue since they were either in the house with her or just outside. In between checking on her and working on an online course, Ryan had been doing some horseback riding, and Sunny had even seen him helping Em in one of the gardens.

Not a whiff of contact, though, from Shaw.

Sunny didn't doubt for a minute that he would come through on the favor of getting men like Bennie off her scent, but Shaw almost certainly had his hands full. From what Em had been able to gather from gossip—gossip that she'd then passed on to Sunny—Shaw was busy dealing with his most recently found sibling.

Shaw might also be giving her some time to rest, something Sunny would have appreciated if she'd actually been able to rest. So far, her body and brain didn't seem fond of the idea.

Hour after hour, minute after minute, her mind kept circling around the surgery. What could have happened. What could *still* happen. And if it wasn't that particular dose of worry, the thoughts were of her latest botched engagement. And Ryan's future. Heck, her own future.

Swishing a woody tail feather was a lot easier than wallowing in all of that.

Her phone flashed again, and unlike the other texts, a familiar name popped on the screen. McCall. Call me.

Sunny reached to do that and then paused. McCall

was a counselor, and Em had likely got in touch with her to press her to send that text. If she phoned her sister back, then McCall would try to pull her out of this dark place. And she might help, too. McCall was just that good. But Sunny wasn't ready to dump all of this on her.

Before Sunny could continue that mental debate with herself, there was a soft knock on the door. It was likely Ryan. He knocked. Em tapped. And Bernice just threw open the door wherever delivering news about the latest suitor she'd been forced to turn away.

"Come in," Sunny said, and Ryan opened the door and stuck his head in.

"Persimmon sesame rice goulash," he threw out there.

Most folks would have had at least a little trouble deciphering a greeting like that, but Sunny figured it out right away. "Lenore Jameson sent over more food."

It wasn't really even a guess. No one else in town fixed dishes like that, and besides Lenore had already sent over two other meals with notes that encouraged Sunny to *eat up and enjoy*. Sunny wouldn't eat up, but she would enjoy simply because Lenore had been kind enough to think of her.

"Working?" Ryan asked, stepping in. He looked at the sketch pad in her lap. Normally, Sunny worked on an easel, but the stitches tugged and pulled when she lifted her arms.

She nodded. "Slackers wakes up in the Amazon jungle. There'll be toucans and other jungle stuff."

As always, she'd keep it simple. As did the author

when he sent her instructions for each of the scenes she needed to illustrate. The story before this one had been Slackers waking up in a Halloween spook house. And before that, Slackers snoozed his way into Venice.

"Uh, that fireman dropped by again," Ryan said. "Bernice threatened to let him in the next time he comes if you don't talk to him and tell him to knock it off."

Sunny sighed. She was betting Bernice hadn't said it so politely. "If Bennie comes by again, let me know." She wasn't good at telling someone to get lost, but that's what she'd have to do.

Sunny's phone lit up with a call. "Dad," Ryan muttered when Hugh's name popped up on the screen.

Crud. This was a call she'd have to take, and it didn't seem right to make it a private one. Not with Ryan looking as if he was starved for any info about his dad. Pulling in a quick breath, she set the sketch pad aside, answered the call and put it on speaker. She was about to tell Hugh that their call wasn't private, but he spoke before she could say anything.

"If this is your way of making me feel sorry for you, it won't work," Hugh blurted out. "You walked out on me, Sunny. You ripped me to shreds, and I'm not going to feel sorry for you."

Sunny considered how to respond to that and settled for, "Excuse me?"

"I won't feel sorry for you," he emphasized. "'When the sun has set, no candle can replace it.'"

Even though she was confused about the call, Sunny wasn't confused about the last thing Hugh had said. "That's a quote from one of the *Game of Thrones* books."

"So? It applies."

Sunny doubted that, but it was a bad habit of Hugh's to start spouting book quotes, especially when he was angry, and she got more proof of his anger when he continued.

"Your grandmother tried to make me feel sorry for you. She called and told me you'd had surgery and some kind of accident."

No sigh this time. Sunny groaned. "Em shouldn't have done that. How'd she even get your number?"

"I'd emailed it to her when we were planning our wedding." Oh, the bitterness was practically seeping through the phone line at the mention of the wedding. "Is it true? Was there some kind of accident?"

"I'm fine," she said to avoid an explanation she didn't want to get into. "There was no reason for her to call you."

"Of course, there was. She wants me to feel sorry for you so I'll ask you to come back. That's not going to happen." The bitterness went up a few significant notches. "You walked out on me at the worst time possible. 'I can't go back to yesterday because I was a different person then.'"

"Alice in Wonderland," she and Ryan muttered in unison.

Hugh must not have heard them because he continued. "The investors in my new stores were coming to the wedding, and I had to tell them that you'd called things off. Do you know how that made me look?"

Sunny couldn't help feeling just a little guilty about

that. Those investors had been important to an expansion that Hugh wanted—three new stores. That's why she'd wined and dined them with Hugh and tried to put on a good front. But a front was still just a front, and in the end, it was like trying to make a quote from a book fit a specific situation.

"Your grandmother has to stop her matchmaking," Hugh ranted on. "We're done."

Something about this didn't make sense, and she didn't think that last comment was a quote. "Em actually said she wants us to get back together?"

"She didn't use those exact words, but I could tell that's what she wanted."

"What did Em say?" Sunny pressed.

Hugh's huff was loud enough to extinguish candles on a senior citizen's birthday cake. "Em said that Ryan was worried about you and that she in turn was worried about Ryan."

Bingo. That's why Em had called. She'd wanted to remind Hugh that he had a son.

"Ryan's here now, and I've had this entire call on speaker," Sunny said. "If you want to talk to him."

Silence. And it went well past the awkward stage. "I can't do this now, Sunny," he finally responded. "You tore out my soul, and I have nothing left to give."

Sunny wanted to press it, to tell him that even parents with torn souls shouldn't give up on their kids, but she doubted Hugh was going to say anything that would make Ryan feel better. And it was possible Hugh could say something to make him feel a whole lot worse. Good thing she didn't have to figure out a way to end the call because Hugh hung up.

"I'm okay," Ryan said, while she was still staring at the phone screen. "That was about what I'd expected him to say. Though I figured he'd quote Tolkien at least once," he added.

That was true on both counts. Ryan had expected it, and Hugh liked to quote Tolkien. But it was Hugh's non-quotes that tore at her soul. She'd crushed Hugh, and in turn he'd crushed Ryan. Now, along with her commitment phobia, Sunny had a shiny new guilt trip.

Sunny eased off the bed. "I'll go downstairs and tell Em not to call Hugh again."

"I can do that," Ryan offered.

"No. Don't worry about that. I'll take care of it." She couldn't help herself. Risking the stretch that would do a number on her stitches, Sunny came up on her toes to kiss Ryan's cheek. "You deserve better," she murmured.

"Who says I don't have it?" He mustered up a smile. "Not every teenager can eat all the persimmon sesame rice goulash he wants."

And that was why she loved him, why she had wanted him here with her.

Sunny was well aware that Ryan kept his steps shorter than was usual for his six-foot-tall body. That was his way of making sure she took it easy. Which she did. Even though she wasn't hurting as much as she had been earlier, it was best not to push things, because she'd end up worrying Em and Ryan.

They found Em in the kitchen at the window, and

as she had the day before, she was peering through the binoculars. There was a large casserole dish on the counter next to her, and the gooey contents—an unappetizing mix of orange and gray white—was oozing over the sides and onto the tiles.

"Josiah brought his cousin with him today." Em looked back at them, her mouth set in a line that was as much of a frown as Em ever had. "I'm going to buy those boys some underpants. I think showing that much hiney is scaring off the bunnies and ladybugs. Want to take a look at them?" Em asked, offering Sunny the binoculars.

It was probably a sad day in a woman's life when she didn't want to ogle two hot guys, but she wasn't up to it. Sunny shook her head and thanked Em.

"Granny Em, Hugh said that you'd called him," Sunny said.

"Yes." She didn't add more about that. "McCall's been trying to get in touch with you," Em added almost casually, and she started to get out plates and silverware.

"She probably just wants to check on me." Sunny went to the fridge to look for something other than the goulash.

"Sounded like more than that to me," Em said. "It sounded important. She said I was to get you to call her right away."

That sent a curl of alarm through Sunny. McCall wasn't the sort to blow things out of proportion, so maybe there was some kind of emergency and this wasn't just a checking-on-her-sister kind of thing. Sunny took out her phone and returned her sister's call, which went straight to voice mail. After leaving a message, she was about to put her phone away when the screen lit up with another call. Not McCall.

Shaw.

It was a good time for her to step out of the room and take this. Especially since Em was dishing up three servings of the goulash. Sunny threaded her way through the rooms and into the parlor.

"You might have saved my stomach lining," Sunny said the moment she answered his call.

"My mom sent over a casserole," Shaw said without her spelling it out for him. "Sorry about that. Other than the risk of possible digestive failure for life, how are you?" His voice was a lazy drawl. Like foreplay. Something she wished she hadn't remembered.

"Better. Better-ish," she amended because, hey, this was Shaw. They had a favor pact, which meant she didn't have to fudge the truth with him. "I got a call from Hugh that shook me a little, that's all."

"Oh?" A little less drawl and foreplay now. She knew concern when she heard it.

"I was just hoping to convince him to see Ryan or at least talk to him. It didn't work out. How about you? Any luck with Kinsley?"

"Yeah, if you count bad luck. It sounds as if your ex and her mom have a lot in common when it comes to their kids. She's left town and isn't answering her phone."

Oh, mercy. Poor Kinsley.

Poor Shaw.

"Look, I just wanted you to know that Em called

me," Shaw said, and before Sunny could groan and apologize about that, he continued. "She invited me over for dinner tomorrow night."

Great day, her grandmother had certainly been busy. "She's worried about me."

"Yeah, got that." He paused. "There's more." And he paused again. "Tonya did the story, and she apparently plans on doing more."

Sunny didn't groan because she'd suspected they hadn't dodged this particular bullet. "Did she use that picture of us she took in the ER?"

"No. Dr. Mendoza threatened to sue her if she did that." Shaw hesitated once again, causing her to get a tingle. Not a good sexual one, either. "Tonya just called me though to give me a heads-up about something else."

"You actually took her call?" Sunny asked.

"Purely an accident. I was doing paperwork and didn't check the screen before I hit Answer." He paused. "According to Tonya, she somehow got her hands on a diary, Sunny. *Your diary*," he emphasized. "Tonya said the cover was purple, and the date on the outside was for the last year you lived in Lone Star Ridge. She said the article and excerpts from the diary will be published tomorrow in a tabloid called *Tattle Tale*."

Sunny felt as if a concrete block had dropped from the sky and landed on her head. Thoughts and memories of that particular diary came flying at her. Pages and pages of private ramblings, and one particular rambling soared right to the front of the others.

Hot Dreamy Shaw and the account of her deflowering.

"That diary's in the attic," she muttered with something she didn't actually feel. *Hope*. Hope that it was indeed still there and that the box it was in had a thick layer of dust to let her know that no one had gotten inside.

Risking the pain from jiggling because she wasn't wearing a bra, Sunny ran upstairs and practically skidded into the hall to go to her brother's room. The closet door was open, which wasn't unusual since Ryan was using it.

"You still there?" Shaw asked. "You didn't faint, did you?"

"No fainting." Not yet anyway, but all bets were off if she didn't find that dusty box right in the far corner where she'd put it. "I'm checking the attic now."

His sigh was loud enough to let her know that he wasn't feeling an ounce of the hope she was clinging to.

Sunny climbed the steep wooden steps and flicked on the light. As it had been the last time she'd been up there, it was cluttered and creepy. Old Halloween costumes dangling from wire hangers, spiderwebs galore, and the multitude of boxes and old furniture where Hayes had told her monsters lived. Of course, he'd said that to keep her out of his secondary sanctuary, but she felt the old chill go up her spine.

The footprints turned that chill into a January Montana blizzard.

Specifically, footprints in the dust-covered floor.

Footprints that led past the creepy stuff and all the way to the back corner.

"Still there?" Shaw repeated. "It sounds like you're breathing funny."

A surprise since Sunny wasn't sure she was breathing at all. She thought maybe the blizzard had frozen the air in her lungs. Frozen her feet to the floor, too, because she stopped when she saw the corner. And the box with "Sunny's Stuff" written in black marker on the side. No dust on the top of this box because it was wide-open.

Oh, God. "Hot Dreamy Shaw," Sunny muttered.

"Yeah," Shaw verified. "That's the title of Tonya's article."

CHAPTER SEVEN

"'His MOUTH WAS so hot, kissing me in places I'd never been kissed before. He kissed my mouth, my neck… and then he got to the good parts.'"

That's what Shaw heard when he stepped into the barn to grab a saddle, and he heard it coming from the mouth of a ranch hand, Zeke Mayhew, who likely didn't know that he was about to have his ass kicked six ways to Sunday.

Shaw turned into the tack room where Zeke was in the process of reading Tonya's article to two other snickering ranch hands. Those two were up for ass kicking, too.

All reading and snickering stopped when Shaw stepped into the tack room, and the two listening hands practically mowed him down trying to get out of there. That likely had something to do with the rock-hard scowl that Shaw knew was on his face, but they wouldn't get off scot-free. Shaw's mood was bad enough to last for hours. Days, even. Plenty enough time to spread the ass kicking around.

"Just doing some reading," Zeke said, lifting the dog-eared tabloid that had published Tonya's article.

Because he was clearly stupid, Zeke smiled. It faded when Shaw's glare and the silence cut through the room. Shaw wasn't staying quiet because it was part of some grand plan. It was because he couldn't unclench his jaw muscles enough to speak.

"Sorry, boss," Zeke finally muttered. "I didn't mean any harm. It's just everybody's reading this, and it's kind of funny."

Shaw's jaw muscles eased up enough for him to bare his teeth. He managed a growl. An honest-to-goodness, scary-as-shit growl.

"Guess it's not real funny to you," Zeke babbled. "I mean, 'cause you were there and all. Well, maybe you were. And maybe all of this is made-up." He paused. "You think I should tell people it's made-up?"

Shaw growled again. That's because he'd already tried to tell his mom it was made-up, but when she'd called Sunny's grandmother, Em had nixed the made-up lie by spilling that Sunshine had stolen the diary. At least, someone had stolen it, and the culprit had to be Sunshine.

According to the last update from Em, Tonya wasn't confirming the identity of her source, but this was exactly the kind of stunt Sunshine would pull. If that turned out to be wrong, Em would let him know. Thankfully, she'd stayed in touch with Shaw so that he hadn't had to bug Sunny about it. In fact, he wanted to avoid Sunny since right now she was no doubt going through even more shit than he was.

"I'll tell people it's made-up," Zeke said, still babbling, placating and attempting to get out of this with his ass un-kicked. "And I'll burn this copy of the magazine. Heck, I can burn any copies I find."

Because Shaw didn't trust himself to grab the hand

by the shirt, he got his jaw muscles to work enough for something more than a growl. He got out one word.

"Run," Shaw muttered.

Apparently, that one word was effective. Zeke tossed the magazine to the floor and ran, not gracefully, either. It was a clomping gait, complete with flailing arms. It would have been funny if Shaw had been able to consider anything funny at the moment.

He couldn't.

Shaw stayed put, but he knew he should make himself move. He should just skip the ride he'd planned and go back to his house. He had an office there, too, but it was a place he didn't want to be because of all the calls and emails pouring in over the twenty-four hours since Tonya's story had come out. It was the reason he'd wanted a long sweaty ride on a mean horse and turned off his phone, too.

Granted no phone contact wasn't good business practice, but he was treading water here to hang on to his temper.

Shit. Why had Sunny gotten so graphic about that night? So…flowery? Hell, she'd called his body "chiseled" and his chest hair "dewed with moisture that carried his musky scent."

He'd been hot, hard and sweaty.

And Sunny had doctored up the rest of the deal, too. They'd been in a barn, for Pete's sake. *This* barn, with the smell of horse piss and liniment. Specifically, in the hayloft, where they'd gone after she'd found him coming in from a late ride. With no one else around, they'd had the barn to themselves.

They'd climbed the wooden ladder, groping and kissing, giving each other bruises and hickeys and nearly breaking their necks when they'd stumbled. Shaw had gotten a skinned-up shin that had taken weeks to heal and so many puncture marks on his ass from the jagged bits of hay that he'd looked as if he had a case of smallpox.

But all of that didn't dampen his other memories.

Yes, he'd kissed her in those places she'd mentioned, including the good parts. Of course on Sunny, all the parts were good.

Shaw tried to force himself to remember that. To remember that he'd tried his damnedest to give her a pleasurable experience. It would have been easier to do that, probably, if she'd at least told him she was a virgin. Or if she hadn't straddled him and impaled herself on his extremely hard hard-on only seconds after he'd gotten on a condom.

He could still feel the sensation of being inside all that tight heat. That blast of pleasure that had nearly undone him. But then he could also hear her gasp of pain. Had seen it in her eyes, too, thanks to the crappy overhead light in the barn that had seemingly never shined bright enough to see squat.

It'd been damn bright that night.

Her eyes had watered. Her face had gone pale and tight. Then Sunny had whispered his name in the breathiest of breathy voices. *Shaw*. As if this had been some kind of betrayal.

Hell, who was being flowery now?

Betrayal? Yeah, right. That was a fancy word for ass-kicking pain. It'd hurt. Bad. And he'd tried to get her past the agony and onto the pleasure by using his fingers to touch her where they were joined. But he'd been twenty and an idiot. Clearly, his fingers hadn't been skilled enough, and when he'd tried to move her off him, Sunny had shaken her head and asked him to help her finish it.

Finish it.

Yeah, not exactly flowery, and that's maybe why Sunny had embellished things in her diary by saying it was the most wonderful night of her life. She hadn't gotten off, although not from his lack of trying.

Apparently, his dick had been stupid that night, too, because after Sunny's constant whispered urgings to finish it—and tongue kissing his ear—Shaw had decided to fake a climax. Something he would have done, too, if Sunny hadn't orchestrated a thrust of her hips that he was certain high-priced hookers couldn't have managed. Getting off had never made him feel so shitty.

He had put up with more pokes from the hay to kiss her and hold her afterward. He'd tried to say in his own fumbling twenty-year-old stupid way that he was sorry, that sex shouldn't be this bad. But she'd said her own fumbling eighteen-year-old stupid thing by telling him that she was glad he was her first. That she hadn't wanted to leave Lone Star Ridge without having been with him like this.

Come to think of it, she'd said some flowery things then, too. Things like she'd never forget him and that it was amazing to live out her fantasy with him like this.

That was BS, of course.

A fantasy should have included at least one orgasm, maybe him going down on her. And it shouldn't have included Sunny leaving town the very next day.

Yeah, it especially shouldn't have included that.

Shaw still felt the sting of her goodbye, and now he could add a new sting. Everyone in town—hell, maybe even the entire country—knew very private details of his chiseled body and chest hair dewed with moisture and his musky scent.

He was about to turn and leave when he heard the rustling sound overhead, and then something fell from the hayloft and plopped on a clump of hay by his foot. Shaw frowned.

It was either a giant rat turd or a Milk Dud.

Since there was suddenly the faint hint of chocolate in the air, he guessed it was the latter. A moment later, he got confirmation of that when Kinsley leaned over the hayloft and peered down at him.

"What are you doing up there?" he asked. Last he'd checked on her, she'd been getting a cooking lesson from his mom.

"Hiding out," she snarled. She pulled the headphones from her right ear. "All people can talk about is that stupid story from Sunny's diary."

Shaw couldn't fault her for wanting to get away from that, and he tried the tactic himself. He went up the ladder and found Kinsley lounging against a hay bale. She had a giant box of Milk Duds, and when he saw her throw one up to catch it in her mouth, he realized that's how the other one had fallen to the ground level.

Candy wasn't the only thing the girl had brought

with her to her makeshift hideout. There was a large bottle of Coke and three photo albums. Each of those albums was open to pictures of Marty. Many of them had been snapped when he'd been performing while holding his trademark acoustic guitar that he'd named Darlin'.

"Your mom said I could look at them," she said, following his gaze to the albums. "I didn't steal them. I didn't steal the candy or Coke, either."

"I didn't think you had." Shaw sank down on the floor across from her. "Milk Duds are my mom's favorite candy, but since they're bad for our teeth, she keeps them hidden in the pantry."

He did consider mentioning that there wasn't any nutrition in her snack choices, but he could say that about so many of the meals that Lenore served. Or rather tried to serve. He made a mental note to have the diner deliver something that would qualify as an actual food group.

"How'd you get all of this stuff up here?" he asked.

Kinsley tipped her head to a burlap feed bag that she'd rigged with a metal hook. It appeared to be one of the hooks that his mom used to hang her macramé projects—which were often just as strange and unappealing as her recipes. "I used the rope to hoist it up."

Shaw also spotted the rope that Kinsley had looped around a post. It was a clever makeshift pulley system similar to the ones that he and Austin had rigged when they'd used this place as a hideout in an effort to avoid doing their chores.

"Did you come up here to tell me that you're making me leave the ranch?" Kinsley snapped.

She was so defensive that it almost put Shaw's back up. But he was feeling sort of whipped at the moment and didn't want to fight with the one person who was seemingly avoiding what he wanted to avoid—anything to do with Sunny's diary. He suspected Sunny was trying to do the same thing because, other than short apologetic texts, he hadn't heard from her.

"No, I didn't come here to tell you to leave," Shaw said. "But if your mom doesn't turn up soon, I'll have to call social services. It's the law," he added.

Kinsley had been about to go for another Milk Dud toss, but that stopped her and frosted her eyes. "I'm a Jameson. I have a right to be here."

"Yes, you're a Jameson," he confirmed. "But legally your mom decides where you have a right to be. That's something we're going to have to get straight with her and have her spell out."

Of course, any sane person could argue that Aurora had given up that right by disappearing, but Shaw was holding out hope that the woman would calm down, come back and beg Kinsley to forgive her. Or at least show some interest in bringing her daughter home. His hope was dimming though because it'd been nearly a week since Kinsley had shown up at the ranch, and Aurora wasn't anywhere to be found.

He hadn't lied when he'd told Kinsley that it was the law that her mom had the right to tell her where she could or couldn't be, but technically Aurora had given the girl permission to be at the ranch. Or rather Aurora had demanded it. That was the sole reason Leyton hadn't already called social services, but as Shaw's cop brother had pointed out, there was no written agreement, and Aurora could come back on them and deny saying that. Or even claim that Shaw and his family had hidden the girl from her. That could land Shaw in legal hot water.

"You'd really let me go into foster care?" Kinsley asked but didn't wait for him to answer. "You want to get rid of me that bad?"

This was tricky. He wanted to get rid of her. Or rather he wanted her to leave. But he didn't want her to go into the system. This was the rock and the hard place he'd been between since she'd shown up.

Shaw wished he could make a rule that no more half siblings could arrive at the ranch until they were eighteen. Better yet, twenty-one. Then, he could buy him or her a beer while they trash-talked Marty and his condom-phobia ways.

"He's not going to come here, is he?" Kinsley asked. No snap and sting in her voice now, and he didn't think it was because her mouth was clogged with Milk Duds. She was looking at a picture of Marty.

Their dad was standing next to a bay mare, the reins gripped in one hand and his other hand lifted in a gesture of "lookee here" jubilation. Shaw didn't know why Marty was so proud of that horse, especially since there were no other photos similar to that one. He'd posed for shots, of course. The Christmas gatherings and such. But Marty hadn't beamed like that in any of them. In those, he'd looked more like someone caged and trying to get out.

"Probably not," Shaw answered honestly. Because he hated that look that came over Kinsley's face, he added, "I'll keep trying to find him. Leyton will, too." He was about to add his sister, Cait, to the list of helpers when he heard her voice.

"Is this a turd or a Milk Dud on the ground?" Cait called out.

"Milk Dud," Kinsley and Shaw answered in unison. "There's more up here," he told her because he knew that would be good news to his sister. She loved them as much as Lenore did. Apparently, as much as Kinsley did, too.

A moment later, Cait came climbing up the ladder, and he recognized the metal sound as her deputy sheriff's badge clanged against the rungs. She would have it clipped to her belt as she usually did.

Cait grinned when her head popped above the floor line. "Are you two hiding out up here?" she asked.

Shaw and Kinsley answered in unison again. "Yes."

"Not a bad idea. Oh, you've got Coke, too." Cait hoisted herself up, dropping down next to Kinsley. "Hand over the goods, little sis." She gave Kinsley a nudge with her elbow.

Kinsley didn't scowl and didn't balk when she *handed over the goods*, and Shaw wondered if that was because Cait had called her *little sis*.

Maybe.

To the best of his knowledge, Cait and Kinsley had only seen each other once before and that'd been three nights ago when Cait had come for dinner. They hadn't eaten anything that Lenore had fixed. That would have in no way enticed Cait to drive over from her place, which was on the other side of town. Shaw had had to lure Leyton and her there with pizza that he'd picked up from the diner.

He was still working on a way to arrange for their brother, Austin, to meet Kinsley, but that wouldn't happen until Austin's two girls got over the "snots" as Austin called their bad colds. Shaw suspected, too, that Austin might not want to attempt an explanation to his kids about who Kinsley was. And there was the fact that Austin just wasn't very social these days. Losing the woman he loved to cancer could do that.

"They're a little melted," Kinsley warned Cait when she dug into the Milk Duds.

That didn't stop his sister. She tossed a candy blob into her mouth and wiped her fingers on the hay. Cait then pulled out something tucked in the back of her jeans. A copy of the tabloid. And she flung it on the ground next to Shaw.

"You had chest hair back then?" Cait asked in a smart-ass way that only a sister could manage.

"Apparently so. It was dewed with moisture that carried my musky scent." He instantly regretted saying that in front of Kinsley, but judging from the girl's reaction—which was no reaction at all—she'd already heard it or read it enough not to snicker or scowl about it.

Cait made a snorting laughter sound. "More like horse pee and liniment."

Exactly, which hit too close to home for Shaw to be amused by her nail-on-the-head assessment.

"So, you're looking at pictures of Dad?" Cait asked, giving Kinsley another nudge.

Kinsley either muttered a yes or else she burped.

Chewing a Milk Dud that was obviously sticking to her teeth, Cait hauled one of the thick albums into her lap. The bubbly plastic covered the pages of yellowing photographs.

Other than Milk Duds and finding bad recipes, another of Lenore's loves had been to take pictures. Lots and lots of them apparently, but that hobby had slowed down some by the time Cait had been born when Shaw was three and a half and Austin was two. Shaw figured that was because Lenore didn't have time to click any pictures what with chasing three kids around and with little or no help from her husband.

"Say, I just thought of something," Cait said, looking sideways at Kinsley. "I'm no longer the kid sister. Marty's other kids are all boys. Well, the ones we know about anyway. But now that we know about *you*, you're the kid sister."

Kinsley eyed her with some suspicion, maybe wondering what that title meant in the pecking order. "You don't expect me to do like chores for you?"

"Absolutely," Cait readily answered. "Along with taking some ribbing and handing over any and all snacks that you sneak from my mom's secret stash in the pantry. She doesn't offer up Milk Duds very often, but she's doing that because she probably wants to make you feel welcome."

Kinsley stayed quiet a moment. "Why? I mean, she should hate me, right?"

"Not Lenore," Cait assured her. "And not us. We don't hate you, either, and we won't judge you for your

DNA or your choice in boots. But those are really bad boots," Cait added in a sisterly voice.

A small smile worked its way onto Kinsley's mouth, but it didn't have time to fully form before someone called out.

"Uh, what's this on the floor of the barn?"

Sunny.

"Milk Dud," Kinsley answered just as Cait said, "It's a really big mouse turd. Don't step on it."

Because Sunny knew Cait, she gave a fake hardy-har-har laugh, and before Shaw could get to his feet, he heard the familiar sound of steps coming up the ladder. Hell. Sunny wasn't in any shape to be climbing into haylofts.

He hurried to the side of the loft. "Stay put. I'll come down."

"It's okay. My stitches don't come out until tomorrow, but they don't hurt. I'll go slow."

She did just that, easing her way up, and Shaw wondered why she was here. It wasn't as if this was a den or game room. Then again, it had been Sunny's choice location for losing her virginity.

Once she was at the top, Shaw took hold of her non-stitched arm and helped her the rest of the way. He watched to make sure there were no signs of pain. There weren't. If she was hurting, she was covering it well.

"Your mom said you were in the barn so I came out looking for you. I wanted to get away from the ranch hands." Sunny sat next to Cait, and Kinsley passed her the box of Milk Duds. "They've obvi-

ously read the story from my diary and they're looking at me funny."

Maybe it was because that was a big-assed under-
statement, Kinsley and Cait looked at her funny, too.
Shaw hadn't quite managed to move on to the stage
where any of this was amusing so he kept the scowl
he'd been sporting pretty much all day.

"So, the cootie queen stole your diary and sold it to
a trashy tabloid," Cait summarized. The cootie queen
was a play on words for beauty queen, Cait's term for
Sunshine, who had indeed once been a beauty queen.
There were other terms, ones not so G-rated, but Cait
likely hadn't wanted to use them in front of Kinsley.

"It looks that way." Sunny was sighing when she
bit into a Milk Dud. "She's not answering my calls
so I haven't actually gotten a confession from her."

"Want me to find her, flash the badge and have
a go at making her regret screwing you over?" Cait
asked.

Shaw was almost sure his sister was kidding. *Almost.* But even if she wasn't, he was hoping just the
thought of it would cheer Sunny up. She didn't look
as if she was in pain, but she looked sad.

"You don't even wear a gun," Kinsley pointed out.

"No need," Cait insisted. "We're not exactly living
in a hotbed of crime." She pulled a small travel-size
can of Mighty Hold hairspray from her pocket. "But
if necessary, I could use this."

"Hard to scare somebody with just a badge and
some hairspray," Kinsley muttered.

Cait lolled her head in Kinsley's direction. "Hey,
one squirt of Mighty Hold will glue eyes shut. Then,

I could go in for the takedown. I was raised in a house with brothers so I know how to defend myself. Mean brothers who used to fart in my face when I was sleeping."

"Not me—that was Austin," Shaw clarified.

Cait shifted, zooming right in on him. "No, but you peed in my shoe."

"Once," he admitted, "and that was an accident. You'd left it by the toilet, and when I went to swat at a fly, some pee went in your shoe. If you'd put your shoe where it belonged, that wouldn't have happened."

And he suddenly realized he and Cait sounded as if they were eight years old. He frowned. Then he saw Sunny's slight smile. He knew instantly that the humiliation of a misdirected pee stream was worth it if he could lighten things up for her. Especially since her humiliation was even greater than his over the diary being leaked.

"Come on, little sis," Cait said, getting to her feet and pulling Kinsley to hers. "Let's give these love-birds some privacy." She reached down, picked up the tabloid and waved it at Sunny. "'Chest hair dewed with moisture that carried his musky scent'?"

Sunny shrugged. "I wrote that when I was watching a lot of *Sex and the City.*"

"Ah," Cait said as if that explained it all perfectly. "It would have taken on a whole different tone if it'd been when she was binge reading Stephen King."

True, but Shaw figured that kind of influence would have sounded better when being read aloud by ranch hands.

Shoving the tabloid in the back waist of her jeans, Cait poured some of the Milk Duds into Sunny's lap. Then Cait helped Kinsley put the albums, remaining candy and Coke in the burlap bag. Once Kinsley had used the rope to lower it to the ground, she and Cait left.

"I'm sorry," Sunny said once they were alone. "And I know I've already told you that, but if I repeat it six million times, it won't be enough."

If she'd said that when he'd been in the worst of his ass-kicking mood, he might have agreed, but she looked as whipped as he did. "It wasn't your fault. It was the fault of a sleazy reporter who used a stolen diary to make our lives miserable."

She nodded, but Shaw didn't see any acceptance of that. She was still carrying this on her shoulders. Crap on crackers. He hated to see her like this, and it made him want to do something stupid like pull her into his arms.

Considering her stitches, that wouldn't be wise.

Plus, she didn't need close contact with him in the very place that would remind her of other close contact. Sunny might have written flowery stuff about their encounter here, but he was betting all of that had now been significantly overshadowed by the gossip and publicity.

"I hired a lawyer." She took a bite of one of the Milk Duds, but Shaw shook his head when she offered him one. "Cora Neely from a law firm in San Antonio. She's a friend of McCall's. Along with trying to get an injunction to stop Tonya from publishing anything else about us, she's pressing Tonya to give up the name of the source."

"The diary was stolen," he pointed out. "You can't file criminal charges?"

"No. At least not now. I can't prove the diary was indeed stolen. Yes, it's missing from the last place I saw it in a box in the attic, but in theory it could have been taken at any time in the past fifteen years. Or even thrown away, though Em doesn't remember ever doing something like that."

Well, Em was getting on up in years and might forget a thing or two, but he still couldn't see her tossing Sunny's diary.

"Tonya's got a lawyer, too. Her brother," Sunny added. "And he's saying that the source who gave Tonya the diary didn't steal anything, that Tonya gained access to the diary through legal means."

"Bullshit," Shaw growled, and he felt that kick-ass mood start to bubble and churn again.

"Definite bullshit," she agreed. "Of course, Tonya's lawyer isn't saying what those legal means were. I'm guessing Sunshine stole it and then sold it to her. That doesn't make it legal. So, I'm hoping when the dust settles, Tonya won't be able to print anything else about us." She paused. "But there's a chance more will come. I could lose this legal wrangling."

"Hell." Shaw tacked on some more curse words and groaned at that possibility. He hoped like the devil that there wasn't anything else like what had already been published.

Sunny ate the rest of the Milk Dud in silence,

wiped her hand on the hay and glanced around the hayloft. "This is where it all took place."

Yep, and he figured her head was full of the memories they'd made here. His certainly was.

"Uh, there were some things not quite true in the diary," she added a moment later.

"You mean the part about my chiseled body and chest hair dewed with moisture that carried my musky scent?" he asked, his tone on the dry side.

"No, that was true," she said, her tone nowhere near dry. It sounded, well, genuine. "It was an amazing experience—"

"I hurt you," Shaw interrupted. "Don't deny it."

"Oh, I won't deny that part. Darn right it hurt. You were huge and I hadn't expected that."

Shaw waivered for a moment between stupid male pride over the *huge* and the less-than-stupid reality of that particular situation. "I was huge because you were a virgin."

"No, you were huge because you're huge. I've been with other men since then, Shaw, and you're what women call a big boy. I had no idea what to do with all those inches."

Well, crud. The stupid male pride won out after all. "You did just fine." And, yes, that was a drawl that he knew complemented foreplay.

"That's your horniness talking," Sunny said, calling him on the drawl and the sizzler of a look he was no doubt giving her. "And don't you smile that smug smile because I gave you a backhanded compliment on the length and girth of your manliness."

"Girth, too?" he asked, just to see her smile.

It worked. For a second or two anyway. She looked up at him, their eyes locking long enough to let him know that she was experiencing some of the same horniness he was. He could have withstood that, letting the fear of her stitches hold him in check, but then her eyes lowered to his mouth, and Shaw could have sworn that she tongue kissed him.

Sunny clearly picked up on the dirty dream kiss, too, because she glanced away and pushed her hair from her face. He was about to tell her that she'd smeared chocolate on her cheek, but she started talking before he got the chance.

"It's a good thing I can't do anything about the old heat because of this," she said, motioning to her chest area and arm. "I suck at relationships, Shaw, and I'm not into casual sex. In fact, I think that's why I jumped twice into getting engaged."

That should have cooled him down. After all, Sunny seemed to be pouring her heart out to him along with clarifying, in no uncertain terms, there'd be no repeat performance in this hayloft. But the impulsive, ignorant part of him behind his zipper, the one with both length and girth, was urging him to kiss her.

Along with giving her that orgasm he'd failed to give her fifteen years ago.

"Did you just hear what I said?" she asked.

Possibly. It was also possible that he'd missed something because his heartbeat had started to thud in his ears. It was keeping rhythm with the thudding in the rest of his body.

"I'm bad news," Sunny said, as if repeating it.

So, that's what he'd missed her saying, and Sunny had likely meant it to be a big turnoff. It had a slightly different effect on him.

Shaw leaned in and kissed her.

Oh, man. This was so much better than the infamous bloody kiss. Her mouth was soft. And familiar. The kind of mouth a man could just sink right into, so that's what he did. Sliding his hand around the back of her neck, he eased her closer and had that mouth for supper.

She tasted like chocolate and sin. All in all not a bad combination, and paired with that soft hiccupping sound of surprise and pleasure she made, it slammed him right back to a different time. Same place, though. He'd definitely kissed Sunny before the bad sex that he now felt compelled to fix. He didn't want that to be her sole memory of his abilities to please her. Shaw wanted to remedy that right now.

Sunny didn't nix the notion, either. Despite the *bad news* lecture she'd just given him, she moved in, her mouth doing its own share of sampling and tasting.

He brought Sunny even closer to him, forcing himself to remember stitches and surgery. Also forcing himself to remember that he didn't want to have sex with her again in a barn but rather a bed. The chocolate scent might be offsetting those other barn smells, but Sunny deserved better. And neither of them deserved hay pricks in their butt.

Keeping away from her breast, Shaw settled his fingers on her waist, touching as much of her as he could. That escalated things for him. Of course, he was already primed, so that wasn't a surprise. He felt like a teenager again. Way too hot. Way too ready.

Way too stupid.

Because hay pricks and smells suddenly didn't seem like such a bad idea.

Without breaking the air-starved kiss, Sunny slid her hand from his hair to his neck. Her body did some sliding, too, and she moved onto his lap. Shaw normally would have thought of that as a move in the right direction, but the whiff of chocolate became more than a whiff. And he was pretty sure the stickiness he felt on his throat wasn't sweat but rather a melted Milk Dud.

Sunny must have realized that, too, because she stopped and pulled back. Looked at him. And cursed.

"I just smeared chocolate all over you," she grumbled.

He'd already figured that out. Figured out, too, that the candy was gobbed and smeared in both of their laps.

"Sorry," she muttered.

Sunny climbed off him, grabbed a handful of hay and started wiping. Unfortunately, she took it upon herself to try to wipe it off his jeans, too, and she would have given him a hand job if he hadn't stopped her.

"Sorry," Sunny repeated, probably because she'd noticed the way he was grimacing.

"Not to worry. It went better than our first kiss." No blood or sore nuts, and that reminder made him smile. Then, chuckle.

"I told you I was bad news." She was smiling, too.

Shaw couldn't help himself. He kissed her again, but this time he didn't go in for the tongue play. He kept it short and sweet. The chocolate helped with that last part.

"You're not bad news," he assured her. "Not when it comes to kissing." He wouldn't touch the commitment-phobia stuff she'd mentioned, but there was another area he could maybe soothe over for her. "Now, that the diary's been printed, the worst has been done. The gossip will die down soon."

She was still using the hay to remove the chocolate from her jeans, and she stopped in midswipe. Actually, she froze for a couple of seconds before her gaze finally lifted to meet his. Not a quick jerk to make eye contact. It was slow, like a striptease.

But without the heat.

There was definitely no heat in Sunny's eyes when she finally got around to looking at him. However, Shaw did see something that he thought might be a whole bunch of regret and an apology or two.

Hell.

"What's wrong?" he managed to ask.

Like the eyeball striptease, she took her time with the words. "There were six of my diaries in that box," Sunny finally said. "And every single one of them is missing."

CHAPTER EIGHT

"BULL BALLS ARE really ugly."

Sunny frowned at the text from Shaw, wondering why he thought she might like to know that particular tidbit about bovine genitalia. She got some clarification when his next text came in.

The buyer for those Angus is here. She's a twenty-year-old city girl who inherited her granddaddy's ranch, and she didn't have a positive reaction to certain parts of the bull. How well do you think our meeting is going?

Now Sunny smiled and answered. I'm guessing it's not going well. Any chance that bull will be covering some heifers for cow sex? That'll really give her an eyeful.

Sunny went back to frowning again when she read the text she'd just sent to Shaw. It probably wasn't a good idea to launch into sexting even when it didn't apply to them.

Not after all the kissing and groping she and Shaw had done in the hayloft.

And especially not after what'd happened after the kissing and groping.

When she'd dropped that nasty little bombshell of the six missing diaries, it had instantly cooled him down, that was for sure. There had been shock. Followed by some creative cursing, including voicing a desire to smother Sunshine in her sleep. Sunny had liked that one, but there'd been no other kisses that day.

Or since.

However, the texts and calls from him had been promising. Judging from his often lighthearted tone, he didn't blame her for the diary thefts and hadn't planned any trips to find Sunshine and smother her. In fact, when he'd talked to her on the phone Shaw had sounded flirty and open to taking more trips to the hayloft.

Sunny wondered just how big of a mistake that would be.

Probably a huge one, but it suddenly felt like a big storm coming. Something that she couldn't stop and hoped she could, well, weather.

She went back to the illustration she was working on. Slackers lounging on the back of a crocodile. Because in theory this was still a story targeted to kids, she minimized the croc's teeth and tried to give him a dopey look that was probably more suited for a cartoon donkey than a deadly reptile. Still, it meshed with the equally lounging, dopey smile on Slackers's face.

However, there was still a problem with the blasted tail feather. Way too phallic. The shape was only emphasized because of its white color against the crocodile green. Maybe she could make the croc an albino?

Not having Slackers lounging was out because that's how the narrative described him. So, how could a duck stretch out and lounge without exposing that pointy little projection between his legs?

Her phone dinged again, and she saw another message from Shaw. Cowboys shouldn't scratch their privates. That's the opinion she just shared with Rowley who might or might not have scratched himself in a private place.

Sunny was back to smiling, something she suspected Shaw and his top hand, Rowley, definitely weren't doing with this particular customer.

Scare her and tell her that bulls sometimes scratch their own ugly privates, too, she texted back, and then turned to the illustration again.

"Fire!" someone yelled.

That gave Sunny a jolt and caused her to slash the pencil over the sketch pad, giving Slackers an even more elongated tail feather than it should have. It looked as if he was peeing. She tossed the pad aside, hurrying to the window, and she saw the shouter.

Bernice.

Sunny saw the fire, too. The flames were shooting up from the oversize concrete birdbath. Sunny figured that the sight would have caused most people to gasp, run and call the fire department, but she'd been down this particular road before and knew there was no need for that. The fire department, or rather Bennie Harper, would be nearby.

She opened the window, still feeling a tug from her incision and the bra injury. A tug was far better than pain. Sunny was about to tell Bernice to go get the fire extinguisher, but before she could even open her mouth, Ryan came running out of the house with one. He took aim at the flames and doused them with the white foam.

"Here, let me do that," Bennie called out. He was running across the yard, no doubt coming out from wherever he'd been hiding and waiting. He, too, had an extinguisher. "Good thing I was driving by and saw the fire."

Sheez. He was stupid. Did he really believe she would buy that? Apparently so, because Bennie gave the already doused flames another hit from the extinguisher and then looked up at her.

"You should come down and take a look at this," Bennie said, giving her what he probably thought was his best lady-killer smile.

Bennie probably thought she'd smile at him in return or at least give him the attention he'd been seeking. In the past she might have toned down the glare she aimed at him, but Sunny wasn't in a generous mood. In the week and a half since she'd come home, Bennie had become a huge pest, and it was time to put an end to it.

"Leave me alone, Bennie." And because that would in no way make him stop, she said, "I'm with Shaw now, and trust me, you don't want to make him jealous."

Even from this distance she could see that had indeed put some concern in Bennie's eyes. Some disappointment, too. "I thought that was a rumor."

"It's not," she assured him, and closed the window. Of course, *I'm with Shaw now* was a bit of a stretch, but there was no denying the attraction between them. He would be a wonderful distraction at a time when so many things in her life weren't so wonderful. But Shaw might get hurt because the one thing that wasn't going to happen was her getting into another serious relationship. Even if Shaw had been inclined toward seriousness—or having children—there'd be no proposals or engagement rings. Her runaway fiancée days were over.

Besides, the aftermath of this whole diary mess almost certainly wasn't over. And it might be just the tip of the iceberg. Sunny had checked the other boxes in the attic, and she couldn't tell if anything else had been taken. There were some of McCall's boxes, untouched. Ditto for Hadley. Only Sunny's had been opened, but that didn't mean Sunshine hadn't taken other things. It was possible there were notes or maybe mementos that could come back to haunt her.

Of course, nothing could haunt as well as those diaries.

It was impossible for her to remember every detail she'd written during those teenage years. All those thoughts, feelings and secrets that wouldn't stay secret once printed. But Sunny could remember the highlights.

Getting her period, for example.

Yes, she'd poured out details of cramps and having to share that time of the month with her sisters. Things had gotten so bad in the house that Sunny was surprised Em hadn't made a PMS-alert flag to ward off anyone who might venture near the puberty- and hormone-crazy *Little Cowgirls*.

There were also pages and pages in the diaries about the embarrassing kiss with Shaw. Dreams and what-if ramblings where she'd imagined kissing him without the injuries.

She'd also written about sexual fantasies. Well, as much of sexual fantasies as a teenage girl could have. But there was one biggie that she had no trouble recalling. The biggest of them all that would be the shocker. It was the page she'd written shortly before she'd had sex with Shaw. Specifically, page 111 of the sixth diary.

Yeah.

That.

The lawyer she'd hired had to get back the diaries before that page was published. In fact, she couldn't figure out why Tonya hadn't zoomed right in on it and made it the headline. But maybe the reporter was holding it back, planning to save it for impact once she'd garnered a whole bunch of readers from this first article.

Since the possibility of that was just plain depressing, Sunny picked up her phone to send Shaw another text. Bennie started another birdbath fire so to get rid of him, I told him we were together and that you'd get jealous if he came over again. Just wanted to give you a heads-up in case gossip gets back to you. How's the meeting going?

She'd tacked on that last question, but the meat of the text was the "together" part. Even though Shaw had agreed to do her a favor by pretending they were a couple, she still felt awkward about it. The awkwardness shifted to uneasiness when he didn't answer right away.

Minutes crawled by. Enough time for her to fix Slackers's feather and add a few tropical-looking insects buzzing around his head.

Sunny hadn't realized just how on edge she was until she gasped when her phone dinged with Shaw's reply. City girl stepped in shit and stormed off. Was sorry to see her go.

Even though it was only a text, Sunny could practically feel the sarcasm. She could also feel her edginess increasing, when the little dots kept blinking on the screen to indicate that Shaw was still writing the rest of the message.

Eons seemed to pass before it finally came. Maybe we should talk?

For only four words, they packed a wallop. Sunny immediately thought that the stolen diary mess had been too much for him, that he wanted to call off the favor.

Sure, she texted back hesitantly just as another message came in from Shaw. I'd like to see you. I want to kiss your.

More dots came, lingering and flashing, and while it was no fun waiting, Sunny was smiling again. Unless this was the start of a joke, it didn't feel like Shaw was ending things.

Sorry about that, he messaged a moment later. I was texting you when Austin came in, and I had to stop. I'd intended to say I want to kiss your mouth that's dewed with moisture, but after the long wait, I should probably say a different part of your body, just to give you more incentive for me to come over and see you.

She released the breath she'd been holding, and her body got that really wonderful shimmering feeling again, the heat tingling and spreading to multiple parts of her. It was delicious, coated in naughtiness. And exactly what she wanted.

Come over, she texted. Any and all incentives are optional.

All right, so that was probably past the flirty stage, but he'd pressed there, too. Maybe would continue to press.

She frowned again.

She had a chastity belt of sorts. Her surgery scar. It was still too tender for full-scale groping, but even if she had been physically grope-ready, she didn't want Shaw to see the scar. She could barely stomach looking at it herself and didn't especially want to share that with anyone. Not even Shaw. Still, she doubted that would stop them from more of those fully clothed kisses.

Sunny was heading to the bathroom to freshen up when her phone rang. Not Shaw this time but McCall. Since this could be about the stolen diaries, Sunny immediately gave herself an attitude adjustment and answered the call.

"I saw the article in the *Tattle Tale*," McCall said. "God, Sunny, I'm so sorry."

Coming from McCall, the sympathy was genuine. "Your lawyer friend is trying to sort it all out."

"Good. I've actually hired her, too. I've heard from another reporter that Tonya's planning on writing an article about Hadley and me. Apparently, there were some things about us in your diaries."

Sunny groaned. She was certain there were all kinds of things about her sisters scrawled on those pages. Everything from whatever squabble happened to be going on all the way to their boyfriends.

"I'm sorry," Sunny muttered, and she wondered how many more times she was going to have to say that. She wished she'd burned the damn diaries when she'd left for college.

"After being followed around by cameras for years, I seriously doubt anything fresh and new can come to light about me," McCall assured her.

Sunny wasn't so sure. "I remember writing about you lusting after and wanting to have sex with Shaw's brother, Austin. For real sex and not the pretend relationship that Sunshine was always pressing for you to have with him." Sunshine had done that because viewers had sent in lots of fan mail the few times Austin had appeared on screen.

"Shit," McCall said, a rare use of profanity for her. "It won't matter to me, but I've heard Austin might be having custody problems with his late wife's parents. They want to raise his girls."

That put a huge fist-sized knot in her stomach. Apparently, that particular tidbit of gossip hadn't made it to Sunny yet. Good grief, tawdry publicity from the diaries definitely wouldn't help with something like that, and she needed to press the lawyer to make sure Tonya didn't get that in print.

"I wrote about Hadley, too," Sunny added.

"Hadley won't care. In fact, she'll say the publicity will help her business."

That was possible. Judging from what Sunny had seen in the box of underwear Hadley had sent, her sister didn't cater to prudish clients.

"And Hayes," Sunny went on. "I also wrote some stuff about him." Though, like Hadley, Hayes hadn't kept many of his escapades secret so there'd be no shocking or sappy revelations about him.

"Actually, that's one of the reasons I'm calling," McCall said. "I didn't want to worry you, what with everything else going on in your life, but Hayes is missing."

This time the knot wasn't from dread but from fear. Not an overabundance of fear, though. Hayes had gone missing before. Well, not actually missing. As Hayes had put it, he just hadn't wanted to be found.

"Apparently, he had some kind of blowup on the set where they were filming a commercial," McCall explained. "He left, and no one, not even his agent, has heard from him."

Sunny didn't ask about the blowup or the commercial. Those were somewhat the norm, too, when it came to Hayes. He had a reputation for being a bad boy actor with a face so alarmingly handsome that it made people give him leeway that he should in no way be given. What someone needed to do was get that chip off his shoulder. Still, Sunny couldn't assume this was another case of her brother just being irresponsible and not wanting to be found.

"I'll make some calls," Sunny assured her. "I'll see if I can track him down." She was about to hang up, but then Sunny remembered something else. "Did you take your silver name necklace with you when you left home?"

McCall made a soft sound of surprise. "No. You know how much I hated that thing. It's probably somewhere in the chest of drawers with the other things I left behind. Why?"

"Just wondering." Sunny thought of her own necklace that had been on the floor the day she'd arrived. A couple of days later, she'd checked the room for McCall's and Hadley's but hadn't found them. Of course, Hadley might have tossed hers. Or she could still be wearing it as Yeldah, the Ukrainian peasant.

When Sunny ended the call, she put aside her freshening-up plans and got started in on tracking down her brother. She went to find Em. Even when Hayes was at his worst, he'd still stayed in touch with Em. McCall knew that, of course, and had almost certainly already spoken to Em about it, but it was possible her grandmother knew some of Hayes's friends for Sunny to contact.

Sunny threaded her way through the house. No Em, but Ryan was working on his laptop at the dining room table. It appeared to be some kind of advanced math homework.

"Em?" she asked.

"She's in the backyard dealing with the fire aftermath. She's making Bennie scrub out the birdbath and fix the mosquito traps."

Sunny thought of the dozen or so lantern-sized stainless steel canisters that Em had sitting around her gardens. "What'd Bennie do to the traps?"

"Some of the foam from the fire extinguisher got on them. Em gave him a bottle of silver polish and said they had to be buffed to a shine."

Well, that would be interesting work considering that the traps were usually filled with mosquitos and other biting bugs.

Thankfully, Ryan didn't ask if she was okay, which was progress. She didn't want him worrying about her, and his concern had seemed to ease up a bit.

Maybe.

When Sunny gave him a closer look, she did see something there in his eyes. "Uh, can I use the SUV tonight? I have a date."

She wanted to smile, but since Ryan suddenly seemed as uncomfortable as a bug on a blistering hot rock, she kept her expression blank. Ryan had been going into town to get groceries and run errands so he must have met someone. However, this was the first she was hearing about it, and Sunny made a mental note to pay more attention.

"Of course, you can use the SUV. Is the date with anyone I know?" she asked.

Sunny didn't think it was a good sign that his glance flicked away. "Kinsley."

Sunny pulled back her shoulders so fast that she got one of those twinges she'd been carefully avoiding. The angry, crying girl certainly didn't seem to be Ryan's type. Not that she knew what his type was, but she certainly wouldn't have guessed it'd be Shaw's most recently discovered sibling.

"Kinsley's having a hard time," Ryan went on, obviously trying to justify this date. "We're just going to go to the ice-cream shop and then hang out."

Sunny paused, considering what wise advice she could give him about this and drew a blank. "Sounds fun," she settled for saying.

It didn't, not at all. It sounded depressing, what with everything Kinsley was going through, but maybe this would help Ryan get his mind off his father.

Still…

It made her wonder if Hugh had ever had "the talk" with Ryan. Since Ryan was almost seventeen, that should have come years ago, but Hugh being Hugh, maybe it hadn't. Good grief. Should she say something now? Maybe. But this certainly wasn't Ryan's first date.

Was it?

She'd never heard him talk about actual dates, though he'd had friends in San Antonio who he went out with as a group. Not especially socially savvy friends but rather those from the smart-kids clubs that he'd belonged to when he'd still been in school. Sunny didn't want to judge Kinsley, but…all right, she was judging her because Kinsley didn't look like the smart-kids-club type.

"Are we about to talk safe sex?" Ryan asked. His mouth twitched as if fighting a smile.

Sunny definitely didn't have to do any smile fighting. She was now the one who was as uncomfortable as a bug on a hot rock. However, she tried not to show it. "Maybe. Do you need to talk about it?"

"No," he quickly assured her. "Do you?"

Coming from anyone else, that would have sounded snarky or even cocky, but the question seemed genuine.

"I just want to make sure things aren't moving too fast for you," Ryan went on. "Kinsley mentioned that you and Shaw had been in his barn."

"Kinsley told you about that?" Sunny hoped she hadn't told anyone else. Even though the horse was already out of the barn, she didn't want Kinsley spilling anything about it. "What exactly did she say?"

Ryan shrugged. "Only that Cait and she had left Shaw and you in the hayloft."

Sunny felt the blush rise in her cheeks and then heard the sound of someone clearing their throat. She whirled around to the parlor doorway, expecting to see Em or even Bennie. But it wasn't.

It was Shaw.

Though he wasn't the throat clearer. Nope, that sound had come from the woman standing beside him. The one with a malarkey-eating grin on her face.

Her mother, Sunshine.

CHAPTER NINE

SHAW HAD HOPED to give Sunny some kind of advance notice about her visitor. That's why he'd told Sunshine to wait in the foyer when he'd seen her going into the house. He would have had an easier time telling dust not to settle because Sunshine had stayed right on his heels when he'd gone in search of Sunny. And he'd found her. Heard her, too.

Talking about being in the hayloft with him.

Oh, yeah. Sunshine had to be mentally jotting that down so she could feed it to Tonya for her next rake-Sunny-over-the-coals article.

Sunny snapped toward them so fast that he was surprised she hadn't cracked a bone or two. Or winced from her incision and recent stitches. But there was no wincing, only a hard look for her mother. Sunny rarely looked mean, but she was managing to do that now.

"You stole my diaries," Sunny growled, the mean-ness making it into her voice, as well.

Ryan got up, going to Sunny's side in a show of support. Maybe willing to do more, too. He seemed ready to rip Sunshine a new one, but the boy was going to have to stand in line. It was his life that had been dragged over the coals with that article, too, and Sunshine had given Tonya the ammunition to do it.

"Well, hello to you, too, Sunny." Sunshine went closer, aiming some air kisses on Sunny's cheek.

The woman wasn't stupid and knew Sunny wanted no such greeting from her, so maybe this was Sunshine's way of twisting the knife. He'd heard plenty of rumors about the ways she'd manipulated and exploited her daughters, but this was low even for Sunshine.

"You must be Ryan," Sunshine said, extending her hand for the boy to shake.

Ryan didn't take her hand, and Shaw had to give it to the boy—he was holding up his end of the mean looks aimed at a woman who deserved every one of them and more.

"You stole my diaries," Sunny repeated, stepping in front of Ryan and pushing her mother's hand away.

Sunshine sighed and used her batted-away hand to give her massive tumbling blond hair an adjustment that it in no way needed. As usual, there wasn't a strand out of place, probably because she'd doused it with hairspray. Ditto for the makeup. It had likely taken hours to make sure both her makeup and clothes suited her former beauty queen image. Today, it was slim ice-blue pants, a matching sleeveless top and silver stiletto sandals. He could practically see the cloud of eau de *whatever* haloing around her.

Or maybe that was the smoke from hell seeping up to claim her miserable soul.

"I didn't steal your diaries," Sunshine said, looking Sunny straight in the eyes. "That's what I came all the way here to tell you. I didn't take them and I don't know who did."

Sunny didn't miss a beat. "You're lying. Who else would have been able to get into the house and up into the attic?"

"Any number of people, I'd imagine." Sunshine's voice was cool and completely unruffled. "Think of all the episodes that were shot in this house." She glanced around, lifting her hand to emphasize her point. "Every inch of the interior of this place was filmed at one time or another. Including the attic."

"The diaries weren't there when *Little Cowgirls* was filmed," Sunny quickly pointed out.

Sunshine shrugged. "In season four, episode two, the cameraman filmed you sneaking into the attic to try to get a peek at what your brother was doing. There were boxes up there then. Boxes marked pictures and such. A reporter like Tonya could have seen the reruns, sneaked in, found the diaries and sneaked right back out without anyone seeing her."

The woman had a point. One that Shaw wished she hadn't been the one to make.

"You were here at the house about the time the diaries were likely taken," Sunny pressed.

Sunshine did another lift of her slim shoulder. "Unless you had a security camera that I don't know about, you have no idea when they were taken. Heck, it could have been a 'fan' who snatched them." She put *fan* in air quotes. "One who slipped in years ago and took them."

"And waited around for years to sell them to Tonya?" Sunny huffed.

"It's possible, and I hope you find who's responsible. I really do. After all, I technically own those diaries. I mean, along with dozens of sketch pads for all that doodling you did, I bought you those diaries and provided them to you so you could pour out your teenage heart."

Sunny closed her eyes, and Shaw knew she was trying to rein in her fury. That kind of stupid Sunshine logic always made people want to punch her in the face. "You—"

That was as far as Shaw let Sunny get. He hooked his arm around her waist, holding her in place when she took a step toward her mother. Sunshine didn't seem the least bit affected by the fact that a) she'd come damn close to being punched or b) the punch could still happen.

"I've talked to Leyton about this," Sunshine went on, "and I've told him I'll make an official statement that I didn't take the diaries, even though they were rightfully mine to take."

That time, Shaw had to take hold of Ryan's arm to keep him where he was. Since he didn't have any spare arms, he hoped Em didn't come in. He might need to hold her back, too.

"You should take a lie detector test," Shaw advised the woman.

For the first time since she'd walked into the house, anger flared in Sunshine's eyes. "I'm innocent until proven guilty, and I won't be proven guilty because I didn't take the diaries."

"What about the silver name necklaces?" Sunny snapped.

At first Shaw drew a blank, but then he remembered the necklaces the triplets used to wear. "Those are missing, too?" Shaw asked.

Before Sunny could answer, he saw it. Not anger in Sunshine's eyes. Not guilt, either. Just a big-assed sheen of *yes, I took them.*

"The necklaces were mine," Sunshine insisted. "The producers had them made for you girls and gave them to me to lend to the three of you. I simply took them back. Well, two of them anyway. I seem to have misplaced yours."

It felt as if the room deflated, like one of those fart-sounding balloons when the air rushed out of it too fast. Sunshine's warped logic was maddening, but it was also so damn frustrating that it wore you down.

"What are you going to do with the necklaces?" Sunny asked.

"I'm looking for the right buyer," Sunshine readily admitted, and she huffed when Sunny did. "Don't stare at me that way. You girls hated those necklaces. They meant nothing to you. For years they've just been sitting around, and I can make good use of them. Along with making someone very happy. You girls still have a lot of fans who'd pay for pieces like that."

"And you've found yet another way to make money off us." Sunny gave Sunshine a dismissive wave as if she couldn't stand hearing anything else the woman had to say, and she turned to walk away.

"Don't judge me," Sunshine called out. "You're still young and have your looks. You have no idea how hard it is for a woman my age. Many people think a beauty queen over the age of thirty is a joke. And I gave a lot to *Little Cowgirls*. Why shouldn't I benefit from it? You girls certainly did."

Sunny kept walking.

"And I thought my dad was as cold as sour owl shit," Ryan muttered.

Shaw muttered something slightly stronger. Well, not stronger than the weird insult that sounded like something Em would have said, but Shaw had perfected a badass tone that Ryan hadn't had time to develop.

"You should leave now, Sunshine." Shaw used the same tone he had with the tabloid-reading ranch hand when he'd told him to run, and he gave Sunny's mother a mean-as-a-snake look.

"I don't have Jameson money like you," Sunshine declared. Shaw wasn't sure if she meant that as a dig or an excuse. Either way, she turned on her stilettos and walked away.

Shaw dragged in a long breath. "Lock the front door after she leaves," he told Ryan. "I'll check on Sunny."

While the boy hurried to do that, Shaw went in search of Sunny. However, he hadn't forgotten that he needed to talk to Ryan about the date he'd had with Kinsley. A date that Kinsley certainly hadn't told Shaw about. Instead, he'd had to hear it from Cait. And while Kinsley wouldn't consider a date with Sunny's almost-stepson to be a big deal, Shaw had wanted to make sure…

Well, he didn't know what he wanted to make sure, but he figured he should have a conversation with

Ryan about it. For now though, Sunny had top priority.

She was probably crying, a thought that twisted him up as much as he wished he could twist up the worthless woman who'd given birth to her. Sunny's defenses were way down, and this confrontation with Sunshine might send her into an emotional tailspin.

Or not.

He found her in the backyard. The spring breeze was stirring her hair and her loose red top, and with a stick in her hand, she was leaning over the sandy walkway that led to the barn.

"I think this might work," she said. Sunny barely spared him a glance, instead continuing to draw something in the sand. When Shaw went closer, he frowned.

She was drawing a dick.

One with a straight line on the left side of it and a thin diagonal line across the tip.

So, maybe this was how Sunny lapsed into an emotional tailspin? Or it could be her way of opening up a conversation about sex with him. Shaw reluctantly admitted that last one might be wishful thinking on his part.

He stooped down to have a better look. As dicks went, it was pretty lame. The shape was right, but it was pointy and stubby at the same time. It definitely didn't mesh with her description of him as a *big boy*. And that disturbing diagonal line looked as if some kind of circumcision was going on.

"Uh, are you all right?" Shaw asked. "Are you mad at me about something?"

There must have been a slathering of concern in his voice because her head whipped up, and she volleyed glances at him and the stick drawing before she let out a long breath.

"It's Slackers," she said. "I can conceal his penis-like tail feather by having him cross his legs. You know, like resting his left leg over the top of his right knee. The perv readers won't like that, but parents will appreciate me not showing off Slackers's duck junk for the umpteenth time."

Okay. Since that seemed to be some kind of creative breakthrough for her, he didn't minimize it, but he couldn't help thinking that this surge of inspiration was a way of coping with the confrontation she'd just had with her mother.

"Do ducks have knees?" he asked. He hadn't actually thought about how stupid and completely irrelevant his question was, but he was glad he'd asked it when Sunny smiled.

"Thanks." She stood upright, tossed the stick aside and gave his arm a pat. "I needed that."

Shaw was betting that she needed a whole lot more than an unintended lame joke. He knew it for certain when her smile vanished and she shoved both hands through her hair. She groaned.

"I don't know why I'm still surprised by anything Sunshine does," she muttered.

"The woman's definitely got a predictable pattern," Shaw agreed. Along with being as cold as sour owl shit. "If it can be low-down, shitty and reprehensible, then Sunshine has done it."

He recalled the times Sunshine had made sure the

cameraman caught the girls doing something embarrassing. Often something embarrassing that Sunshine herself had set up—like stealing McCall's phone, and while pretending to be her daughter, inviting several boys to come over at the same time for a date. Thanks to Sunshine's clever scheduling and the cameraman who Sunshine was likely boinking, the viewers had probably gasped and giggled as a flustered McCall had tried to sort everything out.

Em had tried to run interference, and there'd been a few times when she'd set up Sunshine for something less than flattering. However, Em hadn't had editorial control, and Sunshine had deleted anything that made her look less than perfect.

A couple of times, Em had also tried to get the filming stopped completely. After all, it was her house. But Sunshine had played the "you'll lose the girls" card by simply threatening to leave with Hayes and the triplets. The producers had even considered it a good twist for the *Little Cowgirls* to move to the city, and that possibility had kept Em mostly quiet. Mostly.

"I wonder if Sunshine hates me," Sunny went on, "or if she's just too self-centered to see anything past her cosmetically altered nose."

It could be both, but since Sunny didn't need to hear that confirmed, Shaw put his hand on the small of her back to get her moving to the porch swing. It was impossible for him to take her anywhere on the premises that didn't hold a bad memory or two—Sunshine had been right about every inch of the place being filmed. Other than the ground, the porch swing was the nearest thing, and he wanted her off her feet.

And in his arms.

It turned out that didn't take any maneuvering on his part, because the moment they were seated she settled against him. Sunny slipped right into his arms as if she belonged there.

That gave him a couple of rounds of second thoughts.

Sunny and he were getting close again, like they'd been way back when, and that had led to sex. Something he wanted just as much now as he had then. But Shaw had to keep better hold of the reins this time and not find himself in a hayloft with her again until he was certain he wasn't going to add another heaping of trouble to the plate of trouble she already had.

"Do you want to have sex?" she asked, looking up at him.

And just like that, there were no second thoughts, and he eyed the hayloft of the barn.

"Of course you don't," she said before he could answer with the *okay* that was already forming on his mouth. "Because you know it'd be out of frustration. I'd just be using you."

Shaw couldn't help it. He smiled. Which was probably better than kissing her. "And I'm sure I'd feel taken advantage of afterward. Just how dirty would that kind of frustration be anyway?"

"Dirty," she assured him.

And she kissed him.

One touch of her mouth on his, and Shaw started to convince himself that all this sex talk was just foreplay. Foreplay leading to something that wouldn't be frustrating.

Sunny shifted a little, turning toward him and deepening the kiss. She made it long and dirty, just the way he liked his kisses, but when she eased back to look at him, he saw more than heat in her baby blues.

"God, Shaw," she said, and with only those two words, he could have sworn he heard her heart breaking.

On a heavy sigh and plenty of unspoken cuss words aimed at Sunshine, Shaw pulled Sunny back into his arms. Not for any hanky-panky, either. But for the kind of comfort that only a longtime friend could give. He knew the crap she'd gone through, and despite the thick skin she'd managed to build up over the years, Sunshine could still find a weak spot and slice right through her. No cut was deeper than the one that could come from family.

"I can set Leyton on Sunshine," he offered.

Even though it wasn't exactly playing fair, Leyton might be willing to have Sunshine watched like a hawk if and when she was in town. Still, a ticket for a traffic violation or loitering didn't seem like much payback for what the woman had done this time.

Which got Shaw to thinking.

"Did you believe Sunshine when she claimed she didn't take the diaries?" he asked.

"No." But she went still a moment and then huffed. "I don't want to believe her." Yeah, neither did Shaw. "She didn't deny taking the necklaces," Sunny added.

There was that, and if Sunshine had fessed up to

that, then why not admit to taking the diaries, as well? Maybe because Sunshine had known she could be sued for the diaries and not the necklaces?

Shaw didn't know the fine print of the *Little Cowgirls* contracts, but it was indeed possible that Sunshine owned the necklaces. However, he couldn't see a judge stretching that ownership to a teenager's diaries. Even if Sunshine had been the one to buy them for Sunny. Heck, if that were true, Sunshine could claim she owned Sunny's sketches, too.

"Well, that's taken care of," he heard Em mumble.

That got Shaw's attention. Sunny's, too, because they practically came to attention, their gazes zooming in on Em as she walked from the side yard and onto the porch.

What they saw not only piqued his curiosity but confused him. Shaw was almost positive that Em had one of his mother's casserole dishes tucked under her arm. There were still bits of food stuck to the sides, and some of it dislodged and splatted onto the porch.

It was hard to tell, but he thought it was a blob of Lenore's tuna apricot surprise.

And that wasn't the only thing Em was carrying. She had not one but two of those mosquito catchers, and the white mesh sacks that were usually inside the canisters were missing.

"Granny Em, what did you do?" Sunny asked, getting to her feet.

"Nothing you need to know about." Em smiled. "But I don't think Sunshine will be coming back around here anytime soon."

The words had no sooner left the woman's mouth

than Shaw's and Sunny's phones rang. Leyton's name was on his screen. Cait's on Sunny's.

Shaw was pretty sure that wasn't a good sign, but he pressed Answer at the same time Sunny did.

"Are you still at Em's?" Leyton asked him. Shaw was plenty close enough to Sunny to hear Cait say, "There's some trouble."

"What happened?" Shaw said in a loud enough voice for both his siblings to hear.

"It's Sunshine," Leyton answered.

Cait finished up the sparse explanation to Sunny. "The cootie queen is demanding we arrest Em, Shaw and you for assault."

CHAPTER TEN

SUNNY FIGURED THERE'D never been a more ridiculous-sounding complaint filed at a police department. Assault with mosquitos and tuna apricot surprise. Sunshine's accusations would have been laughable had it not been so serious.

Okay, it was still laughable.

Sunny had gotten some perverse satisfaction when Shaw, Em, Ryan and she had walked into the Lone Star Ridge Police Department and seen Sunshine's face and arms covered with the itchy red splotches from the mosquito bites. Ditto for seeing the remains of tuna apricot surprise in her mother's hair.

The congealed fish mix was turning bad, fast, and it reeked to high heaven. If Sunny had needed any incentive to keep her distance from Sunshine, that would have done it.

However, there was no satisfaction in realizing that Sunshine had indeed filed a complaint. One that Leyton was obviously going to have to do something about.

"Hey, Sunny," Cherry Miller immediately called out to her. "Tell me a joke."

Cherry was the dispatcher, and even though she'd been a couple of years ahead of Sunny in school, she'd always been friendly to Sunny. The woman sat at the desk that faced the door, and she had a big smile of anticipation on her face. Clearly, Cherry wasn't very perceptive if she thought this was the time for jokes. Still, Sunny gave her one.

"What do you call a sad cup of coffee?" Sunny asked and then provided the lame punch line to go along with the lame joke. "Depresso."

Cherry slapped her jeans-clad knee and laughed. No one else did, but Em did give her arm a poke and said, "Good one."

Nothing about this was good, including the fact that they were walking into a police station. Sunny didn't know what'd happened with Sunshine, but it must have had something to do with Em. She doubted it was a coincidence that Em had had the casserole dish and mosquito catchers with her when she'd come onto the back porch. On the drive over, Em had simply said that she'd done what was necessary.

"One of them tried to kill me," Sunshine insisted when they all went into Leyton's office. Cait and Ryan followed them, both of them staying in the doorway.

Sunny was about to insist that no such thing had happened, but Em spoke before she could say anything.

"I did it," Em readily admitted. She didn't sound even remotely remorseful, either.

Leyton looked at Sunny and Shaw for verification. She shrugged. He scowled. Neither of them would implicate Em, especially since they didn't know what was going on.

"Shaw and Sunny didn't have anything to do with

it," Em added a moment later. "And it was fair and square punishment. Parent-to-kid kind of punishment. My daughter's so crooked that she has to unscrew her britches at night, and I just wanted her to get a taste of what it's like to be malarkeyed."

Sunny had to work her way through the Em-ism. She thought that was a good assessment of her mother, but not such a good thing for Em to do. Sunshine wasn't just crooked and greedy. She was also vindictive.

"Could you tell me exactly why you thought your daughter needed punishing?" Leyton asked Em.

"How much time do you have?" But Em didn't wait for an answer. "She took the girls' money, their things and anything else she could get her grubby hands on."

"Anything I took was mine," Sunshine insisted. She scratched at her neck, making the splotches even redder, and then cursed and flicked away a mosquito that sprang from her hair. It was possible the insect had gotten caught on the sticky helmet of hairspray and had just managed to get loose.

Looking very much like the beleaguered lawman he was, Leyton put his hands on his hips while he volleyed glances between Sunshine and Em. "How'd you get the casserole in her hair?" He directed that question at Em.

Em didn't hesitate. "When she was inside talking to Sunny, Ryan and Shaw, I went to her car. It wasn't locked so I smeared the apricot tuna surprise on the ceiling above the driver's seat. That stuff sticks bet-ter than glue, but I knew sooner or later, it'd come plopping down on her."

And it had clearly done just that. Sunny was surprised though that Sunshine hadn't noticed it when she'd first gotten in the car. It was possible that her perfume slathering had masked the scent. Not now though. Nothing could mask that.

"Don't tell your mom that I said the tuna surprise was like glue," Em muttered to Shaw.

In the grand scheme of things that didn't seem important, but even with the risk of being arrested for assault, Em wouldn't want to hurt her friend's feelings.

"What about the mosquitos?" Leyton pressed.

Em shrugged. "It was time to empty the bags in the traps, and I didn't want them buzzing around my ladybugs."

"She put them in my car so they'd attack me," Sunshine snarled.

"And you didn't notice them and the whining little sounds they make when you got in the car?" Sunny asked.

Sunshine huffed. "I wasn't exactly in a good mood when I left. What with being accused of theft by Shaw and you. So, I started the car and drove off. They swarmed at me when I got to the end of the road. That's when the food fell on me."

"It clung to the ceiling longer than I thought it would," Em remarked.

Obviously, that wasn't a good thing for Em to say because Sunshine made a shivery sound of outrage. "I want her arrested. She just confessed to sabotaging my car. I could have wrecked or hit someone else, and it would have been all her fault."

There it was in a nutshell. Even though it was a stupid prank, or rather a stupid but interestingly clever *parent-to-kid punishment,* it could have had dangerous consequences. Of a lesser concern, there had almost certainly been property damage since the tuna surprise would have left stains. And then there were the mosquito bites that Shaw supposed could be stretched to bodily harm.

"You want me to arrest your own mother?" Leyton asked Sunshine.

Shaw had to hand it to his brother. Leyton managed to look shocked. Appalled even. But Leyton knew Sunshine, knew the stunts she'd pulled over the years, knew that appalling behavior was her forte.

"Of course, I want her arrested," Sunshine insisted. "Lock her up and throw away the key."

Leyton's beleaguered look went up a notch when Em held out her wrists to be cuffed. "It was worth it."

Shaw had to put a stop to this and somehow make Sunshine back off. If groveling worked, he would try that, but he suspected cash was the only thing that would get Sunshine to back off.

"Could I talk to Sunshine alone?" Shaw asked his brother.

Shaw glanced at Cait, Ryan, Em and Sunny to let them know that *alone* meant just that. Him and Sunshine. He didn't want Leyton or Cait to have to listen to him bend the law by paying the woman off so she wouldn't press charges. There was no need for Ryan to witness that, either. And as for Em and Sunny, well, it would be like setting off double powder kegs for them to hear that this worthless member of their gene pool was going to profit from Em's antics.

Cait and Ryan moved with only minimal mumblings of protest. Leyton moved, too, but only after giving Shaw a warning glance. Perhaps because Leyton was wondering if Shaw would potentially become another powder keg if Sunshine pushed for as much as she could get out of this.

"Please," Shaw said to Em when she didn't budge. "Let me talk to Sunshine alone." He played dirty and brushed a kiss on her cheek.

Em smiled at the kiss and then turned to Sunshine. "If you mess him and Sunny over, I know a woman in Wrangler's Creek. She does curses and such, and I'll have her brew up something that'll make your hiney and armpits smell worse than the goop that's in your hair."

As threats went, it was bad and in no way helped their current situation—especially because now Sunshine looked as if she was about to throw a hissy fit. The only silver lining was that Em must have thought she'd had her say because she let Leyton take her arm and lead her out of the office.

"I'm not leaving," Sunny insisted when Shaw motioned for her to go with Leyton and Em. Not only did she stay put, she reached behind her and shut the door.

Sunshine folded her arms over her chest and aimed impatient eyes at her daughter. "Are you going to threaten me with warts or something?"

"No," Sunny answered. "But if you back off, I'll give you the necklace with my name on it."

Clearly surprised, Sunshine blinked. It became

somewhat of an awkward gesture though when a fleck of the tuna surprise dropped onto her eyelashes and caused them to stick together. She swiped it away and swatted at the persistent mosquito that continued to circle her head.

"I own that necklace," Sunshine snarled. "I want it and I want charges filed against that crazy loon."

Oh, that was so the wrong thing to say, and even though Shaw wasn't touching Sunny, he thought her suddenly tensing muscles actually caused ripples in the air. "Em's not a crazy loon," Sunny spit out. "She's just frustrated from having to deal with the likes of you."

Sunshine gave her head an indignant wobble that caused more tuna surprise to plop onto her face. That didn't improve her mood. "I want that necklace, and I want it now."

"Tough titty," Sunny fired back. "I want a mother who isn't a certifiable ass, but I've learned to live with disappointment."

While that was a decent comeback, Shaw knew things were escalating and nothing with the word *titty* in it was going to accomplish anything.

"Sunshine," Shaw said, using the tone he did with his own mother when she frustrated the hell out of him. "You can get a lot more money for all three necklaces than you can for just two. I'm sure there's a fan who'd be willing to pay big bucks for the whole set."

He didn't like Sunny turning over that necklace, but he knew she didn't have an attachment to it. Just the opposite. She likely hadn't given it a second thought through the years. Now though, it could be the bargaining tool needed to smooth this over.

"The necklaces are all mine," Sunshine emphasized, turning her frosty eyes back on Sunny. "Give it to me now, or I'll file charges against you."

There was frost in Sunny's eyes, too. "I don't have a clue where it is," she said with a straight face. "And I'll continue to not have a clue where it is until you sign a paper saying that you won't have Em arrested. If you agree to do that in the next thirty seconds, I'll throw in one of my old sketchbooks, the one where I doodled pictures of Shaw."

Shaw turned toward Sunny so fast that his neck popped. "You doodled pictures of me?"

Sunny nodded. "I drew pictures of a lot of things, including us."

Us. That was potentially worse than doodling just him. Or it could be if Sunny had sketched parts of him. Specifically, any part of him that had been exposed when they'd had sex in the hayloft.

"Uh, could I see this sketch pad?" Shaw asked.

Sunny and Sunshine didn't respond. That's because they were locked in a stare down.

"Two sketch pads and the necklace," Sunshine finally said. "And Em has to do some kind of community service. Something humiliating that'll teach her a lesson about messing with me."

Sunny maintained the stare down. "Two sketch pads, the necklace and Em's community service. Agreed."

Sunshine's suddenly smug look didn't last long when Sunny continued.

"In exchange," Sunny went on, "you'll never step foot here again. If one of your toenails crosses into Lone Star Ridge, then you'll not only have to do some humiliating community service yourself, but I'll call Tonya the reporter and do a tell-all story on you. What I spill to her will stir up enough stink that it'll make Em's threatened curse of hiney-and-armpit odor smell like roses."

Shaw watched as Sunshine processed that. Oh, she wanted to fling some snark back at Sunny, but it must have occurred to her that if this particular shit hit the fan, then Em might try to do a repeat performance with tuna surprise and mosquitos.

"It's a deal," Sunshine snarled through clenched teeth. "Get Leyton in here now so we can start the paperwork."

SUNNY TRIED TO force the acid churning in her stomach to stay in her stomach. Being around her mother was never easy on her digestive system, but the last five hours had been particularly acid-inducing. It hadn't been so healthy for her teeth that she'd been grinding.

Five hours of Sunshine haggling over each word of the agreement Leyton and Shaw were trying to work out with the woman. Five hours of listening to Sunshine whine and demand. And all while being in a closed room—Leyton's office—with the reeking casserole and the high-pitched mosquito that had evaded every swat the four of them had aimed at the critter. He'd dodged death so many times that Sunny was starting to gain respect for him and might include him in the next *Slackers Quackers*.

"I still think Em should have a different community service, a harder one," Sunshine said as she read over the agreement that Leyton had typed up. "She should have to pick up trash while wearing a sign proclaiming what a bad mother she is."

Sunny was about to give her a hell-freezing-over look, but Shaw beat her to it. He was better at it, too. The glare he gave Sunshine was sort of a blend of *Scorched Earth* meets the tornado from *Wizard of Oz*. Definitely formidable.

"Em's community service of doing story and art time in the kindergarten class won't be easy," Leyton told Sunshine. "You must remember how hard it is to deal with kids that young."

Touché. It was genius on Leyton's part because Sunshine would indeed see that as grueling since she'd hated spending time off-camera with her own children. She likely thought everyone felt the same way, but Em would love being with the kids.

Which was the reason Sunny had suggested it.

She hadn't done that at first, though. Sunny had let Sunshine babble off a string of other possibilities such as cleaning the toilets in the police station. Or scrubbing the jail floor. Or collecting roadkill. Sunny had countered each one with punishments so light for Em that they were laughable.

No sweets for a week.

Time out in her bedroom.

Limited television privileges.

When Sunny had finally brought up "duties" at the

kindergarten, Sunshine had jumped on it. Her mother didn't seem so eager now that it was in writing, but Sunny spurred her along with a one-word reminder.

"Tonya."

A couple of days ago, the reporter's name had had its own acid-inducing effect on Sunny, but like the mosquito, it was starting to grow on her.

With narrowed eyes, a pinched mouth and a seriously clenched jaw, Sunshine signed the agreement, which Sunny had already done. Em had signed it, too, but Leyton had carried the papers out to her so that she and Sunshine wouldn't have to breathe the same air.

Now that Sunshine had scrawled her name on the bottom line, it was a done deal. Yes, Sunny would have to give up the necklace and two sketchbooks and Em would have to put in ten hours at the school, but all those things were small potatoes if it truly kept Sunshine out of town and away from Em.

"I don't know why I can't just go out to the house and get the necklace and sketchbooks now," Sunshine remarked, getting to her feet.

Sunny tapped the top of the second page of the agreement. "Because I don't want you there. As agreed, I'll go to the post office tomorrow and mail them. You'll have them by the end of the week."

"If I don't, there'll be hell to pay," Sunshine snapped.

"Tonya," Sunny countered, and had the pleasure of watching Sunshine turn on her heels and leave in a snit. It helped, too, that one of her stiletto heels was dragging the net bag from the mosquito trap. It wasn't as good as a trail of toilet paper would have been, but it was close enough.

Even after Sunshine was gone, Leyton, Shaw and she sat there like survivors of a natural disaster. They'd had to do a lot of talking during the negotiations, and when Shaw had offered Sunshine a check. Sunny had nixed that, which had resulted in more talking, more arguing, but in the end she'd won. Shaw wasn't using Jameson money for Sunshine to line her coffers.

"Just how important are those sketchbooks to you?" Shaw finally asked.

Since he was battle worn and didn't need to be weighed down by the truth, Sunny patted his hand. "Not important at all."

But they were, of course. All of her sketches were like little secret windows and mirrors. Pieces of herself and what she'd been feeling or working out when she'd sketched them.

Each one was *her.*

McCall and Hadley might have her face, but they'd never had what she'd seen with her eyes. They could never put her memories down in those pencil marks on the pages.

"Are there dirty drawings of me?" he asked. She saw the slight smile and knew that he was throwing her a bone because she, too, was battle worn.

"Only flattering ones. If they're ever made public, you'll have more women wanting you than you'll know what to do with."

When Shaw leaned in as if he might brush a kiss

on her mouth, Leyton cleared his throat. "I need a drink."

Shaw's brother got to his feet and went out into the squad room where the dispatcher and deputies had their desks. Shaw and Sunny followed, expecting to see Em and Ryan, but they weren't there. Only Cait was at her desk.

"Ryan took Em home," Cait explained. "I figured Shaw could drive you back."

Shaw's F5-tornado look was gone, but he had a glimmer in his eyes. Maybe because of that near kiss. Or maybe he was wanting to get her alone so she could tell him about the *dirty* pictures she'd sketched of him.

It probably wasn't a good idea for her to use those pictures to flirt with him, but after dealing with Sunshine, Sunny felt as if she'd been in the muck too long. There were problems—correction, there were serious drawbacks—to playing around with Shaw, but at the moment she couldn't think of one that didn't erase her itch for him.

And just like that, she became a teenager again.

There wasn't a single memory from her teen years that didn't involve him. She could have gotten past that, but it was hard to come up with ordinary good memories that he wasn't a part of. Simply put, Shaw had been a big part of her life before she'd climbed up those hayloft steps with him.

She'd been in love with him.

All of that was in the diaries, but if he looked close enough, it was in the sketches, too.

Like those sketches, Shaw had been uniquely hers.

Not a necklace or clothes that someone else had insisted she wear. He was the first non-scripted part of her life that she could remember. Perhaps that had been part of the attraction. Sort of forbidden fruit that her mother and the producers hadn't been able to manipulate.

Maybe it was because she'd become that teenage girl again and was thinking like someone who had been a repeat offender runaway fiancée, but Sunny began to consider that maybe it was possible to fall in love with Shaw all over again. And even though there'd be obstacles to anything permanent with him—their baby disagreement, for one—she found herself smiling at the possibility of it.

"You're thinking about those dirty pictures of me, aren't you?" Shaw whispered to her.

Sunny would have answered *absolutely* if Cait hadn't interrupted.

"Oh, and Ryan wanted me to remind you about his date," Cait told her. "He said he might not be at the house by the time you made it back there."

The date. That snapped her out of her teenage fantasies and brought her back to reality. One that involved two actual teenagers.

"Ryan's going to take Kinsley for ice cream," Cait added to Shaw.

"I heard," he said. No glimmer now, and his voice was practically a growl. "I'm not sure it's a good idea."

Sunny wanted to sigh with relief that he'd been the one to say it first. If she had, it might have sounded as if she was dissing Kinsley or maybe worrying that the girl would corrupt the honor student who was the polar opposite of Shaw's half sister. Because of everything Hugh had put Ryan through, she felt very protective of her almost-stepson.

"What time's the date?" Shaw asked.

"Soon." Cait checked her watch. "In about a half hour."

Shaw opened his mouth to say something, but he must have rethought it. Instead, he took Sunny by the arm and led her outside, away from Cait's earshot.

"Want to do something low-down and sneaky that'll make us feel guilty?" he asked.

Sunny didn't think this had anything to do with sex, but if so, Shaw had put an interesting spin on it. "Sure?" And yes, she made it a question.

"Come on," he added, and slipping his arm around her waist, he got them walking. It didn't take her long to see the direction he was heading.

The Lickety Split.

"We're crashing their date?" Sunny asked.

"Not quite. We're going to *observe* their date. We'll get the booth at the back of the shop. The seat's high enough so they won't see us, but we'll be able to keep an eye on them."

"We're crashing," she concluded, not at all certain about this. "I trust Ryan."

"Do you trust Kinsley?" Shaw countered as they walked.

Sunny wanted to say yes, but she hardly knew the girl. "I think Kinsley's just troubled." Which, of course, meant it troubled an almost-stepmother who cared deeply for her almost-stepson.

"Let's just think this through," Sunny went on, but she didn't dig in her heels. "Their date's in a public place. Obviously, if they'd wanted to do something that involved clothing removal, they would have gone elsewhere."

"Ice cream could be the foreplay that leads to elsewhere," Shaw quickly pointed out.

Now she did dig in her heels, but they were already outside the Lickety Split, and they weren't alone. People were on the sidewalk, and some of those people included men who wanted to go out with her. And gossips. Of course, maybe there was so much talk about Sunshine and Em that no one would bother with Shaw and her.

"Foreplay," Shaw repeated, no doubt because he'd noticed her attention wandering. But her mind hadn't wandered that much.

"Ryan's sixteen," she said in as low of a whisper as she could manage. "And I've talked safe sex with him."

Except she hadn't. Sunny mentally brought up that earlier conversation and realized she'd been the subject of that, not Ryan.

"Has he ever been with someone like Kinsley?" Shaw asked.

"I don't think so." And that was the reason she allowed Shaw to take her into the Lickety Split.

They weren't alone in there, either. There were at least a dozen customers, but chatter suddenly stopped when the bell over the door jangled as they walked in. Well, audible chatter did anyway. Sunny noticed some behind-the-hand whispers. Diary gossip, no doubt.

It probably wasn't a good thing to draw attention to herself, especially since this was like a recon mission to observe the date, but Sunny figured her silence would only stir the gossip pot even more.

"Did you hear about the new restaurant on the moon?" she said, tossing out the joke that no one had asked for. "It's got great food but no atmosphere."

She didn't get a cackle like Cherry's, but there were a few giggles, all coming from the customers over forty who actually remembered her *Little Cowgirls* role. The four teenagers just looked at her as if she had gone off her meds.

"Hey, Shaw?" someone called out. Delbert Jenkins, or Jinx as folks called him, who worked at the feed store. "Did your chest hair run into any dew or musky scents today?"

Now, that got some laughter. Even Reverend Carmichael, who was chowing down on a double-decker hot-fudge sundae dropped his normally pious expression for a giggle. Sunny was about to suggest they find a different place for their covert op, but Shaw silenced Delbert and the snickering with a single-word answer.

"No."

That was all it took to stop the merriment, and people were suddenly interested in eating their treats before Shaw melted them with his withering glare.

Shaw led her to the back of the shop, where they saw the booth was occupied by two teenagers who were trying to see how much of their tongues they could get into each other's mouths. The teens stopped and looked up at Shaw with what would have likely been a get-lost protest.

The money stopped them.

Shaw took out his wallet, put a handful of twenty-dollar bills on the table and used his thumb in a take-a-hike gesture. The wide-eyed teens turned to each other, an unspoken conversation going on between them. A very short conversation. The girl scooped up the cash, and the pair hightailed it out of there, leaving behind the banana split they'd been sharing.

Shaw pushed the dish of ice cream to the side, and Sunny and he slid into the seat, with her taking the spot by the wall. If Shaw leaned to his left, he could almost certainly catch a glimpse of the front door. Sunny immediately saw a problem with this plan.

"Someone will tell Kinsley and Ryan that we're here," she pointed out.

"Maybe. But it's just as likely folks will stare, whisper and then gossip. There's a lot of interest in Ryan."

Sunny frowned when she turned to him. "What interest?"

Shaw didn't have a chance to answer because at that moment the twentysomething waitress in the cotton candy pink uniform came over to take their orders. Sunny didn't recognize her, but according to her name tag, she was Misty. Based on the way Misty made goo-goo eyes at Shaw when she leaned over to clear away the banana split dish, she knew him plenty well enough and had a thing for him. Based on the way Shaw ignored her, he didn't even notice. If the man ever figured out how hot he was, he'd have a swollen head the size of Texas.

Shaw ordered a chocolate malt, something he could obviously nurse if this surveillance went on for a while. Sunny glanced at the menu and ordered something called the Deluxe Bite even though she had no idea what it was since there was no picture or description. It sounded like something she could nibble at while they waited.

"What interest do people have in Ryan?" Sunny repeated after Misty had walked away. "People don't think he's our son, do they?"

"No," he quickly assured her. "Apparently, gossips can do simple math. Ryan is sixteen which means he would have been born while you were still living here." He paused and slid a glance at her. "You really want to hear something that could put you in a bad mood?"

Sunny frowned. "No. But tell me anyway."

He dragged in a long breath. "It's really more to do with you than Ryan."

"Now you have to tell me." Though, having lived her life in a fishbowl, Sunny didn't relish the idea of listening to what people were saying. Still, she didn't want her "celebrity" status to affect Ryan.

"You want to hear the commitment-phobic theory that claims you get involved with men only so you can be a mother without having to put up with a husband? Or the one that claims you've never gotten over me and that you brought Ryan here to show me that I could want kids after all?"

What a mix of truth and crap. Yes, both of her

former fiancés had been fathers, but the first one, Eric, shared custody of his daughter Miranda with his ex-wife. Sunny hadn't mothered Miranda. All right, she had when Miranda had needed some substitute mothering. The girl had been so hurt by her parents' divorce and had done plenty of crying on Sunny's shoulder.

And as for the second theory, well, that was way off.

"If I'd felt the need to show you that you might want kids, I would have brought a sweet cuddly baby, not a teenager who'll soon be heading off to college," Sunny insisted.

Though some would argue that it would have been a lot harder to get her hands on a baby than a teenager. Still, it was stupid gossip.

"If there are naked pictures of me in the sketchbooks you'll give Sunshine, there'll be some fuel to the second theory if she makes them public," Shaw said.

It took her a second to pick through theory number two to realize he was talking about the claims that she'd never gotten over him. This part might have a smidge of truth.

And there was still the heat.

Sunny could swear it was a higher temp now than it had been when she was a teenager. Of course, now she had a better idea of how to put his "inches" to good use. Plus, there was no hormonal teenage angst to get in the way and make her mopey and needy like whenever he didn't give her just the right look or smile at her way back when. The needy part was apparently still there though.

She heard the sound of the bell jangling over the front door as it opened. Shaw leaned out a bit and then shook his head, indicating that it wasn't Ryan and Kinsley.

"Why don't we just put ourselves out of misery and have sex?" he asked, confirming for Sunny that he had some neediness of his own.

She smiled, and leaned in to whisper something naughty in his ear, maybe bite his earlobe, too, but the clatter of dishes interrupted them. Misty—who had ditched her goo-goo eyes to give Sunny some stink-eye—practically dropped the plate of ice cream in front of Sunny.

Correction: it was a platter, one big enough to have held a Butterball turkey with all the trimmings.

Every inch of the dish was covered with scoops of ice cream, apparently all the flavors sold in the shop. There were at least thirty of them, and as if that wasn't enough, there was a thick layer of whipped cream circling the platter. And as if that still wasn't enough, the cream was topped with chocolate sauce and haphazardly positioned cherries.

"Enjoy," Misty said in a tone that suggested she had no such desire for Sunny's enjoyment.

Misty then carefully set Shaw's malt in front of him as if it were a fragile art project being presented by a master sculptor. Served in a tall glass that wasn't the size of a platter, the thick creamy chocolate had one dollop of whipped cream and a single cherry, stem up, placed in the middle.

"It's like that night in the hayloft all over again," Sunny muttered while she perused her ice-cream choices. She hadn't actually meant to say that aloud, and she doubted Shaw would get the analogy.

He did.

He grinned at her. It was the cocky grin of a man remembering that she thought he was a big boy.

"Are you actually in any shape for sex?" he asked.

Sunny knew what he meant. Didn't think it was a joke, either. He was asking about her recent surgery, and she might have voiced some concern about that particular area if he hadn't leaned in and kissed her.

That evaporated any concerns.

It possibly evaporated her makeup and nail polish, too.

Oh, the man could kiss, and there was plenty of proof to back up that claim. Like now, it wasn't deep and sloppy like the one the teenagers had been doing in the booth when Shaw and she had arrived. Nope. This was gentle, just a press of his mouth to hers, and still it packed a heavyweight's punch.

She heard herself moan, and there was no mistaking that it was a sound of pleasure. Great day— if she could bottle this, she could make a fortune. However, Sunny was positive she'd want to keep it all for herself.

Shifting a little in the booth, he slid his hand around the back of her neck, turning and angling her so he could deepen the kiss. Still no sloppiness though. But he did use his tongue. She'd never been quite sure why French-kissing was more intimate than regular kissing. Maybe because it sort of mimicked the sex act.

Heat and penetration.

Shaw gave her both, all the while moving her closer to him so that parts of them were touching. Not *the* parts though. That would have taken some doing since there wasn't much room to maneuver in the booth. Still, her leg was against his, and her hand found its way to the front of his shirt so her fingers could dally with his chest.

His hand found its way to her thigh so he could dally there, and Sunny suspected his actions were much more effective than hers. He slid his touch from her knee all the way to her waist. She was mortified that he would do this in public.

She was also very turned-on.

She quickly figured out that staying put and kissing wouldn't tamp down the heat building inside her. And it darn sure wouldn't satisfy this ache that was starting to spread through her body.

Because she had no choice and could take no more, Sunny eased back, taking her mouth from his. That created a different kind of ache.

"Once Kinsley and Ryan are done with their date," she started, about to suggest that Shaw and she could find their way to a bed. But the shadow looming over them got their attention.

Misty.

The waitress had gone well past the stink-eye stage, and she practically slapped a napkin on the table. "For you," Misty snarled before she turned and walked away.

Sunny was a little perplexed as to why Misty would have brought them a single napkin, especially since there was a dispenser full of them on the table. Then she saw the writing and realized it was a note. Maybe Misty was passing her number to Shaw.

But it wasn't that.

"We didn't want to disturb you but wanted you to know that we've decided to go to the diner," the note read, and at the bottom were two signatures.

Ryan and Kinsley.

CHAPTER ELEVEN

THE COVERT OPS mission wasn't over. In fact, Shaw figured it was more important than ever. Because it was possible that in a weird, unintentional way, he and Sunny had given Ryan and Kinsley permission to do the same stupid thing they had just done.

Kiss in a public place.

Yeah, talk about being stupid. Shaw had been so caught up in the kiss that he hadn't noticed the teenagers when they'd come into the Lickety Split and obviously spotted them in the booth.

Heck, Shaw wasn't sure he would have noticed a zombie apocalypse after his mouth had discovered that Sunny tasted just as good and right as she had all the other times he'd kissed her. It shouldn't have felt like a startling revelation, shouldn't have caused him to go hard, but there it was. His life. His reaction to this woman made him brainless.

He didn't mind word of the kiss getting around to the adults—it'd get the suitors off Sunny's back and uphold his end of the favor-bargain. But that kind of public display of hormones wasn't a good example for Ryan and Kinsley.

"There they are," Sunny whispered. "No hanky-panky." Like him, Sunny was at the corner of the large front window of the diner, peering in.

Shaw spotted them, too. Unlike Sunny and him, Kinsley and Ryan sat up front on the red padded stools at the counter—where the other diners and anyone driving by could see them. They each had a menu, likely deciding what to order.

Judging from their body language, what they weren't doing was considering hanky or even some panky. Kinsley was nibbling on her bottom lip, and both had tight grips on those plastic-coated menus that were seemingly riveting, considering how quietly and intensively they were studying them. Everything about them screamed first awkward date with the prying eyes of the town looking on.

Sunny released a long breath and stepped back from the window. "Okay, I feel like an idiot," she said.

"I'm right there with you."

And it was coming on the heels of him feeling stupid for the public kissing. Worse, it was entirely possible that someone had spied Sunny and him spying on Kinsley and Ryan. That would generate another level of gossip that none of them needed.

"Come on," he told her, maneuvering her back toward his truck, which was still in the police department parking lot across the street.

"Are we going to your place?" she asked.

The question threw him so much that he practically stumbled. Shaw stopped and stared at her.

Sunny shrugged, maybe trying to look casual, but he saw some of the same nerves in her body language as he'd seen in Kinsley. Sunny was even doing some bottom lip nibbling. Not on his, as she'd done in the diner. But on her own.

"I figure everyone will assume that's where we're going anyway," she added.

Yeah, they would, and while Shaw thought it was a fine idea to take her to his house, he didn't like that Sunny might be having doubts about it.

So, that's why he kissed her.

Right there on the sidewalk of Main Street.

He reasoned, with an ample slathering of sarcasm, that anyone who'd missed the display of affection in the Lickety Split could see a repeat performance of it. But the real reason had been so he could feel the heat fire up Sunny again.

And it worked.

It worked for him, too, and the kiss was a reminder that idiocy and stupidity were always going to be factors where they were concerned. But this time he wasn't a twenty-year-old being surprised by a teenage virgin. He was thirty-five and had access to a private bed with good-quality sheets. That's where Shaw figured they'd land. After all, at their age, a good making out—and with Sunny, it'd be good—would lead to sex.

Primed and ready for that, Shaw broke the kiss so he could get her across the street and into his truck. He would have kissed her again, but her phone dinged with a text message.

"From Em," she said after she'd taken her phone from her purse and looked at the screen. Sunny groaned softly. "She said next time I should order a cone or a malt like you did because the Deluxe Bite's too much for one person to eat."

So, Em had gotten details, probably from Misty, the disgruntled waitress who'd spent the last couple of years sending off "do me" vibes to Shaw. Vibes that he'd had no trouble resisting. Misty wasn't his type, and the rare occurrences when he'd taken the time for a relationship, he'd looked outside of Lone Star Ridge for it. He hadn't wanted everyone to know his business.

Obviously, that had changed with Sunny.

Horniness could apparently lower a man's standards.

"'Thanks for the advice,'" Sunny texted back, saying it aloud as she typed. "'Are you okay?'"

Shaw started driving as Sunny waited for a response, knowing that if her grandmother showed any signs of distress he'd be turning around and going to Em's.

"'I'm fine, all excited about never having to see your mom's hiney again,'" Sunny read when Em's reply finally came.

Shaw didn't think that was lip service, either. Sunshine had made herself so unwelcome that even Em had given up on her.

"'I'm heading for bed,'" Sunny continued to read from Em's text, "'and I'll be putting on my earphones to listen to some tunes. So, if you're late getting in, real late, I won't hear you. Give Shaw a kiss goodnight for me.'"

That was as good as a hands-on blessing for Sunny to haul him off to bed, but Sunny wasn't smiling when she answered back, "Will do." She stared at her phone for several long moments before she put it away.

"I forgot about…things." She made a circling motion to the front of her top, and he didn't think she was referring to her breasts. More like the incision from her surgery and the site of her recent stitches.

He'd forgotten about…things, too. Well, hell. Being primed and ready to go didn't make it easy for him to cut through the BS pressure his *manhood* was adding to this, but Shaw forced himself to remember it now.

"I'll turn around," he said.

"No." She blurted that out as if it was the start to an explanation or really big protest, but she clammed up for several seconds. "I want to see your place," she said. "I want to see if this is a problem." Sunny made another circling motion with her hand.

Well, it wouldn't be a problem for him, but then he was a guy and few things posed obstacles to sex. But Sunny having doubts would certainly do it. It'd be a big-assed obstacle that would stop him in his tracks.

"I wouldn't push you for something you're not ready for," he said.

She nodded. Nibbled on her lip. "I have a scar. Well, two of them because of the spiked bra. But the one on my breast is really ugly."

"It's still healing," he pointed out. Which was another reminder of why sex couldn't happen. "Most scars fade with time."

Another nod. "I don't have the same body I did when I was eighteen. I'm…jiggly in places."

Shaw wanted to say if that was meant to put him

off, then she'd failed miserably. He was instantly interested in any and all parts of her, especially the
ones that jiggled. But he didn't think that was the
way to go here.

"We'll just have a drink," he said. "At the end of
the drink, if you want, I'll drive you home. And FYI,
my body's also changed in the past fifteen years."

She made a little snort of laughter. "Right. You've
gone the exact opposite of jiggly. You've muscled
out."

Shaw wasn't sure that was a compliment. He'd
never given much thought to his body and didn't own
a single piece of exercise equipment. Still, it was hard
not to gain some muscle when you worked on a ranch.
And speaking of the ranch, he drove past the main
house and threaded his truck through the narrow road
that ran parallel to the pasture fence. They were close
now to his place, and he began to prep himself to keep
his hands off her.

One drink and then he'd take her home.

He stopped in front of his house. Not the sprawling place where he'd been raised. His was more of a
cabin, though he'd had it built with white limestone
to offset some of the logs. He'd also situated it just
back from the creek. Not close enough to flood during a storm, but he still had the view of it from his
kitchen window and back porch.

Since the step-off was high, he helped Sunny from
his truck, and they started for the front door, which
wouldn't be locked. No lights on, either, but there was
enough moonlight that they didn't stumble on the path
that led from the driveway to the porch.

"It's not a big place," he said, so she wouldn't be surprised by the size as most people were.

It was one bedroom, one bath and a combined living, eating and kitchen area. Plenty enough space for him and the rare overnight guest he would sometimes bring there. But it practically screamed that it wasn't a place to raise a family. Which suited Shaw just fine since he practically screamed that he was not a man to raise a family. Cleaning up after his father had seen to that.

He opened the door and stepped in, automatically reaching for the light switch. But Sunny's hand caught his, stopping him.

"Just leave it off," she said, setting her purse on the porch.

She didn't move. Didn't add anything else. Sunny just stood there, and the only sound she was making were several deep breaths.

"Hugh told me I was lousy in bed," she blurted out.

Shaw had considered what she might say, and it sure as heck hadn't been that. He was totally out of his element here as to how to respond so he went with his gut. "It takes two people to have lousy sex."

He wanted to have managed something better.

She shrugged, making him wish she'd laughed or issued a "damn right" so it'd let him know that Ryan's shit bag of a father hadn't put some dings and dents in Sunny's confidence.

"Hugh told you that after you broke up with him?" Shaw tried again. He hoped that was the case so he could then point out to her that guys with broken hearts could be dicks.

She turned and looked at him. The moonlight was angled behind them, almost like a spotlight. Enough for him to see her face. He couldn't figure out what that expression meant.

Then she kissed him.

It came quick and sort of sneaky, like the kiss he'd given her outside the diner to renew the heat between them. This kiss did the same thing to him. It also confused him.

Shaw couldn't help kissing her right back, couldn't help feeling the kick from it. Couldn't stave off the instant pull it had to make him want to take her where she stood. However, he didn't want that if Sunny wasn't ready for it.

He waited, continuing the kiss, and he let it go on even after he felt her tongue in his mouth. He didn't break the lip-lock until they had to gulp in a breath.

"Are you sure you want to do this?" he asked.

Or at least that's what he'd intended to say—it came out sort of garbled because she'd scrambled his brain. Instead, it was more like "you do this?" But at least he'd managed to make it sound like a question rather than the ramblings of a man who wasn't thinking straight.

"Do this," she answered. No question mark. And just in case Shaw had any doubts about that, Sunny dived back in for another kiss.

Good grief. The woman certainly wasn't lousy at this, and it didn't help that her stomach bumped against the front of his jeans. It was a reminder that it'd been way too long since he'd been with Sunny.

Shaw tossed his Stetson on the nearby table and

took her by the shoulders to slow things down a bit. Also, so he could move her and shut the door by ramming it with his boot. The odds of a ranch hand coming out here at night were slim, but it did happen, and he'd already had enough of people gawking at them.

"No," she mumbled when he reached for the light switch again.

He wasn't sure how she managed to have that come through loud and clear, especially since she was still kissing him. But if darkness was what she wanted, it's what she'd have. Shaw simply anchored her back against the door and had her mouth for supper.

Sunny did some devouring, too. And touching. Just as she'd done earlier, she slid her hand between them, moving her palm over his chest. He wanted to do the same to her, but even the suddenly raging ache in his groin wouldn't let him forget that he could hurt her.

Shaw repeated that last part to himself, and it was sinking in.

Sunny's hand didn't stay on his chest. Those clever artist fingers went to the front of his jeans. Her mouth went to his neck. Either she had a good memory as to how sensitive that spot was for him or else she got it right on the first try. Of course, she'd been getting a lot of things right. He wanted her, bad.

Since touching anything above her waist was out, Shaw gripped her hips and moved her closer for some zipper-to-zipper contact. That sent the wanting-her-bad up a few notches, something he would have savored a whole lot more had she not been torturing him with tongue kisses on his neck. Since that was going to make him very, very needy way too fast, he turned the tables and kissed her ear. He remembered that was her sensitive spot...

Still was.

He got verification of that when she cursed him and arched her hips against his. That was clearly an invitation for some deep contact, but her breasts weren't exactly small, which meant he had to get the angle right so he wouldn't smash them with his chest.

Shaw stepped to the side to do that and knocked right into the table by the door. His hat, some keys and the housewarming gift from his mother all fell to the floor, but it was the gift—an alabaster spirit goddess figurine—that bounced off his knee. Since it was basically rock, that's what it felt like when it bashed against his kneecap, somehow ricocheted off his shin and dropped onto his boot.

"Are you okay?" Sunny immediately asked, probably because he hadn't been able to muffle a grunt of pain.

His first thought was to say something along the lines of *Sunny, this would be safer if I could see*. But he didn't. Because that would put an end to this. It didn't matter that something or someone should put an end to it. Shaw wasn't ready for that, and he didn't think Sunny was, either.

"I'm fine," he said, though his knee was throbbing like an abscessed tooth.

So that she wouldn't press him on that lie, Shaw kissed her ear again and made up his mind as to how to handle this. It didn't take him long since he knew he couldn't be the one to lose control here or Sunny could pay the price for it.

He went after her zipper.

Shaw slid it down, opening the fly of her jeans and shimmying them down her hips. Just enough so he had no trouble getting to her panties. Which took him a second to find because they were low and barely there.

He groaned.

His eyes ached to see what his hands were touching. These panties certainly weren't anything like what she'd worn when she was eighteen and in the hayloft with him. Those had been cotton and sensible. These felt more like lace and—in the very best sense of the word—smut. The exact kind of underwear that spurred fantasies and hard-ons.

At least that's what they were doing to Shaw.

Too bad this particular hard-on was going to be wasted because he couldn't risk the body-to-body contact, especially not when he was this revved.

Biting off another groan, he flicked her earlobe with his tongue and kneed her legs apart. In the same motion, he moved his hand into her panties. Not that he had to go far since there was only about an inch and a half of fabric. And there he encountered another surprise. Not a nest of womanly curls. Instead, it was slick skin.

She must have felt him freeze because she stopped kissing his neck long enough to say, "I had a Brazilian right before my surgery."

"It was just an impulse decision," she added as if embarrassed.

Shaw wasn't embarrassed. He was intrigued. So intrigued that he wished again for some light. He'd been with another woman who'd chosen that particular form of grooming, but that'd been years ago. And again, this was Sunny. It seemed much more interesting on her.

"If it turns you off…"

Shaw kissed her so that she couldn't finish that. Because it didn't turn him off. Like the tiny panties, it made him ache to be inside her. His dick started to beg for that, which was a bad sign. He needed to regain control of himself. He did that with his tongue and his fingers.

His tongue went in her mouth though he did consider it might be more fun to use it on that Brazilian. For now, though, he went old-school and slipped his fingers inside her. Judging from the silky moan she made and the way she pulled his hair, he thought that'd been a good decision.

Shaw stroked, kissed, nudged and bumped, and soon Sunny's moans turned to little pleas for release. So, that's what he gave her.

He located the most sensitive part of her and went to it, sliding his fingers through all that slick wet heat. Rubbing. Going deeper. And rubbing some more. She bucked against his hand, but he kept it up until he felt the spasms of her climax.

There.

Shaw couldn't help it. Even though he was in pain, he grinned like a fool.

Maybe it was fifteen years late, but he'd finally managed to send Sunny flying.

CHAPTER TWELVE

THAT WAS CERTAINLY better than her virginal impaling.

That was Sunny's first thought. Well, her first thought when she actually could think. Before that, everything in her head was more primal. *Feels good. So good. So very, very good.*

And Shaw had been responsible for that especially good feeling.

She let herself come back to earth, mentally tiptoeing first to make sure she wasn't going to fall flat on her face. But there was no chance of falling since Shaw still had one of his hands anchored on her hip. As if he, too, were tiptoeing, he eased his hand from her panties, sliding it around her back. Then he kissed her. It was a dreamy kiss that nearly made her forget that all the recent pleasure had been completely one-sided.

Sunny's dreamy-induced eyes flew open, but there wasn't enough light in the room to see his face, which was what she'd requested since she hadn't wanted him to see her body. Now it put her at a disadvantage because she didn't know if he was smiling in satisfaction over giving her an orgasm or if his expression was somewhat pained because he was hard and throbbing against her thigh.

She decided that it was likely a combination of the two and acted accordingly. Sunny slid her hand over the hard and throbbing part of him. "Let's do something about that."

"No," he said. His voice was husky and strained. "I think we need to give this some more time to heal." He leaned down and pressed a whisper of a kiss on her left breast.

She wanted to argue that. Yes, she was feeling fantastic, but the feeling could be expanded to include Shaw.

"More time to heal," he repeated as if he'd heard the argument she'd been about to give him.

"We wouldn't have to do missionary," she pointed out. She didn't move her hand even though his clamped over hers. "In fact, I could do to you what you just did to me. I wouldn't need to use my breasts for that."

Again she wished she could see his face. She thought there might now be some temptation in his expression. If so, it almost certainly faded when they heard the sound of a vehicle approaching his house.

"I'll get rid of whoever the hell that is," Shaw snarled. He moved Sunny to the side and she gave her clothes a quick adjustment. Shaw had to do some adjusting, too, because his erection was seriously testing the strength of his zipper.

"Nuckle Shaw!" someone, obviously a child, called out. A second later, another little-girl voice belted out the same greeting. That was followed by the pitter-patter of tiny running feet on the porch.

"The lights are off. Are you still up?" another voice asked. Definitely not a child or a girl. This time,

Sunny knew it was Shaw's brother, Austin, which meant the earlier greetings had come from his three-year-old twin daughters.

Sunny turned on the light, nearly blinding them both. They probably looked like moles emerging from the ground when Shaw opened the door and they peered out. Austin stopped and grinned when he saw her, but the girls kept barreling forward, practically climbing onto Shaw as he scooped them into his arms. They each gave him sloppy cheek kisses complete with giggling and excited wiggles.

Austin just stood there and smiled like the contented dad that he was rumored to be. But not a contented man, not since he'd lost his wife to cancer. After Sunny's brush with it, she could relate in some small way. But then, she'd never lost someone she loved, and that had to slice Austin all the way to the marrow.

It'd been years since she'd last seen Austin so, of course, he'd changed. He was thirty-three now, the same age she was, but he'd obviously managed to hang on to the Jameson good looks. Tall, lanky and gorgeous.

"Remember, we can't stay long," Austin told the kids. "It's already way past your bedtime."

That brought on a chorus of protests and flat-out refusals. Amid all of that, one of the girls leaned in to Shaw and whispered in a loud voice, "I cutted Gracie's hair."

"I noticed," he said.

"Daddy didn't like it," the other one remarked.

"Granny Lenore neither. She dropped a bowl on her toe and said a bad word."

Cutted didn't tell the whole story. The second girl's hair had been shorn like a sheep. Even though Sunny had never seen Austin's girls before, she assumed that the shorn child had once had dark blond curls like her identical twin sister.

Once again the stylist child leaned in and put her mouth close to Shaw's ear. "The bad word Granny Lenore said was—"

"Don't repeat it, Avery," Austin warned her, but the corners of his lips twitched a little in amusement.

Austin came closer and pulled Sunny into a hug. "It's good to see you," he whispered to her.

"Good to see you, too," she whispered back and held him in the hug for several moments.

"I'm guessing this is a bad time?" Austin asked when he eased away from her. His gaze skimmed over Sunny, then Shaw and then the strange little statue on the floor. It was of a white robed woman, her hands lifted in the air. So, that's what had fallen on the floor.

Shaw did some nonverbal communication with his eyes, as well. He gave his brother one of his mean stares but was all smiles when he blew raspberries on the girls' necks. They giggled like loons.

Sunny suspected any kid would giggle when on the receiving end of a raspberry, but the fact that Shaw had done that puzzled her. He'd made it clear that he didn't want kids yet he seemed so at ease with his nieces. And that put just a slight glimmer of hope in her heart.

Stupid glimmer.

Stupid hope.

Because they were at an impasse when it came to this particular subject. She wanted kids. Desperately wanted them. And even if she somehow could change his mind on this, it wouldn't be fair. It would be similar to the children that the irresponsible Marty had thrust on Shaw over the years.

When Austin strolled inside, Sunny noticed he was carrying a plastic bag, which he handed to her instead of Shaw. *"Slackers Quackers,"* Austin explained. "When I told Avery and Gracie that you drew the pictures, they wanted you to sign the books. Actually, they wanted you to read every one to them, but I convinced them that an autograph would have to do. They're big fans."

Sunny always had a double reaction when a parent of young children told her something like that. Number one was that she hoped the children weren't aware of Slackers's penis-like feather. Number two was that she filled to the brim with pride. She had drawn those pictures, and just like with her sketchbooks, she'd put little pieces of herself into them. It never got old to hear that someone—especially children—enjoyed them.

"Crackers!" the girls squealed in delight, and they began to make duck noises. Obviously, that was their pronunciation of the lazy duck.

Sunny beamed at them and set her purse on the table so she could glance in the bag. There were at least a dozen of the stories inside. "I'd be happy to sign them. And read them to you."

Reading to kids was something she loved doing.

She'd frequently done readings in the children's section at Hugh's bookstores. That had been very popular, especially after Sunny had learned to do voices for the various characters.

"Thanks," Austin said. "No reading tonight though. It's too late, and I need to wrangle them to bed soon. If you can just let me know when you sign them, I'll come over and get them from you."

Sunny nodded in agreement, but then something occurred to her. "How'd you know I'd be here?" she asked Austin.

"Four texts," he answered readily. "A few people saw you at Lickety Split and ratted you out. I figured Shaw would bring you here. Figured, too, that you hadn't got *too deep* into things."

Maybe because the conversation had just taken a turn, Shaw stood the girls on the floor, and they immediately took off toward his fridge. Once they were out of Shaw's line of sight and earshot, he gave his brother a deep scowl. "Slackers couldn't wait?"

"Thought you'd want an update on Kinsley, as well," Austin said, but he didn't add anything else until Shaw gave an impatient huff. "She's back at the house with Mom. Ryan dropped her off about ten minutes ago. Judging from the seven texts I got about them, they didn't carry on the way the two of you did."

Shaw's scowl deepened.

Austin grinned. "By the way, Mom said if it's not already too late, she'll give you the talk about safe sex. She said all you have to do is ask. Oh, and she whispered the words, *safe sex*. And blushed."

Sunny was reasonably sure that Shaw would eat a cactus before he allowed a talk like that. Besides, technically Shaw and she had practiced sex as safe as you could get and still have an orgasm.

"Was Kinsley all right?" Sunny asked. "I mean, did she say anything about how the date went?"

Austin peered around Shaw as if to make sure the girls weren't listening. They weren't. They were still at the fridge, apparently going through Shaw's inventory of possible snacks. Sunny heard them identify— and dismiss—apples, mispronounced grapefruit juice and ucky cheese.

"Kinsley said this whole town was one big noseball," Austin answered, "and that they could kiss her butt. Of course, she didn't use *butt*. I'm paraphrasing because I've learned not to repeat words like that around the girls. Anyway," he went on after a long breath, "it's my guess that Kinsley still has some resentment over Marty not coming forward to claim her."

"Yeah," Shaw agreed. "There's resentment all right. And we're no closer to finding Marty than we were a week and a half ago when she got here. He's not at his house in Nashville, and his manager doesn't have a clue where he is, which is often the norm. Marty often forgets to share info about where he's going and when he'll be back."

"Nothing from her mom, either?" Austin asked.

"Not a word. Leyton's holding off CPS from stepping in by getting Kinsley's school assignments and having her do them, but that won't last."

Sunny felt for the girl and had a fleeting thought

of trying to take her in. But she hadn't worked out things for Ryan. Nor for Miranda, the girl who'd almost become her stepdaughter. So, clearly she didn't have a good track record when it came to such things.

"Time to go, girls," Austin called out.

Gracie, the shorn one, came in with a handful of green grapes that still had bits of stems on them. She was eating them and squishing them at the same time. Grape pulp and juice oozed through her fingers.

Avery, the future hairdresser, came in with a beer. Unopened, thankfully.

Austin took the bottle of beer from his daughter and handed it to Shaw, who leaned down to kiss the girls on the tops of their heads.

"Can we spend the night with you, Nuckle Shaw?" Gracie asked, and her sister quickly echoed the request, complete with jumping up and down in anticipated excitement.

"Did you finish your homework?" Shaw asked so fast that it made Sunny believe this wasn't the first time he'd given that response.

The girls groaned. "We don't got homework," Avery informed him. Which wasn't much of a surprise to Sunny since the girls were only three and were likely in preschool.

Shaw shrugged as if this was out of his hands. "Once you start getting homework and it's done, then you can spend the night."

Judging from the girls' expressions, it was the answer they'd expected, and they turned to their dad. "Can we spend the night with Aunt Cait?" The possibility of that brought on even louder squeals and higher jumps.

Austin shook his head. "Not tonight. The days after Valentine's, Easter, your birthdays and Halloween are when you can stay with Aunt Cait."

The girls groaned, but again it was the answer they seemed to expect. Sunny also suspected Cait would get them those days since that's when the twins would be on a sugar high.

"Bye, Crackers lady," Avery said. "Bye Nuckle Shaw," they said together, and hurried off to the SUV that was parked out front.

"Don't do anything I wouldn't do," Austin said as he headed after his daughters. "Or better yet, do something I would have done way back when I used to do stuff," he added from over his shoulder.

Austin had his hands full, but Sunny could almost feel the love coming off him in waves when he helped his little girls into their car seats.

"You're good with your nieces," she said almost absently, and winced. Because, of course, that sounded like she was trying to steer him toward having one of his own.

"I'm not sure *good* is the right word." Shaw gave a goodbye wave to Austin and crew, stepped back and shut the door. "I love them and they don't like to take no for an answer. Sort of like Kinsley," he muttered.

He handed her the beer. "Here's that drink I promised you." While she had hold of it, he twisted off the cap. "Unless you'd like something else."

"The beer's fine." She had a sip and watched as he went to the fridge to get himself one. She had a nice view when he leaned down, causing his jeans to tighten over his superior butt. It was a reminder that they had unfinished business.

Business that would require her to turn off the lights.

"You obviously like kids," he said, uncapping his own bottle of brew. "Why haven't you had one of your own?"

Sunny wasn't surprised by the question, and it was one she'd gotten more than once from McCall. Heck, even from Miranda.

"I will have a baby. One day. In fact, I'd decided to start checking into sperm banks and such when I found the lump in my breast. Obviously, that had to be taken care of first. Before that, well, I was engaged, and I thought that would lead to marriage and babies. You know, the traditional route."

But Sunny wasn't a fool. Not about things that didn't involve Shaw anyway. She'd been with her first fiancé, Eric, for two years, and since he'd already had a child, Sunny had believed he would want more. However, once Miranda reached her snotty teenage years, Eric had announced he was done with fatherhood. That's when Sunny had ended the relationship with him.

Not with Miranda, though.

Sunny had not only stayed in touch with Miranda, she'd tried to be there whenever Miranda needed her.

Hugh had been less transparent in letting her know he didn't want other children. There'd been no non-fatherhood announcement, but after their months and then years together, she'd come to see that he was just putting in time with Ryan. Almost as if he were waiting for Ryan to go off to college and rid him of any parenting duties. Sunny now had proof that was the case because after she'd broken the engagement with Hugh, he'd stopped seeing his son.

Sunny tried to push that depressing thought aside. Especially since she had a much more pleasant thought after giving Shaw a long look. One that hopefully let him know that she was very much interested in finishing up what they'd started against the door.

She leaned in, putting her mouth on his, but Sunny had barely managed a touch when her phone rang. Knowing that her life had too many important people in it to just blow off the call, she took her phone from her purse and looked at the screen.

"It's Hayes," she relayed to Shaw.

He looked as surprised as she was. It'd been months since she'd heard from her brother. Then she remembered that McCall had said he was missing. Oh, God. He could be in some kind of trouble. Her fingers had already started to tremble over that possibility when she answered.

"Hayes, are you all right?" Sunny blurted. It didn't matter that they weren't close. Or that Hayes could be an ass. He was still her brother.

"Uh, yeah. Fine." He sounded confused by her question.

"You were missing," she pointed out.

"Oh, that. Yeah, I'm fine. Just needed some time to myself. That's not why I'm calling." He grumbled some profanity. "Look, I just wanted to tell you how sorry I am."

Now Sunny was not only surprised but also confused. "Sorry for making me worry about you being missing?" she asked.

"No. Sorry about Tonya."

That did not help with her confusion. "Tonya, the reporter?"

"Yeah, that one." Hayes cursed again. "Sunny, when I got mixed up with her, I swear I had no idea what she'd do. We only hooked up for a couple of days, and I didn't know she was taking notes and making plans."

Many questions went through Sunny's head, but she settled on one. "What exactly did Tonya do?"

No cursing this time. Just the sound of a long blown-out breath from her brother. "She stole your diaries. And I'm the one who told her where to find them."

CHAPTER THIRTEEN

"I JUST GOT the word that Tonya's been arrested in LA," Leyton explained to Shaw. "And she's turned over the diaries to the cops there."

"Good," Shaw said in relief. No more articles about his chest hair, throbbing loins or whatever the heck else a teenage Sunny would have written about him.

Of course, the fallout wasn't over since the first article was still floating around, but at least Tonya had been stopped and would spend some time in jail for criminal trespassing and theft. Sunny and Em could thank Hayes for setting that ball in motion.

Hayes's phone call the night before had accomplished a couple of things. It'd let Sunny know that her brother was okay, info that she'd then passed along to McCall. But Hayes had also alerted Sunny that he'd inadvertently told Tonya about the diaries. Hayes hadn't thought it was more than pillow talk until he'd gotten wind of the article and figured out what happened. During that pillow talk, Hayes had also spilled that Sunny and his other sisters had things stored in the attic. He figured Tonya just sneaked in and had a look around until she found them.

That begged the question—had Tonya stolen anything else? Shaw had enough trouble without borrowing more, but he was going to suggest that Sunny, her sisters and Em do an inventory of the attic to see if they noticed anything else missing.

"I hate to think Tonya was prowling around in the house while Em was there," Shaw commented.

Leyton made a sound of agreement. "The woman really needs a security system. Or she should at least remember to lock her doors. She still gets people driving out there for a look at where *Little Cowgirls* was filmed. A few of them just walk in as if they've been invited."

Yeah, Shaw had heard about that. Even though it'd been a while since the last incident—including a tour bus of seniors—he would talk to Em about security when he brought up the inventory of the attic.

"Did the LA cops give you any idea if the charges against Tonya are strong enough to stop her from doing something else this stupid?" Shaw asked. Because the woman should be punished.

"No, but I know how this works. Tonya would need to be brought back here for trial. If there is a trial," he amended. "I suspect the county DA will offer her some kind of plea deal."

In other words, an hour or two in jail. Maybe some community service. "I guess that's better than Sunshine will get." Sunny's mother had gotten no jail, no community service and had instead walked away with the necklaces and sketchbook.

"Yep. And speaking of Sunshine," Leyton went on. "Sunny was in here first thing this morning."

That got Shaw's attention since just the night before Sunny and he had played around in the dark.

Or rather he'd played around with her. And they almost certainly would have done more if Hayes hadn't called. That had pretty much taken the air out of *doing more* that didn't involve Sunny going to Em so she could take her grandmother in to file charges against Tonya.

"Sunny had a courier meet her here," Leyton continued. "She wanted witnesses that she was turning over two sketchbooks and the necklace." He paused. "I guess you know there's a picture of you in one of the books?"

"Just one?" Shaw asked, feeling hopeful.

"I only saw the first page of one of the books," Leyton clarified, dashing Shaw's hopes. If he was on page one, there could be dozens. Maybe hundreds.

"What was I doing in the sketch?" Though Shaw wasn't exactly sure he wanted to know. "Was I wearing clothes?" he amended.

"Mostly. It was a drawing of you by the corral at Em's. You weren't wearing a shirt."

It took Shaw more than a couple of moments to pick through his memories and figure out when Sunny could have possibly sketched that. He had a dim recollection of the producers of the show asking him to bring over some horses from his ranch for the triplets to ride.

That wasn't unusual.

The producers often contracted the Jameson ranch to provide livestock and even tack. Shaw had been about sixteen at the time, and he had indeed taken off his shirt while he did the sweaty delivery. He'd done that only because the cameraman hadn't been around. Obviously, Sunny had been, though.

"And no, your chest wasn't glistening," Leyton added. "But your jeans were riding a little low."

Great. Sunny might have penciled in a butt crack. Shaw might end up busting some ranch hands' heads when they ragged him about that. And it might put Sunny back into that "lower than a gopher hole" frame of mind. She was already feeling rotten over the diary leak, and Sunshine had the potential to keep smearing their faces in the embarrassment.

"For what it's worth, it was a good drawing," Leyton said, and it didn't sound like a taunt that might end up with a busted head. "Very artistic. It made you look like a cowboy rock star."

Shaw groaned. A rock star. That'd go over well with the ranch hands and the cattle buyers he worked with. The fact that it was a good drawing didn't surprise him. Sunny had always been talented that way. Too bad, though, that for this particular artist's rendition, she hadn't stuck to stick figures.

"I'd really like to stop Sunshine from publishing anything in the sketchbooks," Shaw said. "And, yes, I know she owns them now because of the agreement she signed with Sunny and Em. But I didn't sign anything to give Sunny and especially Sunshine the right to splatter my images from here to kingdom come."

Leyton stayed quiet a moment. "Are you thinking about suing Sunshine? Maybe trying for some kind of injunction? Or are you just venting?"

"All of the above, but especially number two. What

if I go to a lawyer and file some kind of suit against her?"

"I could get that started for you," Leyton said. "I could drop over to Rick's office and have a quick chat with him."

Rick was Richard Downing, one of the town's two lawyers, but he had the advantage of his office being right next door to the police station. Plus, Rick had a thing for Cait and would likely jump to do one of her brothers a favor.

"Maybe Rick can figure out a way to tie Sunshine's hands or stall her with some legal wranglings," Leyton went on. "I'll let you know what he says. Better yet, I'll send Cait over to talk to him."

Cait probably wouldn't like that. She hated when people tried matchmaking, but she'd do it because she knew this could ultimately come back to bite them all in the butts. It was possible there were sketches of her in those books, too.

Shaw ended the call, signed the contract he'd been looking over while he'd talked to Leyton and put it aside to go to the kitchen for more coffee. That was one of the few advantages to having his office in the main ranch house and his childhood home. The disadvantages were plentiful, but Shaw knew if he moved to a different location it would hurt his mom's feelings. Besides, he did like being around to check on her.

He saw one of those disadvantages when he made it to the kitchen. Both Kinsley and his mom were at the stove with their backs to him. They were both wearing mitts and were staring at something in a casserole dish that they appeared to have just taken from the oven. Since they hadn't seen him, Shaw quietly turned, intending to go back to his office rather than risk them wanting him to taste anything.

"Man pudding surprise," his mom said. "See, it's sweet looking because of that rim of brown sugar that we've put around the potatoes, but looks can be deceiving because the center's not sweet at all. That's where all the onions, jalapeños and garlic are."

Even though Shaw knew he should just keep walking, that stopped him in his tracks. God, why had Kinsley agreed to help cook a concoction like that?

"The center's the surprise," Lenore went on, and she turned to Kinsley. Shaw could see only half of his mother's face, but it appeared that she was giving the girl a motherly look. "That's like a man, too. Do you know what I mean?"

"Uh. Not really," Kinsley admitted.

While still wearing the mitt, Lenore gave Kinsley's arm a pat. "Well, men draw you in with the sweet, but it's the center that you've got to watch out for. Understand?"

"Uh, sure." Kinsley would have convinced no one other than his mother with that wishy-washy tone.

"Good." Lenore practically beamed, and she let out a breath of relief. "I wasn't sure if your mom had talked to you about safe sex." She lowered her voice to a whisper for those last two words.

Shaw was now even more puzzled. That had been a safe sex talk? Well, hell. If it was, Kinsley would be confused by it and possibly get knocked up. Which caused him to scowl because he hoped like the devil that she wasn't doing anything that could result in a knocking up. Especially doing something with Sunny's almost-stepson.

"Oh," Kinsley said. He could only see half of her face, too, but that side flared up with a blush. "Yeah, she sort of talked to me about it. Sort of."

Even without that second "sort of" qualifier, Shaw knew he was going to have to chat with Kinsley. And yes, it would have to be *the talk*. He didn't want to pawn it off on Cait, either, but on second thought, it was possible his sister wouldn't mind taking this on. Or maybe Leyton or Austin would. He stepped farther back and fired off a group text.

Any volunteers for talking safe sex with Kinsley? he messaged. Shaw got fast responses.

No way in hell, from Austin.

Shit, no, from Leyton.

Suck it up, buttercup. You're the oldest so do it yourself, just like you did for the rest of us, was the response from Cait.

Shaw wanted to point out that he hadn't actually had the talk with Leyton. They were nearly the same age, and Leyton had figured it out on his own. However, that wasn't the way Shaw wanted Kinsley to come by that knowledge. But he wasn't going to get any sibling help. He was on his own. And apparently Cait thought he had an adequate skill set for it.

He cleared his throat so Kinsley and his mom would know he was there. Kinsley still hadn't recovered from her blush, but his mother smiled. "Just in time to try the new recipe I showed Kinsley how to make. It's sort of like rice pudding but with potatoes and some savory stuff."

Shaw couldn't shake his head fast enough, and he ran his hand over his stomach. "Better not. I ate something last night that didn't agree with me."

Over the years, he'd stopped counting such things as lies. More like self-preservation measures because if he ate what was in that dish, there was a high chance of having real stomach problems.

"Oh, dear. Want me to get you some Pepto?" his mother asked.

"No. I'll just have coffee." While he poured himself a cup, Shaw looked at Kinsley. "I need someone to take a contract to Rowley. I'm pretty sure he's in the barn. Would you do it?"

Kinsley nodded, fast, perhaps because she thought Lenore might insist she sample some of the man pudding surprise. She stayed right on his heels while she followed him back to his office, but the moment they were inside, Kinsley whirled around.

"Don't you dare talk safe sex with me," the girl insisted.

Shaw felt no relief in her offering him an out on this. "Do you need to talk safe sex?"

"No," she spit out, folding her arms over her chest. She sputtered out a few sounds before she finally managed to say, "Sheez, Louise. Who voted you to do this?"

"Leyton, Cait and Austin," he mumbled. "Apparently, being the oldest means I'm better qualified."

Of course, it was more than that. Marty didn't need another child or a grandchild, and he couldn't count on Ryan's dad having had the "always use a rubber" talk with him.

"Look, I don't want to do this any more than you do," he went on when she kept huffing. "So, let's make it quick. You shouldn't have sex, not without your partner's and your mutual respect and stuff."

He hadn't meant for that to sound flippant with the *stuff*, but Shaw honestly hadn't been able to think of another word.

"And stuff?" Kinsley challenged in the way that only a snotty teenage girl could manage. "Do you have *and stuff* with Sunny?"

Shaw considered how to answer that. "Sunny and I aren't teenagers, and yes, there's a mutual respect."

And there was stuff. Not just the fanned flames of scorching attraction, either. They had a history together. He'd been her first lover. He was her friend. Definitely, stuff. However, he got the feeling that Kinsley wasn't talking about any of that. But rather love.

Yeah, that.

Love always felt like deep, murky water to Shaw. The murky kind of water that could hide sharp rocks and things that could bite off a toe or two. Maybe he felt that way because he hadn't had any good role models for it. Relationships failed, and hearts got busted to pieces. His sure had when Sunny had left when she turned eighteen. He'd known all along in his head that she would leave, but his heart just hadn't gotten the message.

He supposed a therapist would say he was now guarding that heart, but it was more than that. Even with all their stuff in common, Sunny and he still didn't want the same things.

Well, one thing anyway.

He couldn't see himself as a father, and she couldn't see herself not being a mother. That wasn't a great divide that they could easily bridge.

"God, you didn't invite him over for this stupid talk, did you?" he heard Kinsley say.

Confused, Shaw looked up and followed her gaze to the window that overlooked the backyard. Ryan was walking in the direction of the barn.

"No, I didn't ask him to come over," Shaw told her. "I suspect he's here to see you." And that was his cue to wrap up this chat. "Don't have sex until you're thirty. Then, make sure the guy uses a condom."

There. He'd done his brotherly duty. Again. And while it wasn't something that would end up in any parent guide, it had been better than the chats he'd had with Cait and his brothers. Which wasn't saying much. Still, it was done.

Ryan had already made it to the barn by the time Shaw opened the window and called out to him. "Looking for Kinsley?"

"No, actually I was looking for you." Ryan began to make his way back to the house. "One of the hands thought you were in the barn."

Shaw had been there earlier, then returned to his office to call Leyton and do the contract. "Come in through the front door," Shaw instructed. That would keep him away from the man casserole in the kitchen. "My office is just off the hall."

Kinsley huffed again, and that's when Shaw realized she'd ducked out of sight when he'd been talking to Ryan. She was now peering around the corner of his door. "You're going to talk safe sex with him?"

"Not under threat of death," Shaw assured her.

No, that was Sunny's area. It was bad enough having to spread the message in his own gene pool. Ryan would be Sunny's responsibility.

"I smell like man pudding surprise," Kinsley said, sniffing at her sleeve. "God, don't tell Ryan I'm here. I don't want him to be around me when I smell like this."

The girl scurried away as if she'd just been scalded. He probably should have tried to reassure her that all was well, that she didn't actually stink, but it wouldn't have necessarily been the truth. Lenore's recipes didn't usually have a mouthwatering effect on people, and stink was always a possibility.

Kinsley was long gone and out of sight by the time Ryan stepped through the doorway of the office. Ryan smiled, but Shaw had no trouble seeing the worry in his eyes. Hell. He hoped this wasn't going to turn into some kind of confession of the things he wanted to do with Kinsley.

"Come in," Shaw offered. He was ready to say something about Kinsley being in the shower, which she almost certainly was to get rid of the smell, but Shaw didn't want the boy to think that was some sort of invitation for Ryan to fantasize about the girl.

"I'm here about Sunny," Ryan said right off.

That didn't cause Shaw to relax any. He definitely didn't want to have to skirt around what'd happened between Sunny and him the night before. Or what

Shaw was hoping would happen between them the next time they were together.

Ryan sat when Shaw motioned for him to take the chair across from his desk. "Sunshine already has a buyer for the sketchbooks."

"How do you know that?" Shaw sat, too.

"Sunshine texted her. Not an FYI exactly. More like because Sunshine wanted to gloat."

That was Sunny's mother all right.

"That's what I wanted to talk to you about," Ryan went on. "If there's a buyer, then it might not be long before the sketches are published. I know Sunny gave her mother those books to keep her grandmother out of trouble, but it could come back to hurt her."

"I'm listening," Shaw said when the boy paused, but he didn't need to hear more to feel that god-awful knot tightening his gut.

Ryan scrubbed his hands over his face and made a sound of frustration. "I don't think Sunny thought about how this would affect her career. Some parents might not be happy if they know the illustrator drew something...not for kids."

Shaw thought of the shirtless sketch Leyton had seen. Since Sunny had done that years before she'd become the illustrator for Slackers, it probably wasn't something that would upset most parents.

Most.

But some might complain and stop buying the books. And that shirtless sketch might be tame compared to others. So, yeah, Shaw could see why Ryan was worried.

"Sunny loves doing those illustrations." Ryan

seemed to be trying to convince him that there was a problem that could blow up in her face. "She's been through a lot already, and if she loses that…well, it might break her."

That was deep insight for a teenage boy. Shaw suspected it was also accurate. Coming on the heels of her cancer scare and the stupid messes that Tonya and Sunshine had pulled, nasty publicity like that might send Sunny running for cover, away from Lone Star Ridge.

Away from him.

Shaw reminded himself that there'd never been any guarantees Sunny would stay. Still, it tightened the knot even more, and this time, it was his heart that felt as if it was being squeezed.

He looked up when he heard the footsteps, and Shaw figured it was Kinsley fresh from a shower. But it wasn't. It was his mother, and she was ushering in a lanky guy in a suit that Shaw didn't recognize. Ryan, however, must have because the boy practically scrambled to his feet.

"Dad," Ryan said, his voice breathy.

Dad, as in Hugh. Sunny's ex-fiancé.

Well, that didn't help any of those knots.

Ryan moved toward his dad and then stopped as if debating what to do. Hugh solved that for him by taking hold of Ryan and pulling him into his arms for a hug. A short one, complete with a fist bump on Ryan's back, but it was definitely a hug.

"What are you doing here?" Ryan asked once he'd pulled back.

Shaw couldn't see the boy's face, but he could sure

see Hugh's. The man was eyeing Shaw in a way that made him think he'd heard some things about Sunny and this particular cowboy.

"I was in town at the hardware store asking for directions to Em's house," Hugh said, "and someone told me they'd seen you driving out here."

Well, that was an explanation all right, but it didn't answer Ryan's question of why Hugh was there. Maybe to reconcile with his son. But there was a look in Hugh's eyes, one that told Shaw there was more to it than that.

"Sorry," Hugh said, his attention on Shaw. "I didn't introduce myself. I'm Hugh Dunbar."

"Shaw Jameson." He shook Hugh's hand when he offered it.

Shaw figured the man was about to launch into questions about Sunny and him. But he didn't. Hugh slid his arm around Ryan and started leading him out of the office.

"Son, we need to talk," Hugh insisted. "I want Sunny back, and I need you to help me do that."

CHAPTER FOURTEEN

"THE BUNNY BALLERINA or the butterfly pilot?" Em asked.

Sunny had been staring at the concrete figures at Hank's Hardware and wondering how such a form of lawn decorations had gone so terribly wrong. She didn't see a single thing that screamed *I'm in a yard in rural Texas*. No sleek horses. No bulls or herding dogs. Heck, not even a cowboy boot or hat. Just a strange assortment of critters that for some strange reason had been given human career choices.

"It's okay if you can't help me decide which one to get," Em said, patting her arm. "Your mind's on other things."

That was true. Sunny was thinking about other things. Things that were best put aside, which was what she'd been trying to do when she'd agreed to come with Em to the hardware store. It would do no good for her to dwell on the taunting text from Sunshine letting her know she already had a buyer for the sketchbooks. Heck, that might not even be true.

But it felt true.

It felt as if soon strangers would be poring over all those private things she'd sketched.

Of course, Sunny had been well aware of that when

she'd struck the deal with Sunshine, but there hadn't been much of a choice. If she hadn't given Sunshine something she truly wanted, something that could cut into Sunny's soul, then she wouldn't have backed off and Em would have been arrested. Having strangers pry into her private things seemed a small price to pay to prevent that.

"I'm going with the ballerina bunny," Em said, heading to the checkout where the owner, Hank Henderson, was behind an old-fashioned cash register. "I'll have Fred or one of his boys bring it out to the house."

Sunny almost offered to lift it. Her chest and armpit were feeling better, hardly any pain now, but the bunny was made of concrete so it was probably best to go with the delivery.

"Say, did that fella of yours find his way to Shaw's?" Fred asked.

It took Sunny a moment to realize that he was talking to her. "Fella of mine?"

"Yeah. A guy in a suit," Fred happily provided. "He said he needed to see his boy, Ryan, and then you. Said you two were supposed to get married."

The explanation was so unexpected, so surprising, and it didn't make any sense. It was as if Fred had just spoken a foreign language.

"Hugh came to Lone Star Ridge?" Em asked Fred when Sunny didn't say anything.

"I reckon that was his name. He asked how to get to your place, 'cause he wanted to see his boy, but I told him Ryan was heading toward Shaw's. He was driving Sunny's SUV, and I spotted him when I was loading some feed. Your fella asked for directions to Shaw's, and I gave them to him. He should be there by now."

Sunny was about to ask for the keys to Em's truck, but her grandmother handed them to her. "Go," Em insisted. "Don't worry about me. I'll get someone here to take me back home."

That was one of the advantages of living in a small town. Someone would indeed give Em a ride. Another advantage was that Sunny had learned Hugh had come to town and that he wanted to see Ryan. That was a positive sign. She hoped. The part about *said you two were supposed to get married* didn't sound good.

Em's truck was practically an antique so it coughed and sputtered when Sunny started it, and it coughed and sputtered the whole way out to Shaw's. She spotted Hugh's silver Audi, which looked as out of place here on the ranch as those weird concrete figures had. Still, Hugh didn't have to fit. He only had to be the father that Ryan deserved.

Sunny parked next to the Audi and her SUV, which Ryan had driven over. She headed for the house, but before she made it to the porch, she saw Ryan and Hugh by the corral fence next to the barn.

And her heart sank.

Because that wasn't a happy father-and-son reunion going on. She couldn't hear what they were saying, but Ryan looked pissed off. He threw his hands up in the air and stormed away from Hugh back toward the house. Hugh was right behind him, but Ryan picked up some speed when he saw her.

"It's bogus," Ryan said with fire in his voice. A fire that immediately died down as if the fit of temper had drained him. "He came here to try to get you back."

Obviously, this was her day for being surprised, but at least this time it didn't seem as if she was hearing a foreign language. She understood every word that Ryan said.

"What?" she snarled at Hugh.

"Just hear me out," Hugh insisted. "You, too," he added to Ryan.

Ryan did no such thing. "Ask him why he wants to get back together with you," Ryan told her, and he didn't exactly whisper it, either. It was loud enough to have Shaw coming to the back door. One look at Shaw's face, and she saw his eyes darken just as she'd seen Ryan's anger. It didn't take her long to figure out why.

Sunny whirled toward Hugh. "Did you tell Shaw you wanted me back?"

Hugh managed to look indignant even with three sets of angry eyes on him. "He might have heard me mention that to Ryan."

"Ask him why he wants to get back together with you," Ryan repeated.

Sunny was betting it wouldn't be a good reason, especially relating to Ryan. This was so not what she'd hoped for, and worse, it wasn't what Ryan *needed*.

"Why?" She aimed that demand at Hugh. "And while you're explaining that, keep in mind that I broke up with you, and I don't want you back."

"Well, you should because this affects Ryan." Hugh let that hang in the air for several moments while he shook his head as if in frustration. "'You never really understand a person until you consider things from his point of view. Until you climb into his skin and walk around in it.'"

Sunny was certain that her frown deepened. "That's from *To Kill a Mockingbird*."

"It still applies to me, to *us*, to our situation," Hugh insisted. "I know you want me to be part of his life, and I will be. I just need this favor from you first. I need you to come back to the store and do some readings for the kids. I know how much you love that sort of thing, so it wouldn't be a chore."

"Tell her the rest," Ryan insisted.

Hugh hemmed and hawed a couple of moments. "I still have those investors lined up for some new stores I'm buying, and they asked about Ryan and you."

Ryan huffed when Hugh didn't add more to his explanation. "The investors want to know why his son and fiancée aren't around. It's making him look bad, and he's worried they might pull out of the deal."

"For Pete's sake," Sunny grumbled.

Now she knew why Ryan had thrown his hands in the air when she'd seen him talking to his father. She didn't want to do any hand throwing, but she considered latching on to Hugh's shoulders and trying to shake some sense back into him. He had a wonderful son, and he was too stupid or thoughtless to realize it.

Hugh put his hands on his hips. "'It's useless to meet revenge with revenge. It'll heal nothing.'"

Ryan and Sunny groaned in unison. "That's from *Lord of the Rings*," Sunny pointed out with Ryan muttering in agreement. "And what does it have to do with your visit?"

Judging from Hugh's flustered scowl, he hadn't expected her to call him on his attempt to use Tolkien. "Well, do you want me to be part of Ryan's life or not?" he threw out there. "If so, then you know what you have to do."

Well, at least Hugh had used his own words, and Sunny didn't have any confusion about that question or comment. It was emotional blackmail. If she said no, it could hurt Ryan. And she couldn't say yes. No way could she tether herself back to this man who had dollar signs where his heart should be.

"You're not giving in to him," Ryan murmured. It wasn't defiance but rather hurt in his voice.

Shaw, who hadn't uttered a word through this, came closer, and he put his hand on Ryan's shoulder. "It's not a book quote and excuse the language, but I'm sorry your dad's a dick."

"What?" Hugh howled. At least that's what Sunny thought he said. It was garbled and filled with what appeared to be righteous anger.

Shaw ignored him, gave Ryan a few consoling pats on the back, then moved to Sunny. "I'm sorry your ex is a dick." Then Shaw hooked his arm around her waist and snuggled her against him.

She appreciated the support, but her heart was breaking for Ryan. Still, Sunny did enjoy the punch of shock—and failure—she saw in Hugh's expression.

"Sunny and I go way back," Shaw said. Coming from Shaw, it didn't sound like mere information but rather a warning.

"I know who you are," Hugh spit out. "I got almost daily reminders of you before Sunny and I broke up."

Sunny hoped she wasn't going to have to explain that now.

"You're back together with him?" Hugh flung an accusing finger at Shaw before he huffed, "There are reasons your relationship with him didn't work out before. Consider that, Sunny."

"There are reasons our relationship didn't work, either," she reminded him just as quickly. And the main one, Ryan, was standing there looking shell-shocked. Shaw must have noticed that, too, because he caught Ryan's arm and hauled him closer to Sunny and him. A united front against a dick.

"All right," Hugh muttered. "Have it your way. But remember this, 'no matter where you run, you just end up running into yourself.'"

"Breakfast at Tiffany's," Shaw and she said in unison. "It's one of the quotes on the menu at the diner," Shaw added and then turned to her. "Does Hugh ever come up with anything original?"

"Not very often." The irony was that once she'd loved that Hugh could recite so many lines from books. That was before she'd realized it was his way of avoiding real conversation.

"Fine then." Hugh was back to snarling again. "Have it your way. But don't come crawling back to me."

Hugh had aimed that at Ryan, not Sunny. The man was about to cross a line that would cause Ryan to lose his father forever. And she had to try to stop that from happening.

Easing out of Shaw's arm, Sunny turned to face the boy. She opened her mouth to say… She didn't have a clue. But she had to do something to let Ryan know she didn't want this rift, that she would help mend it.

"No," Ryan said before she could speak. "I'm not going to let you sacrifice yourself for me." He shifted his attention back to his dad. "Sunny's not getting back together with you. Neither am I. You'll have to come up with something else to satisfy your investors."

Hugh stayed quiet, volleying hard looks at all of them, especially Shaw. Apparently, Hugh was putting the primary blame for his stupid failed plan on him. Sunny doubted that Hugh would ever admit that the failure was solely on his own shoulders.

"Fine," Hugh snapped. He repeated, "Don't come crawling back to me," which had probably come from a book, too.

"You came to them, not the other way around," Shaw pointed out. *Calmly* pointed out. Which was in direct contrast to the flood of temper visible in Hugh.

Hugh stared at him for a long time, perhaps calculating if he could punch Shaw and then not get his own butt kicked. Hugh must have realized his chances were nil, that Shaw was more than capable of giving him a butt whipping, because he shifted his attention back to Sunny.

"'Deep roots are not reached by the frost,'" Hugh snapped.

"Is that Tolkien again?" Sunny muttered, rolling her eyes. "And it doesn't apply to anything that's been said here. If you're going to quote the classics, Hugh, at least come up with something that's sort of relevant."

Hugh glared at her. "You're a hack illustrator with no talent. You can't do anything that isn't scripted for you," he snapped, and stormed off.

Because Sunny was still in the book quote mindset, it took her a moment to realize that Hugh's parting shot had been an original, one that'd been meant to diss her. And it was a particularly sharp arrow that had hit its mark. Not because she believed it was true but because Hugh knew how important her job was to her. He knew the way to get to her was to belittle it.

"Are you okay?" Shaw asked, and after she gave him a somewhat shaky nod, he repeated the question to Ryan, who also nodded.

"I'm not a hack," she muttered as she watched Hugh speed away. The fact that she could earn a living as an illustrator meant that she had talent.

Of course, it was a whole lot more than that to her.

Getting that job to do *Slackers Quackers* had proved to Sunny that she was someone beyond that little girl who'd wanted a weenie like her brother. That she had shaken off the toddler who'd put red panties on her head. It had been one of the best days of her life when J.B. Whitman had wanted her to bring his stories to life, and it meant Hugh was wrong. She wasn't a hack.

She wasn't.

And none of that mattered right now. Not with Ryan standing there with his heart crushed.

Gathering her breath, Sunny turned to Ryan and

reached out to give him a hug. One that she thought they both needed. Ryan stepped back and shook his head.

"I need a minute," he said. "I need a little time to myself." And like his father had just done, Ryan went to the SUV and drove away.

Maybe because she'd just listened to all of Hugh's quote-spouting, another line from *Breakfast at Tiffany's* came to mind. A quote that she hoped Ryan didn't feel.

"Home is where you feel at home. I'm still looking."

CHAPTER FIFTEEN

SHAW FIRED OFF ANOTHER "just checking on you" text to Ryan, something he'd done both days since the boy's father had acted like an ass.

Not only acting like an ass to Ryan, but also to Sunny.

That's why Shaw had been sending her messages, as well. When she'd left the ranch after the blowup with her ex, she definitely hadn't been Funny Sunny, and Shaw hadn't been able to talk to her face-to-face since.

Of course, Shaw hadn't actually come out and asked either Sunny or Ryan if they were truly all right. Or if they were still as pissed as he was about the ass's behavior. But Shaw figured they hadn't had any trouble deciphering the meaning behind his previous messages.

You up for a ride? I have some new horses if you want to try them out.

I'm heading into San Antonio today to pick up some things if you want to come along.

My mom's bringing over a casserole called turnip surprise. Might want to make yourself scarce.

Sunny and Ryan had responded with no, thank you on the first two, adding that they were busy, but he was pretty sure their thanks were heartfelt for the heads-up he'd given them about the casserole. Shortly after that, Ryan had sent him a text that said, I'm all right. You don't need to worry about me.

Oh, if only that were so.

Shaw was troubled not only because he liked Ryan and thought he was a good kid but because Sunny was worried. He hated knowing she was down in the dumps and no doubt trying to get the teenager through this emotional upheaval. Shaw wasn't sure if or how she was managing to do that, but he'd soon find out because Sunny had finally accepted his invitation to come over for dinner tonight.

Since Sunny was no fool, she likely knew the dinner invitation included sex. Or at least the possibility of sex if she was feeling up to it. However, Shaw truly did want to know how she and Ryan were doing, and he'd get the added bonus of having some alone time with Sunny. He missed her. He missed having the peace of mind he'd started to get when she was around.

There are reasons your relationship with him didn't work out before. Consider that, Sunny.

That was what the ass had thrown at Sunny during the heat of their book-quoting argument. Nothing else the wanker had said made a lick of sense, but that comment had given Shaw a kick in the teeth. Because there had indeed been reasons things hadn't worked between Sunny and him.

Some of those things—their young ages, for

instance—no longer applied since they were adults now. Ditto for them both needing to find their places in the world. Shaw hadn't had to look far for his place. He'd always wanted to be a cowboy and run the ranch. After seventeen years with his name on the ranch letterhead, he'd proved he could do that, and Sunny had found a way to turn her love of art into a career.

But there was the kid thing.

However, maybe her feelings about that had changed now that Ryan was essentially her son. Maybe that had cooled down the baby fever.

Shaw was mulling that over when Cait and Kinsley stepped into the doorway of his home office. Today Kinsley's hair was cardinal red and stuck out in feather-like tufts. It looked like a hairdo that Avery would have come up with.

"Can you look me straight in the eyes and say you've used a polynomial today?" Kinsley asked him—after she'd huffed.

He couldn't look her in the eye and say that he'd used that particular form of math on any day since high school, but judging from the way Cait's eyebrows had pulled together, that wasn't the right answer.

"I take it this has something to do with your algebra homework?" Shaw said, though it wasn't really a guess. Kinsley often complained about the assignments that the school was sending her, and algebra was at the top of her list. Plus, she had her math book tucked under her arm.

"Not homework," Cait corrected. "A test. The school wants Kinsley to come in next week to take her finals. I'm driving her to San Antonio today for a study group. While she's studying, I'm hitting Taco Hut."

Kinsley expressed her opinion about the study group and perhaps missing out on the tacos with another huff and an eye roll. "I don't see why I should have to take algebra. I suck at it."

"She does," Cait readily admitted with a shrug. "But finishing the class is part of the deal we settled on. I told Kinsley you'd buy her a bunch of new clothes, but first she has to pass algebra with a C or better."

This was the first Shaw was hearing about the clothes, and while it didn't seem like stellar parenting to offer a bribe for good grades, he couldn't think of a better incentive. Nor could Cait or he step up to tutor the girl. Kinsley wasn't the only Jameson who sucked at algebra. It seemed to be a defect in their gene pool.

However, he did think of something.

"Maybe Ryan can help you study?" Shaw tossed out there. "He's smart."

Judging by her repeated eye roll and even louder huff, that wasn't as good an idea as Shaw had thought it would be. "Then, he'd know how stupid I am. I don't want him to know that."

"You're not stupid," Shaw assured her. He'd seen her grades, and math was the only area where Kinsley struggled. Amazing, considering everything she'd been through. "And Ryan wouldn't think that. It'd probably make him feel good to help."

Or at least get the boy's mind off his own troubles.

On second thought, though, Shaw didn't think he should encourage this sort of get-together.

"Are you still seeing Ryan?" he asked.

Apparently, that wasn't a good response for him, either, because Kinsley looked at him as if he'd turned into a skunk and walked away.

Cait shook her head and whispered, "Ryan's been keeping his distance lately." Then Cait headed off after Kinsley.

Well, hell. Shaw had no idea why he felt the need to fix that, but he did. Fix it in a way that left both Kinsley and Ryan happy but without them actually being involved. He still didn't think that was a good idea. Not only would Ryan be leaving for college soon, both Kinsley and he were neck-deep in emotional baggage. That could lead to sex.

Of course, breathing could lead to sex for teenagers.

It could do that for adults, too, and Shaw got a fast reminder when Sunny walked in. Even though he'd spent a good deal of the morning thinking about her, seeing her still packed a wallop.

"Algebra woes," she said, hiking her thumb in the direction where Kinsley and Cait had made their exit.

He nodded. "Whatever you do, don't suggest that she ask Ryan for help. Kinsley's apparently a little sensitive when it comes to him." The comment was a fishing expedition, with him trying to feel Sunny out when it came to the subject of her almost-stepson.

"Yes." On a sigh, Sunny tucked her hair behind her ear. "Ryan's better but still down. McCall gave me the name of a therapist in San Antonio, and I made an appointment for him."

Good. Because teenage angst was as potent as teenage hormones. "Anything I can do to help?"

She smiled a little. "Offering the horseback rides was nice. Thanks. So was checking on me. I like the duck emoji in the last text."

He'd had to search for that, and it didn't bear much of a resemblance to Slackers. It'd looked goofy enough though that he hoped it'd lifted her spirits. However, other that the brief smile, he got no confirmation that it'd actually helped. Still, he'd keep sending the texts.

"Sunshine's pissed," Sunny went on. "Your lawyer stopped her from publishing any of the sketches of you."

Yeah, he'd received word of that a few hours ago. It was a temporary victory that wouldn't hold, but it had felt good to jab at Sunny's mother. Sunshine would soon get around it once the legal guys read the agreement and confirmed that she did indeed own the sketches, including those of him.

His lawyer had suggested Shaw sue Sunny to try to get the sketches back, but he'd nixed that. It'd only end up generating even more publicity for something he'd rather keep quiet.

"Has Hugh made any other visits?" he asked.

"No." She smiled, then frowned. "He hasn't spoken to Ryan, either."

That sucked, and Shaw wondered if he could try to get Sunshine and Hugh together so they could discuss how many ways they could screw over their kids.

"You're not a hack," Shaw told her in case it needed to be said. "And you can certainly live your life without a script."

"I know." But she sounded a little uncertain about that. Too bad her butt-wipe former fiancé had put that in her head. Of course, considering her childhood, thoughts like that were probably a permanent fixture in her head.

"Are you here to cancel our date?" he asked.

She nodded, and Shaw felt the disappointment slap him in the face. "Ryan's in Austin today doing an orientation for his fall classes. He'll be back around six or so, and I thought I should be there."

Okay, so she wasn't just blowing him off. And besides, he should probably be around, too, after Cait brought Kinsley back from San Antonio. His mom might want to go to her quilting club, which would run late into the evening, and this would save Kinsley from being here alone or Cait having to hang out with her. Cait was already putting in her sister hours for the days and likely had work to do.

"We can reschedule our dinner date," Shaw told her.

"Or we could have it now." Sunny took two energy bars and a bottle of water from her purse and put them on his desk.

While it wasn't actually dinner, the items did intrigue Shaw. So did the fact that Sunny shut his office door and locked it.

"Thinking about you is driving me crazy," she said as she went around the desk, came up on her toes and crushed her mouth to his.

Shaw hadn't seen the kiss coming, but he had no trouble feeling it. All the way to the toes of his boots and everything in between. Suddenly, thinking about her was driving him crazy, too.

He pulled her to him, again mindful of her incision, but Sunny didn't seem to be favoring that part of her body today. She moved deep into his arms, her breasts against his chest. That gave him ideas.

Ideas that involved long slow, kisses to every inch of her.

Shaw started by deepening the kiss on her mouth while sliding his hands over her butt to align her just the way he liked. It was even better than when they'd fooled around at his place because today Sunny was wearing a dress. A soft yellow one that suited not only her name but Sunny, as well. Along with long, slow kisses, he intended to run his hand up her thigh and—

"I need to explain about Hugh," she said, tearing her mouth from his.

Shaw had no interest—none—in discussing her ex. No way, no how did he want that to happen now. But Sunny stepped back as if she was going to insist on it.

"He's an ass," Shaw quickly volunteered, hoping that would suffice and cut off any further talk. It didn't.

"I don't want you to think I'm an idiot for getting involved with him," she went on.

"I don't," he assured her quickly in the hopes of shortening this chat. "He owns bookstores, right?" He'd gotten the gist of that from the argument he'd had to sit through. The rest he'd gotten from Em and town gossip. Hugh was a widower who'd lost his wife over a decade ago. "I'm guessing that sort of lured you in since you've always loved books. Then, there's Ryan. He would have been part of the lure, too."

Her eyes widened, and she was obviously surprised that he could zoom in on it so fast. "I did love him," she said. "I wouldn't have agreed to marry him if I didn't love him. But then things fell apart. It was as if once I accepted his proposal, he quit having anything to do with Ryan. It was as if he wanted to turn over everything to do with parenting to me."

Shaw didn't have any trouble seeing that about the guy, but he was betting Sunny hadn't been aware of it until she was already in too deep.

"At least you ended things before you married him," Shaw pointed out.

"Yes, there is that, but just getting involved with him was a mistake. With Eric, too."

"Eric, your first fiancé?"

She nodded. "He's a lot like Hugh in that he sort of ditched his daughter, Miranda, as well. I'm still fairly close with her."

Shaw figured that Sunny had picked up on the pattern here so there was no need to point it out.

"Anyway, I just didn't want you to think that I was an idiot," she repeated.

"I've known you longer than either of those guys." Something that gave him a smug sort of satisfaction. "And I know you're not an idiot."

She released her breath as if she'd been holding it, which made Shaw want to curse. Had she really thought he was going to bash her for trying to be a mother to two kids? Not a chance.

"Okay," she said, and her smile wasn't so small now, and it was tinged with relief. "That's the conversation part of our date. Do you want to eat?" She tipped her head to the granola bars and water.

"Maybe later. What's the next part of our date?" And he was smiling, too, because he could feel the heat starting to tingle and zap between them. Shaw sent the tingling and zapping up a notch when he pulled her back into his arms.

There was nothing tentative about this kiss, which meant she'd obviously cleared her mind so she could focus on this. Though Shaw wasn't sure just how far this would go. After all, he was in his office, and while the door was locked and the house was empty, that didn't mean Rowley wouldn't come looking for him. It was also possible that Sunny had just come here for a good make-out session.

Or not.

Shaw got his first clue about where this was headed when she stopped again. "Hold on. I brought something else with me." She hurried to her purse and came back with a condom.

So, she wanted more than making out, and his body thought that was a stellar idea. That's why once again he hauled her back to him, and this time he intended to hang on for a while.

He got to work on that long, slow kiss quest, moving his mouth to her neck. Shaw experienced a moment of déjà vu when she went after the buttons of his shirt with a clumsiness that reminded him a little of their hayloft adventure. But after she bared his chest and put her hands on him, he wouldn't have noticed clumsiness if it smacked him in the face.

Shaw had to stop kissing her neck when she dropped lower to kiss his chest. All in all, he thought that was a great trade-off, especially when she flicked her tongue over his nipple. He hadn't especially needed anything to spur him to action, but that did it.

He caught onto the bottom of her dress, sliding it up, up, up. Until he reached the top of her thigh and the leg of her panties. They were just as skimpy as her other ones, and because the lights were on, he could see that these were red. His new favorite color.

Sunny had to stop kissing his chest when Shaw went closer to kiss his new favorite color. Right in the middle of that swatch of lace. Right in the center of Sunny's heat. That tasted so good that he went in for more. He moved the swatch of lace to the side and put a better spin on the dinner date.

Her head dropped back and she moaned, fisting her hand in his hair. She was wet and ready, and Shaw was reasonably sure he could have finished her off with a nibble or two. But he wanted more. He wanted to put that condom to good use and be inside her. Still, he couldn't help himself and he lingered a bit. Until Sunny was seriously pulling his hair and begging for more.

Shaw gave her more.

Sliding her dress up to her waist, he kept on kissing while he dropped back into his chair. Thankfully, Sunny fit right on his lap with her legs spread. Straddling him.

Her face was flushed, her breath gusting when she looked at him. "My clothes stay on, okay?"

He nodded, knowing he would have possibly agreed to a lobotomy at this point, but he didn't like Sunny feeling the need to hide her scar from him. Still, fully clothed sex with Sunny was better than bare-assed naked with anybody else.

Of course, being clothed didn't mean they didn't have to make some adjustments. Adjustments that Sunny helped with when she leaned back and unzipped him. She freed his erection from his boxers and handed him the condom. Shaw took care of that and pushed the crotch of her panties to the side.

Pay dirt.

Everything was lined up just as it should be, and Sunny might have gone for impalement again if Shaw hadn't caught onto her hips. Keeping his eyes locked with hers, he eased her down slowly. Slow enough to make him want to start begging. Slow enough to allow him to feel the gradual slippery slide into her. He felt her body stretch, adjust to take him in.

This was well past the pay dirt stage.

"You're still huge," she mumbled. He froze for a second and was about to ask her if she wanted to stop, but Sunny added, "That's not a complaint."

Shaw managed a chuckle and finished that slow, slippery slide.

Man, she felt good, and Shaw had to squeeze his eyes shut a moment to rein in what his body wanted to do to her. His dick wanted fast and furious. Now, now, now. But since it might be a while before he hit pay dirt again, Shaw went as slow as he could. He clamped his hands on her hips and started moving her forward. Deeper. Until she'd taken all of him.

Sunny didn't have any trouble getting in sync with the rhythm. Probably because her own body didn't give her much of a choice about it. That was the problem with good sex. It wasn't meant to last. It was meant to feed that primal need and release the pressure cooker heat that the friction was building. Plain and simple. It was meant to make them mindless idiots seeking the ultimate thrill.

And the thrill came for Sunny first.

Just the way Shaw had planned it. That way, he got to watch her eyes glaze with the heat. He got to see her mouth open when the moan of pleasure slipped its way through. And he got to feel her wet muscles clamp around him. Not around his fingers this time, either, but a much more sensitive part of him. All that muscle clamping did what it was designed to do, and Shaw didn't hold back.

It'd been fifteen years since the last time Sunny had gotten him off. And in that moment, Shaw decided the wait had been worth it. He dragged Sunny against him and let go.

"Do you hear bells ringing?" Sunny asked.

Because both their breaths were gusting, it took Shaw a moment to figure out what she'd said. "Yeah, I hear them."

He'd never heard post-sex bells before, so maybe it was a first. But then he heard the knock. Not on his office door. It sounded as if it was coming from the front of the house. And it wasn't stopping. Whoever was out there just kept ringing and knocking.

Shit.

This was not an interruption he wanted seconds after "worth the wait" getting off, but it could be some kind of emergency. Maybe one of the hands had been hurt or, God forbid, maybe someone in his family had been in an accident.

Sunny must have realized that was a possibility, too, because she scrambled off his lap. Thankfully, there was a small half bath just off his office, and Shaw hurried there to clean up. By the time he'd managed that, the knocking and ringing had stopped, but he heard Rowley's voice.

"Shaw, you here?" the hand called out.

"I'll be right there." He glanced over at Sunny, who was fixing her makeup with stuff she'd taken from her purse. She crammed everything back inside and followed him out of the office.

Rowley was already in the hall, and he wasn't alone. There was a short older woman next to him.

"Uh, you've got a visitor," Rowley said. He lifted his hand as if he was about to make introductions, but the woman beat him to it.

"I'm Maxine Marbury," the woman said, her voice crisp and all business. She was barely five feet tall, but she had the attitude of a Doberman. Sort of snarly and "don't mess with me" dust-gray eyes. "Are you Shaw Jameson?"

"I am. What do you want?"

She showed him some kind of credentials in a plastic covered sleeve that she wore on a chain around her neck. "I'm from Child Protective Services. There's been a complaint against you, and I'm here to take custody of Kinsley Rubio. She needs to come with me right now."

A couple of words snagged Shaw's attention. *Complaint against you* and *take custody of Kinsley.*

"Who filed a complaint?" he asked. "And what's it about?"

The woman's mouth went tight. "I can't and won't disclose that. Just get Kinsley out here now."

Shaw's own mouth went tight, too. "She's on her way to San Antonio with my sister and mother to attend a study group." He doubted Ms. Marbury would appreciate it if he tried to lighten her tense face with a joke about polynomials. "She won't be back for hours."

"I'll wait," she insisted. "Call her. Get her back here ASAP because she's coming with me."

Shaw had known there was a chance that CPS would show up, but he didn't like the way this was playing out. He took his phone from his pocket to call Cait and then Aurora. Before he could so, Sunny's phone dinged with a text message. He didn't think it was a good sign that Sunny muttered a profanity after she read it.

He wanted to mutter some, too, when she showed him the screen, and he saw the message there.

From Sunshine.

Tell Shaw that if he dicks around with me, I'll dick around right back. I hope he has fun talking to CPS about the complaint I filed.

CHAPTER SIXTEEN

IT WAS TOO bad that her mother's name was Sunshine because Sunny was transferring some of the disgust she felt for the woman on the actual sunshine that was spearing through the windows of the Jameson living room. Judging from the way Shaw was scowling, he was doing some mental cursing, too.

What a mess.

Correction: what *another* mess. And like so many other times, this was her mother's fault. Normally, Sunshine only ended up hurting Em, Sunny or her siblings; this time Kinsley had gotten caught up in it.

Sunny checked the time again. It'd been over a half hour since Shaw had tried, and failed, to get in touch with Aurora. He'd had better success with Cait, and he'd asked her to bring Kinsley back to the ranch. He'd added that they needed to get some things straightened out, but that wasn't a straightening-out look in the social worker's eyes. She clearly didn't want to sit around in the living room with Shaw and Sunny. Ms. Marbury just wanted to take her charge and get the heck out of there. Obviously, the woman believed that Shaw had done something wrong, and they could thank Sunshine for getting that lie-snowball rolling.

"You're sure I can't get anyone coffee or tea?" Sunny asked, trying to stay pleasant.

And hopeful.

Maybe Shaw could indeed straighten this out and Kinsley wouldn't have to leave. In the meantime, Sunny figured it would be smart to get on the social worker's good side—hence the offer of coffee and tea despite this not being Sunny's house. But judging from the woman's scowl, she had no good side.

"No, thanks," Shaw grumbled.

At the moment he didn't have a good side, either. Well, not now, but he'd certainly been *good* when they'd been having sex in his office. Sunny had hoped to spend the rest of the afternoon with him, perhaps using the second condom she'd brought with her, but there was no way that was going to happen now. It would take some doing for Shaw to talk the social worker into allowing Kinsley to stay at the ranch.

If Shaw wanted Kinsley to stay, that is.

Shaw had to be fed up with Marty's other kids showing up and disrupting his life, but Sunny thought that maybe he'd started to make a connection with Kinsley. Cait had, too. Which wouldn't make things any easier for Kinsley if she got placed in the system. The girl could end up living far away from Lone Star Ridge.

"I suppose you're here often?" Ms. Marbury asked, her voice cutting through the silence.

Sunny wished the woman had stayed quiet because that sounded like an accusation. Of course, maybe Sunny was reading into it because, after all, they had just had sex.

"Shaw and I are old friends," Sunny said. "I come here sometimes." She tried not to wince at her word choice of *come*. "I'm not a bad influence on Kinsley," she added when the woman's stare put her on the defensive. "Neither is Shaw."

She needed to stop babbling because Sunny doubted there was anything she could say that would make this better. Thankfully, she didn't have a chance to babble more because the doorbell rang. Sunny automatically steeled herself for Kinsley to come in before realizing the girl wouldn't have rung the bell.

Shaw went to the door, throwing it open, and while she couldn't see who was there, she did see the instant change in Shaw's body language. He pulled back his shoulders, and his hands went to his hips.

"Dad," Shaw said, and it wasn't a friendly greeting.

That brought Sunny to her feet. She hurried to the door to see… Yes, it was Marty on the porch. The grin Marty gave them was definitely friendly even though there wasn't a thing to smile about.

It'd been years since Sunny had seen Marty, but he hadn't changed much. Looks-wise, he was an older version of Shaw, though Marty didn't have his son's seriousness. Nope. He carried himself exactly the way an aging country music star would in his well-worn "I don't have to try too hard" jeans and the T-shirt from his Just Marty tour that he'd done shortly after he'd hit it big.

When he pulled off his Stetson, complete with—naturally—a snakeskin band, she saw that his long, nearly shoulder length hair was threaded with gray. But both that and the wrinkles around his eyes only seemed to add more character to his face. A face that needed no more of that. Simply put, Marty was a good-looking, cocky, irresponsible and charming fool.

"I've been trying to get in touch with you for two weeks," Shaw snarled.

That didn't cause Marty's grin to fade. He stepped in and motioned as if to give Shaw a hug. However, Shaw's "do it and die" expression must have put him off. Marty hugged her instead.

"Sunny," Marty said, pulling her into his arms. "It's good to see you, darlin'."

She wasn't flattered by the *darlin'* because, coming from Marty, it wasn't a term of endearment. It's what he called most women, and she suspected that was easier for him than remembering the names of the string of females who came and went in his life.

Still, Sunny didn't balk at being lumped in with the rest of the women. She didn't know why, but it had always felt good that Shaw's father had been able to tell her apart from her sisters. Few people could do that, especially when they were kids and Sunshine had dressed them alike.

"I've been trying to get in touch with you for two weeks," Shaw repeated, the comment even more of a growl than it had been earlier.

Marty released her, nodded. "I got your messages. Leyton's and Cait's, too. That's why I came." He didn't explain why it'd taken him so long to get there. Instead, Marty glanced around. "Is Kinsley here?"

If Sunny was doling out points, she would have given Marty half of one for at least knowing Kinsley's name, but it was obvious Shaw wasn't in a point-giving mood.

"She's on her way," Shaw supplied. He tipped his head to Ms. Marbury. "And this is the social worker who wants to take her." Shaw muttered a single curse word under his breath. "The kid's had a rough go of it, and you might have helped with that if you'd shown up sooner."

Shaw couldn't put much of a tongue-lashing tone on that last comment though because there were definitely no guarantees of Marty's help even if he had been there.

"Hello, darlin'," Marty greeted, making his charming-scoundrel way over to the social worker. "I'm Marty Jameson, Kinsley's father."

The social worker had no trouble with a tongue-lashing tone, and she aimed narrowed suspicious eyes at him. The woman likely would have launched into a question or two, challenging his fatherhood claim, perhaps objecting to the *darlin'*, too, but the sound of a car engine halted the conversation.

Since the front door was still open, Sunny saw Cait pull to a stop in front of the house. She wasn't sure how much Shaw had told his sisters and mother, but it was obvious they were aware there was a problem because they hurried toward the house with Kinsley leading the pack. She had what appeared to be a text-book under her arm and a puzzled but determined look on her face. When the girl came to a skidding halt, Sunny knew Kinsley had recognized her father.

Behind Kinsley, Cait gave Marty a flat stare. "Oh, good. I can give you that World's Bestest Dad coffee mug I bought for you fifteen years ago."

Sunny didn't know if it'd been that long since Marty had been here, and he didn't react to his daughter's ire. He simply smiled.

"Cait, darlin'," Marty greeted, but he didn't make a move to give her a hug when Cait walked past Kinsley and Lenore and went into the house. Marty had probably backed off because it seemed as if Cait had sprouted invisible porcupine quills. She looked as bristly as Shaw.

But the World's Bestest Dad ire award belonged to Lenore.

"Oh, good," Lenore said in a voice that mimicked Cait's tone. "I can make the whole wheat prune surprise recipe I've been saving just for you." Lenore came closer, too, following in Cait's steps, but she stopped in the doorway and lowered her voice to a whisper. "I hope it gives you the runs you deserve. You should have done better by this girl, Marty."

Marty did hug her despite the fact that Lenore's body went as stiff as her upper lip had gone. Marty chuckled as if that were a fine joke and not the threat Sunny believed it to be. If Lenore could somehow get that colon-blowing food combination into Marty, she'd do it, and that's probably why Lenore made a beeline for the kitchen.

Only then did Marty finally turn his attention to Kinsley.

The girl was eyeing Marty not with venom or intentions of giving him any World's Bestest Dad treatment. She had her teeth clamped over her bottom lip and suddenly looked very, very young. Very, very emotional, too. Her eyes were shining, and even though she was blinking hard, Sunny thought the tears might win.

"You came." Kinsley's voice was small.

"I did. Wanted to meet my girl. Hey there, darlin'."

Marty flashed a smile that Sunny was certain had worked on most people he wanted to charm, and she was surprised when it seemed to work on Kinsley, too. When Marty went to her and hugged her, Kinsley practically melted into his arms.

Part of Sunny melted, too, and not in a good way. Marty didn't seem to have a mean bone in his body, but he was filled with plenty of irresponsible bones. Or at least he had been. Maybe he'd turned over a new leaf. She hoped that was true for Kinsley's sake.

"Dad," Kinsley muttered while she continued to hug him.

"You're as pretty as a picture," Marty muttered right back to her. He kissed the top of her head and pulled away, but kept his arm looped around her waist. "Now, darlin', let's go inside and get some things worked out with the social worker."

Sunny didn't know who was more surprised that Marty knew about CPS being there, but she thought Cait won that award. Of course, her surprise was still mixed with a boatload of skepticism.

"Did you ask her to come here?" Cait said to Marty. She hiked a thumb at Ms. Marbury, who was now standing and eyeing all of them.

"No, but I knew she was coming. Aurora got in touch with me and told me there'd been a complaint. Against Shaw," he added, sparing his son a glance that seemed to imply that he knew such a complaint would be bogus.

"My mom?" Kinsley asked. "She knew how to get in touch with you?"

"No. She found me by reaching out to some of our old friends. I was having a chat with Aurora in San Antonio when she got word from CPS that they were on their way here. They called her to let her know. I figured I'd better come to Lone Star Ridge to meet you and sort things out."

Sunny figured that Marty must have done some BS-ing to talk his way into so many women's beds, but that didn't seem like BS to her. And it had to be a good sign that Aurora was now willing to talk to Marty about Kinsley.

"Am I to understand that you expect me to believe you're Kinsley Rubio's father?" Ms. Marbury asked. "You're that singer, Marty Jameson."

"I'm both *that singer* and her father," Marty insisted, not with the evil eye and sour-lemon mouth that the social worker was giving him. Someone who didn't know Marty might have thought he was turning on the charm with his solar-flare smile, but Marty didn't have to turn it on. He lived in the charm zone.

"See the resemblance?" Marty asked the woman.

While he still had his arm around Kinsley, he caught onto the sleeve of Cait's shirt and pulled her closer. Presumably so that Ms. Marbury could realize that they did indeed look alike. And they did. Even with her eyes narrowed to skeptical slits, the woman had to see that.

"You expect me to take your word on that?" the

social worker snapped. "Because I don't. There's been a complaint—"

"A bogus one," Shaw said, probably wanting to use a much stronger word for the shitty thing Sunshine had done.

"What kind of complaint?" Kinsley said, and some of the "I'm hugging my dad" glow vanished when she turned frosty eyes on the woman.

Ms. Marbury didn't flinch even though she had a roomful of Jamesons and Sunny staring her down. "There's a question about you not being supervised properly, that you've been allowed to run wild and you haven't been doing your schoolwork."

Considering that Kinsley was still holding on to an algebra book, it seemed to confirm the bogusness of the last part of the complaint.

"Trust me, I've been supervised," Kinsley snapped. "And the only time I ran wild was when a bee tried to fly in my hair. Who made those bullshit claims?"

Sunny wished the girl had held back on the profanity, but maybe Ms. Marbury wouldn't hold that against her.

She did.

Volleying accusing glares at the Jamesons—and Sunny—the woman went closer to Kinsley and actually reached out for her. Kinsley stepped back, and Marty moved in front of her like a shield.

"The girl is coming with me," Ms. Marbury insisted.

"No, she's not." That specifically came from Marty, but Cait, Shaw and even Kinsley voiced variations of it. Kinsley went for another dash of profanity. "No way in hell."

"You don't have to go with her, darlin'," Marty told Kinsley as if his word were gospel. He took a folded-up piece of paper from his pocket and handed it to Ms. Marbury. "Kinsley's mother, Aurora Rubio, wrote that. It's permission for Kinsley to spend as much time here at the ranch as she wants. She's a Jameson, and she belongs here."

Wow, Marty just kept ringing up the surprises today, and Cait, Kinsley and Shaw all went to the social worker so they could read, along with Ms. Marbury, what Aurora had written.

"You can see at the bottom that she had it notarized," Marty went on. "That's what Aurora and I were doing when she got the call about CPS coming out here. Aurora and I got together so we could do this for Kinsley, and then Aurora gave me the original papers so I could bring them here to you."

Ms. Marbury didn't respond. She kept reading and apparently rereading because she continued to fix her attention to the page minutes after Shaw, Cait and Kinsley had stepped to the side.

"My mom doesn't want me," Kinsley said.

And that broke Sunny's heart a little. Of course, Kinsley had known that her mother had basically run out on her, but it made things harder to see it in writing.

Still, there was a silver lining here. Marty had cared enough to go to Aurora and get this kind of permission. He was finally manning up, and while he still didn't deserve the World's Bestest Dad award, this was a step in the right direction.

"This permission doesn't address the complaints," Ms. Marbury said after some snail-crawling moments.

Everyone but the social worker huffed.

"None of those accusations are true," Sunny said. "My mother made them because she wanted to get back at Shaw." She could see Ms. Marbury gearing up to argue so Sunny just rolled over her. "Besides, Kinsley will be here with her father, and he'll be supervising her. That's not only what Aurora Rubio wants, it's also what everyone else wants."

"I'm staying," Kinsley snarled. Though Sunny wished the girl had used a more pleasant tone, it did let Ms. Marbury know she would have an uphill fight to take Kinsley. A fight the social worker would lose, thanks to Aurora giving her permission.

More seconds crawled by, and Ms. Marbury took out her phone and snapped a picture of the permission slip. "I'll talk to my supervisor about this. And to Mrs. Rubio. If she has any doubts about her daughter being here—*any doubts*—" she emphasized, "then I'll be back."

Sunny didn't exactly hold her breath while the woman walked out, but apparently that was what Kinsley was doing. The girl made a noisy exhale and then glanced around as if asking—what now?

Uh, what now, indeed?

Sunny had thought it was a good idea for the social worker to know who and what was behind the complaint against Shaw, but she wasn't part of the family dynamics and decisions that needed to be made about Kinsley. Especially any decision that involved Marty. She couldn't see Lenore just welcoming him back into the house, but maybe Shaw's mother wouldn't mind Marty staying there for a while until he worked out something more permanent with Kinsley.

"I'll just be going," Sunny said, picking up her purse. She wanted to kiss Shaw goodbye, but it wasn't the time for that. Sunny had only made it two steps when Marty spoke.

"I need to head out, too," Marty said. "Aurora wanted me to have dinner with her tonight so I have to get back to San Antonio."

The room suddenly got quiet again. Very quiet. And it lasted until there was a loud crash. Sunny's gaze zoomed across the room to see Lenore standing in the archway that led to the kitchen. She'd dropped a dish of…well, something. It was brown, orange and oozy.

"You're leaving?" Lenore asked.

Kinsley asked the same question, but her voice wasn't filled with anger like Lenore's. Kinsley looked and sounded shocked.

"Darlin', I'm sorry, but I can't stay," Marty said as if that'd been obvious right from the start. "I just wanted to come out and meet you and give Shaw that paper so CPS would get off his back. Oh, and I wanted to give you this." Marty took something else from his pocket and handed it to Kinsley.

A check.

Sunny couldn't see the amount, but even if it was

for millions, it wouldn't have been enough. Of course, Marty himself wasn't enough, either.

And he never had been.

"Great to meet you, darlin'," he told Kinsley. "I'll try to get out this way again soon." Marty kissed a stunned and motionless Kinsley on top of her head and looked around as if he might give Cait and Shaw a hug, too. He backed off when Shaw scorched him with another glare.

No glare for Kinsley. With her algebra book in one hand and the check in the other, she hurried past Lenore and the slimed floor, and headed toward the back of the house.

There was so much anger in Lenore, Cait and Shaw that Sunny thought it was possible their muscles had atrophied. They all stood there glaring at the butt hole of a man who'd just stepped on the heart of another one of his kids.

"I'll go check on Kinsley," Sunny offered. Not only did she not want to be part of what was about to happen in this room, she really did want to make sure Kinsley was okay.

But how could she be?

That "permission" basically spelled out that her mother didn't want her, and now Marty had just spelled out the same thing.

Sunny made her way through the house, and when she spotted Kinsley running toward the barn, that's where Sunny headed, too. When she reached the barn, she found the algebra book on the ground, right by the ladder leading to the hayloft.

"I want to be alone," Kinsley snapped when Sunny climbed up into the hayloft and sat next to the girl.

Sunny ignored that and pulled Kinsley into her arms. And just like that, the girl broke. These weren't angry sobs like the ones in the bathroom at Em's. Her tears were almost silent which made them worse. Maybe Marty hadn't just broken Kinsley's heart. He might have broken *her*. If so, maybe Sunny could hold him down so that Lenore could force-feed him that prune casserole.

"He doesn't want me," Kinsley muttered.

Sunny wanted to say something to dispute that. She couldn't. She didn't know what made Marty tick, but there was a definite disconnect in any parental feelings or responsibilities.

"Maybe Marty's just a wuss," Sunny finally said. "Maybe he gets so overwhelmed with responsibilities that he just runs for cover. And he writes checks."

Sunny doubted that helped, but Kinsley's crying did ease up a bit. She fished through her purse and came up with a small package of tissue for the girl. Kinsley was mopping up her face when there were footsteps on the ladder. A moment later, Cait appeared.

"Marty deserves a kick to his nuts," Cait declared. "Since I was perilously close to doing the kicking, I decided to come out here and cool off." She had a huge box of Milk Duds with her and dropped them in Kinsley's lap. Judging from the way Cait was chewing, she'd already tapped into the sugary supply.

Resting her back against a hay bale, Cait sat across from Kinsley and gave the girl's foot a nudge with hers. "Want to stay the night at my place? We can watch movies with hot guys in them and do internet searches on how to put curses on Marty."

"You don't have to be nice to me," Kinsley concluded, but she did eat a Milk Dud.

"Okay. So, you can do my laundry first and clean my house," Cait amended. "Then, we'll watch the movies and read about curses."

Kinsley looked up at her. "He doesn't want me."

"Naw," Cait disagreed. "He wants you. He wants all of us. He just doesn't want to be a real honest-to-goodness father."

Cait was right. But where did that leave Kinsley? Sunny was mulling that over when there were more footsteps. Shaw, this time, and he dropped down across from Kinsley and Sunny.

"Marty needs his balls kicked," Shaw grumbled, helping himself to a Milk Dud.

"Told you," Cait said as if there'd been any doubts about that. "So, what's the plan?" she asked Shaw.

Shaw took a deep breath before he responded. "Leyton will be talking to both Marty and Aurora tonight while they're having dinner. Leyton says he won't let them leave until they've worked out some custody arrangements."

All things considered, Sunny thought that was a good idea. Leyton could be very persuasive. If anyone could talk some sense into Marty, it would be Leyton. Or so Sunny hoped. Because Kinsley desperately needed this to be fixed.

"Okay, let's go," Cait said, giving Kinsley's foot

another nudge. "A sleepover at my house. Bring the Milk Duds."

Cait's gaze met Shaw's for a second, and something passed between them. Some kind of unspoken conversation between siblings. Shaw gave Cait's hand a squeeze before Kinsley and she headed back down the hayloft stairs.

"We keep ending up here," Sunny said, thinking they could use some levity.

She hadn't expected it to work, but Shaw managed a slight smile before he shifted positions and dropped down beside her. Sighing, cursing, he pulled her into his arms.

"Marty and his shit storms," Shaw said. "They're his specialty."

No argument from her on that, and Sunny would have asked him more about this meeting with Leyton, Marty and Aurora, but her phone rang. One look at the screen, and she realized Marty wasn't the only shit storm creator of the day.

Sunshine's name was on the screen.

Sunny nearly hit the decline button, but then she decided it might do Shaw and her some good if they could let Sunshine know that her plan to get back at Shaw had failed.

"Put it on speaker," Shaw said when he saw who the call was from. Obviously, he was on the same venting-and-gloating page as she was.

"Mother," Sunny greeted in the best bite-me tone she could manage. "Guess who just left here?" She didn't wait for Sunshine to answer. "The social worker you sicced on Shaw. But having her come here was a waste of time. Everything was cleared up, and CPS didn't take Kinsley."

Well, most of that was true, but everything was far from being cleared up. Still, no reason to tell Sunshine that.

"Cat got your tongue?" Shaw asked when Sunshine didn't say anything.

"You think you've won?" Sunshine finally snapped. "Well, you haven't. Call off your lawyer, Shaw."

"No," he said without a second of hesitation. "I'm not going to make it easy for you to screw over Sunny by publishing her sketchbooks."

"We'll see about that." Sunshine was still snapping. "There's plenty about my daughter that you don't know. Plenty that she doesn't know about you."

Sunny looked at Shaw to see if he knew what Sunshine was talking about, but he shook his head. Sunny didn't have a clue, either.

"Call off your lawyer," Sunshine repeated, "or Sunny will find out exactly the kind of man you really are."

CHAPTER SEVENTEEN

SHAW WOKE UP the moment he heard his front door open. As usual, it hadn't been locked, but he'd never had someone just walk in at—he checked the clock on the nightstand—three in the morning.

Definitely not normal visiting hours.

If it'd been one of the hands coming to inform him of an emergency, they would have knocked. So, this was family and likely a different kind of emergency. Hell. Considering that he hadn't heard from Leyton as to how his meeting had gone with Marty and Aurora, it could be his brother delivering bad news.

Shaw gripped the covers to throw them back so he could get up, but his bedroom door opened. There was no light on in the room, and he'd pulled the curtains, but there was enough illumination coming from the light over his stove that he could see his visitor.

Sunny.

"Good, you're awake," she said. She closed the door, plunging the room back into darkness, but as his eyes adjusted, he could see that she was taking off her clothes.

So, maybe not an emergency or chat time. She slipped under the covers and managed to locate his mouth, her kiss filled with a level of heat and urgency he had no trouble interpreting. She was horny as all get-out, and it had the effect on Shaw of making him instantly horny, too.

"I couldn't sleep," Sunny said when she paused her kissing to gulp in some air. "So, I decided to drive over here and jump you."

"Best idea ever," he assured her.

Shaw hauled her on top of him. Only then did he remember the blasted incision, and he would have pulled away if Sunny hadn't clamped on to him. "As long as we keep the lights off, I'll be okay."

He hated that the scar bothered her so much, but he didn't get a chance to dwell on it because she ran her hand between their bodies. He was wearing his usual sleepwear, a pair of boxers, but as she'd managed to locate his mouth, she found his erection and clamped her hand over it.

His eyes crossed.

She French-kissed him while she gave him a few squeezes that convinced Shaw that she was in a bit of a hurry. Shaw didn't mind a little hurrying, but they'd done the speed thing in his office chair. He wanted to slow things down a bit so he gently flipped her until she was beneath him.

Shaw French-kissed her right back and then took his mouth and tongue to her neck. He wanted to go lower to her breasts, but that was tricky territory so he kissed his way down to her stomach. Her muscles tightened and stirred there.

She inched her legs apart, and the stirring picked up when he went even lower. Not to the center of her heat. Too obvious. Too fast. Though he was very interested in tasting her there, he'd save that for later. For now he settled on sliding his tongue over the inside of her thigh. And he added plenty of breath.

Obviously, it was having the intended effect because she pulled his hair and called him a bad name. Who knew that Funny Sunny had a trashy mouth when aroused.

Shaw played around awhile with the thigh kisses, making sure he hit every spot that closely surrounded the Brazilian wax. Then, he moved in and took the playing to whole different level.

Sunny moaned, lifted her hips and called him the dirtiest name he'd ever been called. She dug the heels of her feet into his bed, levering herself up. Shaw levered, too, by catching her hips and anchoring her just where he wanted her. He finished her off with a couple of flicks of his tongue.

He'd been right about her tasting good, and it didn't matter that he hadn't been able to see her. Though he wouldn't mind getting an up close and personal look at that part of her later. His dick was throbbing too much for that now, and he wanted to bury himself inside her.

"I'm not good at BJs," she muttered in her postorgasmic silky voice. "But I can try to give you one."

Shaw nearly told her that even a bad BJ from her would be pretty damn good, but then he remembered their first sexual encounter and realized that might be tempting fate.

"No need," he assured her. He groped around in his nightstand drawer and came up with what he was looking for. "I've got a condom," he told her.

Sunny made a sound of approval—a silky, sated moan—and she reached between them to try to help him get it on. He didn't need her help. He'd never had sex without a condom and had never had trouble getting one on. Still, it was interesting torture to have her hands fumbling around his hard-on.

"I think Sunshine saw something in the sketches," she said.

Shaw heard her, barely, but his pulse was drumming in his ears and that dick throbbing was still going on. So were Sunny's attempts to slide the condom on him.

"I think she might have noticed how much I… cared for you," Sunny went on. "My feelings probably came through in the pictures."

"Uh-huh," Shaw managed.

Together they finally got the condom on him in quadruple the time that it would have taken him if he'd done it solo. But he got an instant reward for the insanity-inducing effort. Sunny flipped them, straddling him, and with her knees spread wide, she took him inside her.

Deep, all the way inside her.

If he could have called her a dirty name, he would have, but sadly, his dick wasn't going to spare him enough air to talk.

"I'm not good at BJs," she repeated, "but I can manage this."

Yes. Yes, she could. Apparently, riding the hell out of him was a talent of hers. Shaw could only see a shadowy silhouette of her above him. The shape of her. Her breasts, the curve of her waist and her hips that she maneuvered like a woman on a mission. And that mission was obviously to make him bat-shit crazy.

She anchored her hands on his chest, leaning down to give him a deep kiss to go along with the deep moves she was putting on him where they were joined. He wanted to wait for her to climax again so he had to fight the demand in his own body, the primal push that was urging him on.

"I like your size," she said. No post-sex sultriness now. She was getting a primal push, too. "You can touch me in all the right places at the same time."

Shaw managed a grunt of appreciation, and just in case his dick was missing a key spot, he reached between them and found that extrasensitive nub. He used his fingers now to give her a flick the way his tongue had done minutes earlier.

She flew like a kite.

Sunny stuttered out a gasp of pleasure and slumped forward, her weight on her hands that she still had on his chest. That was his cue to gather her against him and use his size that she liked so much to let her orgasm squeeze and slide him to his own release.

She collapsed onto him, gave him another kiss and then dropped onto her back. "Much better," she said.

Shaw chuckled, kissed her. "Glad I could help."

Because she was stretching and purring in such a way that made him think they could soon go another round, Shaw got up to make a quick pit stop in the adjoining bathroom. He turned on the light and caught a glimpse of himself in the mirror. Now that his brain wasn't muddled with the primal stuff, Shaw began to recall what Sunny had said to him right before she'd given him the ride of his life.

"Uh, what were you saying about Sunshine maybe seeing something in the sketches?" he called out to her.

No response.

He started to repeat his question a little louder but then he looked around the door jamb. She was sacked out on her back with her arms outstretched. Her legs, too, for that matter. He caught a glimpse of that very intriguing Brazilian. And her breasts.

Shaw took a step closer, feeling like a privacy-invading perv, but that didn't stop him from looking at the scar. A pinkish-red line that ran from the side of her left nipple to the bottom of her breast. He didn't see it as ugly, but he knew it was visual proof of something that had scared her. Scared her enough to bring her back home.

Scared enough that she didn't want him to see it.

He went closer, easing down on the side of the bed so that he wouldn't wake her. Judging from the deep rhythm of her breathing, though, that wasn't going to happen. And she didn't stir a muscle when his weight caused the mattress to shift a little.

Shaw leaned down and gently pressed his lips to the scar, and it occurred to him that it was probably the only time in his life he'd kissed a woman's breast when it hadn't been foreplay.

God, he hated that she'd gone through something that had twisted her up and left her feeling less than adequate. Oh, she was adequate all right.

He pulled back when she snorted out a little breath,

and she shifted, moving onto her side. That's when he saw it on her butt.

A heart tattoo.

Sunny certainly hadn't had that when they'd had sex in the hayloft.

The light from the bathroom wasn't cooperating with his getting a better look so Shaw stood and moved around to the end of the bed. He sure as heck saw it then. It was a heart all right, but instead of lines forming the shape, there were words.

Love you forever.

And in the center was Shaw's name.

SUNNY FOUND HERSELF doing some smiling on the drive back to Em's. Mercy, she'd slept well. The best night's sleep in ages, and she could thank Shaw for that. Could thank Shaw, too, for not pushing to turn on the lights when she'd finally woken up, gotten out of his bed and dressed. He'd been tender and amazing.

And a little quiet.

Maybe he just wasn't a morning person, but she suspected it was because he knew what the morning could bring. Right before she'd left he had gotten a text from Leyton, telling him that nothing had been resolved the night before with Marty and Aurora but that he was meeting again with them this morning. Shaw had to know that Leyton could fail.

If he did, that could be disastrous for Kinsley.

Permission for the girl to stay at the ranch might not keep CPS from taking her, especially since both of her parents had essentially abandoned her. That wiped the smile off Sunny's face, and it stayed gone when she pulled in front of Em's and saw the familiar car.

Crap.

What was Hugh doing here?

It was barely dawn, and he was leaning against his Audi, clearly waiting for her. Judging from the big bouquet of red roses he was holding, he had hopes of making up with her. There was also a thick manila envelope on the hood of his car.

Sunny didn't bother trying to comb her hair or look as if she hadn't just climbed out of bed with Shaw. In fact, she hoped that Shaw had left a hickey on her so that Hugh would get the message that she'd moved on with her life and that then he'd leave.

"I've been waiting for you," he said when she stepped from her SUV. It didn't have an accusatory tone. Nor was there the unspoken question—*Where the hell have you been?* He went Mr. Darcy on her with a polite *yes, I've been an ass but please forgive me* smile.

Sadly, that would have worked a few months ago, but Sunny knew now that a smiling ass was still just an ass.

He thrust out the flowers for her to take, but Sunny simply folded her arms over her chest.

"I didn't invite him in," Em said from the front window that she'd opened—probably so she could keep an eye on Hugh and make sure he didn't try to sneak in or something.

Or maybe Em had been waiting up for her. Sunny had left her a note in the kitchen so that her grandmother wouldn't worry if she woke up and found her gone. Still, Em would want to make sure she was okay. Sunny had been more than okay until she'd seen Hugh.

"A guilty fox hunts in his own hole," Em added, giving the window a loud shut that was the equivalent of slamming a door.

Hugh's forehead bunched up. "What does that mean?"

Sunny didn't have a clue, and since she couldn't explain what she was certain had been a diss, she just moved on to her question. "Why are you here?"

Hugh tried that smile again, but it didn't make her think of Mr. Darcy. More like Voldemort. "I have a proposition," he said. "One that will benefit all of us."

Sunny gave him a flat look. "What, your investors are still giving you grief about Ryan and me not being around?"

"They are," he readily admitted. "And that's why what I'm offering you is more of a business proposition." He took a long breath as if gearing up for a sales pitch. "I'll lose a lot of money without these investors, which means I'll gain a lot if the deal goes through."

Hugh tossed the flowers onto the hood of his car, picked up the manila envelope and handed it to her. She wasn't any more interested in taking it than she had been the roses.

"What do you want?" she repeated. "And I'm warning you, that's the last time I ask. If you don't spill all in the next thirty seconds—spill everything without using a book quote—" she emphasized, "I'm going inside. You won't be going in with me."

His next breath was more like a weary sigh. "I'm

offering you everything you want," he said with the envelope still outstretched to her. "It's all there in writing. A contract that I've already signed. I'll spend at least ten hours a week with Ryan. Of course, that'll have to be done with phone calls once he's moved to Austin to go to college. I'll pay for all his expenses."

Her next breath was a huff. "Those are things you should be doing, Hugh. You shouldn't need a contract for it."

"Well, obviously I haven't been doing it or Ryan wouldn't be here with you, and you wouldn't be so upset on his behalf."

He had her there. She still wasn't signing a contract.

"There's more," Hugh went on. "If you do Slackers's reading hours in my stores, I'll pay you well for your time. I'll marry you," he quickly added when she opened her mouth to huff again. "And there'll be no birth control. You can have that baby you've always wanted."

Again, her huff got cut off when the front door flew open and Ryan came out. Maybe the sound of their voices had woken him, but it was obvious that he'd just gotten up. He was still in sleep pants and a tee, and his hair was tousled.

"You're not signing that," Ryan told her, letting Sunny know that he'd heard at least part of their conversation. "She's not signing that," Ryan repeated to his dad.

Hugh shrugged. "That's Sunny's decision, not yours." As if he'd rehearsed it, his expression softened. "I love you, son, and I want the three of us to be a family again."

That was likely rehearsed, too, and the man certainly knew which of her buttons to push. He knew what she wanted—a happy Ryan and a baby. But it couldn't happen, not like this. Sunny would have spelled that out for Hugh, too, if he hadn't tossed the envelope onto the porch.

"I'll give you a day or two to think it over. Think it over," Hugh repeated. "Ryan can have his father, and next year at this time, you could be a mother."

With that, Hugh got in his car and left. The bouquet of roses tumbled off the hood and was crushed by one of his rear tires.

"Don't sign it," Ryan repeated to her. He stood there, staring at the dust that the Audi had kicked up, watching his worthless tool of a dad drive away—no doubt taking another piece of Ryan's heart with him.

Sunny automatically reached for him, pulling him into her arms, and even though Ryan was taller than she was, she put his head on her shoulder. "I'm sorry," she said, knowing the words wouldn't fix anything.

"Don't sign it," Ryan said again. "I don't need his money for college. I can work and get student loans."

"I've put money aside."

He lifted his head, shook it. "You don't have to do that."

"No, but I want to do it."

And there could be even more money if she sold her condo and moved back in here with Em. A few weeks ago that would have been unthinkable, but with the way things were going with Shaw, Lone Star

Ridge was the only place she wanted to be. Plus, it would be a lot closer to Ryan's college than Houston. It could be the perfect solution, and it would give her a chance to see where things were going with Shaw.

"My dad offered to get you pregnant," Ryan said with a tinge of anger in his voice. "He wants to lure you back by giving you something you don't have. By giving you the kid you've always wanted."

Now, here was where words might actually help. Sunny pressed her hand on his cheek. "I've already got a kid, Ryan. I've got you, and I love you."

She saw it immediately. The surprise followed by the smile that let her know she hadn't assumed too much or crossed a line that Ryan hadn't wanted her to cross.

"I love you, too… Mom."

Well, crud. That brought her to tears, but they were definitely of the happy variety. She gathered him back in her arms for the hardest, longest hug she could manage.

Ironically, Hugh had given her a child after all.

No contract or sex needed.

She pulled away from him, dried her happy tears and would have led him into the house for celebratory waffles, but Sunny groaned when she heard the approaching car engine. Good grief. She hoped Hugh hadn't come back, but thankfully it wasn't his Audi. It was a black car that she didn't recognize. Ditto for the man who stepped out from the driver's seat.

"Ms. Sunny Dalton?" the man asked.

She nodded, and he immediately went to her and reached out to give her a thick envelope.

"This is for you," he said.

She groaned. "You can tell Hugh Dunbar I'm not taking that."

He shook his head. "This isn't from Hugh Dunbar. It's from Sunshine Dalton. She hired me to deliver this to you."

Sheez. That was just as bad. Was it her day to get envelopes from people she no longer wanted in her life?

"I don't want anything from Sunshine, either," Sunny snarled.

The man gave a suit-yourself shrug, thrust the envelope into her hands and, much to Sunny's surprise, he left. She debated throwing it in the trash along with Hugh's contract, which was still on the porch, but if Sunshine had launched into a new "make Shaw and Sunny miserable" campaign, then she wanted to know what she was up against.

Sunny pulled out what appeared to be a handful of legal papers. But it was the sticky note on the front of them that snagged her attention.

"Thought you'd like to know the truth about your favorite cowboy," her mother had written. "It was all a sham, Sunny. All a sham."

CHAPTER EIGHTEEN

SHAW HAD PLENTY of hands to ride fence and check for any needed repairs, but this morning he'd given himself that particular chore. He'd hoped the mind-less ambling around on a horse and occasionally getting off to hammer a loose nail or two would clear his head.

So far, it hadn't.

No matter how much fence he checked or how many nails he hammered, he couldn't get the image of Sunny's tat out of his mind.

Love you forever.

Maybe getting it had been some kind of impulse. Sunny's way of remembering losing her virginity to him. Or even a drunken celebration that had ended in a tattoo parlor while she offered up her butt cheek to a tat artist. That didn't seem like Sunny's style, but Shaw had firsthand knowledge that tequila shots and such often led to decisions that reasonable sober people didn't make.

It could also be that at the time she'd gotten it, Sunny had truly felt that she loved him. His feelings for her back then had certainly been deep. Not enough for *love you forever*, but he had been pretty young and not looking for anything permanent. Since Sunny had already been making plans to leave Lone Star Ridge, he hadn't figured *forever* was on her to-do list, either.

So, maybe this was a decision accompanied by a high blood alcohol level. That would have settled a lot better in his mind if it weren't for one big thing.

She hadn't had it removed.

It was still there, highly visible to anyone who ever saw her naked. He remembered Hugh's reaction when Shaw had introduced himself.

I know who you are. I got almost daily reminders of you before Sunny and I broke up.

At the time, Hugh's comment hadn't made much sense, but it sure as heck did now. Any time Hugh had caught sight of his fiancée's ass cheek, he'd seen Shaw's name—inside a *Love You Forever* heart, no less. Being the jerk Hugh was, he'd certainly wanted Sunny to get rid of it, and she hadn't. Why?

Shaw wasn't sure he wanted to ask her that. Because it could open a big can of worms about not only her feelings for him in the past but also her feelings now. He wasn't ready for that, wasn't ready to hear her laugh off the tat as a stupid, drunk mistake, either. Wasn't ready for her to confess that she had indeed loved him forever but couldn't be with him because of the baby issue.

No.

He preferred to stay in the dark at least for a while longer until he could sort out this jumble in his mind. The last thing he wanted was a conversation that would lead to some kind of ultimatum that would send Sunny running again.

Shaw rode back to the main house, figuring that

since the fence repairs hadn't fixed his head, he'd at least get some paperwork done, but the moment he stepped into the barn, he knew head fixing would have to wait.

Leyton was there.

One look at his brother's face and Shaw knew he was in for a dose of bad news. "What'd Marty do now?" Shaw asked automatically.

"Not enough," Leyton said right off, confirming Shaw's premonition. "I had two meetings with Marty and Aurora, and ended up going to see a lawyer to draw up some paperwork. Both Marty and Aurora will sign documents claiming Marty's paternity of Kinsley."

Okay. That didn't sound bad since Marty was her father. "And?" Shaw prompted because he was still waiting for the other boot to fall.

Leyton gathered his breath. "Aurora says she just can't deal with Kinsley, that she needs a break, and she doesn't have a clue how long that break will be."

"Obviously, a candidate for World's Bestest Mom," Shaw grumbled.

His brother made a sound of agreement. "Aurora said Marty could take Kinsley, that she's had to deal with her for the past fifteen years and now it was Marty's turn."

Not a news flash since Aurora had already said something similar. "How'd Marty react to that?" Shaw asked.

"In that *not enough* way of his. He's going to relinquish custody, too, though he will pay child support and set up a trust fund for her."

Yeah, not nearly enough. "Where does that leave Kinsley?"

Leyton didn't have a quick answer for that, but Shaw could see where this was going. "If one of us doesn't take her, CPS will," Shaw said.

His brother nodded, added some profanity, and they both stood there mentally shaking their heads along with wanting to rip Marty a new one. Their cursing ended when Shaw spotted Sunny making her way toward him.

Correction: she was storming toward him.

"What'd you do to piss her off?" Leyton asked, glancing back at Sunny.

"I'm about to find out. Excuse me for a minute," Shaw said, walking toward Sunny.

"Are these true?" she demanded, waving a fistful of papers at him.

Shaw wanted to tell her he needed a tad more information than a fist wave so once he had caught up with her, he took the paper from her hand and had a look. They were legal documents from *Little Cowgirls*, and...

Shit.

Specifically, they were copies of *his* legal documents, the ones Marty had signed since Shaw had been a minor at the time. Any time Shaw was to appear on screen, it had required a signed release that detailed exactly what he was to do in the scene. There were ones for him bringing horses into the corral, teaching Sunny to ride, but he immediately saw the one that had pissed her off.

The episode called "Sunny's Heart-throb."

Where he'd been instructed to kiss her.

"Marty signed that the day before that whole 'sore nuts' fiasco," Sunny pointed out. "Did the producers tell you to kiss me?"

Oh, this was so not going to sound good. "Yes. But I'd been thinking about kissing you." Hell, he'd got hard-ons thinking about her.

She huffed so loud that he doubted she heard anything past the yes. "Did they tell you to spend time with me?"

Again, so not going to sound good. "Yes. But I would have spent time with you even if they hadn't said that. I was attracted to you." Along with trying to resist her because of the age difference. And he was getting those hard-ons.

That earned him another huff. And worse, there was the look of betrayal in her eyes. She marched a few steps away and then turned right back around to spear him with those betrayed eyes.

"Why didn't you tell me?" she asked. Not so much a demand as her other questions, and her voice trembled a little.

Shitting shit shit.

Why had this come back to haunt him now?

Shaw had the answer to that when he saw Sunshine's sticky note. He had just finished reading it and had started to feel the anger and bile rise up inside him when Em's truck came to a noisy, fast stop next to Sunny's SUV. But it wasn't Em who got out. It was Ryan. Obviously, the boy was worried about Sunny.

Welcome to the club. Shaw was worried about her, too.

"I didn't tell you because I was an idiot teenager

when all of this happened," Shaw said. "And I honestly forgot about it."

Apparently, that wasn't the right thing to say to her because the look of betrayal turned to one of heartbreaking hurt. "You forgot that the producers told you to be my boyfriend?"

When she put it like that, it made him want to amend his idiot-teenager label to include that he was obviously an idiot adult. Since he didn't want to continue any idiocy, he settled for saying, "I'm sorry. I'm especially sorry that your mother used me and this to hurt you."

Her mouth trembled again, and she stared at him a long time before she nodded. It didn't seem to be an acceptance of his apology or this situation. More like resignation.

"I have to go," she muttered. Shaw reached for her to maybe pull her into his arms, but she waved him off. "I have to go," she repeated.

She stopped only long enough to say something to Ryan that Shaw couldn't hear. Then she got in her SUV and drove away.

Ryan watched her leave before he walked to Shaw and handed him something. Bloody hell. Not more papers.

"Did I sign away my soul to the devil or something?" Shaw snarled.

"No, but that's what Sunny might do."

Shaw's gaze snapped to Ryan's to see if the boy was making a really bad joke. But, no, there wasn't a joke anywhere in his expression.

"It's a contract that my dad wants her to sign,"

Ryan explained. "He says he'll be a real dad to me and give her a baby. All she has to do is go back to him."

Yeah, definitely no joke, but it was laughable. "Sunny won't go back to Hugh, not after the way he's acted."

"That's what I thought, too, and then she got those." Ryan tipped his head to the release forms that in a way had been like selling his soul. He just hadn't known it at the time.

"Sunny's so upset that she might do something she'll regret," Ryan went on. "You have to stop her from signing her life away."

SUNNY DUG HER pencil so hard into the sketch pad that the paper tore. She had known she was in the wrong mood to draw a children's cartoon character, and the ripped paper proved it. Sunny tossed the pencil and sketch pad aside and went to the window of her bedroom.

It was raining, and the sky was a dull thick gray that mimicked her mood. She was mopey and sulking—she knew that, too—but she just hadn't been able to break out of this pit of despair. What a difference twenty-four hours could make. Yesterday, she'd climbed out of bed with Shaw and had felt on top of the world. Today, she was on the bottom of it.

She was wavering between bouts of cursing Shaw and wanting to douse Sunshine with the prune surprise and mosquito traps. When she wasn't feeling one of those specific things, she was crying.

God, it shouldn't hurt this bad.

Not for something that had happened a lifetime

ago, but it shook her to the core to think that the *Little Cowgirls* producers or—heaven forbid—her mother had convinced Shaw to agree to being with her. Kissing her. Which in turn had made her fall in love with him.

Plenty would say that it was first love and therefore wasn't real, but Sunny knew that it had been. And that every man she'd met or been with since had never stacked up to Shaw.

That was the reality that cut to the core, too.

With her defenses stripped down, her heart on her sleeve, Sunny knew that no man would ever stack up, either. Shaw was her Achilles' heel, her blind spot.

And the love of her life.

Too bad she would have to give up the second love of her life—a baby—to be with him. Of course, maybe Shaw had decided he didn't want to keep dealing with the likes of Sunshine and the crud she kept bringing into his life.

Her phone buzzed again with a call. Sunny didn't even look at the screen because she had no intention of answering it. Sunshine had put out the word about Shaw's *contracted work* on *Little Cowgirls*, and that had spurred the potential suitors to start calling her again. That's why she'd silenced her phone and put it on vibrate, but even that sound was annoying to her, so she reached down and flicked it off. Sunny had no sooner done that when there was a knock at the door.

Em.

She knew it was her before she even opened it. And Sunny immediately took a step back. Because Em was holding a duck. A wet one. Em was wet, too, the raindrops beading on her red slicker, which told Sunny that her grandmother had picked this particular waterfowl from her critter menagerie.

"Brought someone to cheer you up," Em said. "Hard to stay blue with a duck around."

Sunny wasn't so sure about that, but the duck was indeed cute. White fluffy feathers and a bright yellow bill. Sunny reached out to stroke its head, but it made a weird sound. Not a quack. More like a loud, protesting squawk. Not just one, either, but a stream of them that sounded like a distress signal.

"I've named him Slackers," Em went on, ignoring the squawks. "I'm going to take him to the school during my community service reading time. But I also thought he could give you some inspiration for your drawings."

When the duck began to flap around, Em set it on the floor, and with those high-pitched squawks, it waddled with lightning speed underneath Sunny's bed.

"I need to talk to you about Ryan," Em said.

Sunny had been about to go after the duck, but that stopped her. "Is something wrong?" She instantly felt guilty about her moping. Yes, she'd checked on him, had even had pizza with him the night before, but he had to be hurting just as much as she was.

"You could say that. I overheard him talking on the phone to someone at the college," Em explained. "He's got a chance to do some fancy-shmancy summer program in Austin, but he's turning it down because he doesn't want to leave you alone."

Her heart went to her knees. "Ryan said that?"

"Not in those exact words, but that's the gist of it."

For Pete's sake. The duck would have to wait. Sunny went in search of Ryan. He wasn't in his room but rather in the dining room, where he preferred to work. He was on his computer but looked up when she came in and offered her a thin "I'm worried about you" smile. Sunny offered him the same in return.

"Em blabbed," she said. "I know about the summer program you were offered." Sunny sank down in the chair next to him.

"It's no big deal. It's just a series of enrichment workshops for students interested in premed."

"That sounds like the very definition of a big deal." Sunny sighed. "I'm okay. I'm not going to fall apart, and I don't want you giving up anything—even a little deal—because you're worried about me. If you're determined to worry, you can do that in Austin during these workshops. Then I can worry about you worrying about me."

She'd added that last part to put a lighter spin on this, and it sort of worked. He gave her a slight smile.

"Things suck for you right now," he said. "I'd have to leave next week, and that seems too soon."

She slid her hand over his. "Things don't suck all the way for me right now. I'm the mother of a six-foot-tall bouncing baby boy who should take premed enrichment workshops." Sunny paused. "You're concerned about the money."

That put some fire in his eyes. "You're not signing that stupid contract with my dad," he insisted.

"No, I'm not. And I don't need to sign it to pay for your classes and a place for you to stay." Thank goodness for *Slackers Quackers*. "What about Kinsley? Have you told her about these workshops?"

Ryan nodded. "We've talked. She's okay with it. And she's sort of wrapped up in her own stuff right now."

Yes, Sunny had seen the way Marty had reacted to the girl, had been with Kinsley afterward in the hayloft. She was hurting, and Marty and her mom certainly weren't helping. For now, though, Sunny put that aside to focus on Ryan.

"Would you be able to stay in the dorm for these workshops?" she asked. "Because I wouldn't want you moving into an apartment or a place where you'd be alone."

"I could move into the dorm." There was still hesitation in Ryan's voice, his expression.

"Then that's what you'll do." She brushed a kiss on the top of his head.

The hesitation continued, but she could see him working his way through this. "I'll pay you back when I can."

Sunny sighed again. She'd won the kid lottery when it came to Ryan. "I'll take payment in free medical care after you're a doctor. Go ahead. Make whatever arrangements you need to move into the dorm next week."

"Thank you." He stood and hugged her. It qualified as the best hug ever.

Feeling a whole lot better, Sunny turned to go back upstairs, and she practically ran right into Shaw. Her heart did a little flip-flop, and she didn't think it was because he'd startled her. Shaw often had that effect on her. Sometimes, like now, she forgot how to breathe.

He wasn't looking his best today. The rain had soaked his hat, which he gripped in his hand. Had gotten to his shirt, too, because it was clinging to his chest. His hair was rumpled, his eyes were tired, his forehead was bunched up. Still, he ticked off all the "hot cowboy" boxes, especially since she supposed those tired eyes were because of her.

Ryan and he exchanged a glance, one that she suspected comrades would share, and for the first time she wondered if they'd talked after she'd driven away from Shaw.

"I wanted to give you some time," Shaw said to her. "But not enough time to think about accepting Hugh's offer. Ryan showed me the contract," he added.

"I blabbed," Ryan readily admitted.

She gave Ryan a look to let him know that was okay, that it was all part of this package of them having the right to worry about each other. Which meant they had the right to get in each other's business.

"I'll burn the contract if I can find it," Sunny assured Shaw.

"Then, I'll make sure you find it. It's in my truck. I would have burned it myself, but, well, it wasn't my place to do that." He mumbled something she didn't catch and took her by the hand. "Come with me. I want to show you something."

"It's not a duck, is it?" she asked, causing him to blink twice.

"No. It's…not a duck." The way he paused, it made

her think he'd planned to say something else entirely. So, unlike Em he hadn't intended to use a duck to try to cheer her up.

She expected him to take her outside to his truck, but he headed up the stairs instead and led her to her bedroom. The door was closed, but when he opened it, there was no sign of Em or the duck.

"I'm going to call my lawyer and tell him to back off fighting Sunshine," Shaw said, still leading her. He took her to the window, the very one she'd been staring out earlier. "That'll give her the go-ahead to sell or publish the sketchbooks."

Sunny couldn't shake her head fast enough. "No. Don't. If you do that, she wins. I don't want her to win."

Shaw's response was fast, too. "And I don't want her to keep dicking around with our lives."

They were in complete agreement on this. "I called Hayes and told him to try to fix this. I laid a guilt trip on him because all of this started with Tonya and those diaries. Yes, I know that's not a direct connection to what Em did to get back at Sunshine, but Hayes might do something just to stop me from pestering him."

"That's a long shot," Shaw pointed out. "Especially when it comes to your brother."

That was Hayes in a nutshell. A long shot when it came to anything dealing with family.

"Hayes could come through, but even if he doesn't, I struck that deal with Sunshine. Em didn't have to go to jail, and that's what counts."

He searched her eyes as if trying to figure out if

she meant that. She did. But the eye search also meant their gazes were connected. Coupled with the fact that he was still holding her hand, it suddenly felt very intimate between them.

"Want me to tell you about the first hard-on you gave me?" he asked.

She blinked twice. Apparently, it had felt intimate for him, too, and she automatically glanced down at the zipper of his jeans.

The corner of his mouth hitched into one of those smiles. The one that let her know that he had an erection in the making. But he didn't kiss her or try to coax her closer. Shaw put his hand on her waist and turned her so that she was looking not at him but rather outside.

He pointed in the direction of the barn. "I was in there," he said. "I was fifteen, and you were thirteen. You'd been riding a mare I'd brought over, and it started to rain. Your shirt got wet, but you were having so much fun that you stayed with the ride a while longer. And I watched you," he added.

Sunny didn't remember the specific incident. Too bad. "That was the summer I got breasts."

"Yeah," he immediately confirmed. He sighed. "And I guess that makes me a perv."

"No, it just made you a teenager."

She looked at him now, remembering that boy. Remembering them together. And especially remembering that even now her feelings for him hadn't changed.

"I didn't need signed permission or instructions from producers to want to be with you, Sunny." His voice had gone down a husky notch. "That happened all by itself. The contracts and release forms just gave me an excuse to be here around you."

It was as if his words had slapped a gigantic bandage on the hurt she had felt when she'd thought the attention he'd given her had been orchestrated. Scripted. As phony as so much of *Little Cowgirls* had been. But now that she'd gotten over the shock, Sunny knew in her heart that it hadn't been like that.

"Your erection proved it," she said. Perhaps she should have given him some kind of intro to that comment, but it made him smile that lazy, dreamy, cocky smile that caused every cell in her body to want him.

"I can still prove it." He took her hand and pressed it to the front of his jeans.

Yes, he could. Full liftoff had been achieved, and those needy cells of hers moved in for a kiss. Her mouth met his, barely a touch, but it still packed a wallop.

Shaw didn't keep it a touch. He pulled her closer, kissing her deep while her hand stayed pressed to his erection. It was definitely accelerated foreplay, and Sunny felt herself go damp in the right place. Since her right place was so close to his, she moved her hand so their *places* could meet. Body bumping and nudging was old-school, but it still did the trick of spiking up the pleasure and making her want to jump him where he stood.

But where he stood was right in front of the window, where anyone could see them.

Where Shaw could see her.

Suddenly those heated-up cells in her body turned to jangled nerves.

"Uh, Em and Ryan are in the house," she reminded him.

While he waylaid her with another scorching kiss, Shaw backed her across the room, shut the door and locked it.

"You don't want to know how many times I thought about this," he said with his mouth still on hers.

"Nailing me in my bedroom?" The nerves had spread the jangle to her voice. Of course, the kiss wasn't helping with that because she didn't have enough spare breath to manage more than a breathy whisper that made her sound like a sex kitten.

"Nailing you in that bed." He broke the kiss only long enough to tip his head in that direction. It was in the corner, but there was still plenty of light.

"Excuse me a second." Sunny hurried back to the window, yanking the curtains closed, and she turned off the lights. She could still see Shaw, which meant he could do the same.

With a touch as gentle as his earlier kiss had been, he put his hand on the small of her back, eased her to him. Close but not touching. Plenty close enough for him to look her in the eyes.

"I saw your scar," he said. "Yesterday morning at my house."

Oh.

"You were asleep," he went on, "and I didn't mean to see it, but when I came out of the bathroom, the light was right."

Which meant the light was wrong.

"It's not ugly and it doesn't turn me off," Shaw added when she stayed silent.

Sunny didn't stay silent. She huffed. "It is ugly."

"It's a scar. One will that heal. And it doesn't turn me off. Nothing about you turns me off. Let me prove that to you."

When he unzipped his jeans, she thought he was about to show her right then, right there. But he only lowered his boxers and jeans on one side, not to free the erection that was *obviously* still there. Instead, he tapped the white scar on his groin.

"Emergency appendectomy five years ago," he said. "Does it turn you off?"

It wasn't the same. Well, almost not the same. But Sunny had no choice but to answer no.

"Good." He looked her straight in the eyes and shoved his jeans and boxers farther down on his hips. Now, that freed his erection. "Does this turn you off?"

Sunny went hot. A serious wave of heat consumed her and she wished she had better BJ skills or she would have gotten on her knees and done something with that heat.

"No, it doesn't turn me off," she whispered, and she launched herself at him, kissing him and touching him at the same time.

Shaw kissed and touched, too. This wasn't a gentle, slow pace. Nope. This was a hair-pulling, bruising, "take me now, now, now" kind of pace. The bruises happened when they rammed into her bed right before they fell on it.

One thing was for certain—Shaw wasn't treating her with kid gloves, which meant he'd somehow managed to put her surgery and the scar out of his mind. That was possibly because the insane need had pushed everything except sex from their minds.

He landed on top of her and shoved up her dress, pulling it off over her head. The bra came next, and here he did gentle a little when he flicked open the front clasp and her breast spilled out for his waiting mouth.

Oh, yes. She got some tongue kisses on her nipples.

And Sunny forgot about the scar, too.

Next, Shaw went after her panties. Since he wasn't inept at that particular skill, she had to guess that the finger that slipped inside had been meant to take off the top of her head and not because he'd misjudged the position of the elastic legs of her panties.

No, he hadn't misjudged.

Sunny got confirmation of that when he stroked her a few more times, also proving his incredible skill of making sure she was starved for him and his impressive erection.

She whimpered when he stopped the strokes, but then she realized he was fumbling around in his wallet for a condom. His vast skills continued because he had it on in a blink of an eye.

And then he was inside her.

He went still, looking down at her the way a starving man would eye a delicious meal. "Good thing you're not a screamer," he drawled with that smile that only Shaw the Greek god of sexual pleasure could have managed.

At that moment there was a very loud squawk. Shaw looked at her as if she'd been the one to make it. "The duck," she said.

Obviously, Em hadn't taken Slackers with her, but Sunny had no intention of explaining all of that to Shaw right now. The only thing she wanted from him was what he was giving her.

He started to move.

Shaw was a pro at that, too. Long, deep strokes while he watched what it was doing to her. He must have liked what he saw on her face because he somehow managed a smile.

"Go over for me, Sunny. Let me watch you."

She didn't have a choice about either of those things. The strokes turned to thrusts and got faster. Even deeper. Building and building and building until Sunny found herself on that incredible edge between wanting this to last forever and needing for him to finish her.

All the while, she watched him, too.

She had thought of the darkness as a way to hide her scar, but she realized now the too-high price of missing that look in his storm-gray eyes. That look was a big reveal. And she saw that he hadn't lied, that the scar didn't matter, that he hadn't needed a contract to feel the way he did. She saw the hot greedy need that he was counting on her to sate. She saw this incredible man who was giving her the best sex of her life.

The best orgasm of her life followed.

She tipped over the edge, giving in to the need to

finish this. Apparently, Shaw had no trouble picking up on her climax because a moment later, he joined her.

Even though her pulse and breathing were noisy, Sunny heard the duck squawks. She ignored them and gathered Shaw close. That wasn't hard to do since he was still on top of her. However, the ever-thoughtful cowboy was keeping his weight on his forearms so that he wouldn't crush her.

Shaw's breath was gusting, too, but he lifted his head, kissed her and dropped onto his side. Somehow, he managed to turn her on her side, too, even though there wasn't an inch of room to spare in the tiny bed.

"Better," he concluded, and this time when he stared at her, it was the look of a man who'd just finished that delicious meal. He reached around her and patted her butt. "Now, do you want to talk about this?"

Because she was still in a hazy state of mind, it took her a moment to realize he didn't want to have a conversation about butt cheeks or her jiggly muscle tone. This was about the tat.

"I saw it," he added. And he left it at that. Not a question, but there were a couple of big unasked questions in those three words.

Love you forever had just come back to haunt her.

She considered lying and spinning a yarn about the stupid things teenage girls can do, but Sunny was afraid her own eyes would be the big reveal. So, she clamped her hand over his mouth.

"Don't say anything," she insisted. "Agree not to say anything ever about the tat and I'll tell you why I got it."

He stared at her a long time, and other than their breathing, the only sound was the rain on the window and Slackers's squawks. Finally he nodded. Then and only then did Sunny slide her hand from his mouth.

"Five years ago I came back to town to see you. It was your thirtieth birthday, and I thought maybe I could retest some old waters." Translation—she'd wanted to see if he was still opposed to marrying and having kids. "But you were seeing the woman who owns the bakery over in Wrangler's Creek. I saw you two together dancing at your birthday party."

Shaw didn't voice the word, but a curse formed on his lips.

"You two looked very…involved, and no, I'm not bashing you for that. You were single, and she was gorgeous. Like a young Marilyn Monroe." Sunny paused. "I left the party before you could see me, and when I asked Cait about the baker, she reluctantly admitted that things might be serious between you two."

Another *curse* formed on his lips.

"Don't blame Cait for not telling you I was there," Sunny went on. "I made her do a sister-sister pinkie swear."

Which she was glad he couldn't ask her about because it sounded as silly as it was. Still, it was sacred, and Cait wouldn't have ratted her out.

"I left and went back to Houston," Sunny continued. "I got drunk and got the tattoo." She stopped, and it seemed as if his eyes had turned into a lie detector. "Okay, I didn't get drunk. I was sad and thinking about the past. I decided I wanted something permanent—a memento of sorts—something that the perfect, non-jiggly baker didn't have."

She winced because that last part had come out a little angrier than she'd intended. Of course, she'd been plenty angry and jealous when she'd gotten the tat. Really, really jealous. Which was stupid because neither Shaw nor she had stopped living when she'd left town.

"The baker didn't have the history I did with you." Sunny made an effort to slough off the anger. "That's what the tat was about. Our history. My feelings for you. The fact that you'd been my first."

He stayed quiet. Kept his eyes on her. And despite his agreement not to talk about the tat, Shaw asked her a question anyway. "Why'd you decide to put the tat on your ass?"

She scowled at him. "No questions," she reminded him. He opened his mouth and closed it, but only after she narrowed her eyes at him.

Sunny was thankful for his closed mouth. And she was glad she'd made him swear not to ask about the tat, because there was one huge question she didn't want to hear.

Do you really love me forever?

The answer to that would send him running. Because the answer was yes.

CHAPTER NINETEEN

SHAW WAS GLAD he'd managed to have makeup sex with Sunny. Glad, too, that he'd just been able to be with her for an hour or so, because if he hadn't had that he'd be in serious trouble right now.

He was facing the family meeting from hell.

His mood was somewhere between kick-ass and kick even more ass, but without resolving that rift with Sunny, he wouldn't have been fit to be around other humans. Of course, not everything was wrapped up in a neat little box with Sunny. Heck, Shaw wasn't even sure there was a box yet, but at least he had her back in his arms, and for now that would have to do.

Even if he couldn't ask her questions about the tat.

He pushed that aside and glanced into the dining room where the others were waiting. It had taken him many phone calls, some yelling, some threats and plenty of cursing, but he'd finally gotten all the interested parties under the same roof.

Marty and Aurora, who'd arrived only minutes apart. Followed by Cait, Austin, Leyton. Lenore was at the table, as well.

With no threats or cajoling necessary, he'd included his mother in on this because it was entirely possible that she would become the voice of reason they might need. Shaw wasn't counting on Cait to hold her temper in check—especially since she was in the process of sticking pins in a doll that bore a striking resemblance to Marty.

Austin could also end up being a hotheaded loose cannon, which was almost certainly why he'd left his girls with a sitter. Since he'd become a father, Austin had developed a no-bullshit tolerance for his own shitty father and definitely wouldn't be cutting Marty any slack. Hell, he'd find more pins for Cait if she ran low on them.

Then, there was Leyton. He would hold steady, probably, but he'd already had to tangle with Marty and Aurora, and his patience with them had to be wearing thin. Leyton was levelheaded and fair, and Shaw thought he might explode if he continued to come up against the two idiots who'd managed to make a child. Two idiots who were hell-bent on screwing that child over six ways to Sunday.

And that's why Kinsley wasn't at this meeting.

The girl had been through enough, so Shaw had made yet another call to Ryan to encourage the boy to take Kinsley out for ice cream or even a movie. Shaw's treat. That way, Kinsley would miss the little chat session that could turn ugly fast.

There was a knock at the door, and Shaw greeted Rick Downing, his lawyer. As Shaw had instructed him to do, Rick had brought his laptop, papers and pens. Also as instructed, Rick knew that no one would be leaving the house until they'd worked out what would be happening to Kinsley.

"I've made snacks," Lenore said, getting Rick's attention.

She motioned toward what looked to be a plate of brownies in the center of the table. It wasn't. It was something that she called beet-nip bars, which as Lenore had pointed out was a combination of beets and parsnips.

No one had touched a crumb.

"You threatened me," Aurora grumbled, her gaze spearing Shaw's when he sat down across from her.

"Yeah, I did," he admitted. "I said if you didn't come, I'd tell CPS that you'd abandoned your daughter and you could face charges. It's sad, huh, that it took that to get you here?"

"No need to talk to Aurora like that," Marty drawled. "She's doing the best she can."

That got him hell-freezing looks from everyone but Aurora. Cait picked up a huge pin, at least three inches long, and she jammed it into the doll's crotch. Every male in the room winced.

Rick sat, too, introducing himself to Aurora, the only one at the table who didn't know him. "I understand you've said that you no longer want to raise your daughter?" he asked outright.

Aurora pulled back her shoulders. "I shouldn't get in trouble for saving my own sanity. Kinsley has gotten on my every last nerve, and I just can't do it anymore. I can't handle her. It should be against the law for him to try to sic the law on me for that."

The *him* was Shaw, and just in case he hadn't understood that, Aurora jabbed a finger at him. And then she started to cry. Normally, that would have caused Shaw to at least groan. He hated seeing a woman cry, but his sympathy meter for Aurora was pretty low right now.

"And I understand that you also don't want to raise your daughter?" Rick asked Marty.

Marty lifted his hands, palms up. "I just wouldn't be very good at it, dude."

Cait snorted, and Austin added, "You think?" Leyton swore under his breath and scrubbed his hand over his face.

"No one will argue with you about that," Shaw said to Marty. "But the fact remains that someone needs to take care of Kinsley. She's fifteen and still in need of things like food, clothing, shelter and occasionally some love and attention."

"She needs help with polynomials," Cait snarled. That probably wasn't a huge factor here, but it did drive home that Kinsley should have someone who cared enough to know that about her.

"I can't take her back," Aurora said, standing.

"Sorry, no can do," Marty piped in. "Look, you know I wouldn't be good at it. I'd end up doing her more harm than good." He turned to Shaw, his palms up again, his voice pleading. "You and Lenore are better at this. You can do right by her."

And there it was. The straw that broke the camel's back. Or in this case, Shaw's back.

Shaw stood and faced Marty. "For years, you've dumped this kind of shit on Mom and me. On Austin, Cait and Leyton, too. And no, I'm not saying Kinsley is shit. But you sure are. You don't deserve to be a father, so man up and start keeping your dick in your fucking jeans."

Apparently, Shaw himself was going to be the loose cannon today. There was no way for him to stop the avalanche of anger that was slamming down on him. God, this made him boil. Marty had twisted him up for years, pulling crap like this. It was twisting him up and had put one gut-twisting fear in him.

That he could turn out to be as shitty a father as Marty.

"I should go," Marty said. He looked a little shaken, but his voice was steady when he turned to Rick. "Draw up the papers so I can set up child support payments and a trust fund for Kinsley. I can do that much for her."

And Marty turned to leave.

"If you walk out of here, don't come back," Shaw warned him. "Don't ever try to see me again."

"Ditto," Leyton agreed.

"That includes your grandkids," Austin contributed. "If you turn your back on Kinsley, I won't let my girls be around a dick wad like you."

Cait didn't say a word, but with a glare that could have melted Antarctica, she jabbed a pin up the doll's ass.

Marty gave them each a long glance and turned to walk out.

"I'll go with you," Aurora said, hurrying after him.

Marty and she hadn't even made it to the front door when it flew open and Kinsley came running in. Ryan was right behind her, and Kinsley practically came to a skidding halt.

"The waitress at the ice-cream shop said you were here," Kinsley murmured, glancing at both Marty and Aurora.

The girl's glances continued as Shaw and the others came into the living room. She must have seen something on their faces to let her know what had been going on here. And what the outcome had been.

"Oh," Kinsley said. "Oh," she repeated, and this time it wasn't so much an exclamation of surprise as resignation. By the third time she repeated it, the hurt was there. Not the angry, lashing kind of hurt. But the sort that went all the way to the soul.

"You're both here to say you don't want me," Kinsley concluded. Then she focused on Shaw, Cait, Austin, Leyton and Lenore. "And you tried to force one of them to take me."

"Kinsley," Ryan said, going to her side. "Are you okay?"

"Yes." She convinced absolutely no one, and looked up at Ryan. "I'm sorry, but I need to go for a walk or something."

With her shoulders slumped, Kinsley headed to the back door. At least Marty and Aurora had some fiber of decency that caused them to look ashamed of themselves. Good.

"I hope you get infected anal warts," Cait threw out, her words apparently aimed at Marty.

Shaw sighed, turned and went after Kinsley to try to patch up the kid Marty and Aurora had just torn to pieces.

"Wait up," he called out to Kinsley when he saw her heading for the barn and likely the hayloft. He wasn't in the mood for climbing stairs today. Kinsley apparently wasn't, either, because she stopped by the corral.

"I'm okay," she repeated once he'd caught up with her. "I'm not going to cry all over you."

"Too bad. This is my waterproof shirt." Shaw hooked his arm around her neck and yanked her to him. "Sometimes, there's not a strong enough word to describe certain people."

"Flaming assholes," Kinsley supplied.

Okay, those were strong enough words, and Shaw made a sound of approval. "You shouldn't curse, though. Well, not around anyone but me," he amended. He suspected this was the start of many visits from child services, and it was probably best if the social workers didn't hear that kind of language.

"Marty and my mom won't take me," Kinsley said. Even though she'd said she wouldn't cry, she pressed her face against his shoulder. "I'm a screwup, too much trouble."

Shaw had heard enough. "I'll take you."

Judging from her suddenly stiff muscles and the quick lift of her head, Kinsley hadn't had a clue he was going to say that. Shaw had known. He'd figured that out when Marty had stood up from the table. He hated cleaning up after his father, but he hated even more that Marty and Aurora had made Kinsley feel like the screwups that they were.

"My place isn't big enough for you so I'll talk to my mom about you staying here in the big house," Shaw went on. His mother would welcome that as she welcomed all of Marty's kids. "I'm just up the road, and in and out of here all the time. I'll just make a point of being more in than out."

Kinsley shook her head. "You don't want me."

"Yeah, I do." He was about to add, *Or I will want you if you learn polynomials*. But even said in semi-jest wouldn't be good right now for the girl's already battered ego. "You're my sister."

She started blinking hard, trying to fight back those tears. "Why are you saying this? Why are you doing this?"

"Big brother." He tapped first his chest, then her head. "Little sister. Just don't expect me to be nice to you all of the time. I'm only nice to Cait every third Monday of the month. You get Wednesdays."

She lost that fight with the tears, and one went sliding down her cheek. "Really? You'll take me?"

Shaw brushed a kiss on the top of her cardinal red head. "Yeah, I'll take you. But do me a favor and dye your hair a color that doesn't spook the livestock. I'm worried about a stampede."

Kinsley elbowed him in the gut, which was an acceptable form of sibling affection.

He hooked his arm around her neck, ready to take her back to the house so they could discuss this with Lenore, but he saw that Cait, Austin, Lenore and Leyton were in the yard waiting. For that matter, so were Aurora, Sunny and Ryan. He hadn't even known Sunny was there, but Ryan and she were standing with Aurora by the woman's car.

"Kinsley can stay with me," Lenore immediately volunteered when she stepped forward.

"No, she can stay with me." Cait stepped forward, too.

"I have a big place," Leyton added. "You can stay with me. And I'm more responsible than some people." He tipped his head to Cait, who was still holding the doll. Pins jutted out from it in every direction, but there was a concentration of the sharp objects in the very spot where Cait had wished Marty's warts.

"Leyton can't teach you to polish your toenails while blow-drying your hair," Cait countered. "Hey, it's a good multitasking skill to have," she added when her brothers groaned.

Lenore's face brightened, and her smile stretched across her mouth. "I know. All of you can move back in with me. You can have your old rooms."

Silence, followed by some politely muttered noes. Well, polite from Shaw, Leyton and Austin. Cait's "no flippin' way" was louder and had an edge of determination to it.

"All right, suit yourselves, but the offer stands. Anytime…" Lenore trailed off when Aurora walked up to them.

"Could I please talk to you a moment?" Aurora asked Kinsley. "Alone?"

They all waited for Kinsley to give some kind of signal that she wanted either the talk or the alone part, but she stayed quiet. The Jamesons stayed put. Ryan and Sunny came closer, and Ryan moved to Kinsley's side.

Aurora sighed and put her gaze back on Kinsley. "You've been crying," Aurora said.

"Yes," Kinsley admitted in a "what's it to you?" tone.

Aurora didn't get defensive. She nodded. "I'm sorry. I love you, Kinsley, I do, but—"

"There shouldn't be any buts when it comes to love," Shaw interrupted.

Of course, that didn't make sense. People added buts all the time. Hell, he had. He wanted Sunny, wanted to be with her, *but* he didn't want a family. Ironic, since family was what he had the most of. And what was most important to him.

"I'm sorry," Aurora repeated to Kinsley. "I think Marty and I just need some time. I'd like to be able to come out and visit you."

"How do you know I'll even be here?" Kinsley fired back.

Aurora stayed quiet a moment and actually looked guilty. Good. It wasn't nearly enough, but it was a start. "Marty said he has good kids, that they'd do the right thing. Especially Shaw," she added, glancing at him.

That brought on a chorus of groans from all his siblings except for Kinsley. Leyton, Austin, Cait and Lenore walked away, and Ryan, Shaw and Kinsley stayed put. Sunny, too, but unlike Ryan she didn't come closer. She stayed a good ten feet behind Aurora.

"I know you'll think this isn't my place to bring this up," Aurora went on, talking to Shaw now, "but please go easy on Marty."

"On Marty?" Shaw snapped. There went that *start*.

Aurora nodded. "Marty and I talked for a long time. Hours of just catching up with each other's lives. He just wasn't happy here, but he's found himself now. Who would have thought that he'd live out his dream?"

Yeah, that start was definitely gone if Aurora believed Marty deserved to be cut some slack. "He had dreams of fathering children and not raising them?"

She pulled back her shoulders. "No, not that. I meant his writing."

Shaw figured he looked clueless because he was. "What writing?"

"Oh. I just assumed he'd told you. I mean, he did say only a handful of people knew, but I thought you would know for sure since he has so much respect for you."

Shaw just kept on feeling clueless. "What the heck are you talking about?"

Aurora swallowed hard. "Marty…he's an author. He writes those cute children's comics with the duck."

Shaw felt as if the earth had just tipped on its axis. Apparently, so did Sunny because she seemed to be on autopilot when she came closer.

"Slackers Quackers?" Sunny asked.

"That's the one." Aurora smiled now. "He told me all about how he used to make up stories and songs for his kids when they were little."

Shaw got a bad feeling in the pit of his shell-shocked gut. Sunny had gone pale, so maybe she was going through the same thing.

"Then, after Marty left here, he started writing," Aurora went on. "He kept writing when he wasn't recording songs or on tour. When he finally sold one, he asked his publisher to hire this illustrator he liked.

Well, he said he felt sorry for her. But he pushed and pushed, and the publisher finally hired her."

Sunny hadn't had much color left to lose, but that took her from pale to pasty white. "Oh, God," she muttered.

CHAPTER TWENTY

SUNNY STOOD BACK and looked at the shreds of paper that now lined Slackers's duck bed. Well, not actually a bed. It was a Moses basket, the kind parents used for newborns, which Em had found in the attic and brought to the barn. It still had the eyelet lace padding, which had more eyelets—AKA holes—than it had when it'd first been used, but Slackers seemed to like it.

And Sunny definitely liked seeing the shredded paper there.

She couldn't wait until Slackers crapped on them. She'd like the shreds even better then, and the crap would give them the respect they deserved.

Her phone dinged with a text message from Shaw. There was no actual message this time, only a question mark. It was his way of letting her know he was still worried about her and wanted to see her.

I'm fine, she typed, figuring that was a new personal record for repeating those two words.

The lie.

She'd doled out that very lie plenty after her surgery and the bra injury. She was having to say it again now that word had gotten around about Marty being

J.B. Whitman. Word had also gotten around that he'd hired her out of pity.

She wondered if she could give Slackers some prune casserole to make the crapping start sooner. Those slivers of paper were still too pristine, and she could see bits that she would have preferred not to see.

Don't come over, Sunny added to the text before she fired it off to Shaw.

Sunny knew her response would make him sigh and feel worse than he already did. He no doubt wanted to see her, to try to make things better. But he couldn't. Because Shaw couldn't fix this latest mess that Marty had made.

The day before—mercy, had it really only been twenty-four hours?—Aurora had put into motion what was to be Sunny's worst heart stomping yet. The woman hadn't known a stomping was in the works, though, because Marty hadn't told Aurora the illustrator's name. The illustrator he'd hired because he'd felt sorry for her.

Sunny had heard of pity sex, but this was a first for pity duck drawings.

Part of her, the sensible-adult part, wanted to dismiss it and shout from the rooftops that she had talent, that she would have become an artist or illustrator even if Marty hadn't done this.

But she couldn't.

Because at the core of her sensible-adult being, this hit her secret-fear nail right on the head. A fear that everything about her had been just part of a script. The *Little Cowgirls* producers had given her a hobby, a role that they could use to keep the show moving along. McCall had been assigned reading and had been given dozens of books. Hadley had gotten the edgy superhero graphic novels. Sunny had gotten the sketch pad and pencils. She was the only one who'd turned the producers' props into a career.

Or so she'd thought until twenty-four hours ago.

But apparently her career had been part of Marty's script for her. Why, she didn't know and didn't want to know.

Her phone rang, and before she looked at the screen, she knew it would be Shaw. Everyone else had accepted her brush-off and her need to be alone and rethink and evaluate everything about her life. Well, not Ryan. But everything else, including whether or not coming back here had been a massive mistake. If she'd stayed away, she wouldn't have heard what Aurora had said, and Sunny could have gone on living her imperfect but mostly intact life.

Of course, she wouldn't have reconnected with Shaw, either.

Maybe that, too, was preventing her from going back to her mostly intact life. Before this homecoming and Shaw, she'd had a plan. One that had taken the curvy back roads approach rather than the more direct route of an interstate. But that plan had included her having her own family. She'd gotten a start with Ryan, but she still wanted a baby.

Either she had to make a new life plan.

Or give Shaw up.

She pressed the accept-call button, not sure what she was going to say to him, but it turned out that wasn't a problem because Shaw spoke first.

"I don't want you changing your mind and signing that contract from Hugh," he *greeted*.

Now this was an area where she could ease his mind. "I won't. I shredded it and put it in with Slackers for him to crap on it."

"Good." The relief came through in that one word, but the worry was still there, too.

"I also shredded the contracts and release forms that Sunshine sent," Sunny added. "I think there's a spot of duck pee on some of them, but I'm expecting more. Em gave Slackers a massive tub of water to drink and play in."

"Good," he repeated. "Better than just burning them."

So she'd thought, too. Burning would be over much too fast, and these papers—the ones that her mother had tried to use to hurt Shaw and her—deserved a dousing with fowl fluids.

"Sunny," Shaw said. No relief this time in his voice. It was a stew of all the bad emotions. Sorrow, regret, hurt and plenty more of that worry. "I know you don't want to see me, but please don't do anything…"

He paused so long that she started filling in the blanks with words he could possibly say. *Rash. Stupid. Out of hurt.* But that wasn't how he finished it.

"Without me," he said.

Somehow that was perfect and rebroke her heart all at the same time. *Without me* seemed to be a "comfort blanket" offer. One that she would have jumped at if it weren't for just two things.

That baby, for one.

Plus, she didn't want to drag Shaw into the middle of her life unless she could offer him something more than an already broken heart. At the moment, she couldn't. She needed to get back to her plan, get off these back roads, and then pray that Shaw would still be there after she'd pulled her life back together. Or rather after she'd made a new life.

"I won't do anything without telling you," she assured him.

"Let me see you," Shaw pressed.

She sighed. "Tomorrow. I'm getting ready to drive Ryan to Austin to help him get settled into his dorm."

"I didn't think you were doing that for another couple of days."

"Ryan and I moved it up a bit because there's a group of the professors and students getting together for dinner tonight. And he's anxious to get started." Equally anxious, too, to give her a change of scenery that he no doubt hoped would also pull her out of this dark hole she was in.

But Sunny wasn't counting on scenery to do that. No. Along with the dark hole, she was also going to have to stave off other blues over Ryan basically leaving the nest. She wanted him to do that, wanted him to get started making his own life, but the blues would come. There'd be tears. And Sunny had a plan for that.

She thought about the brochure she'd printed out. The start of that plan.

"After I drop Ryan off, I need to make a quick trip to Houston to check on my condo," she added. That wasn't a lie. Nor was it completely the truth. "I'll drive back here tomorrow afternoon."

"I can go with you and help Ryan get settled."

It was a generous offer. One that she didn't have to think about declining because Sunny had already made up her mind about this. "This isn't a good time for you to be away from Kinsley. How is she, by the way?"

"Still hurting," he admitted after a long pause. "But she'll be okay."

Yes, she would, because Kinsley would soon learn that while she had awful parents, she also had the best support system in Texas. She had her Jameson siblings and Lenore. In this case, it wasn't going to take a village to raise a child but rather a family, and Kinsley had family in spades.

"I don't want you to give up your art," he said several moments later. "I don't want this mess with Marty to make you believe you don't have talent."

"Shaw." Sunny sighed again. Along with knowing all of her erogenous zones—he also knew where her deepest wounds were. "Please don't worry," she assured him. "I'm working that out."

Again, it was only a partial lie, and she had another glance at the paper shreds in Slackers's pen. She could still make out some pencil marks and swirls that'd once been Slackers, but she was counting on Em's pet duck to remedy that. Soon, there'd be no physical trace of these particular pages that'd spun off from the props, scripts and Marty's pity.

"Gotta go," she added after checking the time. "Ryan and I will be leaving soon." Not for a couple of hours actually, but she needed to pack a few things. "I'll call you once I'm on my way to Houston."

"Good. Call me before that, too. I just want to make sure you're okay," Shaw added.

She ended the call, gave Slackers—who was living up to his name—a firm warning to "do his business," and she went back inside.

Em was at the kitchen window and obviously had been watching her. She'd also been listening to music. The moment Sunny stepped inside, Em tugged the earphones from her ears and pulled Sunny into a hug. "Did the duck poop on the papers yet?"

Sunny hadn't told Em what she'd done, but she wasn't surprised that Em had figured it out. The antique shredder that she'd found in what had once been Sunshine's office was loud enough that Em probably heard it even over her music.

"Not yet," Sunny answered. "Soon though." Well, unless Slackers found another spot for his toileting. That was a possibility since the duck wasn't confined in the Moses basket and could waddle elsewhere.

Em pulled back but kept her grip on Sunny's arms to hold her in place. "Marty always could cause trouble, even in an empty house."

Sunny wasn't exactly sure what that meant, but it had to be some expression of sympathy for her since that's all she'd been getting lately. Even from Em.

"Tell me a joke," Em said, causing Sunny to automatically frown. "I know you don't like to do them, but I could use a good laugh."

"Well, you won't get it from one of my jokes." It was yet something else she hadn't been good at. It'd simply been another prop. Still, Em was obviously waiting. "What do you call a boomerang that doesn't come back?" Then, Sunny provided the punch line. "A stick."

As she'd done for more than two and a half decades, Em laughed. What she didn't do was let go of Sunny.

"Did I ever tell you that before I met your grand-dad, I once took a shine to a man who was in the Mafia?" Em asked.

Believing this was Em's start to a joke, Sunny shook her head. "I haven't heard this one before." And it stood a 100 percent chance of being funnier than the one Sunny had just told.

"Well, I did. I loved that man to the moon and back, but he was bad. Not bad like Marty, but more in the way you'd expect from someone in the Mafia. Anyway," Em went on after a long breath, "it didn't work out between us. I had to leave him, and I ended up meeting your granddad. If that hadn't happened, I wouldn't have you, your sisters or your brother."

Sunny picked through each word to find the life lesson that Em was obviously trying to give her. "Is this about my art or Shaw?"

Em beamed as if that were the best question ever. "That's for you to decide." Em kissed her cheek. "But my advice—don't get involved with a Mafia guy. No matter what the experts tell you, vinegar doesn't get blood out of clothes."

She gave Sunny a there-there pat on the arm and walked away as if she'd just handed her the secret to happiness instead of the confusing comment with the equally confusing blood thing thrown in. *That's for you to decide* wasn't some new revelation to solve all her problems. For that matter, neither was the Mafia part.

Still mentally scratching her head, Sunny went toward the stairs to check on Ryan. The house smelled like lavender, a sign that Bernice had come and likely gone. For such a sour woman, she certainly left the place clean and smelling sweet. Before Sunny even made it to the stairs, Ryan came down, carrying a suitcase that he set on the floor.

"Kinsley wants to know if I can come over and say goodbye," he said. "I asked Em earlier, and she said I could use her truck just in case you needed your SUV."

"Sure." Sunny paused. "Are you okay with saying goodbye to her and vice versa?"

He nodded, and when she looked for signs that this goodbye would be another upheaval for him, she didn't see any. "Kinsley and I are just friends, and we'll stay friends." Ryan paused. "Are you leaving Shaw? Is that why you're going to Houston after you drop me off at the dorm?"

While some parts of her plan were still in the to-be-determined stage, this wasn't one of them. "No, I'm not leaving Shaw. And I'll be back. I want to be here for Em," she explained. "But you should know that just because I'm not leaving Shaw, it doesn't mean he and I will stay together."

Ryan didn't seem the least bit surprised by that. "Does that have something to do with the brochure you printed out? I saw it next to your overnight bag," he added. "The one for the Emerson Fertility Clinic in Houston?"

Sunny had intended to talk to him about this on the drive, but she could start the discussion now. "I have an appointment there tomorrow morning. I want to find out what the process is for artificial insemination." A few seconds crawled by. "Are you okay with that?"

"Sure," he answered rapidly, but he wasn't so quick on the next part. "If that's what you want." Ryan's forehead bunched up. "Does that mean you'd have the baby here?"

"Probably." That would also lead to her selling her condo and finding a new job. Thankfully, the sale of the condo and her savings would give her some breathing room. But the whole job thing was part of the "to be determined." Maybe she could do website designs or become an art teacher. Or even open a small bookstore.

What she wouldn't do was any more illustrations.

And just thinking of that caused a little piece of her to die.

"Go ahead and see Kinsley," she said. Sunny wanted him out of there in case she started crying again.

Ryan gave her a long look, followed by a long breath. "I won't be long." He kissed her cheek and hurried out.

Sunny stood there a moment trying to swallow the lump in her throat. Neither her throat nor the lump cooperated, so she decided to go back out to the barn to check on Slackers. She doubted anyone had ever gotten cheered up from the sight of duck crap, but she thought it might help her.

She went out through the side door, but the moment Sunny stepped onto the porch, someone grabbed her from behind and yanked something over her head.

Her heart jumped to her throat.

Oh, God. Was this some kind of mugging?

She managed the start of a scream before she felt the slam of adrenaline. She couldn't see, but her instincts screamed for her to defend herself. She blindly rammed her elbow into her attacker, connecting with what felt like his gut, and she back kicked him in the shin.

He howled.

She elbowed and kicked him again. With Ryan and Bernice gone, and with Em likely using her headphones, it was possible no one was going to hear her and call for help. She had to do it herself. She got in another elbow and another kick, aiming for his other shin this time.

Cursing and howling, the man—and it was a man—let go of her. Sunny ripped whatever it was off her head. A pillowcase, she realized. And she whirled around to face her attacker.

It was Hugh.

That registered about a half second after she punched him in the face. He howled again and the blood flew from his nose.

"What the hell are you doing?" Sunny snarled.

Hugh snarled something similar, adding, "You punched me."

"And you grabbed me and put a pillowcase over my head. What the hell were you thinking?"

Despite the bloody nose, he still managed to give

her an indignant look. "I was thinking that I needed to talk to you, and you won't take my calls."

Her pulse was still racing, but it was going at a snail's pace compared to the jolt of anger she got. "Because I don't want to talk to you."

"But you need to hear what I have to say. That's why I parked up the road and walked here. I didn't want you to have a chance to lock yourself inside and not see me. You need to hear what I have to say," he repeated.

"No, I don't. God, have you lost your mind?"

Some of the indignation left, and he seemed to be considering how he could put a spin on her question. "Yes, I have lost my mind. I'm crazy over you."

She smacked him on the arm with the pillowcase. "You're crazy, period, if you think this would get me to change my mind. What were you planning on doing—kidnapping me?"

His silence let her know that had indeed been the plan. "I just thought if I could get you somewhere alone, that we could talk. And that you would listen to reason. Kidnapping you seemed to be the only way I could convince you to come back to me."

Her anger went well past the boiling point, and Sunny stepped back because, heaven help her, she was about to slug him again. "Go away and leave me alone, Hugh."

He shook his head. "I can't do that."

At least that's what she thought he said. It was hard to tell because at that moment there was a series of very loud, high-pitched squawks. She looked over her shoulder to see Slackers waddling—fast—

toward them. Sunny figured that the duck wasn't actually coming after Hugh, but it certainly looked like a mean, feathered ninja. Hugh must have thought so, too, because he actually jumped back.

"Careful, he bites," Sunny warned Hugh. It wasn't as satisfying as a punch, but she liked the horrified look in his eyes.

"Ducks can bite?" he asked.

At that exact moment Slackers flew onto the porch and right in Hugh's face. The side door did some flying, too. It opened and a broom came out, smacking Hugh on the back of his head.

Em.

Apparently, she'd heard the commotion after all.

"You're not kidnapping my granddaughter," Em declared, and she hit him again. Hugh couldn't do much to stop her, not with Slackers pecking the crap out of the fingers he was using to shelter his face.

Sunny let the punishment go on a few more seconds before she caught the broom to stop Em. "It's okay, Gran." Sunny tried to sound a lot calmer than she felt so she could defuse this situation. She didn't want Em to pull a muscle or have a heart attack.

Sunny was a little more cautious getting Slackers to stop. The duck was clearly agitated, and she didn't want to become his secondary pecking target. She gently took hold of him and kissed the top of his feathered head because, well, that seemed like the thing to do. In a weird, flattering way, he had tried to save her.

"Go poop in your pen," she instructed, and set Slackers on the ground before she whirled back around to Hugh. "If you pull another stupid stunt like this, I'll have Leyton arrest you. And I'll set my duck on you."

Hugh opened his mouth as if he was about to justify his stupid stunt, but he must have realized that this was one war he'd lost. With his shoulders slumped and his nose bleeding like a tap, Hugh limped off the porch holding his hand over his sore gut. However, he didn't go anywhere near Slackers who was still in the yard and giving him a version of the beady eye.

"It's okay," Sunny repeated to Em. "Just go back inside. I'll make sure Hugh actually leaves."

Em checked her over from head to toe and looked in the yard to do the same to Slackers. Her grandmother finally gave a satisfied nod. "I'll get Slackers some treats for being such a good boy."

"Good." That would not only be a reward, but it might also cause him to finally soil those shredded papers.

Sunny went into the yard and headed toward the front of the house. She didn't hear a car engine to indicate Hugh was leaving, but he had said that he'd parked up the road.

"What an idiot," she grumbled. Why he thought that abducting her would make her more amenable, she didn't know, but maybe he'd finally gotten the message that she was done with him.

Still mumbling to herself, Sunny reached the front corner of the house. Just as someone jumped out and snagged her by the wrist. Her first thought—a *very angry* first thought—was that it was Hugh. It wasn't.

It was Marty.

"Don't scream, darlin'," he begged. "I just need to talk to you, and you won't take my calls."

Since she'd heard similar words only seconds before and she still had some adrenaline and anger pumping, she smacked Marty on the arm with the pillowcase. "Let go of me. Are you trying to kidnap me, too?"

He blinked, then nodded. "Sort of. I just wanted to make you sit down and listen to me."

She smacked his other arm with the pillowcase, and even though it probably hadn't hurt much, he let go of her as if she'd scalded him. That perhaps had something to do with the low guttural sound she made in her throat.

"Darlin', did, uh, you just growl at me?" he asked.

"Yes," she said through completely clenched teeth. "And I can and will set a killer duck on you."

After a couple of seconds displaying a confused expression, Marty nodded again and seemed considerably calmer than she did. Considerably sorrier, too. What he wasn't was pissed off. However, he might have been a little confused if he hadn't seen the way Slackers had gone after Hugh.

"Please just listen," he said.

She supposed he'd added that *please* and omitted the teeth-grinding *darlin'* to get his way and have her stand there while he spouted some lame excuse. Sunny shook her head, turned and walked back the way she'd come.

"I just want you to look at this," Marty called out to her. "One look, and if you still want me to leave you alone, I will."

Even though she wanted her feet to keep walking, she stopped. "If it's a first edition of *Slackers Quackers*, be prepared to eat it because that's the kind of mood I'm in."

"It's not *Slackers Quackers*," he said. She heard his footsteps behind her. Heard him stop, too, and pull something from his shirt. "That's why I asked for you to be the illustrator for my stories."

She didn't want to see anything he was offering her, but Sunny looked. And her heart melted a little. It was a sketch of Marty and Shaw, one that she'd done during one of Marty's visits back to the ranch. Shaw and he were at the corral, their poses identical while they looked at a mare. There was absolutely nothing special about the sketch.

Or so she wanted to tell him.

But even now through the filters of the anger, she could see that she'd captured something. A moment between father and son. A rare moment. Which was why she'd sketched it. Marty had always been kind to her, and she'd wanted him to have that memory.

"I hadn't actually written a story yet when you drew this," he went on. "But, darlin', I could see you had talent. Heart," he amended. "So, when I did get around to doing the *Slackers Quackers* story, I wanted you to do the illustrations."

Sunny kept her back to him, but she had questions. Big ones. "Why didn't you tell me you were J.B. Whitman?"

"I didn't tell anyone. I hardly have the sort of background that's ideal for being a beloved children's author. Ironic, isn't it, that such a bad father can do something like this?"

It was many steps past irony, and because she was starting to lose her anger edge, she looked away from the sketch. "You didn't tell Aurora that you hired me because you felt sorry for me?"

"I did feel sorry for you," Marty readily admitted. "You had parents who were worse than me, and that's saying something. Something bad. I know I'm a shitty person."

Sunny whirled around to face him. "Why? Why are you such a shitty person?" she amended when he gave her a blank stare.

He shrugged as if the answer was obvious. And painful. "Because it pushes people away. It pushes my kids away." Marty groaned softly. "It just feels like too much having a kid's life in your hands. Being responsible for them. Not just the food in their mouths but for everything. Doing one wrong thing can mess them up for life."

"Yes, and that one wrong thing could be not being there," she quickly pointed out. "And if it's so overwhelming, why not just use birth control?"

"I do. Most of the time." He scrubbed his hand over his face. "It's like a cycle. I start to get depressed at what I've done so I push it down as far as it'll go. Women help with that. I really like women," he added, as if that were some kind of revelation.

"I think a lot of straight men do," she tossed back, not bothering to tone down the sarcasm.

"Yes, but I don't think they're using them to forget all the stuff I've done wrong." Marty looked her straight in the eyes. "Shaw doesn't use you."

"No," she quietly agreed.

In frustration, she smacked the pillowcase against the side of the house. She didn't want to give Marty an inch, but a little of what he was saying was getting through. A little. That didn't mean she'd ever understand him or accept what he'd done to his kids.

"Shaw doesn't use me," Sunny went on when she had more control of her voice. "More like he resists me. I think Shaw gets overwhelmed with the responsibility, too. Responsibility that you've put on him."

"I know. I know," he repeated, groaning. "Shaw was born old. He always put more on his shoulders. Once I saw that he could run the ranch, I knew it was time for me to leave."

Sunny turned on him again. "And that makes you a shit."

"Agreed. But, darlin', it makes me a shit without an illustrator for my stories. Please don't let your disgust for me get in the way of that. I might have felt sorry for you way back then, but I could also see how talented you were. I also believe you love doing the sketches. I can see your heart in the pictures."

Her heart was indeed in those sketches. "I didn't mean for that tail feather to look like that," she snapped. Then she realized this probably wasn't the time to bring that up.

He gave a hint of a smile. "Well, it's sold a lot of copies to drunks and perverts."

"Yes!" Sunny said that a little too loud, a little fast,

and she didn't want to agree with him on anything, including the obvious.

The next few seconds crawled by. "Just consider staying on as the illustrator," he finally said. "I would offer you a huge bonus or a raise, but that'd probably feel like a bribe to you. Unless it's a really big bonus or raise."

She scorched him with a fresh glare. Sunny didn't want any humor in this. She wanted him to suffer... but she didn't know exactly why. It'd probably been a smart business move not to let the world know that the world's worst father was putting stories out there for kids. And as for the illustrator part, it was possible that she was the only artist he'd known. It was as if Marty had considered that sketch she'd given him to be an audition of sorts.

But that didn't mean everything between Marty and her was resolved. There was the part about his feeling sorry for her when she'd been a kid. Heck, he probably still felt sorry for her. After all, she had Sunshine for a mother, and Sunshine's parental flaws were legion.

Marty and she looked up when they heard footsteps coming around the side of the house. Shaw. He stopped, eyed them both, his stony gaze settling on Marty.

"Don't worry, I'm leaving," Marty said to his son. He lowered his voice and added to Sunny, "Just consider staying as the illustrator, darlin'. The bonus and raise are optional."

Marty walked away, moving past Shaw, but Shaw

spared him only a glance. He kept his attention on Sunny as he made his way to her.

"Are you here to kidnap me?" she asked.

"Uh, no." Shaw's forehead wrinkled. "Do you want me to do something like that?"

His question had a sexual edge to it. Of course, Shaw always had a sexual edge. Even now, with the kidnapping attempts and arguments, Sunny wanted to slip into his arms and kiss him. She resisted because if she did that, she'd be using him. He likely wouldn't object—who was she kidding? He definitely wouldn't object. But it wouldn't be right, not with her mind in tatters.

"Ryan said you were going to a sperm bank to get knocked up," she heard Shaw say.

Well, Ryan hadn't kept that secret for long. Then again, she hadn't really said it was a secret.

"He's worried about you," Shaw added. "He just wanted me to make sure you'll be okay. Plus, I'm guessing he didn't want to talk to you about sperm."

"Understandable," she muttered. It wasn't what she wanted to discuss with Shaw, either. Still, she was in love with him, and this was something he needed to hear. "I want to have a baby. This is the first step."

He nodded, and she could practically see him gearing up to do the right thing. To step up to the plate, something he'd been doing his whole life. Well, Sunny was going to put a stop to that.

"I don't want you to be my baby's father," she threw out there before he could speak. "I don't want you to ever feel you have to do something with me that you don't want to do. That includes kidnapping sex," Sunny tacked on because she couldn't help herself.

She hated to see him twisted up the way she was.

He didn't smile. In fact, despite her attempted humor, his expression didn't change. "Give me twenty-four hours," he said.

Sunny shook her head. "For what?"

"Twenty-four hours before you go to the sperm bank. After you drop off Ryan, come back here. I want us to talk. When we're done, if you still want to go to the sperm bank, I'll drive you there myself."

With that, he turned and walked away.

CHAPTER TWENTY-ONE

SHAW WAS PRETTY SURE he wouldn't die from the pain, but it might be a while before he could sit down. Or sleep. Or not take a step without wincing.

Or wonder if he'd just done the dumbest thing in his life.

He was certainly doing plenty of wincing now as he came out on his porch with his coffee to wait for Sunny.

As promised, she had driven back to Lone Star Ridge after getting Ryan settled in Austin, but she'd arrived so late that she had said she'd come over in the morning. That had turned out to be a good thing because it had allowed him a little more time to get some things done. However, the delay had eaten into the twenty-four hours he'd given her. Maybe she wouldn't hold him to that deadline. Maybe she'd listen to what he had to say.

And what he had to show her.

If it didn't work, then the limping and pain were the least of his worries. At least one thing would strike a good chord with her; everything else could be a gigantic bust.

He drank his coffee and glanced around at the place he'd made his home. A month ago, it had been everything he'd wanted. He had a job he loved. Family that he mostly loved with the big exception of Marty. However, even Marty had come through—sort of—when it came to Sunny.

Shaw's stomach clenched a little when he saw Sunny's SUV approaching. She got out, looking better than any woman had a right to look. A body-skimming blue dress…and carrying a duck. Yes, a duck. She had tucked it under her arm like a football and walked toward him.

"There are some repairs being done on the barn this morning, and it was freaking out Slackers," Sunny said. "Em asked me to bring him with me."

"Slackers?" he asked, staying put on the porch. He wanted to go to her, wanted to pull her into his arms, but he didn't want her to see him limp. Plus, this way he got to enjoy the view of watching her walk toward him.

"Em named him." She didn't say that with a smile, and Shaw didn't know if the disapproval was because she'd been assigned duck-sitting duty or if the name was one big bad memory.

Maybe both.

Maybe, too, because she was here to tell him that she'd kept that appointment at the fertility clinic in Houston.

"How's Ryan?" he said, not only wanting to know but to get it out of the way. It was possible some of Sunny's lack of smile was because of the boy.

"All moved into the dorm. Now I know how moms feel when their kids leave the nest. But I didn't get all sixteen years with him before that happened." She glanced away for a couple of seconds. "I miss him."

Yeah, he'd figured she would. "Kinsley asked if I'd drive her up to see him in a couple weeks. Maybe we can all go together?"

That put a little light in Sunny's eyes, and she nodded. Smiled, even, but it wasn't a full-fledged Sunny smile. The kind of smile that made you believe life could truly be, well, sunny.

"Come in," he offered. "I'll get you some coffee, and we can talk."

She looked down at Slackers. "I can't leave him out here. He might waddle off."

"Bring him in with you."

She continued to look down at the duck. "He can get...aggressive if he thinks I'm in trouble so you might want to keep your voice pleasant."

Shaw frowned and looked down at the duck. He had no intentions of yelling or such. "Aggressive?" he asked, wondering what the heck had happened for Sunny to learn that about Slackers. And what exactly was aggressive about a duck?

"He went after Hugh when he tried to kidnap me yesterday to convince me why I should get back together with him." Sunny said it in an almost matter-of-fact tone, but there was nothing matter-of-fact about it.

The rage came like a fast storm. "I'm going to kick Hugh's ass."

She lifted her head, met his gaze and gave another of those little-bitty smiles. "If he comes back, I'll let you do just that. Then I'll have Leyton arrest him. I filed a restraining order against Hugh this morning."

That soothed the rage a little. However, it was a gut punch of surprise that Sunny had had to do something like that and that Leyton hadn't told him about it. Of course, maybe Leyton had wisely figured the info had best come from Sunny. Anything was better coming from Sunny.

"I didn't file a restraining order against Marty," she went on, stepping onto the porch. "He tried to kidnap me, too."

Well, shit. No wonder Sunny had asked Shaw if he was there to kidnap her when he'd shown up yesterday at Em's. He'd thought it was some kind of sex game she wanted to play. He should have pressed for more info, and then he could have kicked two asses—Hugh's and his father's. And here Marty hadn't mentioned anything about an attempted kidnapping when Shaw had talked to him the night before.

"Marty showed me a sketch I'd done of you and him," Sunny continued. "I'd given it to him as a gift when he'd been visiting. He said the sketch was the reason he'd wanted me to do the illustrations. It wasn't just because he felt sorry for me."

"Yeah, he explained that to me," Shaw admitted.

And Marty had put a good spin on it, too, making it sound as if Sunny might keep on doing the graphic novels with him. Now, Shaw had to wonder if Marty had left out anything else.

"Marty said he'd make sure you got a raise," Shaw added, and judging from her nod, his father had told the truth about that. "So, will you keep on working with him?"

"Maybe. Probably," she said. Then she sighed. "I

just hate that I let Aurora and him take a whack at my self-esteem like that. I can draw pictures." Sunny added almost defensively, "I'm a good artist."

Shaw leaned in and kissed her. "You're better than good. You're freaking amazing." And that included the kiss, too. She tasted like sex and sin.

And Sunny.

That was the best part.

The worst part was the annoying loud squawks the duck made, and Slackers gave Shaw a non-friendly peck on the chin.

When Sunny pulled back from the kiss, she smiled again and ran her tongue over his bottom lip as if to gather up his taste. That caused his body to do a little clenching and begging. He might be able to do something about that, but first he had something to give her.

"Come inside," he repeated. "And bring the duck." Considering the critter's crappy attitude, that was a concession for him. Still, Shaw would do whatever it took to get her to stay long enough to hear him out.

"What happened?" she asked when he turned to walk inside. "You're limping."

He waved that off, and once they were inside, he shut the door.

"You're in pain?" she pressed, but Shaw silenced her question by picking up the package on the entry table and handing it to her.

"It's from Hayes," he said.

Her eyes went wide with surprise, and she set the duck down on the floor so she could take the package. Her eyes went even wider when she saw what was inside.

"My sketchbooks." Her voice was mostly breath and came out as an awed whisper. She quickly flipped through the one on top. "These are the ones that I gave Sunshine in the plea deal. How'd you get them back?" Her surprise turned to wariness. "You didn't steal them, did you? Or did Hayes steal them?"

"No theft involved," Shaw assured her. "Hayes traded for them and then had them couriered to me so I could give them back to you. He also got Sunshine to sign a release, saying they're yours and that she has no claim on them."

He enjoyed that openmouthed stunned look she was giving him. In part because he knew this was good, that it was going to make her happy. And also because if her mouth stayed that way, it'd make it easier for him to French-kiss her.

"How?" Sunny managed to say. "What did Hayes use for the trade?"

This was a good part, too. A sweet little comeuppance for her witch of a mother. "Apparently, when he was about sixteen, Hayes put a nanny cam in the attic because he thought someone was sneaking up there. He ended up getting a recording of Sunshine giving head to one of the cameramen. Apparently, it wasn't a very flattering video of Sunshine and didn't capture her good side."

Sunny's mouth dropped open again.

"Hayes traded the sex tape for your sketchbooks," Shaw went on, "because he wanted to make up for Tonya stealing your diaries."

Now he kissed her open mouth, and without the duck there to peck him, he went in for something longer and deeper. He didn't stop until the duck pecked him on the leg. Apparently, he was going to have to bribe the stupid thing if he wanted to finish up things with Sunny. Shaw went to the pantry, took out a box of Cheerios and dumped some on the floor.

"Uh, that could lead to duck poop," Sunny pointed out.

He didn't care. Shaw went back to her, pulled her into his arms and finished the kiss. Unfortunately, he didn't finish it without wincing again.

Sunny stepped back and stared at him. "All right, what's wrong with you?"

He'd wanted to get in a little more kissing before he launched into this, but it was obviously time for him to let her know what he'd done. "I need to show you my ass," he said.

Clearly, she'd been expecting him to say something else, but that didn't stop Shaw. He hadn't bothered with a belt, so that was one less thing to work through to get to the zipper of his jeans. He lowered his jeans, and boxers, as well, with as much care as he could manage. He still winced. Then he turned so that she could see his butt cheek.

When Shaw had planned the big reveal, he hadn't taken into account that for him to see her reaction he would have to crane his neck and look over his shoulder—both of which caused pain. Still, it was worth it to see her "you nailed this" expression and hear the soft, sighing way she said his name.

"Oh, Shaw," she repeated, going closer for a better look.

Since he'd already checked it out in the mirror, he knew that his butt cheek was inflamed and an angry red color. But Sunny would look past that and see the tattoo.

It was a heart with the shape formed by the words on her own tat.

Love you forever.

And in the center was Sunny's name.

He didn't point out that his name was one letter shorter than hers and therefore had likely been less painful for her, but Shaw did mumble, "I'm so glad your name wasn't Penelope."

"Do you really love me?" she asked in that breathy voice.

Holding on to the waist of his jeans with one hand, he eased back around to face her. "Do you think I would have gotten an ass tat if I didn't? That *Love you forever* isn't lip service. Or in this case, ass service. I love you, Sunny."

Risking a duck pecking and pain from just moving around, Shaw drew her back to him for a kiss. Judging from the enthusiastic way Sunny kissed him back, the tat—or maybe it was the *I love you*—had hit the right mark.

"Oh, and as for the sperm you want, I just happen to have that," he told her. "No charge. Let me be your sperm donor, Sunny."

He winced, not from pain but because that hadn't sounded as good aloud as it had in his head.

"You do know that sperm could lead to a baby?"

She winced a little, too, probably because of the way that'd sounded.

"That's what I'm counting on." If his swimmers were a tenth as potent as Marty's, he could knock her up today, and they'd have that baby shortly after Christmas.

She didn't exactly jump into his arms or rip off his clothes. "Are you really, really sure?"

This was the easiest question of all for Shaw to answer. "Yeah, I'm really, really sure."

Sunny smiled and proceeded with the clothes ripping while she kissed him and backed him toward the bedroom. Shaw ignored Slackers's protesting squawks and pecking attempts, and closed the door in the duck's face. Sunny and he had a baby to make.

And the start of a new life.

"You're going to need a bigger house," Sunny muttered, right before she hauled Shaw's sore ass to her and Frenched him out of his mind.

* * * * *

*If you enjoyed Shaw and Sunny's story,
you won't want to miss Austin and McCall's
rekindled romance in* Chasing Trouble in Texas,
the second book in the Lone Star Ridge series from
USA TODAY *bestselling author Delores Fossen.*

Keep reading for a special preview!

CHAPTER ONE

IN HINDSIGHT, AUSTIN JAMESON realized he should have taken off the pink tutu and matching tiara and ditched the disturbing-looking stuffed bunny before he answered the door. After all, he was a cowboy with a hardworking reputation that didn't involve such things.

Live and learn.

He'd just been in such a hurry to make sure the knocking wouldn't wake up his twin girls that he'd forgotten about the "costume" that the twins had talked him into wearing for their bedtime story. But Austin remembered it now when he faced the visitor at his door.

The sun had already set, but the porch light made it easy for Austin to see the tall lanky guy in a white Stetson and jeans, complete with a giant's eye–sized rodeo buckle. The light also made it easy to see the big truck and horse trailer parked all the way at the end of his driveway. It wasn't surprising that Austin hadn't heard the truck what with the voices—and yes, hopping around—he'd come up with to make the otherwise dull story, *The Fairy Princess's Magic Rabbit*, a hit with his girls.

The man who'd no doubt driven that truck had

his right hand lifted in midknock. He looked dumb-founded, too, and that was when Austin got that hind-sight and remembered what he was wearing.

Austin supposed he could take off the tutu and tiara and offer some kind of explanation to dispel any rumors about him going off the deep end, but his dignity had already been shot to hell and back. Besides, this guy—this stranger—wasn't anyone he felt the need to impress.

However, Austin couldn't say that about his visitor.

Obviously, this guy had come to impress, or *some-thing*, since he was holding on to the reins of a Shet-land pony that was standing by the porch steps. The pony was draped with a flower garland and wearing a straw hat and yellow cardboard sunglasses. Austin wasn't sure what to make of that getup. Judging from the expression on the Shetland's face, it didn't know what to make of it, either.

Apparently, the pony had had its dignity shot to hell, too.

"Uh, I must have the wrong house," the guy said, shaking his head and backing away.

"Yeah," Austin agreed.

And he wondered why the guy hadn't checked that little detail before getting the pony out of the trailer. It wasn't as if Austin's ranch was on the beaten path. Heck, neither was his nearby hometown of Lone Star Ridge. People who usually made it out this far knew where they were going.

"I was looking for Austin Jameson," his visitor added a moment later.

Austin gave the guy another once-over. He still

didn't recognize the pony whisperer, but since Austin raised horses, he had done business with a lot of people in the six years that he'd owned his ranch. Sometimes, folks brought him horses that needed adoption, but he didn't think that was the case here.

"I'm Austin Jameson," he said. "And you are?"

The confusion vanished from the guy's face, replaced by what Austin was certain was a flare of anger in his eyes. "You're the guy McCall left me for?"

Now Austin was the one who was confused. He only knew one person named McCall, and she hadn't left any guy for him. In fact, he hadn't seen McCall in years. This idiot had to be talking about someone else. "McCall Dalton?"

"That's the one," he snapped, jabbing a finger at Austin's chest.

Again, Austin regretted the tutu and tiara because it obviously gave this lunatic the impression that he couldn't kick ass. He. Could.

"Who the hell are you?" Austin snarled. He tossed the bunny in the foyer and stepped out on the porch so he could close the door behind him. He didn't want his girls, Avery and Gracie, hearing any of this.

"I'm Cody Joe Lozano." The guy spat it out as if that was something Austin should have already known. He hadn't known, but it did sound kind of familiar. "And you're gonna tell me where McCall is."

"Lower your voice," Austin warned him, and he tried to get a whiff of the guy's breath. No scent of alcohol, but that didn't mean he wasn't drunk. Or high. "My kids are asleep."

"Kids?" he snarled. "You're married?"

"I'm a widower, not that it's any of your business. Why would you think I'd know where McCall is?"

"Because you were her boyfriend," he said without hesitation.

As explanations went, it was more than a little thin.

"I saw you two on TV, on the reruns of *Little Cowgirls*," Cody Joe added with a curl of his lips.

Again, it was thin on the explanation. "So did thousands of people," Austin pointed out.

Hell, Austin hoped he wasn't dealing with one of those "fans" of the reality show, *Little Cowgirls*, that had indeed starred McCall and her sisters, the three of them triplets and therefore even more intriguing. It had been a while, years, but every now and then a fan would come around. And, yeah, Austin had been her boyfriend.

Sort of.

McCall's very brief, occasional TV boyfriend anyway.

But *Little Cowgirls* had been canceled eighteen years ago when McCall was fifteen. She'd left Lone Star Ridge after high school graduation, and Austin could count on one hand how many times he'd seen her since then.

The last Austin had heard, McCall was a counselor of some kind and living in Dallas, but he wasn't about to tell this idiot that. Austin didn't want Cody Joe going to look for her.

"Where's McCall?" Cody Joe demanded, jabbing his finger at Austin again.

"Get that finger away from my chest and get off

my porch. Take your pony with you. And for Pete's sake, get that stupid-assed hat and glasses off him. You're humiliating him."

Cody Joe looked back at the Shetland, and it was as if that glimpse drained the fight from his body. "McCall likes horses." His breath was now a weary sigh.

Well, she had when she'd lived in Lone Star Ridge, and it was possible that she'd wanted a pony when she was a kid. But Austin didn't think she would appreciate this particular gift from this particular guy.

Cody Joe swatted at a mosquito buzzing around his head and used his forearm to swipe sweat off his forehead. It might have been nearly eight thirty, but the June temperature was still in the high eighties.

"I've got to find her," Cody Joe went on, his voice more of a whine now than a snarl. "I've got to tell her how sorry I am. I still want her to marry me." He fished around in his jeans pocket and came up with an engagement ring, one with a diamond so big and sparkly that it could have triggered a seizure.

Austin was torn between just kicking this moron off his porch and trying to get to the bottom of this. If Cody Joe was some kind of stalker, then he needed to call the sheriff, who just happened to be Austin's brother.

"Are you saying you were engaged to McCall?" Austin asked.

Cody Joe shook his head, leaned against the porch railing and groaned, the sound of a man in misery. "I was this close to getting her to say yes." He held up a small measured space between his thumb and index finger. "But I messed things up, *bad*. Miss Watermelon just looked so good in that red bikini bottom and watermelon-seed pasties, and I lost my head."

Austin didn't bother to get more details on that story. He got the picture.

While Cody Joe kept up his "pit of despair" mutterings and sank down onto the porch, Austin texted his brother, Sheriff Leyton Jameson, to come out to his place and bring a Breathalyzer. And some handcuffs in case Cody Joe objected to a sobriety test. He added for Leyton to keep this quiet. No way did Austin want this getting around when he had so much at stake.

Hell. His whole life was at stake.

Anything that hinted trouble could come back to bite him in the ass, and Cody Joe had *trouble* written all over him. So did the pony.

"Help me find McCall," Cody Joe grumbled on. "I know she came back here to her hometown 'cause I heard Boo talking to her on the phone."

Again, Austin didn't ask for clarification, not even who the heck Boo was. He'd never heard anyone, including a toddler, whine this much, and since he was the father of two three-year-old girls, he was more than qualified to ID an excessive whiner.

The Shetland started eating the petunias—after it pissed on the walkway. Austin ignored that and used his phone to do a search on Cody Joe Lozano in case the guy was an escaped convict or something.

But no. It was worse.

Cody Joe was a stinkin' rich champion bull rider who'd been dubbed Hot Steel Buns. That meant he was just an ass. In Austin's experience, whining, heartbroken, cheating asses could be more unpredictable and dangerous than anyone. Especially when the ass had an obsession with the woman he'd cheated on.

While he continued to search, Austin spotted a tweet about Cody Joe and Miss Watermelon, but before he could get much past the picture of the blonde with Dolly Parton breasts and, yes, indeed, watermelon-seed pasties, he heard rustling on the side of his house. His first thought—a really bad one—was that either Avery or Gracie had woken up and come out through the back door. He definitely didn't want his girls to see or hear any of this.

It wasn't Avery or Gracie though.

It was a brunette who was using the flashlight on her phone to navigate the yard. She was dressed more like the fairy princess who'd been in that lame story he'd just read to his kids. Her long white shimmering dress hugged her breasts and billowed out over her hips like the top of a soft-serve ice cream cone. She also had a tiara, one a heck of a lot better than his, and a satin sash angled over her chest that proclaimed her Miss Watermelon Runner Up.

"Austin," she murmured.

If the bunny from *The Fairy Princess's Magic Rabbit* had come hopping around the corner, Austin wouldn't have been more surprised.

"McCall," Austin murmured back.

"McCall," Cody Joe said. It wasn't a murmur, more like a whine of relief, and he sprang up, heading to the side of the porch toward her.

"No," McCall snapped, narrowing her eyes at Cody Joe. It probably would have looked more menacing if she hadn't had on a kilo of sparkly eyeshadow lighting up her eyelids. "If you try to touch me again, so help me, I'll kick you in the nuts, and I'm wearing very pointy, very hard shoes."

Wisely, Cody Joe stopped in this tracks, proving that he perhaps wasn't a complete idiot after all.

Austin didn't make a move to go to her, either. In part that was because he was stunned. Not only because McCall was indeed at his place, as Cody Joe had thought she would be. Not only because of her strange outfit, either. But what was the most surprising of all was that he'd never heard McCall sound as if she might do some actual nut-kicking. When she'd been on *Little Cowgirls*, she'd been dubbed the nice one of her triplet sisters. Later on, folks had called her Prissy Pants.

Too prissy for Austin, that was for sure, which was why their "relationship" had never gotten past the peck-on-the-lips stage.

Well, she'd definitely shed some of that prissiness.

"But, McCall—" Cody Joe tried.

"No," she repeated. "You don't speak to me unless I say so, and I'm not saying so. And you won't grab me again, either."

She pointed to the bruises on her left arm. Fingerprint bruises. Since the marks had no doubt come from Cody Joe, that made Austin want to kick his ass, and he wouldn't need pointy shoes to do a damn good job of it.

Still huffing, McCall turned toward Austin. "I can explain," she said, motioning toward her clothes. She eyed his tiara and tutu. "I'm guessing you can, too."

"I was reading to my girls."

He yanked off the tiara, tossing it into the rocking chair on the porch, but there wasn't a dignity-saving way for him to get out of the tutu without tearing it—something that would make Gracie cry. It'd taken some time and effort to shimmy it over his jeans.

"It's a costume for a charity fund-raising beauty pageant," McCall said, pointing to her sash. "It's pinned on from the back, and I can't get it off. I didn't want to rip the dress because I can eventually put it in a charity auction."

Unlike some of the things Cody Joe had said, Austin wouldn't have minded hearing the story behind that, but he was pretty sure the tale would end with Cody Joe nailing the winner of the contest and getting caught.

And then bruising McCall.

"I bought you that pony you always wanted," Cody Joe blurted out. "I called a friend after you left, and he brought it right over for me. It's a peace offering."

The look McCall gave him was the Super Bowl and World Series winner of earth-searing glares. "Shut up. And get the ridiculous hat and sunglasses off that poor animal. It's humiliating."

"That's what I said," Austin agreed.

While Cody Joe took care of the de-humiliation of the pony, McCall again turned back to Austin, and he could see her fighting to rein in her temper and turn off the laser rays she'd just shot at Cody Joe.

"I'm sorry," she said to Austin. "The contest was in San Antonio, and when…things got ugly…" The laser rays drilled into Cody Joe again. "I decided to come home."

That made sense. Sort of. San Antonio wasn't that far from Lone Star Ridge, but his house sure wasn't her home. Home for her was her Granny Em's place on the other side of town. It was the ranch where *Little Cowgirls* had been filmed and where McCall and her siblings had lived until they'd each moved away to go to college.

"While I was driving to Granny Em's," McCall went on, "I realized I didn't want her to see me like this. It would have upset her."

True, and since Em was in her late seventies, Mc-Call probably hadn't wanted to risk an upsetting. "So, you came here?" Austin asked that tentatively, letting her know that he would indeed like some filling in on this part.

McCall nodded. Apparently, her tiara was pinned on, too, because it didn't shift even a little on her long cocoa-brown hair. "I left my rental car on Prego Trail and walked here."

She fluttered her fingers in the direction of said trail. It was on the outer edge of his property, and it hadn't gotten the name from that particular brand of spaghetti sauce; rather because it was where the local teenagers went to make out, which had resulted in some of them getting knocked up.

"Uh, why exactly did you come here?" Austin came out and asked her.

"Temporary insanity," she muttered, but then he saw her do some steeling up to look him straight in the eyes. "I thought about going to my sister, but Sunny isn't home."

No, she wasn't. That was because Sunny was away on a romantic weekend with his eldest brother, Shaw. And since Sunny and Shaw were now engaged and planning to marry and have kids, it was almost certain that there were some knocking-up rehearsals going on.

"I didn't have any other clothes with me and didn't want to go walking into the inn like this." McCall motioned to her dress again. "I knew if I did, word would just get back to Granny Em. So, I decided to come here. I know you've got kids, but I thought maybe I could stay on the sofa or something until morning."

"You didn't have to hide out from me, McCall," Cody Joe declared. "You should have come to me so we could talk things—"

Hiking up her dress in a way that no one could call ladylike or fairy princess–like, McCall climbed onto the porch and aimed her foot at Cody Joe's balls. And, yep, those heels were definitely pointy.

"Say one more word to me," she warned him, "and it'll be months before you can ride another bull or screw around with another beauty queen. You made an embarrassing laughingstock out of a charity event that would have pulled in thousands of dollars for troubled kids." She didn't yell, but the intensity grew with each word. "And it was all caught on camera."

She rummaged through a side pocket of the dress, came up with her phone and thrust the photo on the screen at Cody Joe. Whoever had taken the picture had captured his Hot Steel Buns in action, complete with a watermelon-seed pasty stuck on Cody Joe's cheek. The beauty queen's tits were visible, too. Of course, it would have been hard for them to not be seen, even if it hadn't been a wide angle shot.

The caption on the picture was: "Little Cowgirl's cheating cowboy sampling some melons at the annual Saddle-up for Tots fund-raiser. Hope the tots didn't get a peek at this!"

"One more word," she emphasized to Cody Joe.

Oh, Cody Joe wanted to say something. Austin could see the man practically biting his tongue, but he kept his jaw locked and mouth closed. Good thing, too, because he must have known there was no excuse he could give her that would allow him to leave with his nuts intact. But even if McCall didn't hurt him, Austin might still kick his ass for putting those bruises on her.

"Anyway," McCall said as she shifted back to Austin. Clearly still fighting for her composure, she lowered her dress. "I really am sorry. I didn't know Cody Joe would come after me here."

"He said something about hearing you talking to *Boo* on the phone," Austin provided.

McCall nodded and looked as if she wanted to give herself a kick for allowing that to happen. "Again, I'm sorry." She paused, met him eye to eye. "I'm sorry about your wife, too. Zoey was a wonderful person."

Yeah, she was, and despite the "distraction" going on around him right now, Austin had to put up a fight to keep himself from slipping back into that dark place with just the mention of Zoey's name. Grief was greedy, and even though Zoey had been dead for a little over a year now, it wasn't done getting a pound of flesh from him.

McCall broke the eye contact and murmured another apology, making Austin think that she could see right through him. Well, she was a counselor after all so maybe that gave her some kind of insight. If so, he'd shut it down. He'd had fourteen months of pity, and it didn't help. It only dragged him back to places he didn't want to be.

"Cody Joe will leave now and take the pony with him," McCall went on. "He won't come back, and he won't try to contact you or me again. I'll go back to San Antonio and get a hotel room."

She aimed another glare at Cody Joe. "I want to end all of this—*quietly.*"

At that exact moment, there was the sound of approaching vehicles. It didn't take long for those vehicles to come into view. Leyton's cruiser was in the lead, no sirens or flashing lights. Right behind it though was a San Antonio PD cruiser with its blue lights slashing through the darkness.

And right behind that were two news vans from TV stations in San Antonio. Broadcast vehicles, complete with satellite dishes that would no doubt make it easy to turn all of this into a breaking news story.

Any chance of *quietly* had just bit the dust.

CHAPTER TWO

"Don't worry, McCall," the woman in the stripper outfit called out when she stepped from one of the news vans. "Everything will be okeydokey."

McCall was reasonably sure that nothing about this situation would be okey or dokey.

Austin must have realized that, too, because he started muttering curse words under his breath. While he propped his hands on his hips, he stared out at the circus that was now playing out in his driveway and front yard. It didn't matter that this wasn't his circus, nor his monkeys. Before this was over, McCall was going to owe him a thousand apologies along with cleaning up some metaphorical monkey poop. First though, she had to defuse a very ugly mess.

Wadding up the sides of her dress so she could walk without tripping, McCall started out toward the people who were pouring out of the vehicles: three cops, two cameramen and two people that she guessed were reporters because they had microphones.

Leyton was a welcome sight—especially since he hadn't arrived with sirens blaring, and unless he'd changed a lot over the years, he'd be levelheaded and reasonable. That wouldn't make this hunky-dory, okeydokey or less poopy, but at least it wouldn't add any more monkeys to the circus.

Her assistant, Rue Gleason, aka Boo, might be of help, as well. Definitely not a circus monkey on most days. Too bad though that Boo was giving this tawdry mess even more tawdriness in her stilettos, sequined halter top and red micromini leather skirt that stopped only an inch below her crotch. Since Boo still had on the "Miss Watermelon Participant" sash, maybe it had been pinned to her outfit, too. Of course, knowing Boo, maybe she just liked wearing it.

"Why are the San Antonio cops and news crews here?" McCall asked her. She tried to keep her voice to a whisper and hoped that Boo did the same.

Boo didn't. "I wasn't going to let that weasel-balled turd get away with grabbing you like that. I told a cop friend that I met at the fund-raiser, and he said he'd come and arrest Cody Joe. A reporter heard me talking to the cop and offered me a ride out here. The reporter said he was coming even if I didn't give him directions or anything."

Boo sent a steely look at Cody Joe, who was heading in their direction. So were Austin and the Shetland pony. That only upped the urgency to get rid of the problem—the cop—that Boo had obviously seen as a solution.

McCall didn't want a San Antonio cop to arrest Cody Joe because it would just end up making more news than it already had. Plus, he hadn't "grabbed" her for the purpose of bruising her but rather had tried to hold on when she'd turned to walk away from him. Yes, that was pretty much the same thing, but if Mc-

Call had thought for a second that he'd been trying to hurt her, she would have kicked his nuts all the way into his throat.

"I'll issue a statement in the morning. For now, I want you to respect my privacy and leave," McCall said, aiming that at the reporters.

She kept her voice level and noncombative because she'd already had enough bad press for one night. While flying off the handle would feel good temporarily, it could end up costing the foundation even more money in donations.

"I want you to go, too," Austin added, "and since I own this property, and you're trespassing, that leaving will happen right now."

"Say, that's the guy from *Little Cowgirls*," one of the cameramen said.

McCall groaned. In all the years *Little Cowgirls* had been on the air, Austin had appeared on screen only about a half-dozen times, but he'd gotten a ton of fan mail. His good looks had played into that. Still would with that tousled nearly black hair and sizzling blue eyes. The man looked like a rock star—even in that tutu.

"I'm sure you want to tell your side of the story as to what happened between Cody Joe, you and Miss Watermelon," one of the reporters shouted to McCall.

"Leave now!" Leyton snarled, tapping his badge and holding up a pair of handcuffs that he took from a clip at the back of his jeans. Unlike McCall, Leyton didn't bother with a level or nonconfrontational tone. He was all pissed-off cop.

The cameramen didn't stop filming, but they did

walk backward to their vans, and once they were inside, they slowpoked their way down Austin's driveway. Heaven knew how bad the spin would be that they'd put on this story, and first thing in the morning, McCall really did need to do some damage control.

"I'm Officer Gary Hatcher," the cop said. "I'm here to take Cody Joe Lozano into custody for an incident that happened at the Miss Watermelon beauty contest in San Antonio jurisdiction.

"I was in pursuit," he added to Leyton, "so that's why I crossed into Lone Star Ridge."

Officer Hatcher grinned at Boo, and McCall instantly knew why he'd taken such an interest in going in *pursuit* and bringing Cody Joe to justice. He was lusting all over Boo. Of course, plenty of men did.

"Sorry, but I gotta take you in," Hatcher told Cody Joe. He shook his head, scratched it, smiled. "But I gotta tell you, I'm a hell of a big fan of yours. That ride you did on Gray Smoke up in Austin was one of the best I've ever seen."

"Well, thank you. I appreciate that. Always good to hear from a fan." Cody Joe turned on his thousand-watt smile that McCall suspected he'd been practicing since he had first cut teeth.

Of course, he'd had to practice that smile around that silver spoon in his mouth, and it had paid off. He was a trust fund rodeo champion with movie-star looks and charm that often got breaks mere mortals didn't. However, it appeared getting out of his arrest was one break Cody Joe wasn't going to get.

"But I still gotta take you in," the cop added to Cody Joe with plenty of regret. Regret that eased up a little when Boo winked at Officer Hatcher. "Just come on with me, and we'll try to get this all straightened out as fast as we can." He shifted his attention to Mc-Call. "You'll need to come, too, and press charges, 'cause Boo here said that Cody Joe assaulted you."

"I didn't. It was just a misunderstanding, that's all." Cody Joe didn't lose an ounce of his charm with that denial. "I didn't want her to leave before I explained things."

"No explanation needed," McCall countered. "I got the picture when I saw your jeans hiked down over your hips and your hand in Miss Watermelon's bikini bottom."

There'd be actual pictures of that, too, since Mc-Call hadn't been alone when she'd gone into the ladies' room at the rodeo arena and found Cody Joe on the verge of banging the contest winner against the feminine hygiene products dispenser. A few attendees who'd just needed to pee had been right behind her. So was one of the biggest donors of the fund-raiser, Elmira Waterford, who'd simply wanted to powder her nose before the next round of publicity photos.

Elmira, who was the mother of the contest winner that Cody Joe had been about to nail, hadn't taken things well and had ended up needing medical attention because of hyperventilation and a panic attack.

It'd been while Elmira was breathing into a discarded Chick-fil-A bag that McCall had gotten out of the trash that Cody Joe had insisted this was all a misunderstanding and that he needed to speak to McCall alone. McCall had resisted telling him to do anatomically impossible sex acts with himself and had held her ground about not leaving with him. That was when he'd grabbed her. That was also when she'd stomped on his boot to get him to back off.

While the drama of the night was still playing out in her mind and would continue playing out in the press, McCall started that damage control now. "I won't be pressing charges if Cody Joe leaves and agrees not to come here again."

And once Cody Joe was gone and she did some serious groveling to Austin, McCall would do the same.

"But, McCall, I really need to talk to you," Cody Joe protested. He started to move toward her, but Leyton blocked his path. "I need to make things right," he hollered over Leyton's shoulder.

Apparently, Cody Joe was going to continue to act like a fool tonight, but McCall didn't get a chance to show him her shoe as a reminder of what would happen if he touched her again. The sound behind them caught everyone's attention.

Girl squeals.

McCall turned to see the twin girls in pj's run out the front door, onto the porch and then down the steps. The girls were identical except for their hair. One had a halo of dark blond curls bouncing around her head. The other had a choppy bob that appeared to be in the growing-out stage.

That gave McCall a déjà vu moment of when her own sister, Hadley, had cut McCall's hair. It'd been used in an episode that the producer had joked was "why Badly Hadley can't be trusted with scissors."

"A pony!" the girls squealed in unison. That was

accompanied by giggles, jumping up and down and immediate attempts to pet the pony.

Obviously, these were Austin's kids, and it was also obvious that this wasn't something he wanted them to see because he hurried to them. McCall did the same. Well, she hurried as much as the dress allowed, but she wasn't sure if the Shetland was skittish and might knock the girls down.

Austin made it to the girls well ahead of her, and he scooped them up like footballs in each of his arms. "You should be in bed," he said, but there was no anger in his voice.

"But we woke up 'cause we heard loud talking," the girl with the longer hair proclaimed. "Santa got us a pony!"

The twin with the shorter hair gave her a puzzled look as if she might have realized Santa didn't bring gifts in June, but then her gaze landed on McCall. Her eyes widened. "It's the fairy princess," she said with the awe of someone who might be witnessing the real deal coming toward her.

McCall smiled at her but didn't get a chance to explain that she was merely a fake fairy princess before the other girl asked, "Where's your magic bunny?"

"She brought her magic pony instead," Austin answered without missing a beat. "Princess McCall, this is Avery." He kissed the nose of the one with longer hair. "This is Gracie." He gave the other a kiss on her cheek. "But now that you've met the princess and her pony, you have to go back to bed. That's the fairy-tale rules, and we can't break them."

The girls groaned, of course, and the one with the longer hair declared that "Rules suck."

"Yeah, they do on many occasions," Austin agreed. "You still have to obey them."

He turned and headed toward the porch, holding the girls in such a way that he was clearly trying to keep their little eyes and attention away from what was going on beyond the pony and the *princess*. But the "rules suck" Avery pointed at the driveway. "Nuckle Leyton," she squealed. "I wanta see Nuckle Leyton."

"Tonight, Uncle Leyton's part of the fairy-tale police. So is the other guy in the uniform. They're here to make sure we don't break fairy-tale rules." Austin didn't offer explanations for Cody Joe and Boo.

Avery gave her father a flat look as if she clearly wasn't buying that. Gracie gave a little wave and shy smile to Leyton, who was now walking toward them.

"Let me put them back to bed," Leyton volunteered. "Then you can finish up here with... Princess McCall. I'll read you a story," he said to the girls when they started to protest about having to go to bed.

All protests stopped, even though the twins both cast longing glances at the pony. Since Austin raised horses, McCall would have thought a pony wouldn't have been a big deal, but it obviously was. Maybe because it'd been a surprise and was still wearing the flower garland. The "magic" part might have played into it, too.

"I'll talk to your dad and the pony and see if it can visit you sometime soon," McCall said to try to console them. It worked. The girls cheered.

"Read us two stories," Avery insisted. She cuddled against her uncle when Austin passed off the girls to Leyton. "And we get ice cream."

"Nice try." Leyton took hold of Gracie, too. From the looks of her droopy eyes, the excitement for her had run its course, and she'd likely be asleep as soon as her head hit the pillow. "Yes to the two stories, but nope to the ice cream."

"FYI." Leyton lowered his voice and leaned in closer to Austin. "Howie and Edith will get wind of this."

Austin nodded, groaned and looked as if he wanted to start digging the hole to bury himself in. It took McCall a moment to realize that she recognized the names. They were Howie and Edith Marygrove, Zoey's parents.

"Shit," Austin muttered once Leyton had the girls out of earshot and back in the house.

She didn't know the specifics as to what was going on, but McCall remembered Granny Em mentioning something about Zoey's parents wanting to raise the twins. Crap. If there was some kind of custody struggle going on, this free-for-all certainly wouldn't help.

"I'm so sorry," McCall said. "I honestly didn't mean to involve your girls in this."

He didn't give her a "that's okay" or any other sign that he wasn't riled to the bone about it.

"If you think it'd help, I could talk to Mr. and Mrs. Marygrove and explain none of this was your fault," McCall pressed.

Austin slid glances at her, Cody Joe, the cop and

Boo. "Just wrap this up. I want as little getting back to them as possible."

That was her cue to get moving again, so with Austin on her heels, McCall went back to Cody Joe and Officer Hatcher.

"As I was saying, if Cody Joe leaves now, then I won't press charges." McCall motioned toward the Shetland. "And if Austin agrees, you'll leave the pony for his daughters. Send me a bill and I'll reimburse you for the cost."

Even with the blue lights from the cruiser swirling on his face, McCall saw the glimmer go through Cody Joe's eyes. A glimmer that let her know he thought this was a time to bargain with her.

"The kids can have the pony as a gift," he said, "if you'll give me another chance and forget all about what happened in San Antonio."

It was such a ridiculous bribe attempt that McCall couldn't even muster up another round of temper. Boo could though. She made a sound of outrage and lunged toward Cody Joe, but Officer Hatcher hooked an arm around her waist and held her back.

"You were going to marry this guy?" Austin said, tipping his head to Cody Joe, who was attempting his "gotta love me" grin.

"No." McCall couldn't say that fast enough. "But we were a couple," she was forced to add.

"A couple of what?" Austin asked.

A burst of air left her mouth, not quite a laugh, but as close as she would come to one tonight.

Austin turned and looked at her. The blue lights were swirling on his face, too, but she didn't see a glimmer there. However, she did see the hot cowboy that'd once been her crush.

"Cody Joe and McCall are cofounders of the Saddle-up for Tots foundation," Boo pointed out. "Cody Joe's the poster-boy celebrity, and his name brings in a lot of money."

Austin made a sound to indicate that that explained a lot. It did. But it didn't explain why the foundation was so important to McCall. Or that she'd known from the get-go that Cody Joe was irresponsible. However, this was the first time he'd put the foundation in the center of what would almost certainly be a scandal.

"Me and you together can still pull in a lot of money for those kids," Cody Joe went on, obviously trying to sell an unsalable plan. "I love you, McCall. Just give me another chance."

Deciding that he just wasn't going to get it, that he'd done something that couldn't be undone, McCall shook her head and turned to walk back to Prego Trail. Cody Joe made another move toward her, and this time it was Austin who stepped in. He caught onto Cody Joe's arm, but all of Cody Joe's charm vanished, and he tried to push Austin away.

Enough was enough.

McCall turned to give him another "kick to the nuts" threat, but Cody Joe took a swing at Austin. He missed. Then he pulled back his fist to try again. Boo, McCall and Officer Hatcher all went rushing in.

And Cody Joe's punch caught the cop right in the face.

A wise man would have stopped right there and started apologizing, but Cody Joe decided to lunge at her again. Since now both Austin and Officer Hatcher had hold of him, his momentum sent them forward.

Toward Boo and McCall.

They all went to the ground, landing in a tangled heap of bodies. McCall's shoe did indeed land in the area of a man's nuts, but not Cody Joe's. Instead, she connected with the cop's. He howled in pain, and McCall wanted to do the same when Boo's seriously hard elbow slammed against her cheekbone.

There was some cursing from all of them, coupled with the sound of the pony, who was neighing over the melee. But there was another sound, too. A car engine. A moment later, a sleek silver Mercedes came to a stop, the tires kicking up the gravel in the driveway, and the headlight spotlighting the human heap.

McCall managed to crawl out on all fours. So did Austin. His mouth was bleeding, the tutu practically ripped to shreds, but he'd clearly fared better than Officer Hatcher. His nose was gushing blood, there was a cut on his forehead, and he was using both hands to clutch his balls while he writhed in pain and rolled from side to side.

"Shit," Austin grumbled, and he groaned as the two people stepped from the pricey car.

Howie and Edith Marygrove.

His former in-laws.

And McCall could tell from their horrified expressions that this circus had gotten a whole lot more monkey crap.

Don't miss Chasing Trouble in Texas
by Delores Fossen,
available July 2020 wherever HQN books
and ebooks are sold.

www.HQNBooks.com

Moving back home to his grandmother's ranch was not what
Cody Wyatt had envisioned for his adult life.

Despite being the youngest of six, despite having five bossy,
obnoxious older brothers, Cody had never excelled at people
telling him what to do. He accepted it from his grandmother—
she'd raised him and his brothers, had saved him and his
brothers. There was no challenging Grandma Pauline.

But he was pretty sure he was going to punch Dev's lights
out if his brother kept criticizing the way he took off a horse's
saddle.

It wouldn't be the first time he'd gotten in a physical fight
with his brothers, but rarely did he get frustrated with Dev.

With six brothers, certain smaller relationships existed. The
oldest, Jamison, had saved all of them from their father's biker
gang and secreted them out to Grandma—their late mother's
mother. Jamison had tried to father him, and Cody had allowed
it and chafed at it in turn. He looked up to his oldest brother,
but there were so many years between them and such a feeling

of responsibility on Jamison's shoulders that Cody hadn't understood when they'd been younger.

Brady and Gage were twins, their own playmates and companions—operating on their own frequency. Cody loved them, respected them, but they were two sides of the same coin who spoke their own darn language half the time.

Tucker, closest in age to Cody, idolized Jamison. Tuck shared that core goodness about him that Jamison had, with a little less martyrdom weighing him down.

But Dev had shared that angry thing inside of Cody. A darkness the other brothers didn't have or didn't lean into the way Dev and Cody did, or had. That darker side had almost gotten Dev killed years ago—and Cody had vowed to hone it into a different kind of weapon.

It was a little harder these days now that he was back at the ranch after his last mission with the North Star Group. Too many truths about his involvement in the secretive operation had been revealed.

He missed North Star and his confidential work there. It had become vital to the man he'd built himself into. But he'd also been very aware his time with North Star was temporary, just as everyone else's was. It was what made the group effective in taking down large, dangerous organizations.

Like his father's.

Don't miss
Covert Complication *by Nicole Helm,*
available April 2020 wherever
Harlequin Intrigue books and ebooks are sold.

Harlequin.com

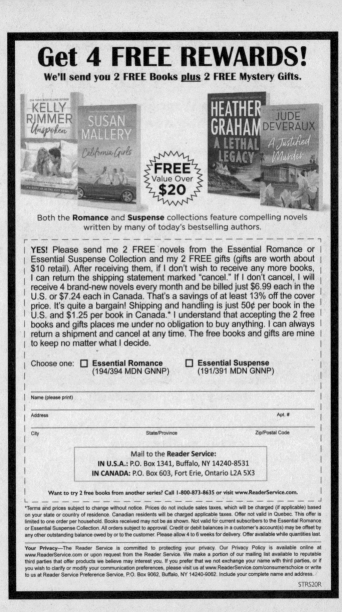